Martin Edwards was born in Cheshire. He read law at Oxford and then trained as a solicitor. He is married with two children, and is currently a partner at Weightmans LLP, a leading national law firm. He writes the hugely popular crime series set in the Lake District, featuring *The Coffin Trail*, which saw him shortlisted for the Theakston's Crime Novel of the Year Award. He is also a critic and has edited various short story collections.

www.martinedwardsbooks.com

By Martin Edwards

LAKE DISTRICT MYSTERIES

The Coffin Trail

The Cipher Garden

The Arsenic Labyrinth

The Serpent Pool

The Hanging Wood

The Frozen Shroud

HARRY DEVLIN NOVELS

Waterloo Sunset

The Frozen Shroud

MARTIN EDWARDS

Allison & Busby Limited
12 Fitzroy Mews
London W1T 6DW
www.allisonandbusby.com

First published in Great Britain by Allison & Busby in 2013.
This paperback edition published by Allison & Busby in 2014.

A CIP catalogue record for this book is available from the British Library.

10 9 8 7 6 5 4 3 2 1

ISBN 978-0-7490-1465-0

Typeset in 10.5/15.5 pt Sabon by
Allison & Busby Ltd.

The paper used for this Allison & Busby publication has been produced from trees that have been legally sourced from well-managed and credibly certified forests.

Printed and bound by

CPI Group (UK) Ltd, Croydon, CR0 4YY

Dedicated to my cousins
Mark, Barbara, Heather and Nigel,
and to the memory of Mona,
who died while I was writing this book

FIVE YEARS AGO

CHAPTER ONE

'Do you believe in ghosts?' Miriam asked.

Shenagh Moss stretched in the ancient armchair. Oz Knight had once said her every movement possessed a feline grace. Shenagh had moved on – gracefully, of course – from Oz, but he wasn't wrong. Where she came from, nobody cared about elegance, but these days, poise came as naturally as breathing. Even with no admiring man around, just an elderly housekeeper with anxious eyes.

'Ghosts are about the past. Look forward, not back, that's my philosophy.'

Miriam frowned at a mud-stain disfiguring the carpet she'd cleaned for so many years. Thinking about her long-dead husband? Poor, stuck-in-a-rut Miriam. Sixty was no age, but to look at her you'd think she had one foot in the grave. At least she'd made the effort to dye her hair, but why that dismal shade of mousy brown? Her beige cardigan, shapeless grey skirt and thick stockings were a perfect match for this room, with its faded furnishings, and faint aroma of mothballs.

Yet it was never too late to change your life. Look at Francis, twelve years older than Miriam, and a martyr to osteoarthritis. From the moment they met, Shenagh knew she could put a smile back on his face. Life was short, got to grab your pleasure when you saw the chance.

'We can't ignore the past.' Miriam rested a hand on Shenagh's shoulder, gripping bone through thin silk. 'Remember the Faceless Woman.'

'Our very own ghost?' Shenagh giggled. Forget the rotten weather, life was good. She wanted to cheer Miriam up. 'Hey, after haunting Ravenbank all those years, you'd think she'd get bored. Forever prowling up and down the same lane, where's the fun in that?'

'You may laugh, pet, but Mrs Palladino once caught sight of the Faceless Woman. Gave her the shock of her life – and she wasn't given to flights of fancy.'

Shenagh glanced at the framed photograph on the sideboard. With her long nose, pursed lips and pointed chin, the late Esme Palladino looked as though she disapproved of imagination, and anything else smacking of self-indulgence. You'd never guess she'd drunk herself to death.

'Spooky!' Shenagh pretended to shiver. 'Makes you wonder why she carried on living in Ravenbank.'

'Why ever not? This is the loveliest spot in the Lakes – ghost and all!' Miriam brightened. 'You could be so happy, pet, living here permanently. This is your home.'

'Thanks. You're very kind.'

Yet Miriam was also wrong. Home for Shenagh should be Katoomba, high above her native Sydney in the Blue Mountains. Or maybe a big house at Double Bay or Vaucluse, with views of the harbour. Not a decaying mausoleum on the edge of Ullswater. She wasn't nostalgic for Sydney's outer western suburbs, of course. No one could be sorry to leave behind that weatherboard hovel by the train track in Jannali. But she needed room to breathe. Ravenbank was suffocating her.

'Well, you're one of us now.'

There was no higher praise that Miriam could bestow. Shenagh was the daughter she'd never had, according to Francis. And for sure, she'd have been a massive improvement on Shenagh's actual Mom, a surfie chick who gave birth at fifteen, and was run over by a truck one night when she was out of it on cocaine, looking for business on the streets of Caringbah instead of looking after her daughter.

'You're very kind.'

'You're not fretting about that dreadful man Meek, are you, pet?'

Miriam *cared*, that was the difference. She'd never even met Craig Meek, but already she was worried sick about what he might do, now he was out of prison.

'Hey, it's fine. Craig isn't any sort of ghost. Just a selfish, troublemaking bully. Nice as pie as long as everything is going his way, but when it isn't . . .'

Miriam peered at her, as if straining to decipher a message written in code. 'Promise you'll be careful. Now he's back in Pooley Bridge . . . well, it's too close for comfort, when he has a history of violence.'

'I'm not running scared,' Shenagh said. 'I wouldn't give him the satisfaction. And that is a promise.'

The velvet curtains weren't thick enough to deaden the lash of rain on the flagstones outside. The clock struck six, but it felt like midnight. This vast sitting room was draughty, despite the crackling fire. Shenagh reckoned the whole house needed a makeover to bring it into the twenty-first century, but she wasn't going to hang around, waiting for it to happen. Who could blame her for counting the days until she landed back at Kingsford Smith?

Miriam tossed another log from the wicker basket onto the flames, and Shenagh reached out to warm her hands.

'Why do you ask about ghosts?'

'Don't say you've forgotten? Today is Hallowe'en.'

'I wanted to go to a party.' Shenagh feigned a pout. 'Francis wouldn't hear of it. I told him, you don't have to believe in ghoulies, it's only an excuse for a piss-up. But he'd rather stay at home, the lazy sod.'

'One thing he isn't, pet, is lazy.' Miriam seldom ventured to contradict Shenagh, but she'd defend Francis to the death. 'He's absolutely tireless. That's why he reached the top of his profession.'

'Yeah, I hear the nurses worshipped him. No wonder he expects everyone to jump when he says jump. Sometimes he makes me feel like a stupid kid.'

Shenagh smiled. Both of them knew she was anything but stupid. Francis wouldn't want to spend the rest of his life with an airhead, whatever she looked like.

'It's just his way.'

'He thinks the world of you, and no wonder. During that terrible time, when Esme was ill, he couldn't have got through it without you.'

A pink tinge appeared on Miriam's leathery cheeks. This was another of Shenagh's gifts, her lavishness with praise. It cost nothing to make people feel good, and sometimes they were generous in return.

'You always say such nice things, pet, but I was only doing my job.'

'Francis shouldn't have stayed on in this house,' Shenagh said. 'Even though he doesn't believe in ghosts any more than I do.'

'Mr Palladino's a man of science.' Miriam shook her head. 'He doesn't believe in anything he can't see and touch.'

Shenagh clapped her hands. 'How's this for an idea? We can celebrate! Commemorate the occasion. I mean, we can't just ignore our very own legend. It wouldn't be fair on poor old Gertrude. Let's mark the Faceless Woman's anniversary with champagne!'

'Oh, pet, I don't think it's . . .'

The sitting room door creaked open, and the words died on Miriam's tongue. The man who walked in carried a stick, and winced with every step he took. His sparse grey hair was wet, his Barbour coat dripped onto the carpet.

'Filthy night.'

A voice of authority, unaccustomed to dissent. How he must have relished making the nurses swoon. He claimed he missed the world of medicine, but Shenagh suspected he missed not the patients, but the power. Even she'd been startled by his reminiscences of life and death in hospital, and a God-playing former colleague known as Morphine Morris: 'No bed-blockers in his wards, I can tell you, not after one quick squirt of his trusty syringe!'

'Dreadful, isn't it?' Miriam said.

No wonder Francis had kept Miriam on after Esme's

liver finally gave up the unequal struggle. Miriam served the same purpose as the adoring nurses. *Yes, Mr Palladino, no, Mr Palladino, three bags full, Mr Palladino.* And it wasn't only Francis; her son was someone else she spoilt rotten. No doubt it was the same with her husband, the late lamented Bobby. Big mistake. Let a man get his own way, and he'd walk all over you.

'Is your back hurting? Your own silly fault, Frankie. I warned you not to overdo it.'

Her easy familiarity shocked Miriam, adding to the fun. The older woman helped Francis remove his coat, and hurried off to hang it up in the hall. He hobbled over to Shenagh's chair, and bent to brush his lips against her hair.

'Why are you keeping Miriam here?' he murmured. 'There's a storm brewing. She needs to get back home.'

'We were talking about the Faceless Woman.' She kissed his cold cheek. 'It's my first Hallowe'en in Ravenbank, and I've paid no attention to the story about Gertrude Smith till now.'

Francis Palladino made the sort of scornful noise he usually reserved for people campaigning for more wind turbines in the Lake District. 'You don't want to bother, it's a load of tosh.'

'Miriam didn't want to go until she was sure you were safe and sound.'

'I'm not a bloody invalid.'

She ran her fingertips along his tweed-clad thigh. 'You'll be sacking your masseuse, then?'

'Somehow,' he murmured, 'I don't think so.'

As Miriam bustled back into the room, he said, 'So you

and Shenagh have been discussing our little legend?'

'Well, it is Hallowe'en, Mr Palladino,' Miriam said.

'Spook night!' Shenagh cried. 'You know, I really ought to check out this Faceless Woman. Will I find her with a Google search? Does she have a Facebook page in her memory? Or is that a contradiction in terms, given the – uh – face shortage?'

'It's no joking matter, pet!' Miriam's eyes widened. 'Gertrude Smith was murdered on Hallowe'en, and the person who killed her wasn't hanged. That's why her spirit is tormented. Justice was never done.'

Outside the house, someone hammered on the old oak front door. Miriam jumped at the very moment that Shenagh dissolved into a fit of helpless laughter.

'You gave me the fright of my life.' Miriam was only pretending to scold her son. In her eyes, Robin could do no wrong. 'We were talking about the Faceless Woman.'

'Sorry to make such a racket.' Robin Park chortled, not looking sorry at all. 'The doorbell needs fixing. Want me to sort it out when I get a moment, Francis? I was telling Shenagh the other day, if the gigs ever dry up, I'd make a pretty decent handyman.'

Palladino's reply was a non-committal grunt. Robin never would get a moment. The offer was for his mother's benefit, one more thread in the tapestry she'd woven, depicting Robin the Virtuous, a man kind and generous to a fault. Shenagh thought him lazy and self-obsessed, but she'd met fellers a hundred times worse. He was good-looking, good company, and a pretty good jazz pianist. She'd have been tempted, definitely tempted, but at the cocktail party where Oz Knight introduced them, she also met Francis. And Francis might not be a lean hunk with startling blue eyes, but he was a civilised and childless old-school Englishman who owned a mansion. No contest.

Robin grinned. 'Gertrude Smith, eh? She's part of Ravenbank's heritage. Like Mum, really.'

His mother frowned. 'It's no joke, dear. What happened to that wretched young woman was pure wickedness. It makes my stomach heave just to think of it.'

'Take it easy,' Shenagh said. 'It was a long time ago.'

'Gertrude Smith never could rest in peace.' Miriam swallowed hard. 'On dark nights in the cottage, when Robin is away, I can't help thinking about that poor young creature, walking down Ravenbank Lane, without a face.'

Robin put his arm around her bulky shoulders. 'Not to worry. Nobody left alive has ever seen her ghost.'

'What exactly happened to Gertrude?' Shenagh asked.

Miriam cleared her throat. 'Someone battered her face with a heavy stone, and kept on until all that was left was a bloody pulp. No eyes, no nose, just a mashed-up mess.'

Francis frowned, and opened his mouth to speak, but there was no stopping Miriam in full flow.

'And that's not all. Gertrude's face was covered with a woollen blanket, like a shroud. The men who found her had to rip it off. The cold had frozen the shroud to her flesh.'

CHAPTER TWO

'You don't suppose Miriam was frightened of being attacked as she walked home?' Shenagh asked, an hour later. 'Is that why Robin came, to keep her company?'

'Miriam is perfectly capable of looking after herself, on Hallowe'en or any other day. Besides, who would want to murder her?'

'Oh, I dunno. A homicidal ghost, thirsting for vengeance because of the wrong done to her?'

Breathing hard, Palladino shifted his position in the bed. The sudden movement of his crumbling joints caused a spasm of pain to cross his face. 'Miriam doesn't have an enemy in the world. She deserved better than a good-for-nothing husband, let alone that idle lad of hers. Calls himself a musician, but does nothing except take advantage of her good nature.'

In fact, the idle lad was thirty-plus, and Francis's distaste stemmed from the way Shenagh let him flirt with her. Not that either she or Robin meant anything by it. He wasn't into commitment, frustrating Miriam's dream of surrounding herself with grandchildren she could spoil. The old lady had even tried a bit of unsubtle matchmaking between the pair of them. But although Miriam would be the ideal mother-in-law, she was wasting her time. As far as Shenagh was concerned, Robin's role in her life was to divert attention from her latest bit of fun. Like Mom, she'd never been a fan of monogamy. Francis didn't have a clue about what she was up to, thank God. Anyway, it was harmless enough. No way would this latest dalliance interfere with her plans for the future.

She nibbled Francis's dry lips. He was such a well-dressed man that it always came as a shock when he shed his clothes to reveal this scrawny body. His flesh felt like pudding pie, and the wonky vertebrae cramped his style as a lover. Massage helped, but it couldn't make him young again. Not that she was complaining. Long ago, she'd learnt you can't have everything, though it didn't stop her trying.

Over his shoulder, she stuck her tongue out at a photograph in an ornate ironwork frame standing on the bedside cabinet. Esme, again. In this black-and-white, head-and-shoulders portrait, she was in her thirties, hair in a bun, wearing her irritable schoolmarm face. The mirthless smile betrayed impatience, as if she wanted to scold the photographer for being so slow to take the picture. It amused Shenagh that Esme was gazing at her, in bed with her husband. Sort of a turn-on, having a dead wife as a voyeur.

'Miriam won't come to any harm.'

'Hope not. She's petrified of ghosts.'

'So was Esme. But only when she was four sheets to the wind. Claimed she saw Gertrude Smith at Ravenbank Corner one Hallowe'en, and managed to convince Miriam it wasn't a hallucination. She's extraordinarily credulous, for such a tough old boot.'

The tough old boot was younger and fitter than Francis, but Shenagh kept her mouth zipped. She'd learnt not to tease him about his age.

Her hand sneaked between his legs, but when he didn't respond, she murmured, 'Hey, it's Hallowe'en. A night when all sorts may happen.'

'A feeble excuse for shops making money, and children making a nuisance of themselves.' He'd lapsed into grumpy old man mode. 'I blame the Americans. Thank God we don't have trick-or-treating in an out of the way place like this.'

'I'm still glad Robin walked Miriam back to her cottage, made sure she's all right. She'd have a seizure if she caught a glimpse of the Faceless Woman.'

'Superstitious claptrap, that's the top and bottom of it.'

Sure was, but Francis needed contradicting, every now and then. If he couldn't handle contrariness, he should've signed up for the senior citizens' tea dance down the road in Penrith, not started shagging a red-headed westie from Penrith Valley on the other side of the world.

'Several people have seen Gertrude's ghost over the years. Jeffrey Burgoyne told me so.'

'When were you talking to Jeffrey Burgoyne?'

He sounded disgruntled, but surely not even Francis could be jealous of Jeffrey? 'Must have been back when we first met. He asked if I knew about the legend.'

Francis snorted. 'Pay no attention to Jeffrey. Fellow's an actor, spends too much of his time prancing around like a poor man's Ian McKellen. And he's a dreadful gossip.'

Was there a touch of homophobia there? Probably, but Shenagh didn't intend to make an issue of it. She knew something about Jeffrey that Francis would never guess, but she wasn't in the mood for gossip. The last thing she wanted was to start a conversation about Jeffrey Burgoyne and his partner.

'Sweetheart, this is Ravenbank. What else is there for people to do? That's why I want to escape.'

He squeezed her right breast. Hooray! His fingers were cold, but at least there was life in the old dog yet.

'Can't wait,' he said in a throaty whisper.

The eight-day mahogany mantle clock was an heirloom. A wedding present to Francis Palladino's great-grandfather, with floral decorations and brass bun feet, and topped by a gilded cockerel perched on two books. Shenagh loathed its extravagant ugliness.

The clock struck each hour on a gong; at one in the morning, it woke him. They'd shared a couple of bottles of claret over dinner; Shenagh had waved away Miriam's offer to do the cooking, and Francis found that fine wine always helped compensate for his lover's lack of culinary expertise. The combination of the alcohol, the fire, and their exertions in bed had made him drowsy, so he hadn't accompanied her when she said she would take Hippo for a walk.

'With any luck, I'll come face to face with Gertrude's ghost.' She giggled. 'Hey, I guess that's a contradiction in terms if the ghost doesn't actually have a . . .'

'Don't stay out too long,' he muttered. Within five minutes, he was snoring.

One o'clock? She must be back by now. After locking up,

she'd gone straight up to bed. Might she be waiting to offer him her own special version of trick or treat? He levered his protesting body out of his armchair, switched off the light, and stumbled upstairs.

The bedroom was empty. No sign of her in the bathroom, either.

'Shenagh?'

He called her name twice more. She didn't answer.

Puffing and grunting, he made his way back down the steep staircase. Hippo's basket was empty. Surely Shenagh hadn't had an accident while taking him out? She was young, fit, and fearless. Yet a lifetime in medicine had taught him that nobody was invulnerable. Disaster often struck out of a clear blue sky. Or out of a dark, starless sky.

What could have gone wrong? Hippo – properly, Hippocrates – was an Irish Setter, five years old and full of energy. Too boisterous for his owner's taste, but he had been a present for Esme after she fell ill, and after her death, Miriam, ever the sentimentalist, begged him not to let the dog go.

Shenagh loved Hippo too, a case of one tactile extrovert bonding with another. She used to say she enjoyed nothing better than being licked by a wild, panting animal. When, in the damp of autumn, Francis's arthritic back started playing up, she'd volunteered to take Hippo for walks by herself. Ravenbank was an ideal place for a dog to roam, whether on the muddy track by the lake shore, or along the secluded lanes and overgrown pathways criss-crossing between the scattered houses.

No choice but to go and look for her. Shuddering with dismay, he pulled on his Barbour coat and thickest lambswool scarf, and shoved his age-spotted hands into leather gloves. Before grabbing his torch, he donned the garish woollen hat Shenagh had bought as a birthday present. He'd avoided wearing it until now, because it made him look foolish; at least nobody else would be out there to see it.

He knew better than to panic. Thirty-five years as a stroke physician had accustomed him to distress. From student days, he'd cultivated a cool fatalism. Speculation was the enemy of medicine. Doctors traded in facts, unlike patients who made themselves sick and unhappy by allowing their thoughts to roam. Imagination ranked with superstition and religion. A rational man could have no time for any of them.

The moment he stepped outside, the cold sank its teeth into his cheeks. Ravenbank was a small and isolated peninsula jutting out into Ullswater, at the mercy of gales roaring down from Helvellyn. The rain had slackened to a malicious drizzle, but swirls of fog kept blowing in from the lake, and the wind howled through the trees like a creature in pain.

He headed for the path to the ruined boathouse. To his left lay the grave of the woman who had once lived here. The jealous wife who had battered Gertrude Smith to death. This part of the estate had become a wilderness, the old lichen-covered tombstone invisible beneath a tangle of dripping ferns, serpentine brambles, and stinging nettles. What had possessed Clifford Hodgkinson to bury the rotting remains of his disgraced spouse in the grounds of the Hall? Morbid sentimentality, that was the top and bottom of it.

'Shenagh!' he called.

No answer. What the hell was she playing at? Once or

twice he'd wondered about her new-found enthusiasm for taking Hippo for a walk late at night. It wasn't the form of exercise she usually favoured. Francis had warned her to be careful. Craig Meek knew where she lived, and a crude thug like that was capable of anything. But Shenagh was stubborn, and insisted she'd never let Meek mess her about again. She refused to become a prisoner in her own home through fear of anything he might try to do.

Once or twice, Francis had asked himself if walking the dog was a subterfuge, an excuse for getting out of the house so that she could meet someone in secret. Namely, that conceited lecher, Oz Knight. But he'd dismissed the idea out of hand. Knight was history as far as Shenagh was concerned; besides, he'd never be able to explain any nocturnal absences to that wife of his. Francis knew better than to give in to paranoia. Shenagh was a lovely woman, and any red-blooded male was bound to lust after her, but she knew which side her bread was buttered on. He was confident of that.

The worst case scenario was that Shenagh or Hippo had finished up in the water. He'd start by eliminating this possibility; a reassuringly scientific approach. Shenagh was sure-footed, and a strong swimmer. Her early years had been tough; he'd never pried into details, but she'd developed an instinct for self-preservation. Much as she cared for the dog, if it got into difficulties, she'd not risk her life on a rescue. The lake was deep and excruciatingly cold. Nobody could survive its icy embrace for long.

Rain spat in his face as he limped along the muddy track. On the far side of Ullswater, lights glimmered behind curtained windows as Hallowe'en parties staggered to an end. Headlamps flickered as vehicles on the main road to Glenridding passed between the trees on the west bank. The east side of the lake was silent but for the melancholy hooting of an owl, and the muffled scrabbling of an invisible fox. His torch beam picked out the way ahead. The rest was blackness.

The air smelt of damp leaves and wet earth. The lakeside path was bumpy, and he needed to watch where he put his feet. It didn't help that the gale was making his eyes water, and his vision was blurred. How easy to trip over a tree root, and snap his Achilles, especially when he was hampered by this damnable pain in his back and knees. Gritting his teeth, he followed the path's curve around the promontory. No sign of Shenagh or Hippo.

Reaching a gap in the mass of trees, he began to climb towards the heart of Ravenbank. The downpour had made the ground treacherous, and his boots kept sliding as he struggled up the slope, but he pressed on. He knew this place like the back of his hand, and since Esme's death he'd found comfort in the familiar, yet Shenagh was right. He was too set in his ways. If he didn't change them now, he never would. She had opened his eyes to fresh horizons that he was desperate to explore, before it was too late.

Where the hell was she?

His boots pinched, and he could feel blisters forming on his heels. The wind blew a thin, spiky branch into his face, almost taking out his eyes. He brushed it out of his face, and carried on until he reached the spot where a stony lane petered out into a rough track.

'Hippo! Hippocrates!' He whistled twice before he called

again. 'Are you there, boy? Shenagh, where have you got to?'

The fog clutched at his throat as he approached the Corner House. Wheezing noisily, he stopped to rest his aching back against the For Sale sign. In case Shenagh had taken shelter inside the empty cottage, he peered through the cobwebbed windows, but saw nothing. Taking a deep, rasping breath, he limped on down Water Lane. His torch beam picked out Watendlath, the whitewashed home of that pansy Jeffrey Burgoyne and his boyfriend. Francis didn't care for the boyfriend, or the way he looked at Shenagh when he thought nobody else could see. Was he wondering what it would be like with a woman? People nowadays hadn't the faintest idea of how to behave.

A tall hawthorn hedge marked the boundary of the Hall's grounds. He decided to retrace his steps, and follow one of the paths that led through the wooded area. Near to the beck, not far from where the two lanes crossed at Ravenbank Corner, Gertrude Smith's corpse had been discovered. And this was where Esme insisted she'd seen Gertrude's ghost, a shimmering white phantom with a bloodied, unrecognisable face.

Absolute bunkum. Esme had downed too much gin while he was at the hospital, that long ago Hallowe'en.

'Hippo!'

At last his patience was rewarded. His tired eyes detected a movement in the distance, moments before a familiar bark ripped apart the silence of the night. Within seconds his torch fastened on the big, awkward dog, bounding towards him. Relief washed through him as he bent down, and patted Hippo. The fur was sodden.

'So what have you done with Shenagh, old fellow?'

Hippo whimpered.

'Is she hurt? Don't tell me she's taken a tumble, and fractured her ankle?'

The dog pulled away from him, and loped over the grass towards a clump of silver birch trees. Francis hurried after him, stumbling in his efforts to keep up. Somehow he managed not to lose his balance, but his heart was thudding and the throbbing of his back made every movement a test of will.

Suddenly, the narrow beam of light from his torch caught a huddled shape on the ground.

He'd found Shenagh.

'For God's sake, what has he done to you?'

He'd forgotten that he didn't believe in God.

Hippo stood panting over the motionless form. It took Francis an age to catch up, but he recognised Shenagh's black anorak, jeans and boots. They were designer cowboy boots; he'd bought them for her birthday, stifling his horror at the ridiculous price.

As he drew closer, his torch beam moved up towards her neck and face. They were covered by a rough woollen blanket. He pulled it away and hurled it onto the sodden ground.

Shenagh had lost her face. The lovely face he had so often kissed.

As he stared at the bloody, ruined features, he let out a howl of rage and pain. A fearful noise, the cry of a beast with a mortal wound.

NOW

CHAPTER THREE

'Murder for pleasure was invented by a man who lived down the road from here,' Daniel Kind told his audience. 'Thomas De Quincey moved into Dove Cottage a year after the Wordsworths left for Allan Bank. You can understand why the tourist board highlights the poetic daffodil fancier. Better PR than a self-confessed opium eater obsessed by serial murder.'

Laughter drowned the rain drumming on the skylights of the lecture theatre. Two hundred and fifty paying customers had come to Grasmere for a Saturday conference on Literary Lakeland. Daniel had turned down countless speaking invitations since quitting academe and starting a new life in the Lake District. In Oxford, he'd lost his zest for lecturing, but the sea of faces in front of him gave him that old adrenaline rush.

'De Quincey wasn't a monster, any more than people who enjoy a good murder – any more than Mr Wopsle in *Great Expectations*, or people flocking to watch

The Girl with the Dragon Tattoo, are monsters. The world in general is, De Quincey said, bloody-minded. "All they want from murder is a copious effusion of blood . . . but the enlightened connoisseur is more refined in his taste." De Quincey was no different from me or you. We all like a good murder.'

He always made eye contact with his audience, and now his gaze was drawn to a woman in the front row. Wherever she'd sat, you couldn't miss her. Not among the grey hair and cardigans, and not only because she was olive-skinned, not white. Glossy black hair, black eyes, high cheekbones. Her lipstick and nails were crimson, the silk blouse dazzling yellow. A tablet computer rested on her lap, but her tiny hands were motionless.

'He was an eccentric, De Quincey, a mishmash of contradictions. A solitary soul who fathered eight children. A satirist with a morbid cast of mind. An addict who was also a notable journalist – though come to think of it, that might not be such a contradiction after all.'

The woman tapped into her tablet. Oops. For all Daniel knew, she worked for the *Westmorland Gazette*, whose long ago editor was – Thomas De Quincey.

'I'm not saying De Quincey lacked sympathy for victims of crime. He points out that Duncan's graciousness, his unoffending nature, makes his murder in *Macbeth* all the more appalling. But what fired the man's imagination was the nature of murder. Macbeth, and Lady Macbeth, intrigued him more than their victim. He was the first writer to focus on a burning question. A question that has fascinated people ever since.'

Daniel paused. The woman leant forward, lips slightly parted. Their eyes met.

'The fundamental question about the ultimate crime. The question that haunts us all. Just what is it that drives someone to kill?'

As Daniel inscribed a hardback for the last woman in the queue, he spotted through the crowd the leonine hairstyle of Oz Knight. Tall, tanned and trim, he was making for the authors' table. That hair was unmissable – waves so sweeping you could almost surf them. He wore a hand-tailored black jacket – Charvet, at a guess – and a white shirt, unbuttoned to the waist. For a man close to fifty, his physique was enviable, and he relished giving people a chance to envy it.

'A fabulous lecture, and an even more fabulous book! Treasure that personalised copy, madam, it's one for the pension fund!'

Oz's voice was melodious, if unnecessarily loud. A touch of humorous self-parody made his egotism almost tolerable. Yet it was lost on the woman, a slim redhead who was obviously no fan of chest hair. She rolled her eyes, and hurried off in search of refreshments.

'Great audience today,' Daniel said.

'Sold every ticket months in advance!' Oz gave a theatrical bow. Over-the-top dandyism was part of the package he'd constructed to create a high-profile business, the events management company which had organised this conference. A past master of the technique of persuasion, he was charming and persistent enough to tempt even Daniel to be a speaker. 'But it's not simply about putting bums on seats. It's about creating a buzz, and a wonderful experience for everyone here. To miss the chance of talking about De Quincey in the village where he made his home would be – simply criminal.'

Daniel had woken up wishing he'd never agreed to take part. The conference had seemed like a good idea at the time – but why return to a past he'd escaped? Yet he'd enjoyed the day, and the audience's enthusiasm gave him a buzz. Now he wanted to unwind.

'It was fun.'

'Now, it just so happens that one of my clients is recruiting speakers for a month-long luxury cruise. Sail from Southampton to the Caribbean, the itinerary is incredible. Money no object for the right lecturers, and invitations are only going to Europe's leading—'

Daniel held up his hand. 'Stop right there! I've not been bitten by the bug all over again, you know. Today's a one-off. When I quit the television series, I decided—'

'Of course. I understand. You moved to the Lakes for a reason. Forgive me, I should never have mentioned it.' A smile flashed, vivid as lightning. 'You won't blame me for trying, I hope?'

'No problem.'

'I'll leave you to head back for the green room and a well-deserved break. I must find my wife. We need to schmooze the sponsors.' Oz clapped him on the shoulder. 'Forget what I said about the cruise, it was crass of me. A colossal opportunity, incredible exposure, and an itinerary to die for, but you don't want to spend your life back on the treadmill, do you? The global speaker circuit. You have other fish to fry. Fame and money aren't everything, you're absolutely right. Catch you later, eh?'

Oz waltzed off, leaving Daniel – probably like most

people he talked to – feeling his head had been pummelled. He doubted he'd heard the last of this cruise; it felt more like the opening skirmish in a campaign destined to become a battle of wills. Was this what it was like to fall prey to an accomplished seducer? Oz was legendary for his conquests, in his private life even more than in business; Daniel had asked around, after Oz made his original approach, and persisted after being turned down flat. The gossip was that he'd run wild until, at forty, he'd tied the knot with a girl who worked for his company. Not that marriage had cramped his style.

Money, Daniel presumed, made up for a lot, along with the mansion on Ullswater and holiday homes in Mykonos and Zermatt. One other thing he'd learnt was that Oz stood, not for Oswald, or even Osbert, but for Ozymandias. For God's sake, what sort of parents would do that to a child? No wonder he had a healthy self-image, he'd have needed it to cope with the mockery at school.

He watched Oz greet the olive-skinned woman from the front row. They embraced, and Daniel noticed the woman's wedding ring. So that was Melody Knight. As she held forth, Oz listened without a word. The king of kings had transformed into a dutiful husband.

Daniel squeezed into a seat where he could listen to the last presentation of the day. The speaker was Jeffrey Burgoyne, his topic the supernatural stories of Hugh Walpole. In the green room, Jeffrey had proposed a quick drink at the end of the day. He described himself as a jobbing actor, part of a two-man theatre company, and lived in Ravenbank, like Oz and Melody Knight.

Jeffrey didn't stand at the lectern, or bother with notes. He strode up to the edge of the platform, determined to hold the audience in the palm of his hand. Overweight and red-faced, he looked more like a gentleman farmer than the Lake District's answer to Kenneth Branagh. But he had presence.

'When I listened to Daniel talking about Thomas De Quincey,' he said, 'I was reminded in a strange way of Hugh Walpole. Once the poor devil was a household name, now he's forgotten. If people think of him at all, they pigeonhole him as a writer of sugary Lakeland sagas. Look beyond the Herries Chronicles, and you see a man who led a weird life, and wrote even weirder stories. If you fancy a masterpiece of the macabre, read Walpole's last novel. A landmark in psychological suspense, yet few people know it. It was only published after he died, and it's called . . . *The Killer and the Slain*.'

You could tell Burgoyne was an actor. This wasn't so much a talk as a performance. Daniel saw Melody Knight note the book's title.

'As with De Quincey, the contradictions are mesmerising. Walpole lived in Brackenburn, his "little paradise on Cat Bells". He designed his own lovely terraced garden, and was a generous host to everyone from J.B. Priestley to Arthur Ransome. He had the gift of friendship. Sadly, he also had a fatal flaw. He wanted everybody to love him.'

Jeffrey cleared his throat. 'There was a dark side to Walpole. Something deeply unhappy about . . . the way he felt the need to keep so many secrets. When he proposed to a girl, he was heartily relieved when she turned him down. Even after his death, his biographer was tediously discreet. All he said was that Walpole found visits to Turkish Baths provided "informal opportunities for meeting interesting strangers". But his stories give us clues to the terrors that came to him at night. He was obsessed with ghosts.'

The supernatural sparked Walpole's imagination, Jeffrey said. In one story, a woman is condemned to spend her last days in the company of a clown's mask, grinning at her in derision.

'And then there is my favourite.' Jeffrey beamed. 'Shameless plug coming up, by the way, for the Ravenbank Theatre Company. Our latest production combines a trio of macabre stories, linked together like that wonderful old movie *Dead of Night*. We're touring venues across the North, starting next week, with our premiere in Keswick, at the Theatre by the Lake. We call the show *Tarnhelm* after Walpole's finest supernatural tale. Who knows, it might become the new *The Woman in Black*! But I'm not going to spoil things by telling you much more . . .'

He beamed, allowing himself a suitably histrionic pause. 'Except to say that the stories we've chosen are sure to make your flesh creep. Like "Lost Hearts" by M.R. James, about a young boy sent to stay with a cousin, a reclusive alchemist obsessed with making himself immortal. "The Voice in the Night" describes a sailor's dreadful encounter with a mysterious oarsman. But my favourite is "Tarnhelm", based on a legend of terrible misdeeds. Tarnhelm is a skullcap. Put it on your head, and it works a sort of magic. At once, you become an animal. And you become as wild as the animal you want to be.'

'Time to come clean, Daniel. Do you believe in ghosts?'

Jeffrey Burgoyne's voice penetrated the hubbub in the crowded bar. The Solitary Reaper took its name from

Wordsworth's poem, and was one of the busiest pubs in Grasmere, as well as the tiniest. People in the village nicknamed it the Grim Reaper, as oxygen was usually in short supply.

Daniel swallowed a mouthful of Old Speckled Hen. 'I'm a sucker for stories of the uncanny. I must read *The Killer and the Slain*.'

'Indeed you must, but that's still an evasive answer. You sound more like a lawyer than that sister of yours.' He waved a fleshy hand in the direction of Louise Kind, deep in conversation at a nearby table. 'Nail your colours to the mast! You say a historian needs to dig up facts, like a sort of scholarly archaeologist. I bet you don't think there's enough hard evidence to justify a belief in ghosts – am I right?'

'If you'd asked me a few years ago, I'd have said so.'

Jeffrey Burgoyne's protuberant eyes scrutinised him from behind rimless spectacles. The loud, plummy voice, striped blazer and MCC tie suggested a cricket spectator from the fifties. Fixing a stern gaze on Daniel, he morphed into counsel for the prosecution.

'But now you're not so sure?'

Daniel gave a lazy grin. 'The older I get, the less sure I am about anything. What about you, Jeffrey? You believe in the returning dead?'

'Certainly.' Jeffrey leant closer, and lowered his voice. 'Perhaps I just have an unfashionable belief that old sins cast long shadows.'

The trouble with actors, Daniel thought, was that they never stopped performing. As a student, he'd had a six-month relationship with a girl who was a star of the

Dramatic Society, and he'd never been sure he really knew who she was. Giselle was sweet and pretty, but unpredictable, trying out personality traits like changes of clothes, forever agonising over which suited her best. She said actors needed to be a mass of contradictions, adaptable yet bloody-minded, sensitive yet thick-skinned. Wherever they went together, she watched people. Studying their turns of phrase and their body language. Trying to peer inside their minds. As Jeffrey Burgoyne was doing now.

'Monday is Hallowe'en.'

'Indeed. As it happens, Quin and I have been invited to a Hallowe'en party by Oz and Melody Knight. Their home, Ravenbank Hall, is magnificent. I'm sure they'd love you and your sister to come.'

'Very good of you, but—'

'You must say yes!' Jeffrey Burgoyne boomed, before Daniel could invent an excuse to say no. 'You'll both have great fun. Besides, Quin is making his special recipe mulled wine, and that simply has to be tasted to be believed.'

'Sounds terrific.' Daniel had been introduced to Quin at the end of the conference. Young enough to be Jeffrey's son, he was his partner in life as well as in the theatre company.

'Believe me. And if all that isn't enough, as an added bonus, we supply a Hallowe'en legend of our very own. A ghost story involving not one terrible crime, but two! Given your interest in the history of murder, you'll find the story riveting.'

Daniel's curiosity stirred. Maybe there was no need for an excuse to avoid a party with a bunch of Lakeland luvvies. His fascination with mysteries of the past had led him to become a historian, and make a career out of being inquisitive.

'Tell me more.'

Jeffrey was in no hurry to spill the beans. Like any storyteller, he loved building suspense. 'You live in Brackdale, I saw from your bio in the conference brochure. A fair stretch from Ullswater, but no need for you to drive home in the early hours. Stay overnight, we have two spare rooms. Save the misery of having to go easy on the booze.'

'Louise went house-hunting in Glenridding last week.'

'Oh goodness, we're much further off the beaten track. I don't expect you've visited Ravenbank?'

Daniel shook his head. 'I haven't lived in the Lake District for long, and Louise is an even more recent arrival.'

'No need to sound apologetic, old fellow. I grew up in Carnforth, spent seven years at Sedbergh School, and moved to the Lake District after coming down from Peterhouse. Not good enough – one of my neighbours maintains I'm still an incomer. On her sixty-fifth birthday this summer, she was boasting that she's never visited London, and a few months in Belfast are the closest she's come to travelling overseas.'

'If all you've ever known is the Lakes, you might decide there's no need to settle for second best.'

Jeffrey chuckled. 'You're a man after old Miriam's heart. She loves the place, insists the only way she'll ever leave is when she's carried out in her box. Mind you, Ravenbank is so isolated that plenty of born and bred Cumbrians have never made it that far. Frankly, it suits us to stay a well-kept secret, we'd hate to become the last leg of a tourist trail.'

'I bet.'

'Believe me, it is one of the most beautiful places on God's earth . . .' Jeffrey paused for five seconds, a performer to his fingertips. 'Yet amazingly, Ravenbank has witnessed two savage murders.'

'Statistically a rival for Baltimore, then?'

'You're teasing, Daniel, naughty, naughty. We even have our very own ghost. The Faceless Woman. All the best phantoms have a suitably macabre moniker, don't you agree? Her real name was Gertrude Smith.'

'What happened to her?'

'She was a young Scottish housemaid who worked at Ravenbank Hall before the First World War. The master of the house, a man called Hodgkinson, seduced her. Unfortunately, he had a mad wife who wasn't confined to the attic. Letitia Hodgkinson found out about her husband's affair, and on a suitably dark and stormy Hallowe'en, she crept up behind Gertrude, and knocked her down with a stone plucked from the rockery in the Hall grounds. Then she battered the young woman's beautiful face into a pulp.'

On the far side of the bar, a man who'd had too much to drink guffawed at one of his own jokes. Daniel picked up a beer mat, and crumpled it in his palm without thinking. His mind was on the story.

'Go on.'

'When Gertrude's body was discovered, her ruined face was covered with an old woollen blanket. It entered Ullswater's folklore, as the Frozen Shroud.'

'What happened to the wife?'

'She committed suicide within hours of the murder, so there was no trial. The whole business was hushed up. Justice wasn't seen to be done.'

'It often isn't.'

Jeffrey took another sip of gin and tonic. 'Indeed. People were sorry for the Hodgkinsons' daughter. Dorothy was only thirteen. Nobody cared much about Gertrude, the real victim. No wonder her spirit was restless. A story gained currency that each Hallowe'en, Gertrude would patrol the lane that leads to Ravenbank Hall, seeking retribution for the wrong done to her. Terrifying anyone who chanced upon her – because there was nothingness where there ought to be a face.'

'Pity you and Quin haven't managed to catch a glimpse of her.'

'I'll say! After the First World War, Ravenbank Hall became a care home run by a charity, but when it closed down, a wealthy hospital consultant turned it back into a private residence. His wife was the last person who saw Gertrude's ghost. The Palladinos are dead now, but the legend persists.'

Daniel sat back, inhaling the Grim Reaper's beery air. 'And the second murder?'

'Five years ago, and a strange echo of the first. Again, justice was cheated, and the man responsible never stood in the dock.'

Jeffrey Burgoyne lowered his voice, his manner unexpectedly intense. Impossible to picture this plump and pompous fellow, even in his younger days, as a leading man. But he was an accomplished actor.

'Unfit to plead?'

'No, Craig Meek died before the police caught up with him. His victim was an Australian woman. Flame-red hair, with a personality to match. Stunning, if your tastes ran in that direction, and plenty of men's did. But then, a jaguar is a beautiful creature, isn't it, until it rips out your throat?'

'I'm guessing you weren't a member of her fan club?'

'She was out for herself, first, last and always. Her name was Shenagh Moss, and she liked to describe herself as a therapist with a speciality in massage.'

'Uh-huh.'

'Draw your own conclusions, and you won't go far wrong. She spouted a lot of drivel about reiki therapy and heaven knows what. At least she was skilled enough to make an impressive conquest. Francis Palladino was more than twice her age, but shortly after they met, Shenagh moved in to Ravenbank Hall. Francis was an intelligent chap, but lonely. Strange to say it of a successful man with pots of money, but he was vulnerable.'

'Where did Meek fit in?'

'He was one of Shenagh's former lovers. His name was misleading – he had a violent temper, and had recently served time for GBH. He ran a club in Penrith, but he ended up bankrupt after fiddling his tax. Shenagh had a fling with him, but when she moved on, he felt betrayed.'

'The jealous type?'

'Yes, he was a bully. Refused to let go, and began stalking her. Following her home, making silent phone calls at all hours of the day and night. Francis paid for her to take the best legal advice, and a judge slapped an injunction on him, preventing him from making contact with her. The plan backfired, because for Meek, the court case was the final straw. One Hallowe'en, Shenagh took the dog out for a walk and never came back.'

'What happened?'

'Francis found her body, poor fellow. Meek had bashed her face in, then covered it with a blanket. Just as Letty Hodgkinson had left Gertrude Smith's corpse. It was as if Meek had made a crude attempt to update the legend of the Frozen Shroud. If the plan was to throw the police off his scent, it was doomed to failure.'

'You said Meek died. Suicide?'

'No, he was killed in a head-on crash with a lorry on the A66 that same night. Fleeing the scene of the crime. The stretch near Threlkeld is an accident black spot, and Meek careered onto the wrong side of the road. So justice wasn't seen to be done. Except in the crudest way.'

'I suppose there was no doubt that Meek did kill Shenagh?'

Jeffrey frowned. 'Absolutely none. A neighbour saw him leaving home that evening, and later his car was seen in Howtown, heading back towards Pooley Bridge, where he rented a flat. Obviously making a run for it after killing Shenagh. Nobody else died in the crash, but Meek was responsible for two deaths apart from his own.'

'How come?'

'Francis Palladino never recovered from the shock of finding Shenagh's corpse. Within a year, he was dead too. Officially, double pneumonia, but anyone with a trace of romance would say he died of a broken heart.'

'Murder is like that.' Daniel glanced at Louise. His sister's former lover had been killed shortly after she'd moved up to the Lakes. 'One death creates countless ripples. It isn't just the victim. So many lives are changed forever.'

'I suppose so.' Jeffrey considered. 'Though the callous might say that every cloud has a silver lining. Take Oz and Melody Knight. They were set on buying Ravenbank Hall, and after Francis died, their dream came true. Not that they would have wished him any harm, needless to say.'

'Jeffrey! I can spot that mischievous gleam a mile off. You're not being bitchy about anyone, are you?'

The mellifluous Irish accent belonged to Alex Quinlan, who had been sharing a table with Louise Kind and Melody Knight. A svelte figure in a purple shirt and white trousers, he shimmied towards them, sinuous as a dancer.

Jeffrey stroked Quin's cheek. 'Bitchy, *moi*?'

'You'll be telling me next that butter wouldn't melt in your mouth.'

'Don't listen to him, Daniel. I'm always well behaved.'

'Not always, love.'

The people at the next table were leaving, and Louise and Melody came to join them. Melody was probably in her thirties, but her skin was so flawless, it was hard to tell. Her lovely face made Daniel think of a screensaver; you could only guess what hid behind the surface.

'Daniel, such a treat to meet you in person! And thank you for giving such a wonderful talk.' She shook his hand. 'I was telling your sister, I used to work pretty much full-time in the business, setting up events like today's. But recently Oz took on someone else, to give me more time to pursue my secret passion.'

'Which is?'

'The same as yours!' A full-wattage smile, blinding in its intensity. 'I love to write, and I've started freelancing, covering the conference for *Cumbria World*. I've been dying to talk to you. Any chance you'd let me interview you about your new book about the history of murder?'

'*The Hell Within*? Publication isn't due until next year.'

'So much the better – I can get in first! What do you say?'

Before he could answer, Jeffrey butted in. 'I've taken the liberty of inviting Daniel and Louise to your Hallowe'en party. Hope that's all right?'

'Of course,' she said. 'You've been telling Daniel about the Frozen Shroud, I suppose?'

'It's an extraordinary story. Poor old Gertrude, eh?'

Quin said quickly, 'Not forgetting poor old Shenagh.'

'Yes, Jeffrey was telling me about her,' Daniel said.

'Oh yes?' Quin's eyes narrowed. 'She came from Penrith Valley in Australia, a world away from our own Penrith. A beautiful extrovert, Shenagh. She loved life, she was full of fun. Did Jeffrey mention that, by any chance?'

'Well, I gather she wasn't everyone's cup of tea?'

'No,' Quin said. 'She certainly wasn't.'

Melody compressed her lips. 'I suppose with a murder victim, that's stating the obvious.'

Jeffrey's brow knitted, but when he spoke, his tone was breezy. 'Anyway, there's no better place to be in the Lakes on Hallowe'en than Ravenbank. You'll find Oz and Melody are fabulous hosts.'

'You're too kind.' Melody seemed glad he'd changed the subject. 'At least there will be no kids making a nuisance of themselves, just plenty to eat and drink, good company, and an outside chance of seeing a phantom housemaid. In fact, Jeffrey, you read my mind. I'd just mentioned the party to Louise. Please say you'll both come.'

Daniel glanced at his sister, who gave a quick nod.

'Thanks, we'd love to.'

'Perfect! Don't get the wrong idea, it's nothing glitzy. A few neighbours, and a handful of people we know through work. Strictly no celebs – you'll be the one and only exception! It's not so long since you were a fixture on the television screen, is it? I never missed one of your programmes.'

'Those days are long gone,' he said. 'I concentrate on writing now.'

'I've always dreamt of publishing a book of my own. But I'm just a beginner.' She smiled again. 'Do bring your partners along tomorrow night, both of you.'

'I'm single at the moment,' Louise said.

'Me too,' Daniel said. 'So it'll just be the two of us.'

'Fine, like I say, you won't be overwhelmed with loads of people you don't know. We organise so many events, we like to keep our private parties quite – intimate. By the way, Jeffrey,' Melody turned to him, 'did you mention the masks?'

He shook his head, and she threw another smile at the Kinds. 'This is the third time we've held a party at this time of year, and we've developed a little tradition of our own. Lots of people come in Hallowe'en themed fancy dress, and that's fantastic. But what we do hope is that every guest will at least wear a mask.'

'What sort of mask?' Louise asked.

'Oh, a ghost, a vampire, a creature from myth and legend,

whatever takes your fancy. It all adds to the atmosphere, Hallowe'en is such a special night. Especially in Ravenbank.' Her eyes gleamed with mischief. 'It seems only right that none of us should wear our own face.'

Fastening her seat belt in the car, Louise said, 'You could invite Hannah Scarlett to the party. Why do you keep shutting her out of your life?'

Daniel switched on the engine. 'Hey, you're not in court now.'

'I'm not a bloody trial lawyer, don't muddy the waters. It's obvious, I'm cramping your style. If I haven't moved into a place of my own by Christmas, I'll rent somewhere, get out from under your feet.'

'You're not cramping anything. Honest.' He patted her knee. 'Stay at the cottage as long as you like.'

'I can't fault you for generosity, but life in Brackdale is too comfortable, for both of us. You need to get out more. Whether or not with Hannah, that's up to you.'

He groaned. 'You know something? You're starting to sound like Mum.'

Not so long ago, the jibe would have provoked anger. Instead, Louise laughed. He was glad; she was loosening up at last.

'Oh God. Perhaps that's every woman's fate. To finish up talking and acting like their mother.'

'There are worse fates. You're wrong about Hannah, anyway. She's shut me out, not the other way around.'

'You're imagining it. Trust me, Daniel. For a smart guy, you're really not that smart when it comes to women.'

'After I last met Hannah for a drink, I rang a couple of times, and left voicemail messages. Sent her an email. She did reply in the end, very brief. Said she was up to her eyes with a couple of cases, and she'd get back in touch soon. That was five weeks ago.'

Five weeks, two days, in fact. Not that he'd been counting.

'She's a senior police officer. Her life isn't her own.'

'I'm not complaining. Hannah and I are still mates, always will be.'

'You fancy her like mad, I can tell.'

'She needs space. Don't forget, she's had a rough year. Splitting up with Marc, finding that mutilated body on the farm. Horrible.'

'Don't be so bloody altruistic. You'd do her good. A lot more good than Marc Amos, for sure. For all I know, he still nurses the fantasy she might take him back one day. As if. She'll never forget what he got up to with that girl who worked for him.'

Louise's last lover had also been a philanderer. She was determined to scrub him out of her memory, and his name was never mentioned. Marc Amos was a dummy target for the scorn she felt for the man who had hurt her.

He knew better than to argue with her. You could never win. He manoeuvred the car down the narrow passage leading out of the car park, a task complicated by defunct bulbs in several of the lamps fixed on the pub wall. Suddenly, he braked, before putting his foot down after a few seconds, so that the car shot forward and out into the lane.

'Wow!'

'What's the matter?'

'You'll never guess.'

He felt a stab of astonishment at what he'd seen. Two figures in the shadows. Jeffrey Burgoyne had slammed the side door of the Grim Reaper behind him, and then slapped Quin's cheek so hard that he staggered backwards and almost lost his footing. A stinging blow on the same cheek Jeffrey had stroked a few minutes earlier.

CHAPTER FOUR

Hannah Scarlett stuck out her tongue at the computer screen, trying to make sense of rows of figures on a spreadsheet. The numbers made her brain hurt. To round off her Monday, she was due to see the Assistant Chief Commissioner for a meeting she was sure to hate. Only one thing occupied Lauren Self's thoughts at present. Costs must be cut. Where to swing the axe?

The silence was broken by the opening bars of the theme from *Doctor Who*. She'd forgotten to switch off her personal mobile. Any interruption was welcome, but her finance report was overdue. Swearing, she delved into the Aladdin's cave of her bag and fished out the phone. This had better not be Marc. Each conversation with him felt like tiptoeing around the rim of a live volcano. If he wasted her time, she might be the one to explode.

The caller's name made her blink in surprise. *Terri.*

Her oldest friend, and the world's worst gossip. Terri was capable of driving Hannah to distraction, but not so selfish as to gatecrash a detective chief inspector's working day simply for a natter.

'Hannah?'

No apology for the interruption. The way Terri spoke her name made Hannah's skin prickle. Terri's dad wasn't in good health, and though they'd been estranged for a long time, if anything had happened to him, she'd be distraught.

'Something wrong?'

'You could say that.' Deep breath. 'Actually, I'm scared shitless.'

Hannah's stomach knotted. 'What's happened?'

'It's Stefan.'

Terri claimed to have only three faults. Eating the wrong kind of food, drinking the wrong kind of booze, and shagging the wrong kind of man. She wasn't fat, and she wasn't an alcoholic, but it was a miracle some of the creeps she'd fallen for hadn't screwed her up permanently. Stefan Deyna worked in a bar, and after a good start, their relationship had sped downhill. He was now beating off strong competition to top the league table of Terri's all-time worst mistakes. So many of her exes were lazy, feckless, two-timing wastes of space. But Stefan, unique among them, had a violent streak. As well as a not-yet-divorced wife back in Poland whom he hadn't thought to mention until a co-worker let the cat out of the bag. His reaction had been to bluster with Terri, and break the co-worker's cheekbone. His employer sacked him on the spot, leaving him with time on his hands to make her life a misery.

'Has he hurt you?'

'No, but the bastard keeps insisting I see him. I tell him

to piss off, but he won't take no for an answer. Last night, he followed me home in a car. He doesn't own a car, so I'd guess he nicked it. We had a row and I ended up scratching his face.'

Good for you, but . . .

'What happened?'

'We were arguing outside my front door. He was angry, and pushed me hard enough to make me fall. I grazed my knee, you should see the bruise, but I picked myself up and launched myself at him. Dug my nails across his cheek, as hard as I could.'

Hannah winced. Terri had very long nails.

'Let's just say, he won't be winning a beauty contest any time soon.'

He never would have done, but Hannah found it impossible not to give Terri a silent cheer. For courage, if not common sense.

'You took a hell of a risk. What did he do?'

'While he was mopping up the blood, I whipped my key out of my bag and ran inside. He was banging the door so hard, I thought he'd break it down. Or break his knuckles.'

'You should have called me.'

'I was about to, but the racket stopped. I thought he'd gone away, but when I looked out of the window he was sitting there in his car. In the dark. Just watching and waiting.'

'How long did he stay?'

'About an hour. Finally, he decided I wasn't going anywhere, and drove off. It was barely eight o'clock, but I went straight to bed, I was knackered.'

She must have been. Terri's head seldom hit the pillow

before midnight. Most of the calamities she'd got herself into over the years had happened in the small hours, after too many Bacardi and cokes.

'You're not at work now?'

'No, I invented a trip to the dentist. Bit of a risk, since I only started there ten weeks ago. But my boss is sweet, and we're not busy, so it'll be fine.'

'How are you feeling?'

'Pretty crap, if you want the truth. This morning, Stefan phoned again. Of course I didn't talk to him. He kept ringing, so I took the receiver off the hook.'

'You said you were going to buy a new phone, and change your number.'

'I know, I know. I've a lot happening in my life at present, you've no idea. My head's in a whirl.'

Hannah glared at the numbers on the spreadsheet, which didn't improve the figures or make them go away. She pressed a button, and the screen went blank.

'Get the phone sorted for a start. Will you do it today?'

'Don't be bossy, Hannah, please. I'm not in the mood, all right?'

'Sorry, it's only that—'

'You're trying to do the right thing?' An exaggerated sigh. 'Good old Hannah. You always do the right thing, don't you?'

If only. 'Listen, Terri, I want to help.'

'I've got so much on my plate. I'd love to see you, if you're not otherwise engaged.'

'I can get away by six. I'll have had enough of this place anyway by then.'

'Are you sure? I mean, I know I've been lousy at keeping in touch lately.'

'Like you said, you've had a lot on your plate.' As she uttered the words, Hannah realised she didn't know exactly what was on Terri's plate. This new job, yes, but she never let work get in the way of fun and friendship – that was Hannah's failing. 'Not a problem.'

'More than you can possibly imagine.'

Terri was calming down. It was a good sign that she was indulging in a pastime that had been a favourite since her teens: making her life sound mysterious and exciting. Hannah prayed that, if a man was involved, he was a massive improvement on Stefan, but she wouldn't bank on it.

'Any room to put a pizza on that plate this evening?'

'Love to. How about we try Balotelli's, that classy new Italian on the road out of Ambleside? It has a big bar, even a dance floor. A . . . friend of mine recommended it. Live entertainment most weekday nights, singers, stand-ups, you name it.'

'Perfect.'

A rap on the door. As it swung open, Lauren Self's immaculately coiffured blonde head appeared; it wasn't her style to wait for a response. The ACC was waging war on closed doors – in fact, a war on doors generally. She was threatening a revamp of the office, ripping down every wall in sight to create 'a more open environment'. She portrayed it as a chance for Hannah to get closer to her team. Hannah wasn't status-conscious enough to regret losing her personal space, but she knew a PR ploy when she saw one. This was a neat way of saving money under the guise of democratising management and promoting an ethos of teamwork. Not that Lauren was moving into open plan herself. Someone of her seniority had far too much sensitive and confidential business to handle. Democracy and teamwork had their limits.

Hannah glanced at her watch. Shit, she'd lost track of time. First the budget figures, then Terri's call. She'd been due to see the ACC five minutes ago, and Lauren made up for her lack of other skills by turning punctuality into a fetish.

'Sorry,' she mouthed, cradling her mobile.

Lauren disfigured her lovely features with a scowl. Hannah guessed she was mentally flicking through the small print of the Proper Use of Technology Policy even as she gave a curt nod and disappeared again. Probably to ask the long-suffering folk in Human Resources to draft a Showing of More Respect to Top Brass Procedure.

'Abject apologies,' Terri said. 'I suppose I'm snarling up the machinery of justice, calling you at this time.'

'You did the right thing, ringing me.'

Terri sighed. 'Sooner or later I had to do the right thing. Law of averages, eh? See you tonight, sweetie.'

It was almost impossible not to feel a sneaking admiration for Lauren Self, but Hannah did her best. Lauren had risen to her current eminence without trace. Cumbria Constabulary was one of the most successful forces in Britain, and somehow she contrived to claim more than her fair share of the credit. Canteen cynics hailed it as a triumph for the fifty-page Equality and Diversity Policy she championed, in that lack of experience at the sharp end was no bar to advancement. She compensated for hardly ever having locked anyone up, with a flair for politics that cabinet ministers would kill for, and a genius for being all things to all people, especially if they were journalists. Lauren scented a photo opportunity quicker than a pig smelling muck. Her gleaming smile was a regular adornment of regional news bulletins and front pages of the local papers, while her chatty blog, tireless social networking and constant stream of tweets turned self-promotion into an art form.

Yet as Hannah walked into the office destined to remain an oasis of calm in the brave new world without walls, Lauren's body language suggested a beaten tennis player at the post-match inquest. Her desk was spotless – a triumphant example of leadership in terms of the Clear Desk Policy – but her PC screen was so crammed with numbers, most of them red, that Hannah felt dizzy just looking at it.

'Take a seat while you can,' Lauren muttered. 'It's only a question of time before I'm asked to put the furniture up on eBay.'

Money, money, money. Researchers said crime was falling – for the moment, at least – but in the age of austerity, that wasn't enough. The government wanted eye-watering cuts to police expenditure – without touching front-line policing, naturally. Even the most efficient forces must embark on a strategic review, also known as slash-and-burn. Vast chunks of the police estate were to be flogged off at bargain prices – assuming any developer could persuade the banks to lend them funds to buy. A hatchet had been taken to pension benefits and working conditions. Morale among the troops was on the floor, and heading down.

At first, Lauren had embraced the new agenda with gusto,

and masterminded an upbeat video presentation called 'No Pain, No Gain'. But then came a decision from on high to halve the force's public relations spend, and Lauren was still reeling from the shock. Worse, a national phone hacking scandal had led to fresh scrutiny of police links with the media. Professional Standards warned against reporters who got close to cops so as to wheedle out information. It was only a question of time before someone rapped the well-manicured knuckles of pretty senior officers who flirted with hacks in return for positive coverage. Lauren's progress up the greasy pole was hampered by the fact that the people blocking her way happened to be very good at their jobs. Rumours had swept through the force that she'd applied for a couple of top posts in the south of England. In the Cold Case Review Team, there was genuine sadness that she hadn't talked her way past the shortlist.

'You wanted to see me.'

'Yes, thanks.' Lauren gestured at the numbers on the screen. 'Unhappy reading, I'm afraid.'

Hannah made a sympathetic noise, and braced herself.

'In times like these, Hannah, we are bound to take difficult decisions. None of us would choose such a path willingly. But we have to face up to reality. We're all in this together.'

She coughed. Hannah waited.

'I'm sorry to say that we simply can't sustain the current level of resource we allocate to non-core activities that don't fit the parameters of conventional work-in-progress.'

Listening to Lauren, Hannah sometimes regretted the absence of an interpreter fluent in management-speak. Even so, she saw where the conversational labyrinth was leading.

Lauren paused, allowing Hannah the opportunity to make her task easier. When she sat tight, the ACC murmured, 'All that has consequential implications for the Cold Case Review Team, I'm afraid.'

Hannah found her voice at last. 'You're dumping us on the scrapheap.'

Lauren frowned, like a torturer finding a captive has committed suicide just before the branding irons have heated up. 'Please don't jump the gun. The team has done good work since I set it up. And you'd expect me to fight tooth and nail to look after my people, wouldn't you?'

Well, not really, to be honest.

Hannah settled for a cowardly nod.

Lauren threw a glance at a poster commissioned from an advertising agency six months ago. It said simply 'We Deliver', but also featured a natty logo in seven different colours, so Hannah presumed it was money well spent. At least by the standards of the time of plenty.

'The answer is to work smarter. We need to do more for less. It's tough, but then, life's tough. You only have to look on your television screens to see what's going on all over the world. We have to do our bit.'

Get on with it, the suspense is killing me.

Lauren picked up a paper clip that had escaped from its appointed niche in her desk tidy. 'Here is what I've proposed to the Police and Crime Commissioner. Your direct reports will be reduced to one DS, one DC, and two admin assistants. The consultant's fixed-term contract will not be renewed on expiry.'

Okay, then. Deep breath. May as well be hanged for a sheep as a lamb.

'Why not get rid of us once and for all?' Hannah demanded. 'Do the job properly rather than inflict death by a thousand cuts, and simply prolong the agony. The workload is crushing the team already.'

'I never said it would be easy.'

'You're getting rid of Les Bryant, our most experienced man.'

'He's retired once already, he can spend more time with his allotment or whatever they do in Yorkshire.'

Hannah bit her tongue. How easy to say something that sent her career whirling into oblivion. Was that what Lauren wanted?

'The rest of the team – who chooses the people who stay, and those who go?'

'You do, Hannah. It wouldn't be right for me to interfere. You're in charge, after all.'

So I wield the axe, and all those difficult decisions become my fault.

'Everyone who leaves the team moves to another team? No job losses?'

'Absolutely. Except for the consultant, of course, he isn't on the permanent strength. And there's more good news. The people at risk are going to be pooled. You might want to bring someone else in to replace a current post-holder. When things are tight, it makes sense to freshen things up.'

'It's a great team. Why would I want to lose any of them?'

'As I say, it's entirely up to you. But you might wish to think about asking Greg Wharf to move on. They are short-handed in Public Protection after the recent early retirements.'

'Greg as a minder for visiting politicians? Why on earth

would I want to lose him? And why would he want to make the move?'

Lauren allowed herself to reprise her perfect smile.

'I'm only thinking of your reputation. Greg's is a lost cause. I've heard a whisper that the two of you are becoming . . . quite close. Sounds to me like you're perched at the top of a slippery slope, Hannah. Take a tip from me. You'd be well advised to scramble off that slope. As soon as.'

Head buzzing, Hannah returned down the corridor. She was unsteady on her feet, as if she'd been smacked about by Stefan rather than just had a talk with the brass about finance and staffing.

'All right?'

A grizzled figure limped out from the kitchen, his battered shoes squeaking on the tiled floor. Les Bryant, cold case consultant, and both guru and team mascot. A man she, and everyone else who mattered, would trust with their lives.

'Not really.'

'Audience with her ladyship?' Les put his hand on her arm, an uncharacteristic gesture. 'Don't fret. I've had a good innings. Two good innings, as a matter of fact.'

Hannah caught his hand and squeezed it briefly. Even more uncharacteristic.

''Sides, I seem to need a season ticket for the GP's surgery nowadays.' He flexed knobbly finger joints to emphasise his point. 'It's no fun getting old. Suppose I'm ready for the bloody pipe and slippers after all.'

After dropping the bombshell, Lauren had sworn Hannah to secrecy. The commissioner hadn't signed off her proposals yet. Though she'd never have shown her hand unless she was confident that she held the aces.

'What do you know?' Her voice was hoarse with emotion.

'When you've been a detective as long as me, it's not what you know, it's what your gut tells you.'

'There won't be a formal announcement for another week.'

''Course not. Takes time to draft a news release, doesn't it? Any road, the formal stuff is always the last link in the chain. Office grapevines work faster than any intranet.'

'I'm sorry.'

'No need. I'm not dead yet. And my contract isn't over, either. I don't suppose a payment in lieu is on the table, and I wouldn't take it even if they offered. The ship may not be sinking, but you still need all hands on deck.'

'Thanks.'

'Nowt to thank me for. Promise me one thing, Hannah.'

'What's that?'

'Don't destroy your own prospects over this. Look after number one, that's my advice. Do yourself a favour, go with the flow.'

Hannah looked into his bloodshot eyes. 'My old boss once told me the best detectives don't waste their time going with the flow.'

'Right, but Ben Kind came close to drowning once or twice himself. And one day you might find you don't have a lifebelt.'

Half an hour later, Greg Wharf waltzed into her office. He'd spent the day in Barrow, checking on a possible link between half a dozen sexual assaults dating back to the nineties. As he finished his debrief, he added, 'By the way, you don't need to say anything.'

'What about?'

'You know, the cuts.'

'I'm not saying anything.'

'Fine.' He stretched his legs. 'I wouldn't mind Public Protection. Bodyguard to nubile young pop stars? I can handle that.'

'Oh yeah? Don't plan your life around it, that's all.'

His mouth folded into a grin, as if to remind her what a good-looking sergeant she had. Not quite as good-looking as he thought. But not bad.

'I'll take my cue from you, ma'am.'

'That'll be the day.'

'Didn't we agree to have a bite to eat sometime? What are you doing after work?'

'Sorry. I'm going out tonight.' Better make clear it wasn't with Marc. 'I'm seeing Terri. Remember that Polish barman? He's giving her a hard time. Apparently he's done time back in Poland for assault, and now he's awaiting trial for punching a guy he worked with.'

'Why doesn't that surprise me?' The grin vanished. 'I smelt the anger on him when we met. Mister Nice Guy as long as everything suits him, but ready to turn nasty any time his nose is put out of joint.'

'I'm worried for Terri. She's hopeless at looking after herself.'

'She's a big girl, Hannah.' Greg looked as though he was about to make a breast-related joke, then thought better of it. 'You can't live her life for her. Tell her to see one of m'learned friends. They'll slap an injunction on the bastard.'

'Mmmmm. You know what lawyers are like. Only ready to move if the evidence stacks up, and the case is handed to them tied up with pink ribbon.'

'Let me know if I can do anything to help.'

'Thanks,' she said, uncertain what kind of help he had in mind. Perhaps a quiet word with Stefan, possibly something more direct. Like Terri, he was a risk-taker. Was that why, against all the odds, she'd taken a shine to him?

'If you're busy tonight, how about dinner tomorrow?'

Persistent, or what? 'I might be washing my hair.'

He laughed. 'It's fine as it is.'

'Don't think flattery will get you anywhere.'

'Hey, I wasn't trying to appeal to your vanity. Just your stomach.'

'I need to lose pounds, not add them.'

A sidelong glance. 'You could have fooled me.'

She reminded herself what she'd just said about flattery. 'Not dinner. A quick drink. Maybe.'

After Greg had left the room, Hannah scowled at the spreadsheet for five more minutes before giving it up for the day. Forget what Lauren had said about her and Greg. The gossips could fuck off. She clung to the belief that with him, she'd always been one hundred per cent professional.

Was that enough? Perception often mattered more than reality. The temptation to do the opposite of Lauren's bidding was almost impossible to resist. It wasn't so easy to brush aside words of wisdom from Les Bryant. If people started to hint that she was shagging Greg, her career would soon go into freefall.

His reputation as bad news had preceded him; when he'd joined the team, he already had one broken marriage to his credit, and God-knew-how-many broken hearts. He was a Geordie Jack the Lad, and like most of the people the brass moved into cold case work – including Hannah – he'd blotted his copybook. The team was widely regarded as a bunch of misfits, yet to everyone's surprise, they had bonded into a cohesive whole. Best of all, they'd solved crimes that had festered in the too-difficult pile for years.

Doctor Who interrupted her mental time-travelling. Her heart skipped a beat; her first thought was that Terri was calling again. Had Stefan caught up with her? Was she in danger?

A glance at the caller name turned apprehension into anger.

Marc. Oh, for God's sake. Did some men never learn?

CHAPTER FIVE

Louise left Tarn Cottage for work, still munching her toast. Cutbacks had led the university to offer her only a part-time contract this academic year. She'd taken the financial hit for twelve months, as a quid pro quo for a better work-life balance, yet a sadistic twist of timetabling fate had landed her with a nine o'clock lecture on Monday morning. Insider trading for a bunch of half-asleep first years. No wonder she was monosyllabic over breakfast. Neither she nor Daniel was a morning person, and after a few weeks of careful politeness, they'd eased back into territory familiar from their teens. Arguing about what to watch on television, and whose turn it was to load the dishwasher.

The air in Tarn Fold was damp as Daniel trundled the wheelie bin along the rough track. The trees that formed a thick summer canopy were shedding their leaves, the birds flitting through twisted branches had lost the urge to sing. Somewhere in the distance, a sheep bleated as if in mourning. After a rainy summer, the autumn hues remained vivid, but winter was inching closer, ready to clutch Brackdale in an icy embrace. He parked the bin at the lane end where the refuse lorry stopped, and scooted back to the centrally heated sanctuary of his study.

A deadline loomed for an article commissioned by an American journal, but he excelled at displacement activity. Anything to put off the moment of truth: fashioning the first sentence that set the tone for everything that followed.

Louise had developed a passion for tidying the cottage, so he found it too easy to fritter away time trying to find where she'd hidden the keys or book or CD that he wanted. She could never understand the strange comfort he found in chaos and clutter.

He made a fresh mug of coffee, dug out an album of Dusty Springfield covers by Shelby Lynne, decided against answering a stroppy email from his accountant about his tax return, and finally flicked on to Google, wanting to learn about the Frozen Shroud while listening to a breathy paean to the joys of just a little lovin', early in the morning.

Too right, Shelby; it beat a cup of coffee any day. Daniel turned up the volume a shade. He'd been celibate for too long; another thought to push out of his mind. He forced himself to focus on the screen.

The wealth of knowledge available on the internet amplified Jeffrey Burgoyne's account. Clifford Hodgkinson, a builder from Blackburn, moved to the Lakes at the turn of the century with his wife Letitia, and their newborn daughter. He bought a stretch of land on the east bank of Ullswater, known as Satan's Head. Fearing the old name might depress property prices, he rechristened the area Ravenbank, and set about creating a private fiefdom beside the lake. Long before planning laws and National Park regulations prevented large-scale speculative development, his dream was to preside over a small, exclusive community with its own village shop, post office and pub. He started by rebuilding a half-derelict house on Ullswater's shore, and transforming it into Ravenbank Hall, a testament to his wealth and status. Two roads were laid out, and individually designed homes built. The fifth was completed a week before Gertrude Smith's murder.

The housemaid had come down from Glasgow in search of work, and Hodgkinson offered her a job at Ravenbank Hall eight months before she died. She had been 'courted', as the old reports quaintly put it, by Roland Jones, a tutor hired to teach Dorothy Hodgkinson at home, but Hodgkinson admitted he'd been having an affair with her. According to some websites, Gertrude was pregnant, but whether the father was Jones or Hodgkinson wasn't revealed. What was certain was that, less than twenty-four hours after the discovery of Gertrude's corpse, Hodgkinson's scorned wife took a fatal dose of veronal.

Letty Hodgkinson had a history of jealous rages, and she'd suffered from depression since Dorothy's birth. She'd spent time in a sanatorium, and the police took her suicide as proof that she was guilty but insane. There was mention of a suicide note in which Letty admitted killing Gertrude, and the authorities were quick to treat the case as closed. Letty was buried, not in the graveyard at Martindale, but in the grounds of Ravenbank Hall. That was why Gertrude's ghost was supposed to walk endlessly down the lane leading to the Hall. She wanted to know why she and her unborn child had to die.

The scandal wrecked Hodgkinson's reputation, and his plans for Ravenbank collapsed. He died of heart failure not long afterwards, 'a broken man'. Dorothy never married, but became well known in the county for charitable work. After the end of the First World War, Roland Jones rose to prominence in the field of liberal education. And that was pretty much that.

The phone rang just as Shelby launched into 'Wishin' and Hopin''. He pressed pause and said, 'Hello.'

'Daniel? This is Melody Knight. I hope I'm not disturbing you?'

'Glad of an interruption.' He gazed through the window. Beyond the rambling back garden rose the slopes of Tarn Fell. A view he loved at any time of year, although a fleecy mist obscured Priest Ridge, and he couldn't make out the dark outlines of the Sacrifice Stone. 'Any excuse not to write.'

'We agreed to get together so you could tell me more about your book. It just so happens that this afternoon I'm in your neck of the woods, picking up supplies for the party in Brack. We could have a cuppa and a chat about *The Hell Within*. If you can spare the time.'

Spending an hour with Melody would be no hardship. Perhaps he could kill two birds with one stone.

'As a matter of fact, I was meaning to visit Amos Books. I wondered if they had anything on Ravenbank, or that legend of the Frozen Shroud. They have a cafeteria there, if that suits you.'

'Oh, I adore that shop! Not just the books, did you know their cakes have won awards? Not that I dare gobble many of them. I'd need to buy a whole new wardrobe. Or rather, talk Oz into buying it for me.'

'Three o'clock suit you?'

'I'll look forward to it.'

After she rang off, Daniel googled Shenagh Moss. Tales of Gertrude Smith's ghost, coupled with the murderer's decision to cover Shenagh's face with a blanket, had been a gift for the media. The crime was a nine days' wonder. Craig Meek, the ex who turned into a stalker, was described by an unnamed 'friend' as 'a bit of a lunatic, really' and 'sort of a Mr Angry', which made Daniel wonder what his enemies thought of him. Nobody suggested that Meek might not have killed Shenagh.

And so, despite the link with a pleasurably macabre ghost story, Shenagh's murder soon slipped out of the headlines. The presumed killer was dead, the narrative complete. There was nothing more to say.

Yet five years after Shenagh's murder, something kept alive Jeffrey Burgoyne's scorn for her. Possibly others felt the same. Daniel couldn't help wondering if Ravenbank was home to more than one ghost.

He arrived at the converted mill occupied by Amos Books in time to search for books about the Faceless Woman before Melody arrived. He loved the shop, with its sloping floor and narrow aisles threaded between rows of crammed shelves, loved the mustiness of the old tomes even more than the seductive smell of coffee and cakes wafting from the cafeteria. Hidden away in his office, Marc kept his computer, and even an e-reader, but the shop remained a temple for worshippers of the printed word. This afternoon, it was quiet except for a group of voluble German walkers examining a set of signed Wainwrights, and the usual stream of people wanting food and drink rather than books. He was leafing through a dusty volume called *Ullswater*

Lore and Legends when a hand clapped him on the back.

'Daniel! How are things?'

Marc Amos sounded glad to see him. They enjoyed each other's company, and even though Hannah had confided that her former partner was always jealous of her friendships with other men, he seemed to make an exception in Daniel's case.

'Good, thanks. How's business?'

Marc pushed a hand through his thick fair hair. 'Keeping the wolf from the door. Footfall is steady, and revenue from the cafeteria is on the up. When you see what's happening to retail in this country, let alone to second-hand bookshops, we've got plenty to be thankful for.'

'Glad to hear it. I can't be the only person who still loves wandering around a bookshop.'

A woman in a blue uniform waved hello as she walked past the far end of the book stacks. Leigh Moffat, brisk and businesslike, was in charge of catering. She and Marc had gone into partnership, and Hannah reckoned that one fine day, the two of them would move in together.

'I should have joined forces with Leigh years ago,' Marc said. 'I used to be a control freak, thought I'd only be happy if I stayed in charge of everything. But Leigh's far better at the business side than me. Not just the finances, but negotiations with the landlords, marketing, all the crap I hate. She actually enjoys it. Thanks to her, I can focus on scouting out rare books, and tracking down collectors who might want to pay good money for them.' He grinned. 'It's like marrying a pristine first edition with a fine dust jacket from a second impression copy. The two are worth more together than apart. Now, what do you have there?'

Daniel flourished the book. 'Someone told me about the legend of the Frozen Shroud. And do you have any books dealing with the real-life murders at Ravenbank? Not just the killing of Gertrude Smith, but the Shenagh Moss case too?'

'Check out the true crime section. We're more likely to have something about the old case. Shenagh was the Australian woman, wasn't she? Your best bet is the newspaper archives. I remember Hannah talking about the investigation, though she wasn't involved directly. Fern Larter was on the team, but she wasn't the SIO.'

Daniel nodded. Hannah had introduced him to Fern, a friend as well as colleague. 'I gather the killer died in a car crash.'

'Well, if you accept that the obvious solution is almost always right. The man's name was Meek, I remember. What sticks in my mind is that Fern wasn't happy about the case.'

'Why was that?'

'She didn't care for the SIO, said he was idle and far too quick to close the file. You've met Fern, haven't you? Once encountered, never forgotten. And never afraid to say what's on her mind. She had a row with her boss, and finished up with her wrists slapped, and forced to toe the line.'

Daniel leant forward. 'Didn't she believe Meek was guilty?'

'They were presented with a story that was too neat. Her theory was that someone took advantage of the old legend to settle a score with the woman who died, and used Meek as a scapegoat. Unfortunately, she had no evidence, she was relying on gut feel.'

'And what did Hannah think?'

Marc sighed. 'You know Hannah.'

'She agreed with Fern?'

'She trusts her instinct. They both hated the idea that someone might just have got away with murder.'

One coincidence about the two murders in Ravenbank had already struck Daniel. In each case, the prime suspect died within a day of the victim. Case closed. Neat and tidy, and convenient for everyone.

A woman whose appearance and demeanour reminded him of the trout who wanted to swallow Jeremy Fisher accosted Marc. She demanded to know where she might find a biography of Beatrix Potter costing no more than two pounds. The answer was the biography shelves, but Marc dressed it up with such tact and charm that by the time she strutted off, she'd morphed into a beaming Mrs Tiggy-Winkle.

Daniel grinned. 'Ten out of ten for customer care.'

'You think that's a daft question? Trust me, it's high-level compared to some. People constantly ask for books whose titles they can't recall, written by authors whose names they have forgotten, about subjects they are rather vague about. Not to worry, they are our lifeblood. Mind you, we'd never survive if I only sold books to people who call in looking for a bargain. I have clients all over the world. Collectors based in countries whose currency rates make the price of rare books from England a snip. To say nothing of women recently divorced from millionaire husbands, who want to invest their alimony in something more interesting than stocks and shares.'

'Or toy boys?'

'Hey, you don't have to worry about your age or your looks when you curl up with a rare first edition. And books cause you less hassle and heartache in the long run.' Marc frowned, his thoughts wandering elsewhere as the pair of them strolled through the topography section. 'Seen Hannah lately?'

Daniel shook his head. 'You?'

'She's seeing someone else, did you know?'

'We haven't spoken for more than a month.'

Marc was watching for a reaction, and he kept his expression neutral, although the news made him want to bang his head against the wall. He'd been so sure she wanted time to herself before even thinking about a new relationship. Louise's words echoed in his brain. *For a smart guy, you're really not that smart.*

'Seriously?'

'Seriously. Last time we were in touch, she was worried about cutbacks. She sounded overwhelmed with work.'

'In more ways than one,' Marc said softly. 'The bloke she's seeing is her DS. That guy Wharf.'

'Greg Wharf?' This time Daniel wasn't able to hide his surprise. Hannah was professional; why had she let herself get mixed up with a subordinate?

'You'd think she'd have more sense, wouldn't you?'

Daniel wasn't feeling too sensible himself. He didn't answer, and Marc luxuriated in a long sigh.

'I'm disappointed, to be honest with you, Daniel. I've heard the two of them go out drinking together.'

Two colleagues going for a drink? Maybe there was nothing in it, and Marc was jumping to jealousy-fuelled conclusions. Before Daniel could say another word, someone called to him.

'There you are, Daniel! And Marc too. Lovely to see you both!'

Melody Knight waved at them. Daniel returned her smile, his gaze lingering on the slanted eyes and high cheekbones. With a stab of surprise, he realised that he'd hardly ever seen anyone in this shop who wasn't white. Nor any more beautiful. Wrapped up against the cold in a white coat, multicoloured woollen scarf and matching hat, Melody looked exotic and out of place, like a rare orchid in an overgrown garden.

'How long have you two known each other?' Marc asked as they shook hands.

'We met on Saturday, at a conference Oz organised,' Melody said. 'Daniel gave this wonderful talk on De Quincey and murder, and he agreed to be interviewed about his new book, to help my career as a budding journo. He and his sister are coming to our Hallowe'en party, by the way.'

'A trip to Ravenbank? Now I understand your sudden interest in the Frozen Shroud.'

Daniel nodded. 'One of my fellow speakers turned out to be a neighbour of Melody's. He told me about Gertrude Smith, and Shenagh Moss.'

'You'll love Ravenbank, if you've never been that far. Gorgeous spot, and the Hall is marvellous.'

'You're so sweet, Marc,' she said. 'Why don't you change your mind and come to the party too? Bring Leigh, if you like.'

Marc shook his head. 'Sorry, can't make it. Now, I'd better leave you to talk about Ullswater spectres, while I price up a collection I've just bought. It came from the executors of a critic for a literary magazine who never parted with a single review copy. Bliss.'

As he disappeared towards his office, Melody said, 'Such a shame. You can tell he isn't over the break-up yet. Ever met his ex? She's a detective. Very nice, by all accounts, but a workaholic. Can't be easy for Marc.'

'Yes, I know Hannah.'

'He was potty about her. Still is, I'd say. Last year, he was going to bring her along to ours for Hallowe'en, but she was called away at the last minute, something to do with her job. He was furious, though of course we understood. Now she's dumped him, he realises what he's . . . lost.'

Melody's voice trailed away as she stared into the flames. Daniel guessed she wasn't thinking about Hannah Scarlett, but within moments she pulled herself together. 'Oh well, he's a very good-looking man, and he won't be on his own for long. Come on, I'm dying for a hot drink. To say nothing of a slice of that fabulous cake.'

'I starved myself at lunchtime, simply to justify treating myself like this,' Melody said, as she polished off the last of Leigh Moffat's home-made lime and pistachio zucchini cake. She'd also indulged in a large glass of Chablis. 'And I'm going to have to starve myself all over again if I want to squeeze into my party outfit.'

'Bet it was worth it.'

Daniel had pigged out on the chocolate fudge gateau while answering her questions about *The Hell Within*. He'd worry about his cholesterol count another day. At least he'd stuck to Earl Grey; he wanted to keep his head clear. Melody wasn't the most incisive interviewer, more like a rich woman playing at being a writer. But he was filling his face in a bookshop in attractive company. There were worse ways to spend an afternoon.

'Absolutely. Leigh is a genius. And here she is!'

Leigh Moffat was on patrol, brisk and businesslike as always, keeping an eye on whether her customers were content. 'Everything okay here?'

'Need you ask? I really must beg the recipe for this cake from you, it's utterly divine.'

As Leigh moved to the next table, Melody whispered, 'I don't know why she and Marc haven't shacked up together yet. Only a question of time, if you ask me.'

'You reckon?'

Melody giggled, and he wondered if the Chablis was her first drink of the day. 'You must think I'm a horrid old gossip. Poking my nose into other people's business like a latter day Miss Marple. I'm even passionate about knitting, as well!'

She pointed with childlike pride to the scarf and hat squatting on the spare chair next to her. Daniel duly admired her handiwork before switching the subject.

'So Ravenbank was the scene of two separate murders. You knew Shenagh Moss. What was she like?'

'Very pretty.'

'Is that all?'

'Shenagh was engaging company.' Melody considered. 'She . . . certainly had the knack of making herself popular.'

Hardly the most fulsome obituary. 'Nobody disliked her, apart from Craig Meek?'

'Why do you ask?'

'Marc told me that one or two police officers weren't sure that Meek was guilty.'

Melody pulled a face. 'They can't be serious.'

'A friend of Hannah's was on the team, and she had doubts.'

'That's the first I've heard of it.'

'Even as a local journalist, someone who was on the spot?'

'Hey, I'd never published anything at that point. It's only lately that I've built up the courage to submit pieces to the local press. It's not like I'm trained, or anything. I never made it to uni, I spent a few years as a model, would you believe?' Yes, Daniel could easily believe. 'I even tried a bit of acting, but I wasn't much good, not in the same street as Jeffrey or Quin. At the time Shenagh died, I was helping Oz to build up the business. I found myself copywriting, and that led to an interest in journalism. I've had a little more time for writing since we employed someone to help with the work.'

He dragged the conversation back to Shenagh Moss. 'So you never heard any whispers around Ravenbank, nobody hinted that that Craig Meek might have been innocent, after all?'

'Not a dicky bird. Craig Meek was a nasty piece of work, by all accounts. Besides, if he was innocent, someone else must have been guilty.' A wary smile. 'It could be anyone. Goodness, even me.'

'But you didn't have any reason to kill her.'

She considered. 'As it happens, an outsider might think I had every right to kill poor Shenagh. You see, before she turned her attention to Francis Palladino, she'd been shagging my husband.'

Follow that, her disarming smile seemed to say. Daniel was supposed to be good at diplomacy, but her pleasant candour left him choking on his cake. And groping for a suitable response. Two elderly women at the table on their left were debating the best way to make treacle toffee; to their right, a well-dressed couple were moaning about the cost of their kids' student fees. A cafeteria in a second-hand bookshop in the Lakes wasn't an obvious venue for a confessional about adultery and murder. Melody Knight was testing him.

'Did I shock you?' Her eyes stretched wide in pretend astonishment.

'I was wondering if you were equally frank with the police after Shenagh died, that's all.'

'Ouch!' She grinned. 'Oz reckons I talk too much. He says so much for ethnicity, I'm the polar opposite of an inscrutable Oriental. Though I was born in Morpeth, would you believe? Yes, yes, it's true. My dad was a Geordie, my mum came over from Singapore when she was seventeen. Unfortunately, my dad ran off with a barmaid when I was a baby, and Mum died when I was five, so I finished up living with my uncle and aunt.'

Daniel wasn't prepared to be sidetracked. 'About Shenagh . . .'

'What happened between Oz and Shenagh was an open secret. I'm not telling you anything you wouldn't find out if you speak to anyone at Ravenbank.'

'Uh-huh.'

Was Melody's frankness misleading? Why had she wanted to meet today? She'd learnt little more about his book or the history of murder than she'd heard in his lecture. A quick internet search could have answered the biographical questions she'd asked.

'Oz is fantastic, but he's also notorious, he's the first to admit it. When he and I got together, he did make it clear I was buying into the whole package, not just the lovely bits. His affairs never last long. But you know something? I'm the only woman he's ever stayed with for more than eighteen months. Let alone married.'

'Must be love, eh?'

'Whatever it is, it works.' Protesting too much, Daniel thought. 'Anyway, Oz wasn't the only notch on Shenagh's bedpost. But in my honest opinion, it's barking up a blind alley to suggest Meek didn't murder her. The case of Gertrude Smith was much more puzzling and macabre.'

'Although everyone thought it was open and shut?'

'Exactly. But I'm sure you'll agree, it's an intriguing case.' Her expression suggested an angler, about to reel in her catch. 'The build-up to this Hallowe'en started me thinking about it properly for the first time. And the more I mull it over, the more I'm convinced Letty Hodgkinson suffered an injustice.'

'Why's that?'

'I don't believe she battered Gertrude to death. No wonder the housemaid's ghost walks at Hallowe'en. The culprit escaped scot free – but not by committing suicide.'

'Let's get this straight,' Daniel said. They'd strolled back into the bookshop, ensconcing themselves in the old leather armchairs thoughtfully positioned close to the inglenook fire. 'Your theory that Letty was innocent is based on a hazy, second-hand account of a conversation between her daughter Dorothy and her old tutor when they were both in their dotage?'

'Roland Jones was Gertrude's lover. Nobody was more likely to know the truth about her death. And I suspect he killed her.'

'Why?'

'That's what I'd like to find out. I suspect he was jealous because of her affair with Hodgkinson, but that's supposition.'

'Did he confess to Dorothy?'

'He may not have made an outright confession, but if Dorothy had already guessed the truth, he didn't need to. When they met, he was dying. If the crime had weighed on his conscience all those years, he might have been glad of the chance to let her know she was right, and that her mother was innocent.'

'You'd need evidence to make that stack up.'

'Who knows? There might even be a book in it.' Melody leant across the table, her fingers almost touching his. Her eyes shone. The Chablis had energised her, and he found her enthusiasm infectious. 'I'd like you to talk to Miriam Park. She holds the key.'

'Because she overheard what Roland Jones said to Dorothy Hodgkinson?'

'When she was working at the Hall all those years ago, when it was a care home.'

'What did she tell you?'

Melody sighed. 'To be honest, it was her son, Robin, who told me the story. Miriam keeps herself to herself, and she's incredibly discreet. But she told Robin and . . .'

'He's not discreet?'

Melody laughed. 'Robin has the gift of the gab. Plays jazz piano, and likes to have a good time.'

'Does he believe Letty Hodgkinson was innocent?'

'He couldn't care less. Robin lives in the here and now,

he only mentioned the story in passing. When I quizzed him, he told me to pump his mother instead. But she gave me the brush-off.'

'She might do the same to me.'

'I don't think so. You're well known, you've published books and appeared on the box. Miriam is bound to be impressed.'

'Will she be at your party?'

'Of course, all our neighbours are invited. I'm sure you'll have more luck than me. When I tried to interrogate her, she made me feel like a nosy cow for prying.'

'Why doesn't she like talking about what she overheard in the care home? Does she think it's unseemly?'

'Yes, there is that. But if you ask me, she's afraid.'

'Afraid?'

'Superstition, plain and simple. The poor old thing is convinced that the Faceless Woman still walks down Ravenbank Lane on Hallowe'en. She'd rather let sleeping ghosts lie. Yet I'm sure poor Gertrude would want the truth to come out.' She checked her watch. 'God, is that the time? I really must dash. It will be dark long before I get home, and I have pumpkin lanterns to get ready and God knows what else to do. We can talk again about Gertrude Smith at the party.'

He held out his hand. 'See you on Hallowe'en.'

She curled her warm fingers around his. 'Don't forget your mask.'

CHAPTER SIX

The last time Hannah and Marc had met, the simmering tension between them almost exploded into all-out war. After Marc moved out of the house they shared, Hannah swore to herself that the break-up would be civilised. No ranting, no finger-pointing, no blame game. Even though the split was his fault. He'd cheated on her, but what made her determined to dump him wasn't his betrayal – a symptom, not a cause – but his selfishness. It was in his DNA. People can apologise, and make amends; she even knew a couple of murderers who, on release from prison, had led lives as decent and worthwhile as others who never so much as nicked an office biro. But Marc would never change.

He didn't get it. He wanted another chance, and was willing to beg. They'd been together so long that she could read him like one of his books, and he'd persuaded himself that if he grovelled for long enough, she would give in. A tried-and-tested tactic, but she'd stopped falling for it. Ditching him hurt, because he was a good companion, as well as good in bed and good to look at. But all good things came to an end. The decision was made, and if he put it down to stubbornness, too bad. And so, despite her best intentions, their skirmishes were becoming hostile. She hadn't seen or spoken to him since a huge row about putting Undercrag on the market.

'What do you want?' she snapped.

She heard him choke off a grunt of exasperation. 'Bad day at the office?'

'Yes.'

'Sorry to hear it. I heard on the radio about cuts in police spending. Hope you're not directly affected.'

On his best behaviour, then. He was seldom so sympathetic about her work. Last time, she'd made the mistake of venting about Lauren Self and her demands for 'efficiencies', provoking Marc into a homily about the cosseted life led by public sector workers. People in the private sector, who actually made and sold things, weren't blessed with gold-plated pension benefits, taxpayer-funded early retirement schemes, and long-term occupational sick pay. She retaliated by asking if he really believed that selling second-hand books would kick-start economic recovery, and the conversation plummeted downhill from there.

'Lauren is downsizing the team. I'll be left with two detectives and a couple of kids in the back office.'

'Jesus, after all you've done.'

'Yeah, well.' She'd blundered by giving him the chance to offer moral support. 'You didn't answer my question. What do you want?'

'I saw Daniel Kind a few minutes ago. He asked after you.'

'You rang to tell me that? Thanks, but I can't see my desk for paperwork.'

Not literally true – otherwise, she'd have committed a hanging offence under the terms of the Clear Desk Policy – but she still had plenty to do before heading home for a quick shower and change before her rendezvous with Terri.

'Hannah, I've been thinking. There's so much we need to sort out. Talk over. There's Undercrag, and everything else. Why don't we get together, over a drink, or a meal if you're up for that?'

'We tried that, and nearly came to blows, remember?'

'My fault, I'm sorry. I'll keep my stupid mouth shut next time. Promise.'

'Then it will be a rather one-sided conversation, won't it? The estate agent will email you about the sales particulars, to check you're happy with them. As for your books in the loft, we can sort out a date for you to come and collect. You still have your key, so I can make myself scarce while you're shifting stuff.'

'The last thing I want you is for you to make yourself scarce. Hannah, listen, I'm pleading here. Won't you reconsider?'

'I've done plenty of considering. My mind's made up. End of.'

The brush-off sounded more brutal than she'd meant. His tone changed into something wintry and quite unlike Marc.

'So who is your urgent appointment with? Not Daniel Kind.'

Who did he think he was? 'You're right. And you also need to start minding your own business.'

'You are my business.' His voice was clotted with anger and distress. Oh Jesus, was he about to burst into tears? 'You're seeing Greg Wharf, aren't you?'

Hannah didn't trust herself to answer without making things worse. He didn't have a monopoly on anger and distress. She killed the call.

She still had her head in her hands when Les Bryant looked in to say goodnight.

Hannah stood at the door of Balotelli's and scanned the bar. Terri was perched on a high stool by the counter, as unmissable as a bird of paradise on a dry stone wall. Since their last get together at a curry evening during the Kendal Festival of Food, she'd dyed her hair a vivid red to match her lips and fingernails. To have poured herself into that tiny skirt, she must have lost close to a stone in quick time. But then, Terri never did things by halves. She was wearing lashings of musky perfume, and she'd already finished her first Bacardi and coke of the evening. At least, Hannah hoped it was her first.

'Sorry I'm late.'

'No problem. Someone's got to keep the thin blue line intact, eh?'

'Easier said than done. The ACC is downsizing my team. Left to her, the cold cases would freeze.'

'Stupid bitch,' Terri said. 'What are you drinking? Please, not orange juice again.'

'I was planning to drive home tonight, stone cold sober.'

'Forget it. Call a cab, like me.'

'Okay, you win. I'll have a glass of Sauvignon Blanc. Small one.' This might just turn into a very long evening.

'Stay with me at Undercrag overnight. It's safer than going home. What if Stefan's lurking in the shadows when the cab drops you at your front door?'

'It's okay, thanks, I'm sorted for tonight.'

So that explained why she'd gone overboard on the perfume. Hannah peered at her friend. 'What have you arranged?'

'God, I wouldn't like to be a suspect you took in for questioning. No third degree, please, I'm not in the mood.'

'There's something different about you. Not just your hair colour. Which I love, by the way.'

'Thanks, sweetheart. I refuse to think about all the petrochemicals that go into caring for it. As for what else has changed, you're the detective, I'll give you three guesses. Sorry, deductions.'

'You haven't . . .'

Terri smirked. 'I might have.'

Well, well. So she'd finally gone for it. Those bags under Terri's eyes, legacy of countless late nights and chip suppers, and cause of more angst than all her cellulite, wrinkles and weight issues put together, had vanished. There was still a touch of swelling, but any bruises that remained had been skilfully camouflaged. The pair of them had often debated cosmetic surgery. Hannah had no time for it, and she'd given Marc short shrift when he made the mistake of wondering aloud if implants might be worth the money. Terri was more than happy to give Mother Nature a helping hand, if only she could afford it.

'How much did that cost, if you don't mind my asking?'

'My lips are sealed – and not because I've gone in for a trout pout!' Terri was gleeful. 'Honestly, I can't imagine why I've waited so long. It's not that I'm such a horribly vain old cow. Deep down, I'm shy and retiring, happy to fade into the background.' This last was an outrageous untruth, and Hannah struggled not to gasp. 'It's about changing my life, and boosting morale, and the plan has worked a treat. A single day being treated like royalty in this posh private hospital, and hey presto! I look ten years younger and feel like a teenager on the pull again.'

'You look fantastic. Then again, you always do.'

Terri squeezed her hand. 'Thanks for not scolding me, Han. I know you disapprove.'

'I'd never do it myself, but everyone has to make up their own mind. Free country.'

'Is it? Sometimes I wonder. But really, the surgery has made such a difference. Especially with this palaver about Stefan and everything.'

'The big issue with Stefan Deyna is how to kick him out of your life.'

Not that Hannah was necessarily well qualified to advise on dumping a troublesome ex-partner, given how hard she was finding it to ditch a second-hand bookseller who, for all his faults, was a thousand times gentler than Stefan.

'Sorry I acted like a wet Kleenex when I rang you. He's behaved like an utter shit, but everything will be fine in the long run.'

A thought struck Hannah. 'He didn't . . . contribute to the cost of the surgeon, did he?'

'No way!' Terri squeaked in outrage. 'What do you take me for? As a matter of fact, he hates my new look. He thinks these changes are about making a brand new me, and for once, he's dead right.'

'Shall we order some food, if you need to get away before it's too late?'

Terri frowned, weighing pros and cons. 'Actually, I'm desperate for a wee. Back in a minute.'

If she did want to blend into the scenery, the crimson lips and talons, tight top and black micro-skirt weren't the right way to go about it. Threading through the salivating office workers who circled the bar, she seemed not to notice the threat she posed to their blood pressure, but Hannah knew she was lapping up the attention. The blink-and-you-miss-it wiggle of the bum was the proof. Oh well, good luck to her. Terri dressed to kill not only because she loved to look great, but as her way of coping. Time after time, life knocked her over, but she never failed to dust herself down and start again.

Hannah took a quick peek at her emails while she waited. The estate agent said someone was interested in Undercrag. Time to think about where to move next. The house was ideal when they were a couple, but too rambling and expensive for either of them to live there alone. A pity, since she adored the solitude, hidden away from the bustle yet only a stiff walk from the centre of Ambleside. Perhaps the truth was that she was a loner, happiest in her own company, and unsuited to the give-and-take of a long-term relationship. Funny, she'd once imagined she would end up in a conventional marriage with two point four children, maybe working part-time behind the scenes for Cumbria Constabulary. But the clock ticked on, and with each passing year the fantasy existence faded further away.

'Would you care for a drink?'

A man resembling a pinstriped Friar Tuck had detached himself from a group of middle-aged men in sleek suits that didn't adequately hide their paunches. They were talking loudly about football, but looked as though they'd never scored in their lives. Bankers out on the razzle after a day spent inflicting further damage on the economy?

'No, thanks.'

After the day she'd had, she wouldn't give Jude Law a second glance. To her relief, she saw Terri weaving her way back to her side. The man permitted himself a leer, and when Terri responded with a look she might bestow on a maggot emerging from a chocolate cake, he scuttled off to the safety of debate about the destiny of the Premier League title.

'They never learn,' she said.

'Perhaps we don't, either,' Hannah said.

'Yeah, well. Change of plan. Can I take you up on your kind offer? I'd love to stay over. I was bothered because you need to work in the morning, but one late night won't hurt, eh?'

What plan had she changed? 'Are you sure it suits you?'

'What could be better than spending the night with my best mate?'

Historically, she'd preferred to spend the night with her latest unworthy loser. The reticence to explain Plan A suggested that Hannah wouldn't approve of it.

'Just like old times, then?'

Terri's face broke into the smile that always melted Hannah's heart, even when they'd been fighting cat and dog. They'd met at school, and bonded as fast as superglue, thanks to a shared hatred of their games teacher. Terri was the daredevil, forever getting into trouble; Hannah provided the shoulder to cry on. She was the one who felt uncomfortable unless she played by the rules. Was the secret of their enduring friendship – that each of them wanted to be more like the other?

'What shall we have, then?' Hannah picked up a menu. 'A poster in the window said a Neil Diamond tribute act starts in half an hour. Let's order a bottle of something, and then if he's hopeless, the booze will dull the pain.'

'You still know how to get round me, kid.' Terri clapped her hands, as enthusiastic as she had been back in Year 7. 'We're gonna have a great night, aren't we? Just like old times.'

Before Marc came along, in other words. They'd still seen plenty of each other, but the combination of long hours at work and Marc's tendency to monopolise meant that Hannah often had to say no when Terri asked her out. Hannah had never married, while Terri had trotted down the aisle no fewer than three times, but Terri was always up for a night on the town, and if her man of the moment didn't like it, he could lump it.

A young and rather handsome waiter called Giovanni found them a table in the restaurant, chatting them up as he did so. Morale duly boosted, Terri demanded to know the state of play with Marc.

'He's becoming a pest. Nothing like as awful as the hassle you're experiencing at the moment, but . . .'

'You're sure it's over and done with between you?'

'Cross my heart and hope to die.'

Terri had gone out for a drink with Marc before things started to get heavy with Stefan, and she admitted to fancying him. Was she was paving the way for a shift from casual flirtation to full-on affair?

Hannah's face gave her away, and Terri put down her

glass and said, 'Hey, don't get the wrong idea. Not many women would kick him out of bed, but we never got further than a peck on the cheek, and we're not going to. Trust me.'

'I wouldn't be upset.' Hannah laughed. 'You'd be doing me a favour. I can't wait for him to get fixed up with someone else, so that he'll stop bugging me. He and I both need to move on.'

'Watch my lips. I'm definitely not moving on with Marc, that's not an answer to your prayers. You ought to try my method. Let him see you canoodling with a new man, so he understands he's history.' She leant across the table. 'Talking of history, where are you up to with Daniel Kind?'

'Not seen him for ages. Too busy.'

Terri swallowed a chunk of garlic bread. 'You're crazy, you know that? Absolutely off your lovely head. The guy used to be on television, for God's sake!'

'Am I that shallow?'

A whoop of laughter. 'Well, I might be. Why not? That ditzy journalist he was shagging has gone back to London. I reckon he only teamed up with her on the rebound after the other girl topped herself in Oxford. If you ask me, he's done his grieving. He'll be looking to settle down with someone else before long, you mark my words. Snap him up while he's still on the market.'

Hannah groaned. 'You're impossible.'

'Come on, sweetheart. Joking apart, you obviously enjoy his company, and he fancies you like mad.'

'You're imagining it.'

'Trust me. I'm never wrong about these things.'

'Of course you are.'

'Well, anyway. I'm not wrong about Daniel. He's only

held back because he's had some bruising experiences in the past. That's why he comes over as introspective. But once you get past the barriers, he's a fun guy. Go for it, kid. Hurry now, while stocks last.'

'It's not that simple.'

'Bollocks. You enjoy making things complicated.' Terri slurped down the rest of her wine and glared. 'Or is that the old inferiority complex? You never think you're good enough, do you?'

Hannah almost choked on the last chunk of her spicy pizza. 'What inferiority complex?'

'Don't pretend you don't know what I'm on about. You always hold back, you're worse than Daniel. Shit-scared of showing your true feelings. This mad idea that you're unworthy. It's why you kept old Ben Kind at bay all those years ago, isn't it?'

'What do you mean?' Hannah demanded.

Terri refilled her glass, and downed most of the wine in a single gulp. 'He fancied you rotten, but you worshipped him and thought you weren't old enough or good enough to lick the great detective's boots. I can't believe you couldn't see it, Hannah, you must have been blind. The man would have loved nothing better than a good licking, if it came from you. And now he's dead, and you're on the way to making the same stupid mistake with his son.'

'Quite a speech.' Hannah tasted her drink. The hand holding the glass was trembling.

'Is that all you can say?' Terri threw up her arms in frustration, knocking the wine bottle to the floor in the process. Giovanni scurried over to check everything was all right, and once he'd been despatched for the dessert menu, she said, 'Sorry to be blunt, but you did ask. And it did need to be said.'

'I suppose I should say thanks?'

'Don't come over all offended. You know I never speak with forked tongue. At least, not to you.'

Terri was actually a seasoned and accomplished fibber when it suited her, and Hannah was sure she was being economical with the facts about Stefan. That was another story. Reluctantly, she recognised enough truth in the caricature of her as a shrinking violet not to start a row. *In vino veritas*.

With exaggerated patience, she said, 'I'm a career police officer. Daniel is an academic who travels the world, lecturing and signing books and all that stuff. Even if he was keen, it would never work. Not long term.'

'Never say never!'

'Isn't that the motto that's messed up your life more times than either of us can count?'

Terri pretended to recoil. 'Ouch!'

Her fit of pique subsiding, Hannah managed a grin. 'Don't dish it out, if you can't take it.'

Terri roared with laughter. She had an alarmingly high tolerance for alcohol, but the amount she'd put away was having an effect.

'Okay, I deserve that. But you get the point? We only live once. Gotta make the most of it. A woman like you should aim high. Higher than that detective sergeant of yours, not to put too fine a point on it.'

'What DS of mine?'

'Come off it! You're not the only smart detective sitting at this table, you know. The way you slag him off is such a red herring. Even that gay cop you used to be so pally with, he never made such an impression on you. Those were the days, when you knew better than to mess on your own doorstep.'

'Quite the amateur psychologist this evening, aren't you?' Hannah's temper was rising again.

Unrepentant, Terri smirked. 'We're like two agony aunts, really, forever looking out for each other.'

'Well, I'm not screwing Greg Wharf, okay? Which means I don't need to take care over him, thanks all the same.'

The intro to 'Sweet Caroline' began to thud out of the overhead speakers and a man in a bomber jacket strode onto the stage. He was wearing a black-and-white striped bob hat and scarf, Newcastle United colours. A couple of middle-aged women at the front of the room whooped with delight as, one by one, he ripped off jacket, scarf and hat to reveal a sparkly shirt and leather trousers at least a size too small. As a stripper, he was no Phyllis Dixey, but his fan club didn't care.

Terri contemplated the wannabe superstar's trousers for a couple of minutes before she said, 'You may not be sleeping with him yet, but it's on the cards, isn't it? I took a peek at your star sign today. It said you were on the verge of a momentous event, one which will shake your world to its very foundations. Well, my advice is, make the earth move with Daniel Kind instead.'

By the time they were in the back of the taxi, easing through the lanes that led to Undercrag, Hannah had mellowed, and Terri seemed, through some metabolic miracle, to be sobering up. The crooning of the wannabe Neil had had a strangely tranquilising effect.

'We need to talk about Stefan,' Hannah said.

Terri gazed into the darkness of the night, humming 'I'm a Believer' slightly out of tune. 'Sounds like the title of a film.'

'Don't dodge the issue. When you called me, you were scared to death. I heard it in your voice, and I didn't like it one bit.'

'Sorry, Hannah. It was selfish of me to disturb you at work, especially when you're under the cosh.'

'All I'm bothered about is making sure that man does you no harm. Stalkers are dangerous. You have to take them seriously.'

'Oh, I am taking him seriously. You're offering me a roof over my head tonight, and tomorrow I'm out at a party with . . . the people I work for.'

'For Hallowe'en? How can you be sure Stefan won't follow you? Trick-or-treaters get everywhere, he may sense an opportunity to make mischief.'

'The party is at Oz and Melody's house, out in the middle of nowhere. Stefan will never find his way to Ravenbank.'

After years of working for herself, Terri had found the going tough in a wintry economic climate. At a jazz concert, she'd met the wife of the man whose events company had organised it, and blagged herself a job. Early days, but she seemed to love it. Once the honeymoon period came to an end, though, Hannah suspected her friend would probably hate not being able to please herself. Most of her jobs had ended in tears; she was suited by temperament to being self-employed and answering to no one. Had so many of her relationships with men fallen apart because – though she would sooner die than admit it – she was better off single?

'You haven't said yet what Stefan did that made you call me.'

'Is this the right turning, love?' the taxi driver asked.

Hannah glanced out of the window. The new security lighting illuminated the area around Undercrag. No sign of that hulking brute hiding among the trees. Not that she expected Stefan to be quite so stupid as to stake out a DCI's home on the off chance that his former lover might show up. She leant forward.

'Yes, if you can drop us off outside the front door?'

Once they were standing out in the cold night air, and the taxi had disappeared off back to Ambleside, Hannah said, 'Well?'

Terri hesitated. 'All right, you did ask. He said he wasn't going to let me treat him the way his wife did back in Poland. If he couldn't have me, why should he let me go to someone else?'

'And if you didn't give in, if he absolutely couldn't have you?'

'Then he would kill me.' Terri turned, and contemplated the moon. 'To show he means business, he's stolen my cat. I daren't think what the bastard has done with poor Morrissey, but he's dropped a hint by sending me a photograph with my head cut off.'

'You need to make a formal complaint.' They were facing each other on the massive sofa in a living room warmed by a roaring fire. A bottle of Bailey's and a couple of half-empty glasses sat on the table in front of them. Hannah had decided not to fret about how she would feel in the morning. 'I'll give you the name of someone who can take steps to sort this out once and for all.'

Terri shook her head. 'We've been through this. It's not a solution.'

'Please, do it for me.' Hannah grasped her friend's wrist. 'This is how violent men get away with it. They rely on terrifying their victims. Women who suffer repeated beatings, women who are raped. Even when they tell us what has happened to them, so often they are too scared to follow through. The CPS need evidence, and witnesses who won't be intimidated, and time after time we see cases fall apart and the guilty walk free. So they can do it all over again.'

'You make it sound like I'm letting the side down.' Terri pulled her arm away. 'I'll be fine, promise. I just need a little time. Breathing space.'

'Stay here as long as you like, that's not a problem. But you must do something to protect yourself.'

'Stefan is already up for trial after smacking the lad he worked with. Chances are, he'll be deported soon.'

'Don't bank on it. His brief will wheel out the Human Rights Act and before you can say Strasbourg, he'll be issuing a writ for false arrest. And how long will it take for the case to come to trial? There's a massive backlog in the courts.'

'Then what difference would it make if I did file a complaint? You've moaned so many times about how bureaucracy complicates the job of locking people up, and right now I don't need any more stress. Anyway, the papers are full of people being let out of prison because they've run out of room. Stefan will go apeshit if some spotty young constable knocks on his door and says I've shopped him.'

'And what about Morrissey?'

Stefan had given Morrissey to Terri. Not that Terri was an animal lover; she'd never so much as kept a goldfish in the past. When Hannah was introduced, she couldn't help thinking Morrissey was even more obsessed with his looks than his owner, but at least the gift seemed to mark a promising start to the relationship.

Not for long. Since the break-up of her third marriage, Terri had rebounded from man to man. She'd taken this new job because hairdressing, make-up and all her other business ventures never made enough to finance her extravagant spending. Her shoe collection alone would turn Imelda Marcos green with envy. A shrink would have a field day with Terri. The men, the boozing, and now the facelift were all down to a search for something lacking in her life, something she'd yet to find. Hannah had no doubt that secretly, she craved stability. Her mother was dead, and her father had emigrated after falling for a Spanish-American woman who drank even more heavily than he did. More than ever before, she was on her own. Other than Hannah, her closest friends were all in steady relationships, and she'd managed to antagonise most of them, or their partners, at one time or another. 'Me and my big mouth' was a favourite phrase. In moments of self-awareness, Terri was at her most vulnerable, and that was when Hannah loved her most.

At other times, she felt like shooting her.

'It makes me sick to think of what has happened to the poor creature. Confession time, I'm not really a cat person. Morrissey and I didn't really get on, he obviously thought I was common. But even so.'

Hannah wasn't a cat person either, but cruelty to anyone

or anything made her gorge rise. 'Are you sure Stefan has taken him?'

'The woman who lives next door told me she'd seen him picking up Morrissey in the street when I was out at work. Said she didn't think any more of it till I came round asking if she'd seen my cat. She's as daft as a brush, thinks I'm after her husband because I took round cakes I'd baked one day when she was out.'

'And are you after him?'

'Give me a break. The feller's seventy, he's got one leg, and he keeps pigeons. I mean, I know you think I'm desperate, but honestly.'

Terri always made her laugh, even at times like this. 'This photograph you mentioned, when did it arrive?'

'I was only working a half-day today. I came home and found it stuffed through the letter box. It's a snap Stefan took of me at Bowness. I was looking rather tasty in my bikini top, though I say it myself. Anyway, it was a head-and-shoulders snap – converted into *just* shoulders. He'd cut off my head, from the neck up.'

'Did any witnesses see him posting the photo?'

'No, the neighbours were out. Pigeon Club annual meeting, more than likely. It had to be Stefan, who else? But it's only a photograph. He's not actually harmed anyone. Well, at least not me.'

Hannah fought back a yawn. She wasn't bored, but shattered. The clock said twenty past one, and she'd been up since six. She'd drunk too much, her temples were roaring, and if she didn't go to bed soon, she'd crash out right here. How to make Terri see sense? One last heave.

'If you won't talk to the police, will you see a solicitor? I'll come along too if it helps. Take out an injunction. Stalking is a crime these days, but there are civil remedies too. You could seek compensation.'

'I'm not interested in money.'

In the pantheon of Terri's breathtaking statements, this was up there with 'I don't know why I was barred, I'd only had a couple of small vodkas' and 'He reckons he's gay, but if you ask me, he's open to persuasion.'

'You wanted help,' Hannah snapped, 'but every suggestion I make, you throw back in my face. All right, I give up. I'm going to bed.'

'Already?' Terri's face fell. 'There was something else I thought I might . . .'

Hannah groaned. 'What?'

A loud sigh. 'Doesn't matter, it'll keep. I hadn't really meant to bother you yet anyway. Sorry, Hannah. You've been brilliant, as always. What would I do without you?'

'I don't need thanks. What I need is to be sure you're okay.'

'Hey, I'll be fine. When I found that photograph on the mat, it spooked me, but I'm over it now. Stefan won't turn my life into a train wreck, believe me.'

'Goodnight, then.'

'G'night, sweetie.'

Hannah blew her a kiss, and hauled her weary body up the stairs. Unlike Neil Diamond, she wasn't a believer.

CHAPTER SEVEN

Terri was up first the next morning, looking bizarrely immaculate as she popped her head round the door, shrilling 'Wakey, wakey!' She insisted on cooking breakfast, and her exuberance was such that, despite her hangover, Hannah's brain creaked into action. At last she realised what she'd been too knackered to figure out the previous night.

'You've met someone else.'

Terri switched down the volume on the radio. She'd retuned it to some unfamiliar station playing gangsta rap. At least it made a change from 'Cracklin' Rosie' and 'Love on the Rocks'.

'What makes you say that?'

'Someone you think will protect you from Stefan. When really you should go through the proper channels.'

'Fuck the proper channels!' Terri pretended to scream. 'I mean, I'm sorry, sweetheart, but you can't live your life going through the proper channels.'

'I only want you to be safe. Not go blundering into one disaster after another.'

'I can look after myself, thanks very much.' Terri considered Hannah's rumpled appearance. 'Which is more than everyone can say.'

'So who's the man?'

'I'm not uttering a peep. At least not for a day or two.'

'Come on. You trust me, remember?'

Terri dunked her bacon in the swimmy egg yolk. 'The diet resumes tomorrow! You know, Hannah, it's been lovely, just being with you. The two of us, together again, like the old days. And I nearly told you everything last night, but now I've sobered up. So don't spoil things, huh?'

Hannah suppressed the urge to bang her head on the breakfast bar with frustration, but only with an effort of will. 'Aaaaaaagh! I give up.'

'Thank you. And don't feel bad about it,' Terri mumbled with her mouth full.

Hannah drank some coffee, not caring that it scalded her tongue. 'He's married, isn't he?'

A hunted look came into Terri's eyes. 'Leave it, won't you?'

'That's why you're so enigmatic, because you've hooked up with someone who hasn't unhooked himself yet. Meanwhile, that bastard Stefan wants revenge for being given the elbow. Oh, Terri, will you never learn?'

Terri ripped the top off a pot of yogurt. 'You don't have a clue, Hannah. Listen, I've no intention of starting the day with a row, especially with a poor wretch who looks half-dead after a single late night, so why don't you just finish your breakfast, put on some lippy, and comb your hair properly before we go, huh? You're an incredibly gorgeous lady, and I'm luckier than I deserve to have you for a friend, but you do yourself no favours by not looking your best.'

Hannah swore, and said again, 'I give up.'

This time she meant it.

They took a cab to Ambleside, where Hannah had left her car. The short journey was controversy-free, as they kept away from the subjects of Stefan, Marc and Greg, and talked about Terri's new job instead.

'Oz and his wife Melody live in this fabulous old house on the far side of Ullswater. Think Wuthering Heights, but with all the mod cons you could possibly imagine. I'd never even heard of Ravenbank till they invited me round for a meal one evening. Can't wait to get back there for tonight's party.'

Oh God. Surely not even Terri was capable of carrying on with her own boss under his wife's nose? Hannah feared she knew the answer. Better not speculate. Let Terri tell her about the mystery man at a time of her own choosing.

'Have a fantastic time.'

'You bet I will. It's such a perfect venue for Hallowe'en. Really creepy. They even have their own ghost. A housemaid was battered to death there, about a century ago. Now a woman without a face prowls the lanes at dead of night.' Terri feigned a shiver. 'Wonder if she'll do the rounds this evening?'

Hannah swung into the car park. 'Enjoy.'

'Thanks.' Terri dropped a kiss on her cheek. 'So what are you doing for Hallowe'en?'

'Nothing much.' No way would she mention seeing Greg

Wharf. Not after last night. Two could play the game of keeping quiet about encounters with unsuitable men.

Terri, well versed in the art of deception, had disbelief scrawled all over her face. 'Well, don't do anything I wouldn't do.'

'So I've got plenty of latitude, then?'

Terri grinned. 'I'm right about Daniel Kind, by the way. Trust me.'

Hannah patted her friend's hand. 'If you change your mind about talking to someone about Stefan, let me know.'

'The proper channels? Well, maybe. I'll be a good girl, and think it over, okay?'

'Fine.' Hannah grinned. 'And if you can't be good, be careful.'

'You bet.' Terri tottered off in her high heels. 'See you soon.'

On the way to the kitchen at HQ for another shot of caffeine, Hannah bumped into Greg. When he asked after Terri, she found herself telling him about Stefan, and Morrissey the cat.

'I feel bad about it, but what can I do? I can't get involved personally, or I might find myself carpeted by Professional Standards, and that won't help Terri. If she doesn't make a formal complaint, we don't have a leg to stand on if someone tries to talk sense into Stefan.'

'Sounds to me like your mate's crying out for a bit of Alternative Policing. Want me to speak to a couple of people I know? They could have a quiet word with him in a dark alley.'

Every now and then, Hannah glimpsed something below Greg's rather appealing surface. Something dark and dangerous. One of her DCs, Maggie Eyre, reckoned he ought to come with a government health warning.

'Definitely not.' Sure that he thought her a wimp, she made a conscious effort not to say they must go through the proper channels. 'Too risky.'

'I like cats,' Greg said unexpectedly. 'We had one when I was a kid. I wept buckets when she was run over by a Ford Fiesta. The driver raced off without a second glance. I swore to kill the bastard, but of course I never found him. Pity. I was below the age of criminal responsibility – they'd have let me off with a pat on the head, and a few sessions with a social worker.'

'Maybe that's why you became a detective.'

He grinned. 'Wasn't for the money or the working conditions.'

'Anyway, we don't even know for certain that Stefan has harmed the cat. There's nothing we can do unless Terri changes her tune.'

'Sure.' He shoved his hands in his pockets. 'But that's how bullies get away with bullying.'

'And vigilante justice is how innocent lives get ruined.'

He opened his mouth to argue, but before he could speak, a nervy girl from Media Relations clattered down the corridor on her wedges and accosted Hannah.

'It's the ACC, ma'am. She asked to see you. Right now, please.'

Lauren Self was white with fury. A newspaper had phoned to demand how the police budget cuts would affect the county's well-regarded Cold Case Review Team, and the Media Relations people were wetting themselves. The press must have inside information. Leaks from the police happened constantly, but not on Lauren's watch, unless she did the leaking. Time for rapid rebuttal. A suitably bland, reassuring and mendacious news release insisted the proposals were not cut and dried. Everyone was determined to build on the extraordinary successes the team had achieved since being set up on the ACC's personal initiative.

'Brief the troops in the next half hour,' she told Hannah, 'but brief is the operative word. Don't be lured into discussing matters of detail. Refer anyone who asks about the implications for themselves to HR. We'll draw up a set of FAQs to set minds at rest.' A pause for effect. 'Though naturally FAQs can never be definitive.'

'Yes, ma'am.'

'And Hannah, one other thing.' For once, Lauren looked almost dishevelled. Lipstick smudged, errant blonde hairs straying into her eyes. 'This isn't merely a breach of security, it's a breach of trust. Believe me, when I find the person responsible, they'll wish to God they'd kept their trap shut.'

'Of course, ma'am.' She knew Lauren suspected she'd had a hand in the leak, but she wouldn't dignify the slur with an attempted denial. 'If there's anything else I can do . . .'

'Thank you.' Lauren in Ice Queen mode. 'That will be all.'

The briefing was an ordeal, for Hannah and for everyone else in the team. Her attempts to put a positive spin on the fact that cold case reviews would continue sounded hollow even to her own ears. Their work might go on, in some guise, but most of those who had built the team's reputation would no longer be part of it. Even stolid, dependable Maggie Eyre was close to tears. Only Les Bryant remained as phlegmatic as ever.

She fled to her room and shut the door. Thank God they weren't yet in open plan. At one point, she'd feared her voice was about to break with emotion. But the respite lasted no more than two minutes.

Greg Wharf marched in, slamming the door behind him. 'Are you okay?'

'Do I look okay?'

'You had the worst of all worlds out there. You're forced to toe the party line, and so the junior team members want to shoot the messenger. At the same time, I bet Cruella is making your life a nightmare. I wouldn't put it past her to blame you for tipping off our pals in the fourth estate.'

'But I didn't.'

'Never dreamt you did, you'd worry it was disloyal. And before you ask, it wasn't me, either. But hats off to whoever's responsible.'

'It won't make any difference, you realise. The money has to be saved somehow.'

'Yeah, but more fun to go down with a bang not a whimper, eh?'

She forced a smile. 'I suppose you're right.'

'Believe it or not, sometimes I am. Are you still on for that drink?'

'I said maybe, remember?'

'You meant yes.'

Another smile, genuine this time. 'I meant maybe. And absolutely not in any of the usual pubs, either. I don't want to bump into any of the DCs drowning their sorrows.'

'There's a pub out your way I quite like. The Cricketers, know it?'

When Hannah shook her head, he said, 'Exactly. The landlord is the ultimate party-pooper, he makes Les Bryant look like Paris Hilton. You'd think he was paid to make customers feel unwelcome.'

'And why would I want to go somewhere like that?'

'Hey, I thought you liked peace and quiet. There'll be no Hallowe'en crap, trick-or-treating is sure to be banned. No danger of running into any of our chums at the Cricketers, let alone the ACC. She wouldn't be seen dead in such a dive.'

'You're really not selling it to me.'

'The ale is brilliant. Have a glass of their Lakeland Lager, it's nothing like the weasel pee that supermarkets sell. Leave your car at home, that stuff packs a punch. Half six suit you?'

'I'll let you know this afternoon.'

'I'm off to Whitehaven in ten minutes, to interview that witness, remember? So it would help to fix up now, if you can bear it.'

How neatly he'd trapped her. If she said no, she'd come over as sad and self-pitying.

So she said yes.

It was half one before she grabbed a sandwich, and took the opportunity to ring Terri and ask how she was.

'I'm good, honestly,' she shouted. A drummer was

practising in the background; she was at a concert venue in Keswick, making sure everything was ready for a Hallowe'en gig. 'Thanks again, kid, for everything.'

'Thought any more about making a formal complaint?'

'Yep. The answer's the same as before. Enough about me, what's this I heard on the local news about your team? I thought the cutbacks were still under wraps at present.'

'Best laid plans, and all that. Lauren's on the warpath. She thinks I alerted the media. I almost wish I had. Might as well be hung for a sheep as a lamb.'

'My philosophy exactly! It's only taken you twenty years to catch up.'

'Some people never learn.'

'Speaking of which, have you called Daniel Kind?'

'No.'

Terri tutted. 'What about your DS Wharf?'

'He's not my DS Wharf. We're colleagues, I like him, that's as far as it goes.' Hannah took a breath. 'I'm having a drink with him tonight. Only one, mind, before you start getting ideas.'

'Yeah, right.'

She didn't rise to the bait. 'Have a good time tonight.'

'And you.'

The Cricketers lived up to its advance billing as a misanthrope's dream. The landlord spoke in surly monosyllables, and the men gathered around the bar looked like extras from *Deliverance*. The only other women apart from Hannah were two elderly women drinking stout in a dusty corner. This was the antithesis of those fancy gourmet places springing up all over the Lakes; if hunger struck, you had to make do with peanuts or pork scratchings. The only concession to Hallowe'en jollity was a carved pumpkin face on a jack-o'-lantern perched on the bar counter which looked less sinister than most of the customers. At least the saloon was quiet, and a bit of peace was all Hannah craved after a second successive day from hell.

She'd spent the afternoon closeted with the Deputy Director of HR, poring over staff costs and career records, trying to figure out whom to redeploy, whom to retain. Like any manager, Hannah knew in her own mind the outcome that would work best, but wasn't so naive as to try a pre-emptive strike. This was one of the lessons Ben Kind had taught her. When dealing with back office staff, far better to reach a consensus, than to try to force something through and then face long and debilitating guerrilla warfare. But the consensus had to be viable.

Greg lifted his glass. 'Here's to the Cold Case Review Team. Bloodied but unbowed.'

'Yes, I keep telling myself, it could be worse. I was afraid Lauren might scrap the whole project and transfer our caseload to Major Investigations.'

'Nah.' He closed his eyes for a moment, savouring the bite of the ale. 'It was never a risk.'

'What makes you say that?'

He ticked the points off on his fingers. 'One, the media love cold cases, and she has too much credibility tied up in our work. Two, cold cases are a safe haven for misfits like me, who aren't easy to sack and might cause her grief elsewhere. Three, she shunted you into a siding to make sure you wouldn't get in the way of her relentless march to the top of the greasy pole.'

'The great Lauren Self isn't afraid of me.'

'You don't think so? She's not stupid, she knows better than anyone that she's been over-promoted. So she's determined to shore up her position, and that includes pushing potential rivals overboard.'

Hannah savoured her lager. He was right, the taste was dangerously addictive. 'And I gave her the perfect excuse by messing up on the Rao trial?'

'Precisely. Putting you in charge of Cold Cases must have seemed like a masterstroke. And then you go and ruin it by making such a success of the job that her only option left is to cut you, and your team, down to size.'

'You flatter me.'

'I don't do flattery, Hannah.' He wiped his fleshy lips. 'Trust me.'

One quick drink turned into three slow ones, and when they were ready to leave, Greg suggested they call at Fryer Tuck's chippy on the way back. Hannah had planned to dig a ready meal out of the fridge, but he suggested they share a cab to Ambleside before he made his way to Kendal, where he had a flat. It was only good manners to suggest in turn that they eat the chips at Undercrag.

After lighting the fire, she left him in the living room while she made coffee. It wouldn't be a good plan to offer the option of alcohol. Or share the sofa with him. No way did she intend to send out any wrong signals.

Over the simple supper, she discovered a new side to Greg

Wharf. The revelation that he liked cats wasn't the last shock disclosure. He played and watched tennis, and during his annual pilgrimage to Wimbledon, he made a point of taking in a West End musical. Not just *Les Mis* or the latest Lloyd Webber, but edgier stuff like *Spring Awakening*.

'You kept that quiet.'

'Do you blame me? I'd never hear the end of it if the lads got to know.'

The horrible thought struck her that she'd written him off as a brawny hunk whose brains were in his pants. A Flash Harry who wasn't that much different from the villains he'd hunted when he worked in Vice.

'I still can't get over the musicals.'

'Hey, I love music. As a kid, I sang in the school choir, and got as far as Grade 7 with the piano.'

Greg Wharf, a choir boy? What next, Les Bryant as a teenage Romeo, Lauren Self a tireless worker for the underprivileged?

'So what happened?'

'My dad died, and I needed to earn a living. Also, I discovered girls and beer.' He grinned. 'Downhill all the way from there.'

'Don't worry, your secrets are safe with me.'

'What about you, Hannah, what are your secrets?'

'Me? I'm an open book.'

'Yeah, written in Sanskrit.'

'Ouch.'

'Sorry. I meant to say, you're admirably discreet.' He watched as she threw another log on the fire. 'And you have a lovely house to be discreet in.'

'Only half of it is mine. Much less once you factor in the mortgage. And soon none of it will be mine. We're selling up.'

He nodded. The break-up with Marc was common knowledge; the disastrous betrayal leading up to it was the stuff of legend back at HQ.

'When Zanny and I split up, I didn't know what had hit me. In the space of a weekend, I lost a wife, the woman I'd been seeing behind her back, and the roof over my head. And my job went west, quite literally. Within a week, I was kicked over to the other side of the Pennines.' Greg's matrimonial catastrophe was equally celebrated; he'd been married to a high flyer in Northumbria Police before getting far too close to a girl from Community Support. 'Everyone said I reaped what I sowed. Fair enough, but when you shoot yourself in the foot, it still hurts like hell.'

Hannah watched the fire. The flames writhed like exotic dancers. 'I'll get over it.'

'Of course you will. You're strong. Where are you looking to move to? Closer to HQ?'

'Not sure. I did wonder . . .'

'What?'

'If the time was right to make a fresh start. All this shit at work is hard to take, day in, day out. Perhaps I ought to try something else.'

'Like what?'

'Oh, I dunno.' She tasted the coffee. Too bitter. 'I'd just . . . like to feel I'm getting somewhere, instead of just running faster and faster to stay in the same place.'

'You've achieved a lot.'

She put down her mug. 'Sorry, I'm rambling. I shouldn't have had that last glass of lager.'

'Even DCIs are allowed to unwind sometimes.' He stretched in his chair. The fire was blazing, the room felt warm at last. 'Now you know the worst about me, when you're ready to look at staffing cuts.'

'You reckon that's the worst?'

'Well, your face was a picture.'

'It's not the image you've cultivated.'

'Fair comment. I've always liked being one of the lads.' He dunked his one remaining chip in a puddle of brown sauce. 'Blokes who like musicals are usually as camp as a row of tents, aren't they?'

'Marc once made me sit all the way through *South Pacific*. And he might be many things, but he isn't camp.'

'What's he up to now? Still licking his wounds after you kicked him out?'

She pushed her plate to one side. Half the fish and most of the chips and mushy peas lay untouched, but she'd had enough. That empty feeling inside was nothing to do with hunger.

'He wants another chance.'

'Who could blame him?'

'It isn't going to happen.'

She was talking to herself as much as to Greg, eyes fixed, not on him, but on the brooding screes of Wasdale in the watercolour on the opposite wall. Marc loved the picture, and she couldn't wait for him to take it away. The dark hues reminded her of a long ago afternoon they'd spent on the slopes above Wastwater, slipping and sliding as the treacherous black rocks shifted beneath their feet. She'd seldom felt as scared in her life; they'd taken a wrong turning at Marc's insistence – he always knew best – and came close to becoming cragfast in the wilds of Great Gully.

'It isn't going to happen,' she said again.

She hadn't drunk that much, yet her head was in a whirl. So much was changing, all around. Her lover gone, her house going, her team slashed to ribbons. What next?

'Hey,' Greg said softly, 'are you okay?'

'Sorry. It's not been the best of weeks so far.'

He swallowed the last of his coffee, and stood up. 'I'd better go.'

Tears pricked her eyes. Oh shit, she'd allowed him to see how feeble she could be. This was so fucking pathetic, she was acting like an emotional teenager, not a head-screwed-on DCI. All those years, she'd worked at painting a portrait of herself in people's minds, and now she was ripping up her own picture. And why? Because she couldn't handle this strength-sapping sense that everything she touched fell apart.

She cleared her throat. 'I'll get your jacket.'

As she stepped past him, he reached out and put his hand on her shoulder. She kept looking straight ahead. It would be a mistake to turn to face him. Any moment now, those tears would start running down her cheeks, and she didn't want to allow him a glimpse of her flimsiness.

'You don't have anything to prove,' he said. 'Not to me, not to the team, not to Lauren Only-Thinks-Of-Her-Fucking-Self.'

'Thanks.'

'You've got nothing to thank me for. It's the other way

round. They dumped me on you, which must have been a total pain, but you just got on with the job. And with me.'

She couldn't avoid looking at him any longer. 'Someone had to keep you in order.'

He smiled. 'You do it well.'

Her mind was a useless blur, no longer in control. Her body seemed disconnected from it. She moved closer to Greg, drawn by his sheer physical presence. Afterwards, she could never quite get the sequence of events clear in her head, but within moments they were on the sofa. His arms were tight around her, as he kissed with a tenderness she'd never have imagined. She smelt beer and a musky aftershave, felt his bristles against her cheek. His hand slid over her jersey. She didn't stop its progress, didn't want to. It had been a long time since she'd been touched like this.

'Hannah.' His breath was hot on her face. 'Are you okay?'

She moved so that she was almost lying on the sofa, head propped against a leather cushion as he eased forward so that his face was above hers. He tugged her jersey over her head and let it fall onto the floor. She saw him drinking in the sight of her. When she'd come back here to change before going out to the pub, she'd put on a black bra and knickers in fine silk, bought a month before the break-up with Marc and never worn since. Not because anything was going to happen with Greg, but because she was sick of feeling like a harassed people manager and wanted to feel like a woman again.

And now something was happening with Greg.

He slipped the straps off her shoulders, and fumbled with the hooks. Funny that he seemed clumsy – wasn't he supposed to be the expert seducer? A light glinted in his wide open eyes, as if he couldn't quite believe what she was allowing him to do.

As for Hannah, she'd given up on believing. She was so sick of careful, diligent, do-the-right-thing Hannah, the inadequate toer-of-lines who believed in going through the proper channels, yet somehow still managed to screw everything up. Life was short. She wanted, yes she wanted, to behave badly.

Her nipples stiffened at the touch of his fingers. For once, she wasn't worrying her breasts were too small or too freckled or the wrong shape. No time to wonder if, now he'd finally broken through her defences, he'd find her disappointing.

Greg bent forward, his tongue moving delicately from one breast to the other. She started to unbutton his shirt. It slid off his shoulders, revealing a chest covered with fine hair. He had a sportsman's arms, muscular and firm. As he breathed harder, she felt the intensity of his excitement. His hands slid to her starchy new jeans, loosening the belt, yanking at the zip. She closed her eyes and waited.

Somewhere outside the room, a door creaked. Her mind was empty of everything except the man she was with; she'd surely imagined the noise. But she felt Greg's body become rigid with tension.

'What was that?'

'Just the wind.' This was a fib, she had no idea really, but she couldn't bear the moment to end. 'It's nothing.'

'No, it's something.'

Then she heard it too. Footsteps, hesitant footsteps, but definitely footsteps, in the hall. Right outside this room.

'Hannah?' The cry was strangled. 'Hannah?'

'Oh fucking hell,' Greg muttered. 'Fucking, fucking, fucking hell.'

The living room door swept open. Hannah closed her eyes.

This is a nightmare, all I need do is open my eyes again, and everything will be all right.

She looked up, and beyond Greg. In the doorway stood Marc, the man she'd lived with for so long. He was staring at the two of them, half-dressed on the sofa.

For a few seconds – or was it years? – nothing happened. The three of them might have been wax dummies in a weird tableau, silent, rigid and cold. Hannah's temples pounded; she thought she was about to scream. Her mouth opened, but not a sound came out.

Marc was the first to move. As he turned to go, he gave her a lingering look over his shoulder, before shutting the door behind him with extraordinary care.

CHAPTER EIGHT

Louise wasn't timetabled for work on Hallowe'en, and she and Daniel stopped in Kendal to pick up their party costumes before driving over the Kirkstone Pass. After overnight rain, the skies had cleared, and as they descended into the valley of Ullswater, the sun sidled out from behind the clouds like a bashful schoolboy. In the old mining village of Glenridding, they parked near the public hall, and Louise pointed out the house she wanted to buy. A cottage built of green Lakeland stone, perched at the foot of Helvellyn, looking out towards the steamship pier and the serpentine lake beyond.

'You'll have the most beautiful commute imaginable,' he said.

'Only snag is, the pass will be closed in the worst of winter.' Her laughter reminded him of the mischievous girl she'd once been, before their father left home, and she grew a spiky skin for self-protection. 'Plenty worse places to be snowed in.'

Three miles on, they stopped again, and entered the labyrinth of woodland paths beneath Gowbarrow Fell. The route wound past the Money Tree, a toppled beech trunk into which people had hammered thousands of coins from all over the world. Once these were private pleasure grounds, landscaped for the family of a wealthy landowner. These days everyone could stroll through the glades on a pilgrimage to Aira Force, retracing Wordsworth's footsteps. Here the great man had found poetic inspiration in the daffodils, but on this last day of October, the flowers were long gone, and the paths were treacherous with mud and wet leaves.

Aira Force made itself heard before they set eyes on it. The waterfall's roar reached a crescendo as they walked onto an old stone packhorse bridge spanning the top of the cascade. Luckily, neither of them suffered from vertigo. The spectacle of the water crashing into the chasm below was dizzying. A chattering Italian couple, kitted out for the Antarctic, squeezed past. Daniel caught the name Sir Eglamore. The woman was telling the story of the valiant knight's beloved, whom he awoke from sleepwalking, only for her to plunge to her death in Aira Force. A legend Wordsworth turned into yet another poem.

'It's an unlucky place we're going to,' Louise said. 'Two women murdered. Do you think Melody's hunch is right, and the mad Mrs Hodgkinson was really innocent?'

He watched the swirling patterns made by the foaming water. 'With murder, like most things, the obvious explanation is usually right. On the face of it, there's even less mystery about who killed Gertrude Smith than who battered Shenagh Moss to death. Letty Hodgkinson's suicide looks like a confession of guilt, Craig Meek died before he could be questioned. But what if things aren't what they seemed?'

'So Melody's succeeded in stirring your curiosity.'

Something in her tone made him look up. 'What are you getting at?'

'She told you her husband was unfaithful. Better watch out, in case she's in the mood to pay him back.'

He shook his head. 'Have you ever known me get involved with married women? She wasn't chatting me up. What Melody fancies is the idea of collaborating on the Gertrude Smith story.'

'Oh yeah?'

'Yeah. She's decided my name might help her sell a book. Probably it's just a rich woman's passing whim. But she has interested me in the Ravenbank murders. Both of them.'

'Don't let her use you.'

Closing his eyes, he listened to the deluge rage below, as he puzzled over the contrast between Melody's conviction that Letty Hodgkinson was innocent, and her refusal to accept the same might be true of Craig Meek.

After lunch in a tea room overlooking the River Eamont at Pooley Bridge, they followed pony trekkers along the road that clung to the east bank of the lake, and past the small harbour at Howtown, before zigzagging up the hairpin bends of the Hause towards Martindale. Parking at St Peter's Church, they climbed the gentle contours of Hallin Fell to the stone cairn at the summit. Mist clung to the distant fells, far below the steamer chugged away from Howtown pier, and an instructor in a wetsuit bellowed commands at a group of teenagers with dinghies.

As the sun dipped out of sight, Louise waved a hand, indicating a small, wooded promontory poking out into the lake to the south of the fell. The peninsula was shaped like a human skull, connected by a neck of land to the valley of Martindale. The trees formed a copper, brown, and green mosaic. Close to the water's edge stood a large triple-gabled house. Even at this distance, Ravenbank Hall looked lonely and bleak. Somewhere in the grounds, Letty Hodgkinson, the supposed murderer of Gertrude Smith, was buried. From their vantage point, it was impossible to make out the design planned by Letty's husband. The Hall was undeniably imposing, but its design was curiously irregular and idiosyncratic, so that it seemed slightly strange and out of kilter. Ravenbank's other buildings were invisible, and so was the lane prowled by the Faceless Woman. A century after Hodgkinson had set out to master the landscape, Nature had reclaimed most of its own.

'So that's why Ravenbank was originally called Satan's Head,' Daniel said. There was scarcely a breath of wind, but he felt a chill. 'Seems to me that Clifford Hodgkinson was an Edwardian Canute, trying to push away the darkness of the past. Even when the sun is out, Satan's Head seems like its rightful name.'

'Oh well, we all know you should never fight against the tide of history.'

Her teasing amused him. After so many years when the slightest provocation had her at his throat, today they were at ease in each other's company.

'The peninsula was always distinct from the valley. People viewed it with suspicion and fear. Its sinister reputation predates all talk of faceless women and frozen shrouds. So the story goes, pagan rituals were commonplace at Satan's Head. Animals were sacrificed to appease the gods, and maybe not only animals.'

Louise, the rational lawyer, made a sceptical noise. 'You'll be telling me next that the place is cursed.'

'People used to say so, long before the murder of Gertrude Smith, let alone the death of Shenagh Moss. Hodgkinson took no notice, and paid the price. Like his successor at Ravenbank Hall, Francis Palladino.'

The sun reappeared as they scrambled back down the fell-side. Tiny and remote Martindale might be, but it boasted two churches. They stopped to look at the ancient chapel of St Martin's. The font had once been part of a Roman altar, a wayside shrine; the gnarled yew outside was supposed to date back to Saxon times. People had worshipped on this site for a thousand years. Had they prayed for protection from the dark forces of the nearby headland?

Britain's oldest herd of red deer roamed in the upper part of the valley, where public access was forbidden. Daniel's researches had yielded the titbit that Kaiser Wilhelm II once visited Martindale as a guest of the Earl of Lonsdale. He'd come here to take part in a deer shoot. Four years later, the Kaiser's war brought about an even bloodier slaughter.

Half a mile from St Martin's, a wooden signpost to Ravenbank directed them along a narrow, uneven lane winding between two fells. Bad for the car's suspension, but once they had bumped over a small humpbacked bridge, Daniel caught glimpses of Ullswater between the sombre mass of trees. He pulled up beside the moss-covered drystone wall, and they walked on a little way for their first close look at Ravenbank. Hodgkinson had planned a boulevard by which to approach his estate, but the straight edges of his proposed boulevard had long since vanished beneath grass and brambles. All that remained was a country lane. A heavy fall of snow would cut Ravenbank off from the valley. This was as isolated a spot as anywhere he'd found in the Lakes.

'So this is where the Faceless Woman walks,' Louise said. 'Perfect for a ghost. Even in broad daylight, you can't help feeling shivery.'

'I wonder why Gertrude's face was covered with a shroud. To say nothing of Shenagh's.'

'Presumably Shenagh's was a copycat killing?'

'Aren't copycats usually psychos who murder for the sake of it, not stalkers with a personal axe to grind against the victim? Craig Meek had it in for Shenagh – but why bother covering her face with a blanket in imitation of a crime from the past?'

'A mark of respect?'

'After smashing her features beyond recognition? I don't think so.'

The only signs of life were a rabbit scuttling across the lane into the undergrowth, and the mournful cawing of a crow. Daniel understood how the people of the valley had regarded this small, secretive enclave as alien and frightening, set apart from the civilisation they knew. Solitary by instinct, he found the quiet desolation of Ravenbank, and the sense that time had passed it by, weirdly exhilarating. He felt shivery too, but with excitement. Ravenbank had an air of mystery. Anything might happen here.

'Have you brought Jeffrey's sketch map?'

Satnav was redundant in Ravenbank, so Jeffrey had drawn a map with directions to the cottage he shared with Quin. Louise dug the sheet of paper out of her bag. Their destination stood close to the lake, at the end of a narrow lane intersecting with Ravenbank Lane, which ended at the gates of the Hall.

'Their cottage is called Watendlath,' she said. 'Why does the name seem familiar?'

'It's a pretty hamlet above Borrowdale, where Hugh Walpole set part of his Herries stories. Jeffrey named his house in honour of his hero.'

'I've never read Walpole. Any good?'

'He was famous in his day, and incredibly prolific. Even earned a knighthood, and how many writers can say that? The Herries books were popular, but Jeffrey Burgoyne is right, his darker stories have worn better. He was snobbish and thin-skinned, and when Somerset Maugham caricatured him in *Cakes and Ale*, the ridicule tormented him. Once he was dead, his books vanished from the shelves, and they've stayed out of sight ever since. Sobering, when you think his admirers included the likes of Conrad, Eliot, and Virginia Woolf.'

'You're such a bloody know-all.'

'You did ask. Okay, now we're in the mood for the macabre, let's press on for Tarnhelm Towers.'

Watendlath stood in a large wild garden of tall grasses, creeping ivy, and rotted tree trunks. It was a sturdy stone cottage with mullioned windows and an old-fashioned bell push. Quin answered the door, and ushered them in through a low-beamed hallway festooned with colourful posters and photographs from past productions of the Ravenbank Theatre Company.

'Each of our shows is a two-hander, and we play multiple parts. Jeffrey does the writing, then we block it – that is, work out our movements – together. It's scarcely Ibsen, just light entertainment, but plenty of fun.' He gave a suggestive wink and pointed to the photographs. 'That's us as a *very* Butch Cassidy and the Sundance Kid. And here is Jeffrey playing Raffles, the Amateur Cracksman, with me as his faithful chum Bunny.'

The living room bore such a strong resemblance to a set for *The Antiques Roadshow* that Daniel was tempted to peer at the mahogany sideboard and say, 'Marvellous example of late Chippendale, if it wasn't for that tiny nick, it would be worth thirty thousand.' A single shelf held calfskin-bound books by Lakeland writers: Ruskin, Walpole, and the poets. Logs crackled on an open fire; the warm, heady aroma of mulled wine filled the air. Jeffrey was due back soon, Quin explained as he waved them onto a deep leather sofa, he'd stayed in Keswick for a meeting with their financial adviser.

'Rather him than me,' he grinned, pouring wine into three huge glasses. 'In another life, Jeffrey would be a top-notch accountant, like his father and grandfather before him. Business is bollocks, as far as I'm concerned. I hate it when money gets mixed up with art. Cash exists to be spent, end of story. Probably explains why I've never had a penny to my name.'

Nice not to need to worry about the sordid realities, Daniel thought. Presumably financial security made it worth tolerating the occasional slap when Jeffrey was in a bad mood. Quin had done well to find a partner who could keep him in style. For Watendlath was undoubtedly stylish, every touch of decor demonstrating impeccable taste. A painting hanging above the fireplace made a vivid splash of blue and sea-green against the white stone wall. Quin pointed out the signature, and Louise gasped. It was a Hockney original.

'Jeffrey's parents bought it at auction thirty years ago. God knows how much it's worth. When he told me how much he pays for the insurance premium, I almost had a stroke.'

'Surely you needn't worry too much about burglars,' Louise said. 'There must be easier pickings, posh houses in villages that are much more accessible.'

'That's the beauty of Ravenbank. Only one way in, only one way out. If you exclude a marine landing, that is, and the currents can be tricky enough to test Admiral Nelson. But Jeffrey's cautious. It's the accountancy in his genes. Never takes anything for granted, that's why he spent a fortune on the alarm system, let alone insurance. Fair enough, I suppose. Ravenbank is hardly a capital of crime, but since we do have the occasional savage homicide, I guess we can't take anything for granted.'

'Melody and I were talking yesterday about Shenagh Moss,' Daniel said.

Quin raised his eyebrows. 'Oh, really?'

'I gather she wasn't a paid-up member of Shenagh's fan club?'

'Understatement of the century, my friend. Don't get me wrong, Melody's a sweetheart. But Ravenbank isn't big enough to accommodate two beautiful women. Robin Park's mum is an old battleaxe, so no worries there, and his latest lady friend is too loud and in-your-face to be serious competition for Melody.'

'But Shenagh was more of a threat?'

Quin nodded. 'Seriously glamorous, and Melody didn't care for her. She aspired to be the lady of the manor, even when Francis Palladino still owned the Hall. Shenagh's arrival put her nose out of joint. Even before . . .'

He paused, seemingly irresolute. As if encouraging Daniel to quiz him, to drag out gossip he didn't want to seem eager to share.

The mulled wine burnt Daniel's tongue. 'Even before Shenagh had a fling with Oz Knight?'

Quin sniggered, but Daniel sensed irritation that his thunder had been stolen. 'Oh, you heard?'

'Melody's very frank.'

'When it suits her. Everybody this side of the M6 knew about the affair. Oz hasn't a discreet bone in his body, and Shenagh was too thrilled by her conquest to keep it quiet. The whole thing fizzled out once she realised Palladino was smitten. So Melody has nothing to lose by being upfront about what happened. And she gains marks for honesty.'

'You're a cynic.'

'And you're not?' Quin pursed his lips. 'Come on, Daniel, you're fascinated by murder, curious to the point of obsession. That was clear from your lecture. Am I right, Louise?'

She nodded. 'Our dad was in the CID, nosiness runs in the blood.'

'Well, then. Isn't that why you've come to Ravenbank for Hallowe'en? Neither of you strikes me as a party animal. But who wouldn't be fascinated by the legend of the Frozen Shroud, and Ravenbank's history of murder most foul?'

Daniel said, 'Melody wants to persuade me that Gertrude Smith wasn't killed by Letty Hodgkinson. She thinks there might be a book in it.'

'Hodgkinson's wife confessed to the crime, didn't she?'

'I don't know what her suicide note said.'

'Well,' Quin said. 'We do know she took an overdose by way of reparation, which seems pretty conclusive to me. So what does Melody base her theory on?'

Daniel outlined what Melody had told him. 'Of course, it's guesswork. There may be nothing in it. And one thing did strike me. Keen as Melody was to talk about Gertrude, she clammed up when I asked about Shenagh's murder. Any idea why that might be?'

Quin rubbed his chin. 'Melody's an unusual woman, not easy to read. Perhaps she felt guilty about Shenagh.'

'Guilty?'

'She's a gentle soul, but I suppose she wished Shenagh ill when she was alive. But the horrific way Shenagh died . . .'

His voice trailed away, as if he were reliving the past.

'Did you ever meet Craig Meek?'

'Never. By all accounts, he was a loser who couldn't control his temper or handle rejection. She should never have got involved with him. Big mistake, and in the end, she paid for it with her life. Desperately sad, but . . . it happens.' He looked Daniel in the eye. 'For the rest of us, life went on.'

'So you accept that Craig Meek killed Shenagh?'

'Of course. Everyone does.'

'I've heard that at least one of the police officers on the investigating team had doubts.'

'Based on what, for goodness sake?'

'There you have me.'

Quin breathed out and laid a hand on his shoulder. His fingers were thin and bony, his grip tight.

‘Idle speculation, if you ask me. Pointless, and potentially hurtful.’ His tone was clipped, as if he were choking back anger. ‘Craig Meek battered poor Shenagh to death. Anyone who suggests otherwise is making mischief.’

‘Getting into the mood for the horrors of this evening?’ Jeffrey asked, peering over Daniel’s shoulder at the book he was reading.

He’d returned in high spirits, proclaiming that advance bookings for the tour exceeded all expectations. Quin had disappeared upstairs, to try on his party outfit, while Daniel was leafing through an anthology of Gothic stories he’d picked off the bookshelf.

‘I see you’ve made margin notes on this story. “The Voices in the Night”.’

‘An old favourite. Still gives me the heebie-jeebies whenever I reread it. And joy of joys, there’s even a Ravenbank connection. So I simply couldn’t resist adapting it for the middle section of our show, in between the tales by M. R. James and Walpole. Amazing the atmosphere you can conjure up with two actors and a few eerie sound effects.’

‘What’s it about?’ Louise asked.

‘A sailor’s encounter with a lone oarsman in the middle of the ocean,’ Daniel murmured, ‘one dark and starless night.’

Jeffrey said softly, ‘In a strangely inhuman and throaty voice, the oarsman describes the catastrophe that has befallen him and his fiancée. As he rows away . . .’ He indulged in a theatrical pause. ‘As he rows away through the mist for a final reunion with the woman he loves, the sailor sees the horror of what has happened to the oarsman, and understands why death will be a welcome release.'

Louise pretended to shiver. 'And the link with Ravenbank?'

'The author, William Hope Hodgson. In the early years of the last century he ran a forerunner of a health club, and challenged Harry Houdini, of all people, to an escapology contest. Not only that, he won.'

'He sounds like a real character.'

'Very much so. All this happened in Blackburn, Clifford Hodgkinson's home town, and when Hodgkinson built the Hall, he invited Hope Hodgson to stay.' Jeffrey gave a casual wave towards a Chippendale sideboard. 'In there is the copy of *The Blue Book Magazine*, where the story first appeared, which Hope Hodgson inscribed to Clifford and Letty. Oz sold it to me for a song after he bought the Hall.'

Daniel whistled. 'A good buy.'

Pleased with himself, Jeffrey poured more mulled wine. 'Needless to say, I haven't scribbled on that copy. Oz never realised the magazine's value, but my conscience is clear. Oz spends money like there's no tomorrow, and for all the literary events he organises, he understands as much about culture as the average Premier League footballer.'

'You're just like Daniel,' Louise said, with a touch of malice. 'A mine of information.'

Jeffrey chortled. 'You must excuse my *braggadocio*. It's not every day we entertain an expert in murder and the macabre. Now, is everything all right with your rooms?'

'Perfect, thanks,' Louise said. 'This is such a delightful home.'

'Our very own bijou residence!' Jeffrey's token effort

to make fun of himself was hampered by his supreme self-satisfaction. 'We're very lucky to have it. Houses in Ravenbank rarely change hands.'

'How long have you lived here?'

'Ten years. Before then, I lived with my dear old mater in Cockermouth, when I wasn't traipsing up and down the country, playing chief inspectors or lascivious uncles in stagey old thrillers and comedies. I did odd bits of telly, nothing you'd remember – a slithery alien in *Doctor Who*, a chap killed by a hedge-trimmer in *Midsomer Murders* before the first commercial break. When Mother died, I was ready for a change, and fortunate that I could pay over the odds to snap this place up the instant it came on the market.'

Daniel put down the book. 'You and Quin were together then?'

'No, we met a couple of years after that, during a production of *Les Liaisons Dangereuses* at the Theatre by the Lake. We discovered we had so much in common. Not only writing and acting, but a passionate desire for creative control. I had this dream of forming my own company, and when I suggested to Quin that he join me, he leapt at it.' An indulgent smile. 'He's always so impulsive.'

Creative control, yes, Daniel understood its appeal. He'd become sick of the demands of the television world, and nauseated by its shallowness. Moving to the Lakes had given him a fresh start. At last he could please himself, not just other people.

Aloud, he said, 'You have so few neighbours. Claustrophobic, surely, when you're snowed in together?'

'Very *The Mousetrap*, eh?' Jeffrey chortled. 'We don't all live in each other's pockets, thank heavens. Two of the six houses here are empty most of the year. We saw precious little of the property trader who owns Hallin House, even before he ran into trouble with the taxman. Same goes for the Bresnans who own the Corner House; they spend most of their time abroad in the sun. But the Knights are sociable, and so is Robin Park. As for Miriam Park, she's a decent old stick in her way.'

'Robin's house is where Oz and Melody used to live?'

'Fell View, yes, it's on the far side of Ravenbank Corner. The Knights moved there a year or so before Shenagh Moss died. At that time, Robin lived with his mother at Beck Cottage. It's the smallest house in Ravenbank, but she'll only leave when they take her away in a box. Miriam's husband was a musician who fancied himself as a businessman, but he ran up big debts. The only smart thing he ever did was to buy the cottage, and put it in her name. When he eventually went bankrupt, his creditors were powerless to force a sale. He died of a coronary, but at least Miriam kept a roof over her head. Working at the Hall as a housekeeper helped her to keep Robin in the style to which he'd become accustomed.'

'So how did Robin come to buy Fell View?'

'He didn't. When Francis Palladino died, he left most of his estate to medical charities, but a fifth of the residue went to Miriam, in recognition of the kindness she'd shown, especially in caring for his late wife.'

'A lot of money.'

'Money doesn't mean much to Miriam.' His eyes twinkled, and he couldn't resist adding, 'If you saw the clothes she wears, you'd realise that. She stayed put in Beck Cottage, and used the legacy to buy Fell View for Robin.'

'It was still a very generous bequest.'

'Nobody was surprised. Francis didn't have any other family, and Miriam was very good to Esme, as well as to him.'

'Were she and Palladino . . . ?'

Jeffrey guffawed. 'You must be joking. Miriam wasn't in the front row when good looks were handed out, and after he was widowed, Francis didn't look at another woman until Shenagh Moss came on the scene. After Shenagh died, Miriam did her utmost to look after him, but he went into a steep decline.'

'The murder broke his heart?' Louise asked.

'You could say so. For Miriam, it was an ordeal, watching him fade away. The money couldn't make up for that. I didn't care for Shenagh, but there's no denying that Francis was besotted.' He sighed. 'No fool like an old fool, I'm afraid.'

'She was a mercenary?'

'Oh, I don't want to speak ill of the dead.' Jeffrey's tone suggested he'd like nothing better. 'What Craig Meek did to her was dreadful.'

'You knew about Meek before the murder?'

'Everyone did. Shenagh was a brash Australian, no British reserve about her. Frankly, she gave us far too much information about Craig Meek and how horrendously he'd treated her. As for her behaviour with Oz Knight, it was shameless. Melody is such a sweet girl, I felt so sorry that she was humiliated by a woman like that. It was inevitable it would all end in tears.'

'But it wasn't inevitable that Shenagh ended up battered to death, with a rough blanket thrown over her face?' Quin was barefoot now, and he'd come down the stairs so quietly that none of them had heard him enter the room.

Jeffrey flushed, and downed the rest of his mulled wine in a single gulp. 'Of course not. It was a human tragedy. I didn't mean to suggest that she deserved to die.'

Daniel saw Quin's eyes narrow, and guessed what was in his mind.

Yet that's what you really believe, isn't it, Jeffrey?

'You look vile,' Daniel said.

'Really?' Louise asked.

'Creepy, disgusting, sinister . . .'

'Flatterer!'

She laughed and did another twirl in front of her brother. Their large and airy rooms occupied a self-contained part of the house, accessible from a separate staircase leading out to the back garden. Jeffrey had explained with a shudder that the previous owners had actually taken paying guests.

'I must say you're pretty unpleasant yourself.'

'Thanks.'

He bowed stiffly. The waistcoat of his Grave Groom suit was tight, perhaps because he wasn't as skeletal as the ribcage overprinted on his black polyester top. The outfit was grey-brown cotton, with tattered gauze fabric. Overprinted gloves, bloody necktie, and a soft fabric top hat lay on his bed.

Louise had morphed into a Skeleton Bride, the perfect companion for a Grave Groom, or so the people at the fancy dress shop assured them. Black and white dress with a tie bodice, spooky veil, choker and glovelets.

'You'll knock 'em dead,' he said.

'You don't think we'll be bored out of our skull masks, trying to make small talk with a load of events management zombies?'

He laughed. 'I know it's not your sort of thing, but thanks for coming along.'

'I'm probably making a huge mistake, pandering to your curiosity about those old murders. Mum would have been furious.'

After their father deserted them, Mrs Kind hated any mention of the police or criminal investigation. Whenever Daniel started watching crime shows on the television, she insisted on changing channel. Louise had been in her mother's camp, until her own close brush with murder brought them closer together.

'I've spent years writing and lecturing about historians acting as detectives. Since coming to the Lakes, I've found digging into past crimes is as fascinating as making sense of social history, or how the Empire worked, or . . .'

'You're a murder addict, worse than Dad ever was.' She hesitated. 'What do you make of the fact that such a small place – barely a hamlet – has seen two murders? It must be coincidence, but . . .'

'One thing is for sure. Even if neither Letty nor Craig Meek was guilty, as everyone thought, the same person didn't commit both murders. But it is a bizarre coincidence, and the fact that a blanket was put over Shenagh's face indicates a connection. What it might be, God knows.'

'Shenagh Moss's death is a cold case. Tailor-made for Hannah Scarlett.'

He refused to rise to the bait. 'We said we'd join Jeffrey and Quin downstairs at half six.' He checked his watch. 'Ready for the feast, Skeleton Bride?'

CHAPTER NINE

If Marc had ranted and raved, if his volcanic jealousy had erupted as so often before, Hannah could have eased her humiliation by flaying him with her tongue. He had no rights over her, he'd come to stand for everything wrong in her life. If not for him, she'd have put her career first; by now, she might be vying for promotion to ACC. However much he cared for her, it had never been enough.

Just as well it was left unsaid. No need to twist the knife. His aching silence only lasted seconds, but said far more than any protestations about lessons learnt, or promises to mend his ways. Pain and loss crumpled his face. The message was as vivid as a neon sign: *I needed you more than you ever knew.*

The slam of the front door was a thunderclap. Through the window, she heard the frantic roar of his car engine. He was revving like a drunken boy racer. Desperate to get away.

Greg shifted his weight off her stomach, but – thank God – knew better than to utter a word. Heaving herself upright on the sofa, she glared at the watercolour of Wasdale. Had

Marc meant to collect his favourite picture, along with all his other stuff? Shit, why had she let him keep his key? His shock was genuine; of course, he'd never really believed she would be unfaithful to him.

As the shock wave subsided, she felt drenched with dismay, as much at her own stupidity as at Marc. Whatever his preconceptions about her, consciously or otherwise, she'd played up to them. Striving to be all things to all people. At home, the main breadwinner, at work, the single-minded career woman. When she'd had a miscarriage, she'd kept it quiet; hardly anyone knew what had happened. She was mistress of her emotions, blotting out the person she knew herself, deep down, to be. Even Marc, who knew her better than anyone alive, had been deceived.

He'd never dreamt she might succumb to a smooth-talking womaniser, or have a one-night stand with someone like Detective Sergeant Greg Wharf. Except that Greg was more than merely a smooth-talking womaniser, and this didn't feel like a one-night stand. But what else could it be? Not therapy, for God's sake?

'Sorry.' Embarrassment choked her voice. God, she sounded wretched; she daren't imagine what she looked like.

Greg swallowed. 'You've nothing to apologise for.'

Scooping up her jersey, she pulled it on in a swift, decisive movement. 'I didn't mean any of this to happen. Not . . .'

When in a hole, rule one is to stop digging. She let her voice trail away. Anything she said now would only make things worse.

'You're not going after him?'

She winced, said nothing. Chase after Marc? As if.

Greg coughed. 'I'd better make myself scarce. Unless – you want some company? To be with someone, I mean. Nothing more than that, no hidden agenda. Honest.'

She shook her head. 'Like I said, I'm sorry. None of this is your fault.'

He started buttoning his shirt, with a rueful glance at the lacy black pants visible beneath her unzipped jeans. 'Well, some of it is.'

Following his gaze, she zipped up. 'We're both grown up.'

'Yeah.'

She mustered a bleak smile. 'Joint enterprise, then?'

'That's right. Joint enterprise.'

Should she add: *but not to be repeated?* This evening had turned into a disaster. She'd never believed in mixing work with pleasure, perhaps that was why she'd never slept with Ben Kind, though subconsciously at least she'd recognised his yearning. Greg needed to know where he stood. But if she started laying down the law at this precise moment, it would seem false and pathetic. She clamped her mouth shut.

'You left my jacket in the hall cupboard, didn't you? Stay where you are, I can get it myself.'

'Uh-huh.'

If she was in the mood to argue, she might have said: *Don't treat me like an invalid. Five minutes ago, you were about to shag me*. But all the fight had drained out of her. All she wanted was to close her eyes and sink into a long and dreamless sleep.

'Can I use your phone to call a taxi? Once I've rung, I'll walk down the lane, they can pick me up on the main road. No point in hanging around, I'd only be in your way. Besides, I need a breath of night air to clear my head.'

He dropped a kiss on her cheek. Very chaste; he might have been the brother she'd once longed for, and never had.

'Listen to me, Hannah. One thing I promise. Nobody at work will hear about this, okay?' A strained grin. 'What happens in Undercrag, stays in Undercrag.'

'Thanks.' Her voice was scratchy.

He strode out of the room, still the big, confident man she'd shown in here less than an hour before. But Hannah wasn't sure she was the same woman.

'Wonderful to see you both!' Oz Knight was a brash and breezy Lucifer, resplendent in red robe and bronze mask. Resting his trident against a lacquered table weighed down by bottles of Bollinger, he embraced Louise, and pumped Daniel's hand. 'Welcome to Ravenbank Hall!'

'Amazing home you have,' Louise said.

Darkness hadn't disguised the impressive proportions of the Knights' mansion, or the uniqueness of its site, on the crest of a gentle slope above the inky depths of Ullswater. If the setting reflected an Edwardian grandeur of vision, its interior was a no-expense-spared triumph of sleek decor and state-of-the-art technology, while dry ice filled it with more mist than you'd find on Blencathra in the depths of winter. Black-and-white movies starring Bela Lugosi as Dracula and Boris Karloff as Frankenstein flickered on vast screens in the main reception rooms, 'Toccata and Fugue' and 'Carmina Burana' played through concealed speakers, and laser light shows conjured spooky images ranging from diabolic pumpkins and scary skulls to garish reproductions of Munch's *The Scream*.

'Have some bubbly.' He handed them each a glass. 'Here's to the spirits of Hallowe'en!'

'This was your dream house, Melody told us.'

'Too right. Dear old Francis Palladino never realised its potential. He wanted to keep it just as Charlie Hodgkinson intended, but where's the fun in the status quo? You can't go back in time. Throughout the time we lived in Fell View, I was itching to get my hands on the Hall. Make it into somewhere special.'

Daniel savoured the champagne. 'You weren't superstitious?'

A sceptical grunt. 'I never bought the notion this was an unhappy house. Even though poor Letty Hodgkinson is buried in our grounds. Shit happens, that's the top and bottom of it.'

'Melody seems fascinated by the old legend.'

'The Frozen Shroud makes a great backdrop for a party, tonight of all nights. Even if you don't believe in ghosts.'

'Has she convinced you that Letty Hodgkinson didn't murder Gertrude Smith?'

'The woman was off her head, wasn't she?' Oz was loud and boisterous, sounding as though he'd enjoyed plenty of bubbly. 'Killed her husband's mistress in a jealous rage, and then took an overdose because she couldn't handle the guilt.'

'Melody tells me she'd like to write about the case.'

'Yeah, yeah.' He glanced over to his wife, an exotic devil woman in red PVC and velvet with matching wings and horns, making conversation with a couple of paunchy werewolves. 'Melody gets these enthusiasms, but they never last. I worry that someday she'll become bored with me too.'

He guffawed at the unlikely prospect. Daniel decided to venture onto dangerous ground.

'What about Shenagh Moss?'

'What about her?' The bonhomie faded, and Daniel felt Louise tug his sleeve in warning. If only he could see their host's expression; impossible to read anything through the eye slits of his mask.

'Do you believe Craig Meek killed her?'

'Obviously. He was a sicko who couldn't take rejection.'

'Shenagh installed herself here as Francis Palladino's partner. Did she antagonise anyone else, besides Meek?'

'Why would she?'

'Surely a woman like Shenagh raised hackles in a place as tiny as Ravenbank?'

'A woman like Shenagh?' Oz glared. 'She was a . . . delightful lady.'

'And an outsider who stole an old man's heart. Was it a love match, or was there another reason why a nubile woman teamed up with the man who owned this wonderful house?'

Oz picked up his trident. 'Who's been talking about her? Not Melody?'

Daniel felt a kick on his shin. Louise, fretting that he'd tested Oz's hospitality to the limit. Just as well the trident was made of plastic, otherwise he might end up gored by the prongs.

He said, 'Melody goes along with the consensus, that Craig Meek was guilty.'

'Naturally. By all accounts, Meek was a big man with an ego to match, but a conscience the size of a pea. If something didn't suit him, he used brute force to get his own way. The case was open and shut. Now, if you'll excuse me, I'd better circulate. Do come and meet some of our friends.'

Oz beckoned over a stringy-haired zombie and a toothy vampire, who proved to be the Knights' accountant and solicitor, before disappearing into the crowd. The lawyer evidently fancied sinking his fangs into Louise, and his drink-lubricated small talk soon had Daniel's eyes glazing behind his mask, but regular refills of Bollinger helped deaden the pain. He wanted to talk to Miriam and Robin Park. At last he spotted Jeffrey Burgoyne, a hooded Grim Reaper stuffing canapés into his mouth, and edged in his direction, leaving Louise to fend off her admirer. She was more than capable.

'Robin has cried off,' Jeffrey said. 'Taken poorly today, and confined to bed. But his mother's here, and so is his partner.'

He waved to two women in the corner of the room and motioned them over. 'Ladies, a chance for you to meet one of our local celebrities! This is Daniel Kind, the historian. You must have seen his television programmes, he's one of the country's leading historians.'

A sturdy witch gave him a brisk nod. Her companion, an extravagantly attired black widow, exclaimed with delight.

'Miriam Park.' The witch kept a tight grip on her broomstick as they shook hands. 'Pleased to meet you.'

'You don't recognise me, do you, Daniel?' the black widow demanded. 'Is it the wig or the mask that's my best disguise?'

Or perhaps the daringly cut dress, with jewelled belt, three-quarter length arms flaring out into cobweb lace-effect sleeves, and fishtail silhouette formed by another cobweb? A woman who liked to be noticed, and yes, there was something familiar about her cheerful voice. But she was wearing a full-face mask, and out of context, he couldn't place her.

'Sorry,' he confessed with a grin. 'You'll have to give me a clue.'

'This is my prospective daughter-in-law,' Miriam Park said.

The black widow whipped off her mask with a theatrical flourish and crowed with laughter at his astonishment.

'Terri Poynton, Daniel. You remember – Hannah's friend?'

Hannah lost track of time as she lay curled up on the sofa, staring at the fire through half-closed eyes as the flames flickered and died. Each time she shifted position, she felt as if she was dragging a ball and chain. She was too exhausted to make a drink or switch on a soothing CD. Her brain resembled the mushy peas congealing on the plate in front of her. Disconnected thoughts buzzed around her head, irritating and pointless as mosquitoes.

The *Doctor Who* theme roared.

Surely this wasn't Terri? Had Stefan tracked her down to the party and started making a nuisance of himself? Back aching, eyes gummy, she hauled herself off the sofa and picked up the phone.

'Hannah?' Greg Wharf, sounding like he'd never sounded before. Despairing. Fearful.

'What is it?'

'Something has happened. I need to come back to the house to tell you about it.'

'Tell me now.'

'It's better face to face.'

She wanted to scream. 'Greg! Don't do this to me!'

'I'm sorry, Hannah. It's Marc.'

'What about him?'

'He's . . . had an accident.'

'How could I forget?' Daniel's head was spinning: the shock of meeting Hannah's best friend when he least expected to, plus generous quantities of mulled wine and champagne. A funeral knell tolled through the hidden speakers: *Symphonie Fantastique*, 'Dream of a Witches' Sabbath'. 'Though wasn't your surname . . . ?'

'Poynton's my maiden name. I went back to it only a few weeks ago.'

'So you're getting married?' Somehow he managed to avoid saying *again*. Hannah had regaled him with tales of Terri's matrimonial misadventures. 'Pity Robin isn't here, I could congratulate him in person.'

'My fault, I'm so sorry. I jumped the gun.' The elderly witch bowed her head in apology. 'Do forgive me, Terri, dear. I'm simply getting carried away. I've always dreamt of having a lovely daughter-in-law.'

'No worries, Miriam,' Terri said. 'I'm so lucky that you're Robin's mum. When I think of one or two of my mothers-in-law . . . let's just say, they wouldn't have needed to wear a mask for this party. But Robin and I haven't named the day just yet. It's a bit soon, even by my standards.'

'A match made in heaven!' Jeffrey's tone implied: *I give it six months, tops*.

'We have Oz and Melody to thank, we'd never have got together without them,' Terri announced. 'I've only worked for the company since August. I went to a jazz concert, where I met Melody, and Robin was one of the performers. The rest, as you might say, is history.'

'Robin is poorly tonight?' Daniel asked.

Terri swallowed a mouthful of popcorn smeared with red food colouring and butter to look as though it was covered with blood, and refilled her glass with punch from a hollowed-out pumpkin.

'He's got the runs – yuck! Thinks he's on his deathbed, but he'll live. A real shame, he was so looking forward to the party, but he insisted we came along anyway. I offered to stay with him and do my Florence Nightingale bit, but he wouldn't hear of it. I ought to text him, see how he is, but someone has nicked my mobile.'

'Stolen it?' Miriam was aghast. 'Not in Ravenbank, I'm sure. You've mislaid it, that's all. It'll turn up tomorrow, when you least expect.'

Terri put an arm round the old witch. 'You always like to think the best of people. "Hear no evil, see no evil" ought to be your motto.'

Miriam shook her head. 'I'm not soft, Terri. That foreigner you used to know, for instance. He's rotten, through and through. If I had anything to do with it, he'd be thrown out of the country. Never mind all this human rights malarkey.'

'He's also history, thank God.' Terri turned to Daniel. 'You remember Stefan, my ex? I've made it clear I want nothing more to do with him, but he takes no notice. Even though he knows I'm with Robin now.'

'Borrow my phone to text him if you like, dear,' Miriam said. 'Not that it does half the things yours can. I can't keep up. One of these fine days, they'll make a phone that cooks a fried breakfast, mark my words.'

'Thanks, but not to worry. Robin's probably fast asleep by now, if he isn't still squatting on the toilet. I couldn't do much if I'd stayed back. Besides, I didn't like to think of you here on your own. I wanted to keep you company.'

Daniel half-closed his eyes, spellbound by Berlioz's dark masterpiece. No wonder people said the composer, in De Quincey fashion, gorged on opium as he wrote the music. The witches danced, their cauldron bubbled beneath the blasts of wind.

'I hope Robin gets better soon,' he murmured. 'I'd like to meet him.'

'Oh, you must!' Terri said. 'He's gorgeous. And he plays a mean piano too. I'm so lucky. Without him, I'd never have discovered Ravenbank. Brilliant, isn't it? Full of history!'

'I've heard about the legend of Gertrude Smith.'

'Ravenbank's very own ghost? Yeah, she's walked the lanes ever since she was murdered, hasn't she, Miriam?'

Jeffrey turned to Miriam. 'Melody told Daniel about that conversation you heard here all those years ago, when the Hall was a care home.'

'A care home? Wow!' Terri gazed around their glitzy surroundings. 'You'd never guess, would you?'

Jeffrey ignored her. 'Was it a confession to murder? Was Roland Jones admitting to Dorothy Hodgkinson that he, and not her mother, killed Gertrude?'

Miriam gave an apologetic cough. 'Robin should have kept that to himself. It makes me seem like an eavesdropper. I believe in people minding their own business.'

'Of course you do, you're the soul of discretion. The polar

opposite of me, I'm afraid.' Jeffrey beamed. 'An incorrigible chatterbox.'

Miriam wasn't mollified. 'Some secrets are best left buried, if you want my opinion.'

'I doubt any historian would go along with you, my love. Besides, it's utterly fascinating to think that for all these years, everyone might have been mistaken. Is that why Gertrude's ghost kept walking?'

'You believe in the legend?' Daniel asked.

'Why not?' Miriam bristled. 'People think they are so clever nowadays. But they can't explain everything.'

Terri said, 'Go on, Miriam. Spill the beans! What did you hear?'

'It was a very long time ago, dear.' Miriam's resolve was cracking, and Daniel suspected that she didn't want to disappoint Terri. 'I'm embarrassed to talk about it, to tell you the truth. It was only a snippet I overheard, and I'm not sure I can recall what . . .'

'What exactly did you hear?' Jeffrey asked. 'That's what we're dying to find out.'

'There were no private rooms in those days.' There was a faraway look on Miriam's leathery face as she lapsed into reminiscence. 'Just a ward with half a dozen beds. I was making a cup of tea in a cubbyhole next to the ward when they were talking – pretty much where we are standing right now. Of course, they were both getting on in years. Older than I am now. Each of them was as deaf as a post, and they had to raise their voices to make themselves heard. You couldn't help hearing odds and ends, however hard you tried to respect people's privacy.'

Chafing with impatience, Jeffrey was about to interrupt, but Daniel got in first. At last they were getting somewhere, and the woman should be allowed to tell the story in her own way.

'I'm guessing that Roland Jones didn't confess outright to murdering Gertrude?'

'Oh goodness me, no.' Miriam sighed. 'Really, it was no more than a few words that I caught. Only that Mr Jones said Dorothy's mother wasn't a murderer. He sounded very emphatic. And Dorothy agreed with him.'

'Anything else?'

'That's all I can recall. I'm sorry, Mr Kind.'

'Please call me Daniel.' He suppressed his disappointment that the great revelation had proved a damp squib. Melody couldn't conjure a book out of that. 'So he may just have been trying to be kind to Dorothy?'

'I suppose so. He was a nice old chap. Always apologising to carers, not that he was ever any bother.'

'And Dorothy?'

Miriam wrinkled her nose. 'She did a lot of good, I suppose.'

'But?'

'She was a bit . . . aloof. With Miss Hodgkinson, you always knew your place. Of course, you have to make allowances. She didn't have the easiest start in life. What with her losing her mother so young. Family is so important, isn't it?'

She was right, Daniel thought. When Ben Kind had run off with his mistress, it had taken years for the shock waves to subside. Louise had been badly bruised, and the divorce left their mother bitter for the rest of her life.

'If Letty was innocent – someone else must have been guilty.'

'I expect you're right.' Miriam shuddered. 'Can't we talk about something more pleasant?'

'But remember what day it is!' Terri raised her voice. The alcohol was talking now. 'We have had two murders right here on Hallowe'en! You couldn't blame Melody for feeling nervous.'

'What do you mean?' Jeffrey demanded.

'Look what happened to Gertrude after she fell for the lord of the manor, and to that masseuse who snared the last chap who lived here.' Terri's eyes sparkled with glee. 'Think it over. It really isn't safe to be a mistress of Ravenbank Hall.'

'Hush, Terri.' Miriam clutched her broomstick, as if for reassurance. 'You're starting to frighten me.'

But there was no denying Terri the last word. 'Let's hope for Melody's sake,' she exclaimed, 'that lightning doesn't strike three times in the same place.'

Greg rang the bell at Undercrag within five minutes of his call. Hannah hadn't so much as run a comb through her hair, but who cared? She was numb; she could scarcely feel her own hands or feet. And when she flung open the door, she saw a man who had aged ten years inside an hour.

He flung an arm round her, and kissed the top of her head.

'I saw his car from the back of the taxi. Of course, I didn't know it was Marc, I had no idea what he drives. He'd crashed into a tree – you know that sharp left bend, half a mile down the road to Ambleside?'

A wave of nausea washed through her. She didn't trust herself to speak.

'The cab driver and I jumped out, to see what we could do. The driver was bent over the steering wheel, he was obviously in a bad way. When I saw the fair hair, I realised it was Marc. I mean, I'd only ever seen him in the flesh for that half of a minute this evening, but it wasn't an encounter I'm likely to forget in a hurry, know what I mean? We called the emergency services, and did what we could to help.'

He hesitated, and she had a vague sense that he wasn't telling her something. But she wasn't focused enough to quiz him about it.

'He was breathing, that's the important thing. The paramedics were brilliant, and got him out in no time. They'll be checking him out in A&E right now.'

She detached herself from him. 'How badly hurt is he?'

'Too early to tell.'

'Come on, no need to protect me.'

'His face has a few nasty gashes, and I'd guess he's smashed some ribs. Whether it's worse than that, who knows? You know as well as me, it will depend on whether the internal organs have been damaged. The car's a write-off. He must have hit that tree at full pelt.'

She covered teary eyes with a hand, swearing in bitter self-reproach.

'Hey,' he said softly. 'This isn't doing Marc any good.'

For all his good intentions, if he'd touched her, she'd have smacked him, but he didn't make that mistake. Her gorge rose, and she ran to the toilet, retching violently as she locked the door.

By the time she'd washed her face, none of the lager or the chip supper was left inside her. Her stomach hurt, a fierce pain raged in her forehead, her eyes throbbed in their sockets. But she couldn't hide forever, so she pulled back the bolt and stumbled back into the hall.

'I know what's going on in your head,' he said.

'You reckon?' She scarcely recognised her own voice, or the ravaged face she glimpsed in the mirror.

'"It's my fault, I should never have come back here." But you can't blame yourself for what's happened to Marc. You will drive yourself crazy if you do.'

Maybe that's what I deserve.

'Stop it,' he said, though she hadn't uttered a peep. 'No self-pity, you're better than that. All that matters is . . . that he gets through.'

'I need to go to the hospital,' she said through gritted teeth.

'Not yet.' He stood in front of the door with his arms folded, legs planted wide apart, blocking her way out. Would he really hold her back if she was determined to go? 'He'll be in A&E. Maybe they'll need to operate. Use the time to get some rest, and go and see how he is in the morning. You help him best now by not falling to pieces.'

She hesitated.

'I suppose you're right.'

'Had to happen one day.'

For once, there was no humour in his grin.

'I expect you're wondering why I ditched Stefan?'

Ten to midnight, and the crowd of partygoers was thinning. The Knights had hired minibuses to ferry home most of their guests. 'Danse Macabre' whirled and rattled in the background as Daniel was cornered by the Black Widow. On the other side of the room, Quin was regaling Louise and Miriam Park with tales of an actor's life. Jeffrey was with Melody and Oz, exchanging farewells with friends from the Theatre by the Lake.

'I guess it didn't work out.' Daniel had met Stefan briefly in the summer. 'But you seem happy, and that's what matters.'

'He's been an absolute scumbag, to be honest. The man can be utterly scary when he's in a foul mood. He's been stalking me.'

Terri didn't strike Daniel as someone who scared easily. 'Has he threatened you?'

She nodded. 'No woman is ever allowed to dump him without paying for it. God, what did I ever see in him?'

'You've told Hannah?'

'Of course, she's up in arms, wants me to drag in m'learned friends and all that crap. The thing is, she doesn't know the full story yet. I'm dying to tell her about Robin, but I wanted to get tonight's announcement out of the way first.'

'What announcement? That you're getting married?'

Terri took another gulp of champagne. The Knights hadn't stinted; Oz and Melody kept topping up everyone's glasses, but there were still bottles unopened.

'No, it's too soon for wedding bells. Miriam would love to see Robin settled once and for all, with three or four grandkids running around, and being sick over her pinafore. But he's not the sort of feller who likes to feel tied down. I know how he feels, I've been tied down too often for my own good.' She screeched with laughter. 'No, my poor old dad isn't well. We haven't always seen eye to eye, but he's on his own now, and I need to move closer to him.'

'Sorry to hear that.'

'Old age, eh? Not a lot of fun. Why can't we stay young forever? Anyway, looking after Dad will help me forget about Stefan. And it suits Robin, he's perfectly happy.' She laughed again, and he realised she'd drunk even more than he had. 'Mind you, the only travelling he's done today is back and forth to the loo. So – no big announcement, no fanfare. Never mind, eh?'

'You'll tell Hannah now, though?'

'I almost did already, but then I thought I'd wait till after the party.' Terri leant closer. 'I feel a bit guilty, to tell you the truth, but Dad needs all the support he can get. As for Hannah, she ought to get shot of Marc, and that old barn of a house, and make a fresh start. Stop worrying so much about work. Get some fun back into her life.'

'She'll be fine,' he said. 'Hannah's a survivor.'

'More than that. She's a winner. A class act. Believe me, Daniel, she's one in a million. She just screwed up over Marc. Cheekbones to die for, but a self-centred wimp. She deserves better.'

Uh-oh. Daniel saw the way this conversation was heading. He mumbled something non-committal. But Terri wasn't letting go.

'Were your ears burning the other day?' she demanded. 'Hannah and I were talking, and your name cropped up.'

Louise's arrival rescued him. 'Quin's insisting that we all go out in search of the Faceless Woman.'

'Brilliant idea – yeah, let's see if Gertrude Smith is on the prowl!' Terri couldn't contain her delight. 'Who can resist a ghost hunt?'

* * *

In her dream, Hannah was late for a funeral, racing through narrow urban streets towards a strange church with a square tower resembling a campanile. She'd missed the service, and as she reached a gap in the stone wall around the graveyard, she saw that men and women dressed in black from head to toe were following pall-bearers carrying a coffin the colour of blood.

She squeezed through the gap and stumbled down a pathway lined with tombstones, knowing that if she did not reach the graveside before the coffin was lowered into its resting place, something terrible would happen. The mourners blocked her way, ignoring her pleas to be let through. She found herself crawling on hands and knees along the wet earth, muddying her clothes, but not caring about anything except to get there in time.

The priest was chanting something, in a language she couldn't understand. She struggled to her feet, only to see the six burly men stepping away from the open grave, their job done.

She shoved her way past the mourners, and the priest turned to glare at her. Taking no notice, she peered down into the hole. The coffin lid was open.

Marc stared up at her, his chalk-white face wrinkled by hurt and reproach.

The ghost-hunters staggered out into the night. They were in pairs; Quin and Jeffrey led the way, arm in arm, weaving unsteadily between the buxus tubs outside the porticoed entrance of Ravenbank Hall. Daniel and Louise came next, then Miriam and Terri. Melody and Oz brought up the rear of the party, after locking up and sorting out the alarms.

During the party, there had been a torrential storm. The grass was sodden, and they found themselves splashing through large puddles on the driveway. Lamps spaced at regular intervals illuminated the way as far as the Hall's iron gates. Beyond, the lane leading to Martindale was unlit, but the moon was high, and the Knights had supplied everyone with torches.

There was something peculiarly British about a ghost hunt, Daniel reflected. In ancient times, had people believed this misty, twilit land was on the very edge of the world? The Roman legionnaires who strode along the road high above Martindale believed the country to be infested with spirits. But apparitions were untouchable, tantalising those who sought them out. However close they seemed, whatever form and shape they took, they remained forever out of reach.

Louise broke into his thoughts. 'Think of that poor girl Gertrude. What in God's name was she doing outside, the night she was murdered?'

'One account suggests Letty lured her out. Sent a message arranging a tryst, pretending it came from Clifford. Caught her unawares, and bashed her face in.'

'So was Letty strong enough to batter her to death despite her poor health?'

'Her illness was mental, not physical. What's more, Gertrude had a withered arm. If Letty took her by surprise, she couldn't have managed much of a fight to save her life.'

'The disability must have made it tough, working as a maid.'

'Depends on her duties, doesn't it? She had fair hair, blue eyes and a coy smile. All the reports of the case dwell on how pretty she was. I doubt Hodgkinson recruited her just to clean the silver.'

'And then it all went tits-up when Gertrude got pregnant?'

'That's one way of putting it. Question is – who was the father? The assumption seems to have been that it was Clifford, and Letty found out. Suppose the news of the pregnancy drove Roland Jones to fury.'

'You think he killed Gertrude in a rage?'

'Or maybe he was the father, and she wanted to get rid of the child . . . the permutations are endless. But it doesn't look like Miriam Park will be much help.'

An owl hooted in the trees. It sounded despondent, as though contemplating human folly. Otherwise, everything was quiet. Daniel fixed his torch beam on the ground. He needed to watch his step. It would be easy to trip, and sprain an ankle, or worse.

'Nothing could ever be proved anyway, not after all this time,' Louise said.

'A historian can't ever afford to think like that.'

'So are you going to see what you can find out about Roland Jones?' He nodded. 'And what about Shenagh Moss?'

'Everyone here resists any suggestion that Craig Meek wasn't responsible.'

'Can you blame them? Raking over the ashes when the people concerned are dead and buried is one thing. Very different when everyone involved is still around. Nobody likes having their lives put under the microscope. All over again, years after the case was officially closed? Nightmare.'

A fresh gust coming in from the lake rippled the branches.

'I'll talk to Hannah about Shenagh, and see if she's interested in looking into the evidence.'

'Good plan.' He didn't need to look at his sister to picture the told-you-so smile.

'Pity Robin Park was out of action. I wanted to say hello.'

'What's your ulterior motive?'

She knew him too well. 'He may not have met Dorothy Hodgkinson or Roland Jones, but he might tell me more about her than I prised out of his mum.'

Raucous laughter tore through the silence. Terri Poynton's hilarity was noisy and distinctive as she enjoyed one of her own jokes. Could Terri make a go of her relationship with Robin Park? Hannah, Daniel knew, despaired of her friend's judgement of men, though after Marc's betrayal of her, she was in no position to talk.

'Is this the place?'

Louise clutched at her brother's sleeve. They'd passed Miriam's cottage, but Quin and Jeffrey had halted where the road crossed the lane running from one side of the promontory to the other. Hodgkinson planned this as the hub of the development. An empty house stood at one corner, and a shop-cum-post-office was to have been built on another, but all that remained were a few foundations, hidden from view by clumps of stinging nettles and a patch of gorse.

'Gertrude's body was lying under the trees, on the other side of the beck,' Jeffrey panted. 'No sign of her on the move tonight, alas! Not so much as the flicker of a shroud.'

Louise shone her torch around, as Terri and Miriam joined them. The beck ran roughly in parallel with the road for a short distance, before veering off towards the lake.

Two women had died near here. Daniel could hardly bear to picture their final moments. Had they recognised their assailants, had they realised they were about to die at the hands of someone they knew – perhaps someone they had once loved?

And was that someone necessarily the obvious suspect?

'Woo! Woo!' Terri was loving the occasion. Her eyes were glassy, her gait unsteady. 'C'mon, Faceless Woman, let's be having you! We haven't got all night!'

Daniel visualised Jeffrey's sketch map. 'So Fell View is down there, on the other limb of Water Lane?'

'Beyond the trees, that's right,' Jeffrey said. 'Although Gertrude's body was left close to the roadside, this is a pretty safe place to commit a murder. Not overlooked by any of the houses, and at this time of night, no danger of passing traffic.'

The Knights joined them, Melody trudging behind her husband. She looked weary and cold. The rain had swelled the beck and they could hear the rush of water in the distance.

'Don't tell me Gertrude is skiving off tonight?' Oz called. 'No Faceless Woman? Dear me, how disappointing.'

'Shockingly remiss of you as a host, old chap,' Jeffrey said. 'I expected you to put on a bit of a show for us.'

Oz's perfect teeth glinted in the torchlight. 'Absolutely. You all deserved a special treat, and I've let you down.'

'What about Shenagh Moss?' Daniel asked. 'Where was her body found?'

'You seem terribly interested in Shenagh,' Quin said. 'Any particular reason?'

'Both cases fascinate me. Two women, their faces destroyed, then shrouded, on Hallowe'en.'

'Craig Meek must have lacked imagination,' Terri scoffed.

'It's no laughing matter,' Miriam muttered. 'This Stefan of yours, he's no different. Men like that are a menace to decent folk.'

The wind was gathering strength, and in the moonlight Daniel saw branches dancing in the dark. Melody seemed lost in her own thoughts. Her husband waved towards the woodland.

'A network of paths lead from the road to the shore. Shenagh used to walk their dog all around. Francis found her, two minutes from here. Does that answer your question?'

'Thanks.'

Miriam stifled a yawn. 'I'm about done in. Terri, do you mind if I come back with you for a minute to make sure Robin is all right?'

'Course not. I'll walk you back home, make sure you aren't accosted by any old ghost.' The Black Widow linked arms with the old witch. 'Goodnight, all! Oz, Melody, thanks a million, it's been fantastic. I wouldn't have missed it for anything. Robin will be gutted he couldn't make it.'

She'd given the signal for the party to break up. Assorted ghouls kissed and hugged, before Daniel and Louise followed Jeffrey and Quin up the road towards Watendlath.

As they trudged off into the night, they heard Terri's voice, ripping up the silence.

'Woo! Woo!' she cried. 'Woo! Woo!'

And then she dissolved into helpless, boozy laughter.

CHAPTER TEN

Hannah had a phobia about hospitals, dating back to her childhood. It was a dread she'd kept to herself; she'd never shared it with Marc, not even in their earliest, happiest days together. Did that show she'd never really trusted him? It didn't matter now, anyway.

At the age of thirteen, she'd been rushed in for an emergency operation to remove her appendix, an experience more frightening than any of her adult encounters with sociopaths armed with knife, gun, or – a few months earlier – scythe. She'd never forget the heart-pounding fear of being slit open, the dizzying terror of never being whole again. To this day, the squeak of hospital trolleys on tiled floors set her teeth on edge, and the smell of antiseptic made her gorge rise. She'd spent her adult life making excuses to avoid visiting hospitals unless there was no choice. But today she had no choice. She had no hope of getting any rest until she found out how Marc was. After waking from her nightmare, she'd found it impossible to get back to sleep. She needed to know.

As she put herself through the purgatory of an ice-cold shower, she remembered where she'd seen the strange church of her dream. On a wall in Tarn Cottage. Daniel had hung a watercolour that fascinated her. A Jericho, Oxford, street scene; he said he'd lived there as a student, and the exotic architecture of St Barnabas had fascinated him. She'd never given the image another thought, and yet it had lodged in her subconscious.

As she drove through the drizzle along the winding road to Kendal, she focused on psyching herself up for whatever lay ahead. By the time she strode into A&E, she was ready to cope with anything. Even the suffocating claustrophobia that the labyrinth of corridors induced in her. And yes, even big hospital bureaucracy. For all its virtues, the NHS, like the police, and probably any large organisation, allowed systems and process to get in the way of talking to people.

This morning, she had become an irresistible force. Token efforts to fob her off until visiting hours made no more impression than a kid's catapult on a Chieftain tank. Within ten minutes of her arrival, steely determination, coupled with the ruthless deployment of her warrant card, earned an audience with a calm and caring young Asian doctor.

'I'm afraid Marc isn't a pretty sight at the moment, DCI Scarlett. You can imagine, after such a terrible accident. He's . . .'

'What's the damage?' She breathed in. This felt like trying to hold off an avalanche, an avalanche of emotion. A picture flitted through her head of the cool, collected woman she'd once imagined herself to be. Just another figment of her imagination.

'He sustained a nasty gash to his forehead that needed a lot of stitches.' The woman paused. 'The other cuts are largely superficial. It will be several weeks before he's posing for snapshots again, but the scars will heal. Two ribs are broken, and there's a lot of bruising. Fortunately, there's nothing more serious.'

Hannah ground her teeth. 'You think he'll make a full recovery?'

'I'm absolutely confident. He's sleeping now, totally out of it, and he'll be sore and uncomfortable for a while, but he's a fit and healthy man, and he'll get through in decent shape.'

Hannah didn't trust herself to speak.

'Don't let him feel too sorry for himself when he comes back home. You know what men are like.'

Not really, Hannah thought: the more I know about men, the less I understand them. Do Greg, and Marc, and Daniel feel the same about me?

'You're sure . . . ?'

'He's lucky, Detective Chief Inspector. Believe me, it could have been so much worse.' The doctor fiddled with her spectacles. 'How did the accident happen?'

Stupid, stupid idiot! Hannah only just stopped herself screaming in self-reproach. All she could do was mumble something hopelessly incoherent. Why hadn't she prepared for the obvious, the inevitable question: had she completely lost the plot? Lurid visions had swum in her head. Marc in a wheelchair, Marc in a coma, Marc in a morgue. She hadn't slept after waking from the nightmare, couldn't rid her mind of the terror she'd felt when peering down into that open grave.

'Are you okay?' the doctor asked. 'Sorry, silly question. This must all have come as such a shock. Would you like a cup of tea?'

Hannah shook her head again. 'You've been very kind, Doctor Sharma. I know you have to do your rounds. I mustn't take up any more of your time.'

They shook hands, and she made good her escape. As she turned into the corridor, it was hard to resist the urge to break into a run. Anything to get away in one piece. She'd dodged that tricky question, and though others would press her harder than a nice young medic with more important things on her mind, she'd worry about that some other time.

Marc was going to make it, and nothing else really mattered. She'd escaped from the dreaded hospital. Everything was going to be fine.

Outside, the rain was pelting down like tracer bullets, but she didn't care. As she walked through the car park, she felt a sudden urge to sing and dance. Marc wouldn't burden her conscience for the rest of her days. She could wriggle free of the handcuffs of moral obligation. Nothing now could stop them going their separate ways.

The words of an old movie song came into her head. *Because I'm free, nothing's worrying me.*

Breakfast at Watendlath was a classic case of the morning after the night before. Daniel hadn't stopped yawning since the stroke of seven, when Louise roused him with an imperious knock on his door. Her next lecture wasn't due until late afternoon, but he'd promised to drop her off at the campus so she could finalise a paper about shareholder duties. A shower did nothing to invigorate him, and his brain was so fuzzy that he twice nicked himself shaving. It didn't help that Louise looked so good in her pinstriped business suit that you'd never guess she'd been up in the early hours, searching for a ghost that refused to show. Daniel just felt like a ghost; the only bits of him that seemed real were the dry mouth and hangover-induced headache.

By quarter past, he was blundering down the stairs after her. The aroma of fresh toast wafted down the passageway linking their staircase to the rest of the house. The heating was on, and the cottage felt snug and secure from the clatter of the wind and rain outside. In the breakfast-kitchen, they found Jeffrey, plump frame enveloped in a silk dragon kimono, fussing over an elaborate bean-to-cup coffee maker like a fretful mother with a mutinous child.

'Morning, both! Dreadful weather today, and the forecast is ghastly, but never mind. Help yourself to juice – orange, pineapple, cranberry, whatever. Cereals and fruit are on the table, pop a couple more slices of bread in the toaster if you like. Coffee will be ready in a jiffy.'

The over-the-top geniality was pure ham acting, his smile as much a disguise as a Hallowe'en mask. As he turned to resume his anxious scolding of the machine, Daniel spotted red rims around his eyes. Had Jeffrey quarrelled with Quin last night or this morning? The walls of Watendlath were as thick as a castle's. Even if there'd been a screaming match, he'd have heard nothing.

'Pity we didn't manage to see Gertrude Smith on the prowl.' Louise sank her teeth into a plump Orange Pippin. 'I've caught the bug myself now. Do you think Dorothy suspected Roland of killing Gertrude, and tracked him down?'

'Who knows? The possibilities are endless. What if she witnessed the killing?'

'Yes, if she saw Roland Jones kill his girlfriend, she may have been too scared to say a word. Then when her mother killed herself so soon after Gertrude's death, she'd have been even more terrified. Perhaps it took a lifetime for her to come to terms with the guilt of having kept her mouth shut.'

He smeared honey on his toast. 'Plausible.'

'Whoever killed Gertrude, it must have been a crime of passion. The catalyst was Gertrude's pregnancy. It changed things for everyone at Ravenbank Hall.'

He glanced out into the wild garden. After another storm, ferns and shrubs dripped in the shadow cast by the copper beeches marking Watendlath's boundary. The downpour had blurred the windowpanes, distorting the shape of the evergreens, turning them into dark green creatures, sombre and surreal.

'I reckon Melody should collaborate with you on the case, not me.'

'It's your fault if I've caught the murder bug. And what I wonder about Shenagh's murder . . .'

Quin strode through the door. Dark bags hung under his eyes, and the customary charmer's smile was nowhere to be seen.

'Shenagh's dead, don't you think we should let her rest in peace?'

He scowled at Jeffrey's vast rump. His partner ostentatiously carried on pouring coffee into four mugs.

Each of them was emblazoned with insults culled from the works of Shakespeare.

'Sorry,' Louise said. 'That was insensitive of me. I didn't mean to . . .'

Jeffrey wrapped the dragon kimono more tightly around him. His cheeks were bright pink. He handed out the coffees without a word. Quin grimaced at the writing on the side of his mug.

'"Dissembling harlot",' he quoted. 'Actions speak louder than words, eh?'

Louise threw a frantic glance at Daniel. A ringside seat to a domestic row was too close for comfort.

'We'd better get out from under your feet as soon as we've finished our coffee,' he said. 'Thanks very much for your hospitality.'

'Yes, you've been so kind,' Louise said, desperate to ease the tension. 'I'm so envious of you, living in such a . . .'

A ferocious battering on the front door interrupted her. Jeffrey plodded out to see who was calling so early in the morning. Daniel and Louise clambered down from their kitchen stools, but Quin did not move. While Jeffrey fumbled with the mortice key, the thunderous knocking began again.

'Just a minute!'

At last the door swung open. A tall, haggard man whom Daniel had never seen before stood on the outside step. Rain rolled off his blue Barbour jacket, and down his cheeks. He'd been caught in the cloudburst, but didn't seem to notice he was drenched. His blue eyes seemed unfocused, and he was breathing hard.

'Robin, what is it?' There was a tremble in Jeffrey's voice.

'Have you seen her?' The man was hoarse and desperate, as if pleading for his life. 'She's nowhere to be found. For Christ's sake, where is she?'

'How is he?'

Greg Wharf had shut the door after coming in to Hannah's office. She nodded as he took a seat, though they mustn't make a habit of talking behind closed doors. For so many people in Divisional HQ, gossip was as natural as breathing. Essential not to give them any oxygen. Anyway, she could only give him a couple of minutes; she was supposed to be on her way to Lancaster.

'He'll live.' She repeated what the doctor had said.

A theatrical sigh of relief. 'Thank Christ for that. Looks like he's got away with it by the skin of his teeth.'

'Yes, he's lucky.'

'And the breath test was negative.'

'Breath test?' Her brain wasn't functioning.

'Yeah, I – um – didn't mention it last night.'

'What?'

'Hey, you weren't . . . yourself. I called Traffic as well as the ambulance when I saw his car wrapped around that tree. Best play it by the book with an RTC.'

Of course, he was right. There were no such things as road accidents, these days. They were, at the very least, incidents with some form of causation. This was a Road Traffic Collision, and the law allowed the police to breathalyse a driver involved in a collision. In practice, they always did so, in order to feed the Home Office's addiction to statistics. Trees were, in the quaint jargon of police legalese, 'roadside furniture', and Marc's crash, inflicting damage on the old oak, opened him up to prosecution. Driving without due care and attention was the likely charge. They'd never make a dangerous driving rap stick, and driving your car into a tree was solid enough evidence of a lack of due care. It could have been so much worse, but all the same . . .

'Shit.'

'Something new for you to worry about?' He kept his face straight, but she knew he was teasing her.

'You think the CPS will be interested?'

'Dunno. Nobody else was involved, and the tree will get over it. At any rate, the council won't need to chop it down. I gave it a quick once-over this morning before I came in. It's not as if he hit another car or wrote off a signpost or something.'

A smart guy, Greg, more efficient than your typical Jack the Lad. Very good at dealing with a crisis. Of course, his reputation suggested he'd had plenty of practice.

'Do you reckon they should treat it as a specified file?'

Guidelines covered the case of a family member of a serving police officer who was potentially liable to prosecution. Extra care needed to be taken, to avoid any whiff of nepotism.

'Your guess is as good as mine, but chances are, the answer's yes. It's not long since you and Marc were a couple, and you were together a long time.'

'Too long,' Hannah said through gritted teeth. 'I guess the prosecutors will want to avoid any whiff of "he only got away with it because his ex was a DCI."'

Greg contrived an elaborate sigh. 'You really don't find it easy to look on the bright side, do you?'

Already the joy she'd felt in the hospital car park was beginning to evaporate. 'Has it crossed your mind that sometimes there isn't a bright side?'

He rolled his eyes. 'Hannah, what are you like?'

She found herself collapsing into a fit of giggles. Absurdly childish, yes, but she couldn't help herself. Something about him was hard to resist. Better make sure she didn't find him too irresistible. A repeat of last night was off the agenda. Absolutely, definitely, forever.

'That's better.' He looked her in the eye, his face stripped of any clue to what he was really thinking. 'Ma'am.'

Robin Park stood in the middle of the breakfast-kitchen, dripping onto the terracotta tiles, a picture of misery. So this was the man who was planning a new life with Hannah's best friend. Robin was unmistakably handsome, with blue eyes and regular features compensating for the weakness of his chin and limp handshake. Jeffrey fussed around him with the coffee pot, as if not knowing what else to do, but Robin waved him away.

'We have to find her! Please, I can't do it all by myself, and there's no time to lose.'

'Hang on a minute,' Quin said. 'We need to know what we're dealing with here. When did you realise Terri was missing?'

'First thing this morning. Oh, I know it's still early. About an hour ago, I mean. I'd finally managed to get some sleep after spending most of yesterday rushing back and to from the bathroom. My stomach was empty, and I felt like shit.' Quin nodded, as if to say *And you look like it too*. 'I dragged myself out of bed and looked in the other room. Terri had said she'd spend the night there, rather than disturb me after getting back late from the party. Of course, she didn't fancy catching whatever had knocked me for six.'

'She wasn't in the room?'

'No. I assumed she'd stayed over with Mum instead. I rang her mobile, but there was no answer. So I called Mum and she said Terri saw her back to her cottage last night, then came back on her own to be with me. But . . . she didn't.'

He buried his head in his hands. Jeffrey put an arm round him.

'She'll be fine, there's sure to be a simple explanation.'

'What about her car?' Quin asked.

'Still parked outside our front door.'

'You're sure she's not somewhere in Fell View?'

'Absolutely certain. I've looked everywhere, including the coal cellar, just in case she was so pissed she fell down the cellar steps. The garden as well. There's not a trace of her.'

'She can't have gone far.'

Robin rubbed his jacket sleeve across his cheeks. Tears glistened in the blue eyes. He was a professional musician, accustomed to putting on an act, but Daniel was sure there was nothing feigned about his despair. Which didn't mean it was justified.

'Last night was Hallowe'en. You know what happens to young women in Ravenbank on Hallowe'en.'

'Don't talk like that,' Quin muttered. 'There must be some other explanation.'

'I've met Terri before,' Daniel said. 'She is a close friend of someone I know, a police inspector.'

Robin stared at him. 'Hannah Scarlett? Of course! Terri mentioned you to me. You and Hannah . . . well, it slipped my mind. I'm not thinking straight.'

'Have you met Hannah?'

'No, but Terri has . . . talked about her. She was going to introduce us.'

'No need for the past tense,' Daniel said. 'One thing I do know about Terri is that she's a joker. This might all be some sort of misguided . . . well, prank.'

'No! She wouldn't do that to me. Not after Hallowe'en, not in Ravenbank of all places.' Robin's voice was hoarse. 'Two women have been killed here, it's no laughing matter.'

'Have you spoken to the Knights?' Jeffrey asked. 'Could she have gone back to Ravenbank Hall?'

'For fuck's sake, why would she do that?'

Jeffrey smoothed the kimono over his knees. 'We have to consider all the possibilities.'

'We need to mount a search party. Quin's right, she can't be far away. Perhaps she's slipped, fractured an ankle or something, poor thing.'

'On her way back from your mother's place?' Jeffrey considered. 'Yes, it's the likeliest explanation.'

'I walked up to Beck Cottage before I came here, just to check. There wasn't a sign of her. Mum's in a right state. Terri's like the daughter she never had.' Robin caught Jeffrey's sleeve. 'I suppose she did get legless last night?'

Jeffrey's eyes met Quin's for a split second. 'We all had way too much to drink. It was a party, the Knights are perfect hosts, what do you expect?'

'Was there any trouble? Terri can't keep her mouth zipped

once she's started drinking. She doesn't know . . . when to stop.'

'Hey, it was all fine. She was in high spirits from start to finish.' Quin clapped his hands. 'Come on, we need to get cracking, it won't do Terri any good to be stuck outside and unable to move in this fucking awful weather.'

'We'll come with you,' Daniel said.

'Yes,' Louise said. 'The more people looking, the sooner we'll find her.'

'Let me call the Knights,' Jeffrey said. 'Just in case.' A landline phone sat next to a serving hatch, and he punched in a number. 'Hello, Melody, is that you? . . . Fine, now listen, we have Robin here. He's in a state because Terri has gone AWOL. She hasn't by any chance come to . . . Okay, right, just thought I'd check . . . Yes, it is. We're setting out to look for her right now.'

He put down the receiver and shook his head. 'No joy. Let's get a move on.'

Lancaster University was hosting a symposium on cold case investigations. Representatives from a dozen police forces together with a sampling of forensic experts were there, to add a sprinkling of practical experience to academic theory. Lauren Self had decreed that the budget could stretch to allow Hannah to fly the flag for Cumbria Constabulary. Extolling the Cold Case Review Team's successes seemed to Hannah a waste of time and money, given Lauren's determination to rip it into shreds, but at least the jaunt would get her out of the office for a few hours. She'd have the chance to network with oppos from other forces, and might even pick up a few tips to help fight her corner over the cutbacks.

The drive should have taken less than an hour, but the weather doubled the journey time. The ferocity of the downpour had contributed to a couple of accidents on the M6, with three lanes reduced to one, visibility poor, and progress reduced to a crawl. But the hypnotic swish of the windscreen wipers, and the soothing voice of Rumer on the CD player worked as a kind of therapy, allowing Hannah's mind to wander from the wretchedness of the traffic conditions.

The good news about Marc didn't quite wash away her guilt about her close encounter with Greg. But the guilt was about letting down herself, not Marc. He didn't own her; never had, never would. He needed to grow up and get used to the idea of her being with another man.

But what other man? Not Greg, she told herself. It wasn't appropriate, and she wasn't his type of woman anyway. In her head, she heard Terri saying she was protesting too much, but what did Terri know? She hadn't exactly made a success of her love life, and Stefan might be the biggest mistake of them all.

Daniel, then? She tightened her grip on the steering wheel. A long-term relationship was out of the question. Celebrity historian and country bumpkin cop? It didn't compute.

Why not follow Terri's example and live for the moment? Thinking long-term hadn't exactly been a recipe for success, either at home or at work. Look at her now. Relationship shot to pieces, career in suspended animation. Her life was going nowhere, just like the queuing traffic.

With a glance into her mirror, she gave the wheel a sudden

wrench, and swerved onto the hard shoulder, accelerating onto the slip road at the next junction. A change of direction was long overdue. She'd throw away the route map. Time to trust her instincts.

Jeffrey assumed command, announcing he was dividing them into two groups. He would lead Daniel and Louise along the paths that meandered around the Fell View side of Ravenbank. Robin and Quin were to search the area on the other side of the lane. The plan was to meet up outside the entrance to Ravenbank Hall once they'd covered every inch of ground between Watendlath and the Knights' mansion.

'You don't think she and Robin had a row, and that explains why he missed the party?' Louise asked.

Jeffrey stopped in his tracks. 'Can't see it – unless the row was in the early hours, after she left Miriam and went back home. Terri was in great form yesterday. But Robin's an easy-going fellow, and he and Terri seem to get on like a house on fire.'

The wind was driving the rain into their faces, and the paths were thick with mud. Trees swayed like creatures from another world, taking part in a slow ritual dance. The moist smell of autumn earth and leaves filled Daniel's sinuses. Louise thrust her cold hand into his, and he gave an answering squeeze. He guessed she was remembering the ghost hunt, and Terri's boozy cheerfulness.

'We're almost at Ravenbank Corner,' Jeffrey called over his shoulder, and soon they emerged from the wood, close to where they had looked in vain for Gertrude Smith's ghost. 'Given that Robin has already walked up and down the lane, let's take the path by the beck, and follow it round to the lake. We'll come full circle before we cut across to the Hall.'

He stomped over to a well-worn pathway carpeted with leaves. Like the narrow beck, it disappeared into the trees they had staggered past the night before.

'Daniel,' Louise whispered. 'What do you think has happened to her?'

'Let's not waste time speculating. We need to concentrate on finding her.'

'You reckon she's had an accident?'

'It's better than the alternative.'

'You heard what Robin said about women in Ravenbank on Hallowe'en.'

'Come on, we need to catch up with Jeffrey.'

They'd lost sight of him, but as they reached the path on the other side of the lane, they heard a loud shriek of pain, as if someone had shoved a knife into his heart.

'Oh God,' Louise whispered.

They ran into the wood. Jeffrey was twenty feet away, his back turned to them. Head bowed, he stood on the path close to the beck. He was staring at something in a dip in the ground, between the stream and Ravenbank Lane.

'What is it?' Daniel demanded.

Jeffrey turned to face them, his pudgy cheeks drained of colour.

'A body, no signs of movement. I'm sure she's dead.' He was gasping for breath. 'There's something else. I can't believe my own eyes.'

Daniel moved forward. He saw it for his own eyes at the same instant Jeffrey spoke again.

'The face is covered with a blanket. And it's soaked with blood.'

Hannah arrived at the campus in time to catch the tail end of the morning session of the symposium. A rotund Cornishman who looked more like a farmer than a forensic entomologist was speaking. His mission was to explain why the government's decision to close the loss-making Forensic Science Service and contract the work out to the private sector was an enlightened example of forward-thinking, guaranteed to improve crime detection. A glance at the programme revealed that the speaker moonlighted from his university duties as a director of the company which was lead sponsor of the symposium. The firm provided analytical services to the police, and boasted every conceivable kitemark, as well, no doubt, as a fee tariff to match. No wonder the chap seemed so pleased with life.

Over an unexpectedly tasty lunch of *pollo alla cacciatora*, she chatted with colleagues from forces in the Midlands. They were appalled to hear that Lauren was butchering her team, but unsurprised. Nothing and nobody was sacred, given the government's insistence on slashing the deficit the bankers had inflicted on the country. God knew where it was all going to end. As for their pensions . . .

'DCI Scarlett?'

A thin, bespectacled woman, from her badge a member of the university staff, was bending over her shoulder so as to peer at her name tag.

'That's me.'

The woman coughed. Her demeanour suggested a lifetime spent apologising for things that weren't her fault. 'So sorry to disturb your lunch, but there is someone to see you.'

Hannah gave a wistful glance at the meringue sitting in front of her. It was simply begging to be eaten.

'Give me five minutes?'

'I'm afraid she says it's very urgent.' A nervous titter. 'I don't think it can wait.'

The cops from the Midlands exchanged glances. Hannah read their minds. *Sounds like that cow she works for has gone on the warpath*. For God's sake, was there no escape?

Hannah stood up. 'Excuse me, lads. Back in a tick. Don't let them nick my dessert.'

She followed as the woman trotted through the crowded dining area. Lauren must want another chat about the team restructure. It had to be bad news, but Hannah reckoned she'd made it through the pain barrier. She felt in the mood to cope with anything.

But – why drag her out to the phone? Why not call her mobile?

'Your colleague is waiting for you in the overseas admissions tutor's room,' the woman said.

Hannah halted in mid-stride. Lauren wouldn't have come all the way out here. Surely Greg hadn't taken it into his head to turn up?

'Did my colleague give a name?'

The woman tittered again; it was like a nervous reaction. Her manner suggested she'd just been arrested for a crime of which she knew nothing.

'Detective Chief Inspector Larter.'

Fern? It made no sense. Hannah shrugged and the woman led her down a long corridor. At the final door, she ventured a timid knock before stepping back to let Hannah through.

Fern sat on the near side of an imposing teak desk. She'd crammed her considerable bulk into one of a pair of chairs apparently designed for size zero students. Her face was creased with pain, as though every joint in her body hurt. She struggled to her feet, and motioned for Hannah's guide to leave. With a nervous titter of farewell, the bespectacled woman shut the door on them.

'What's all this about, Fern?' Hannah sounded angry, but really she was just bewildered.

Fern put a hand on Hannah's shoulder. 'Sit down, kid. I'm so sorry. There simply isn't an easy way to give you this news.'

'Marc? But the doctor said . . .'

Fern shook her head. 'Nothing to do with Marc.'

Something in her friend's expression, a sorrowful compassion she'd never seen before, frightened Hannah more than any words. She felt a choking sensation.

'What?' she whispered.

'It's Terri.' Fern cleared her throat; tears glinted in her eyes. 'Her body was found near Ullswater this morning. Someone has battered her to death.'

CHAPTER ELEVEN

'Stefan Deyna killed her,' Hannah's voice was flat and lifeless. It was as if Terri's murderer had cut out her heart, leaving a vacuum to be filled with bitter despair. 'He couldn't have her, so he made sure nobody else could.'

'We'll soon have the bastard under lock and key,' Fern promised. 'It's only a matter of time.'

They were back at HQ in Kendal, in Fern's office, with its Lauren-defying Cluttered Desk Policy. A DC in Fern's team had driven them from Lancaster; Fern had insisted on arranging for someone to pick up Hannah's car. She'd turned a deaf ear to Hannah's protests that she was fit to drive.

During the journey back up the motorway, Fern had described the discovery of the body at Ravenbank. Terri had been bludgeoned to death, and her face covered with a rough blanket. She'd been found by a small party of locals; together with two visitors, of all people, Daniel Kind and his sister. Within minutes, interviews revealed that Terri was being stalked by her former lover. Fern, who was familiar with Ravenbank and its inhabitants from the Shenagh Moss inquiry, didn't only have Robin Park's word for it; all the neighbours knew Stefan was refusing to let Terri go. She'd told everyone about his obsession.

There was more. Already Fern's team had picked up a reported sighting of Stefan's hired Ford Fiesta, on the narrow road bordering Ullswater's east bank, at one o'clock that morning. He'd nearly crashed into a Mercedes coming in the opposite direction, not long after midnight. He'd clipped the wing mirror of the other car, but rather than stopping to inspect the damage, and exchange insurance details, had sped off in the direction of Pooley Bridge. Motive and opportunity were in the bag. With a known prime suspect, all Fern needed was to find him.

As the SIO in charge of the case, she had a thousand and one things to do in the first twenty-four hours after the crime, those 'golden hours' on which so much depended. But she'd been determined to break the news to Hannah in person. It wasn't solely a matter of kindness. As Terri's oldest friend and confidante, Hannah might possess information that could help to make a murder charge stick. Sure enough, Hannah had painted fresh detail into the picture formed by talking to people at Ravenbank, including the story of the missing cat.

'So Stefan packed his bags and buggered off?'

Fern nodded. 'In a tearing hurry, by the look of things. He rented a bedsit in Patterdale, and moved in after he and Terri split up. The house is owned by a nice old couple who live on the premises. See no evil, hear no evil types. He left sometime after midnight, owing a month's rent. They were fond of him, and hadn't pressed for the cash. Needless to say, he didn't supply a forwarding address. His car's already been found abandoned in a side road near Oxenholme Station.'

Oxenholme, on the outskirts of Kendal, lay on the West Coast main line. You could reach central London within three hours on a Pendolino train.

'Presumably he'll have headed south rather than to Scotland?'

'I guess so. We don't yet know whether he bought a ticket this morning, but that won't take long to confirm. The first train of the day arrived at Euston around nine in the morning, so he's a few hours ahead of us. London's an ideal place to hide, but we're checking out people he might be acquainted with down there. Hot on the trail, trust me.'

With Terri gone, there was nobody else in the world right now whom Hannah trusted as much as Fern. In the blink of an eye, everything had changed. Strange to think that she'd never again hear that raucous laugh, see that conspiratorial wink, feel a hand tugging her sleeve, urging her to do something against her better judgement. You only live once, was Terri's motto. Too true, love, too fucking true.

'Are you okay?'

'Yeah.' A barefaced lie, and they both knew it.

'Will you let me organise that cup of tea and biscuit for you?'

'No, thanks, I'm not sure I can keep anything down right now.'

Fern gave her a hard stare. 'You're not on some kind of guilt trip, are you?'

'What makes you say that?'

'I know what you're like. You take responsibility. Including when it isn't yours to take. Admirable fault, some would say. Load of bollocks, in my book. You weren't Terri's keeper, you were her mate. I knew her too, remember. She wasn't someone you could ever tell what to do. Don't start torturing yourself because you didn't save her from some sicko who couldn't take no for an answer.'

Hannah gazed through the window at the cascade of rain. Fern's office commanded a view of the force's overflowing dustbins; a tiny act of malice on Lauren's part the last time rooms had been reallocated. In the ACC's eyes, Fern committed the dual sin of being not only highly effective, but also a fellow woman officer – and therefore a potential competitor. She hadn't even given Lauren any chance to kick her into a career cul-de-sac such as cold case work. Hannah suspected that Fern frightened the ACC. Buried within that large, jolly body was an inner core of tungsten. Fern had the ruthlessness to go for the kill, whatever the consequences.

Stefan had better beware.

'I suppose you're right.'

'No suppose about it. I'm always right. Question is, are you going to pay attention, or simply pretend to agree while quietly hating yourself for no earthly reason?'

'Don't worry about me.'

'I don't want you to be alone tonight. I'd invite you to stay at mine, you're more than welcome. But Christ knows what time I'll get back home. You'd be better with someone.'

'I need to visit Marc. No need for your eyes to pop out of your head, we're not getting back together, quite the reverse. Last night he was involved in a car crash.'

'For crying out loud, whatever next? What happened?'

Hannah had thought out her story. The truth, but much less than the whole truth, that was always the best plan. 'He came round to Undercrag last night. Let's just say it didn't go well. He fucked off in a temper, and next thing I heard, he'd wrapped his car round a tree. But he'll live. The damage he's done to himself sounds pretty superficial.'

'Oh God, what a plonker.' Fern shook her head. 'First that, then Terri. No wonder you look so frazzled.'

'You're so good for my morale.' Hannah had glimpsed her pale, grief-stricken features in the rear-view mirror on the way here. She'd have made a suitable model for Edvard Munch in one of his bleaker moods.

'Sorry, but that's my point. When you've finished at the hospital, you don't want to go back to that bloody great house in the middle of nowhere. You could do with some company. And you ought to take a spot of leave, while you're at it.'

'Not a good time. Might come back and find I don't have a desk, let alone an office.'

'Not even Lauren would do that to you.'

'You reckon?'

'She has nothing to gain for crucifying a popular officer for no good reason. Take some time out, you could do with it.'

'I'll think about it,' Hannah said, wondering if she'd ever felt less popular.

'Ever realised you do too much thinking for your own good?' Fern levered herself out of her chair. 'Seriously, Hannah, give yourself a break. Otherwise, you'll fall to pieces. Sorry to be blunt, but someone needs to say it. Now I really must hit the road. I'll keep you posted. The minute we arrest him, you'll be the first to know.'

Hurrying down the corridor back to her office, keen to have a few minutes to herself to get her head straight, she ran into Maggie Eyre. The DC's face was an open book, as usual. Her frantic sympathy said louder than any words that everyone knew the DCI's best friend was dead.

'DS Wharf is looking for you, ma'am. He's heard that DCI Larter brought you back from Lancaster.' Maggie's voice faltered. 'It's shocking news about . . .'

Hannah touched her arm. 'Thanks, Maggie. Let's hope the man who did it is nicked before the day is out, eh?'

She found Greg by the coffee machine. He started to say how sorry he was about Terri, but she cut him short and beckoned him into her room. When they'd last talked, a few hours earlier, it had seemed things could only get better after the debacle at Undercrag, and Marc's car crash. If she could rewind the clock . . .

As the thought entered her mind, she banished it. Fern was right. The past was for learning from, not for living in.

'I suppose there's no doubt that Stefan killed her?' Greg said.

'Not in my mind. I've never known any man scare Terri before.'

'Yeah, but Fern Larter won't have ruled out other lines of enquiry.'

'Such as?' Hannah frowned. 'Terri wasn't someone who made enemies.'

'Didn't you tell me once she'd been married three times?

Makes me look like a novice in the matrimonial stakes. Even if she never knew it, she won't have been everyone's cup of tea.'

Hannah shrugged. 'Terri was no saint, but that doesn't mean anyone else wanted her dead. She wasn't at daggers drawn with any of her exes.'

'How can you be sure? They'll have to be questioned.'

'Not as easy as you may think. One moved to London, another emigrated to Crete, the third died last year of liver failure. Take it from me, Stefan's the man. He was spotted in the vicinity of the murder scene, and promptly did a runner. The facts speak for themselves.'

'Okay, okay.' He was ready to change the subject. 'I hate to say this, but you need to take a break. You look totally knackered.'

'That's twice in ten minutes I've been reminded what an ugly old hag I've become.'

'You'll be fine,' he said. 'But for a day or two, you need to look after yourself. Have you got anyone to stay with?'

Hannah's eyes narrowed. Was Greg about to make her an offer she would have to refuse?

'I'm sorted, thanks.'

He studied her, as if conducting a visual lie-detector test. Evidently he wasn't convinced, but he didn't push the point, and for that she was grateful. He sprang to his feet.

'If I can do anything, even just offer a shoulder to cry on, you only have to call.'

'Thanks.'

She avoided his eyes. Decision made. Last night had been a colossal mistake. She wasn't going to make it again.

* * *

As the door swung shut behind Greg, she dug out her mobile. She'd switched if off after arriving in Lancaster, and the missed calls included one from Daniel Kind. He'd left a message on her voicemail. Hasty, breathless, yet characteristically polite. 'Hannah, could you call me, please? It's about poor Terri, of course. Thanks.'

Daniel, witness to the discovery of Terri's corpse. She must speak to him. Fill in the pages missing from the story Fern had told her.

'Hello?'

'Hannah, thanks for calling back.' He cleared his throat. 'I'm so sorry about Terri. I know how close you two were.'

'Fern told me you found . . . the body.'

The body. This was Terri she was talking about. Her gorge rose.

'I was with the man who did. One of her boyfriend's neighbours.'

'The boyfriend, yes. Tell me about him.'

'All I can say is that Robin is in bits right now. It's obvious he cared a lot for her.'

'I realised there was someone, but I guessed wrong. I thought she'd got mixed up with the guy she worked for. I suppose I gave off vibes of disapproval, and that pissed her off.'

'Oz Knight?' He paused. 'He has a track record as a womaniser, but I didn't pick up any hint that he and Terri . . .'

'The Knights are friends of yours?'

'I only just met them. They organised a conference at the weekend, and I was a speaker. That's how I met Jeffrey Burgoyne, who found Terri. He and his partner, Alex

Quinlan, are actors. They run their own two-man company.'

'And Robin?'

'I met him for the first time this morning. He turned up early, in a distressed state because Terri was missing. That's why we set up the search party.'

'Wasn't Robin Park at this do at Ravenbank Hall?'

'No, he was poorly.'

'Are you saying Terri went without him?' A thought struck her. 'She wasn't on a mission to chat up this man Knight, by any chance?'

'Not as far as I'm aware. She was keeping Miriam Park company. Robin's mother. Look, Hannah, it's not easy talking on the phone. Can we get together this evening, are you free?'

'My social calendar isn't that crowded, to be honest. Though I need to visit Marc. He's in hospital.'

'God, what's happened to him?'

'He only wrapped his car round a tree last night. The silly man is lucky to be alive, even luckier that he's come out of it with not much more than a few scratches.'

'You've had a bellyful.'

'You can say that again.'

'Why don't you come over to Tarn Fold? Louise can cook a meal. Stay over, if you like. After what's happened . . .'

His voice trailed away. Hannah filled the silence.

'That's a kind offer. I'll take you up on it before you have second thoughts.'

Hannah still hadn't absorbed the news of Terri's death, but she knew she couldn't surrender to grief and misery. The choice was to sink or swim. She steeled herself for a return visit to the dreaded hospital, and a difficult conversation with Marc. What, unaccountably, she forgot to bargain for was the brooding presence by his bedside of his mother. Mrs Amos had never taken much trouble to hide her belief that Hannah had never been good enough for her son. Nothing personal, really. Kate Middleton wouldn't have come up to scratch, either.

'Hello, Glenda.' Marc's eyes were clamped shut. Fast asleep, or engaging in a tactical retreat from tricky questions? The latter, more like. 'How's the patient?'

Glenda Amos grunted. Hannah thought the old woman had shrunk since their last meeting. Age and disappointed expectations were taking their toll. The atmosphere in the ward was stuffy, but she hadn't undone a single button of her lime green overcoat. From the look on her face, she hadn't quite worked out how to justify accusing Hannah of causing her son's car crash, but it wouldn't take her long. She was a grand mistress of the blame game.

Marc stirred, and made a little moaning noise, as if contriving a protracted return to consciousness. His mother gave a truculent sniff.

'The journey here was a nightmare. It's a long way from Grange by public transport, you know.'

'Why don't you take a break?' Hannah suggested. 'Treat yourself to a cup of coffee, or a snack from the shop?'

'I had my tea before I came out.' She considered her son's flickering eyelids. 'I think he's coming round. I'll go and powder my nose. Back in a couple of ticks. Don't you go upsetting him in the meantime.'

As she stomped off, Hannah pulled her chair closer to the bed and inspected the patient. The gash was bandaged, and he wasn't instantly recognisable as the good-looking bloke she'd shared a bed with for so long. But it could have been so much worse.

'How are you?'

He opened bloodshot eyes and said croakily, 'They tell me I'll live.'

'How are the ribs?'

'Hurt like hell.' Was he calculating whether self-pity would attract sympathy, or be counterproductive? He really ought to know better by now.

'The doctor tells me you'll be as good as new before long. Thank God.' She took a breath. 'About last night.'

The battering his face had taken made it easy for him to hide emotion. 'Yes?'

'It was a one-off. I'd had a couple of drinks and I was feeling sorry for myself. Stupid. It's not that Greg took advantage . . .'

'No?'

'No! My fault, and I'm not going to make a habit of it. But . . .'

'Uh-huh?'

'Even if I wanted to make a habit of it, that would be my choice. Marc, you need to understand, it's over between the two of us. I'd already made that clear. It's none of your business what I do or who I'm with in my private life. Such as it is.'

Slowly, he said, 'I've had a bit of time to chew things over since I regained consciousness.'

'And?'

'I agree.' He expelled a long sigh, as though the admission had cost a vast physical effort. She wasn't convinced; he often resorted to play-acting when things got tough. Or was she just a cynical old witch who had never deserved a man's devotion? 'I kept hoping, couldn't help it, but . . .'

'But?'

'Last night I finally saw we were finished, and it was forever.'

She sat tight, sure there was more to come.

'It's not about Greg Wharf, is it? It's about . . . me. And you're not going to change your mind.'

''Fraid not.'

'I was furious with you. I felt betrayed, even though I had no right. That's why I drove like a maniac.'

'You could have killed yourself.'

'Last night, I didn't care.' He was gritting his teeth, whether against the physical pain or the despair of admitting defeat, she couldn't say. 'I wasn't drunk, you know.'

'Just as well, you'd have had a court case and a driving ban to worry about, as well as your cuts and bruises.'

She was doing it deliberately, this ostentatious lack of sympathy, so he was in no doubt that playing mind games would be a waste of time.

'Apparently I might still get prosecuted.'

'For driving without due care, yes.'

'Making an example of me, I suppose. No favours shown to a DCI's ex. That sort of thing.'

'What do you expect? You smashed your car into a tree. It could have been so much worse. And for what? No reason.'

'Losing you was a pretty good reason,' he murmured. 'Or so it seemed last night.'

She patted his bruised hand. 'In the cold light of day, you can see how wrong you were.'

'I can't write all those years together off as if they counted for nothing, even if you can.'

'They did count for something. But at the risk of sounding like some idiot counsellor on daytime TV, we both need to move on. All right?'

'All right.' He forced a smile. 'Maybe I'd better ask you for Terri's number . . . hey, what's the matter? It was only a joke. We're friends, that's all. Why are you looking at me like I just spat in your face?'

Driving through Brackdale half an hour later, Hannah took a call hands-free from Fern. Her friend's exultant voice echoed around the Lexus.

'We're getting warmer with every passing hour. There is CCTV footage of Deyna arriving at Euston. We even see him splashing out on a taxi. What a gift! We traced the cabbie, who says he took him to an address in Hammersmith. A lot of Poles live in that part of London, apparently, so maybe he's asking a favour from an old friend. Begging a loan, I suppose, or help in getting out of the country.'

'Fantastic.' If Hannah hadn't needed to keep both hands on the steering wheel to negotiate the winding route that led to Brack, she'd have clenched a fist in triumph. 'Any chance of lifting him tonight?'

'Keep everything crossed. Of course, he may not have stayed all day in the house where the cabbie dropped him off, but with any luck, he won't have gone far.' A pause. 'So where are you off to?'

'Daniel and Louise Kind offered a meal and a bed for the night.' She was making them sound like a married couple. 'I took your advice and said thanks very much. I'm only a few minutes away.'

'Glad to hear it. Daniel and his sister were good witnesses, by the way, as you might expect. Told us all they could, without wasting time. Are you taking some leave, as well?'

'Tomorrow, yes. Right now, I feel like I could sleep for a week. I've just left the hospital. Marc is okay, all things considered. His mother was there, hating me more than ever these days. But it was worth running the gauntlet. He accepts that we're finished, which is progress.'

'About time, if you ask me. Enjoy your evening with Daniel. I'll let you know when we nab Stefan. Oh, there was one tiny piece of good news. I forgot to mention it earlier on.'

'What's that?'

'Stefan didn't kill Terri's cat after all. In fact, he'd been looking after it in Patterdale, and left a note asking his poor old landlord and landlady to take care of the poor little creature.'

'You're kidding?'

'No, but it's weird behaviour for a man who had just bludgeoned his ex-lover to death. The torn photo must just have been his attempt to rattle her. Or maybe he couldn't bring himself to harm an animal. Human nature, eh? You couldn't make it up.'

* * *

'Robin Park,' Hannah said. 'What is he like?'

She and the Kinds were relaxing over a glass of Rioja after a filling dinner: Louise cooked a mean shepherd's pie. Tarn Cottage was a congenial place to spend an evening, far better than lonely, draughty Undercrag. When she moved, she ought to try and find somewhere comparable. If she could afford the mortgage, without a partner to share the financial load.

'Not easy to form an opinion of someone who's experiencing the worst moments of his life,' Daniel said. 'If you're wondering if he was less keen on Terri than she was on him, I think I can set your mind at rest.'

'Yes?'

'Absolutely. He was heartbroken when we found the body. Horrified.'

'But?' Hannah asked.

'What makes you think there is a "but"?'

'Be honest,' Louise said. 'When he turned up at Watendlath, you thought he was overreacting, didn't you?'

'Yes, though I didn't get the impression he was *acting*. If that was a performance, it deserved an Academy Award. He'd lost Terri, and he was desperate to find her. But he seemed more frightened by the legend of the Faceless Woman, and the coincidence that Terri had gone missing at Hallowe'en, than I thought was rational.' Daniel took another sip from his glass. 'My mistake. He was right to be afraid.'

'One thing's for sure,' Louise said, 'he wasn't the only one who was rattled.'

'No?' Hannah asked.

'Quin and Jeffrey quarrelled after we went to bed. It was

obvious this morning, as much from their body language as from what was actually said. At breakfast, you could cut the tension with a knife.'

'Last Saturday evening,' Daniel said, 'I saw Jeffrey slap Quin on the face.'

'What was that all about?' Hannah asked.

'Not sure. It's obviously a volatile relationship. They've been together for years, but it isn't easy, working together and living together as well. Perhaps the pressure tells on Jeffrey, every now and then.'

'Three women killed in Ravenbank on Hallowe'en,' Louise said. 'Even allowing for the fact the murders span a century, it's bizarre.'

'The press are wetting themselves with excitement,' Hannah said, 'especially since they discovered that a former telly presenter with an interest in murder was on the spot when the body was found.'

'We left the landline phone off the hook,' Daniel said. 'Journalists were waiting for us here as soon as we got home after giving our statements. I issued a two-line comment, a morsel for them to chew on, and refused to say any more. Finally they gave up, and went off to file their stories. But they'll be back.'

'After badgering your agent with offers of publicity for your new book,' Louise said.

'Vultures.' Daniel groaned. 'They've got a job to do, I guess. When we last saw Oz Knight, he was slamming his front door in the face of a young woman from one of the nationals. I suppose being in the news for the wrong reasons may harm his company.'

'Not like Oz to rebuff a pretty blonde,' Louise said. 'He isn't exactly the model of a faithful husband.'

'Is that right?' Hannah asked.

'His wife told Daniel that he had a fling with Shenagh Moss before she moved into Ravenbank Hall with Francis Palladino.'

'And Melody Knight? Marc hinted to me once that she's a flirt.'

'I'm not sure she means anything by it. Though Daniel will know better than me.' Louise gave her brother a cheeky grin. 'She's already had a cosy one-to-one with him.'

Daniel blushed. 'She writes freelance for local magazines, a rich woman's hobby, I suspect. She isn't a trained journalist. When she said she was keen to discuss the murder of Gertrude Smith, I was happy to have a chat. We met at Marc's shop.'

'What did she have to say?'

'Her theory is that Letty Hodgkinson was innocent, and someone else killed the Faceless Woman.'

'Based on what?'

'A conversation overheard years ago by Robin Park's mother, when she was working at Ravenbank Hall during its former incarnation as a care home. Letty's daughter, Dorothy, met Roland Jones there when he was a patient, just before he died. He'd been her tutor – and one of Gertrude's admirers.'

'What was said in this conversation?'

'Miriam Park is maddeningly vague. The bottom line is, I'm not aware of any hard evidence to support the view that Letty Hodgkinson didn't kill Gertrude.'

'Coincidentally, Fern Larter, who was on the team when

Shenagh Moss was killed, was convinced she wasn't guilty either.'

Daniel nodded. 'Marc told me.'

'Suppose it wasn't a coincidence?' Louise suggested.

'What else can it have been?' Hannah asked. 'Everybody involved in the Gertrude Smith case was long dead by the time Shenagh was murdered.'

Daniel stood up and raked the fire with a long brass-handled poker. Hannah was mesmerised. Had Stefan Deyna used a similar weapon to smash her friend's face to pulp?

'I suppose,' Daniel said quietly, 'the theory was that Craig Meek simply copied the MO of Gertrude's killer to deflect suspicion away from him?'

'Suggesting a connection with the previous murder at Ravenbank?' Louise said. 'He was an outsider, so it might make sense.'

'Yet nobody seems to have been fooled. As I understand it, whatever Fern's personal reservations, he'd have been arrested if he hadn't died in that car crash.'

As Hannah nodded, Louise said, 'Rather like Stefan. He may have tried to pull the wool over people's eyes, but without success.'

'Exactly,' Daniel said. 'He's the obvious suspect, so battering poor Terri and covering her face in much the same way as happened twice before in Ravenbank was pointless.'

'Killing Terri was even more pointless,' Hannah said. 'She never did anyone any harm.'

'Of course not. But it makes me wonder – why did Stefan bother, why did Meek take the trouble, when it was so futile to imitate the murder of Gertrude Smith? Why . . . ?'

'Two crazy killers,' Louise interrupted. 'Logic matters less to them than to a former Oxford don.'

'I'm a writer, not a don,' her brother said. 'People interest me. Why they do what they do. Now, and in the past. And this copycat MO, I just don't get it. Take Stefan, for instance. How did he know about the legend of the Frozen Shroud? Why take it into his head to indulge in some kind of grisly re-enactment of the old story?'

'He'll have read about it,' Louise objected. 'If he found out where Terri's new boyfriend lived, he'll have looked up Ravenbank, and hey presto!'

Hannah's phone trilled. 'This is Fern. Hopefully we'll soon find out what Stefan has to say for himself.'

'Got him!' Fern whooped in her ear. 'Arrested twenty minutes ago. We're bringing him back to Carlisle this evening. No resistance, no bloodshed, thank goodness, he came like a lamb in the end. I'm told he seemed glad it was over, and wanted to talk.'

'Before the lawyers get at him?' Hannah felt triumph surging through her. A good end to a horrible day, a day she would never forget. 'Brilliant.'

'Well, yes and no.' Fern sighed. 'At the moment, he's in denial. Insisting he didn't touch Terri.'

'You can't be serious.'

''Fraid so. He claims she was already dead when he found her.'

CHAPTER TWELVE

Louise and Hannah were up the next morning, consuming a virtuous breakfast of muesli and grapes, washed down by camomile tea, long before Daniel stirred. Hannah was glad that Louise didn't talk for the sake of making conversation. Daniel's sister was a woman after her own heart, someone who understood the pleasure of the companionable silence. Not like Terri; that relationship had been founded on the attraction of opposites.

Terri, oh God. This time yesterday, with Marc's prospects of recovering from his car crash weighing on her mind, she'd never dreamt she'd seen her friend for the last time. Rewind forty-eight hours, and she couldn't have imagined getting caught pretty much *in flagrante* with Greg Wharf. Terri loved her horoscopes, but who in their right mind wanted to look into the future? Better not to know.

'Why don't you stay here for a while?' Louise suggested.

Hannah's first instinct was to say no. Last night, before she fell asleep, she'd wondered if Louise wanted to create the opportunity for her to get together with Daniel. Even if she did, so what? Hannah was a big girl, able to make her own choices.

Not that you've made many good ones lately, a small voice in her head complained. She fixed on a smile. At least the sun had ventured out, pale fingers of brightness creeping into the kitchen like apprehensive children, expecting to be chastised for staying away too long.

'Thanks, that's kind. One more night would be wonderful, but then I'd better get back to Undercrag. There's loads to do, getting the place in a fit state for showing people round. Although there's no way I can be involved in the investigation personally, I want to keep in close touch with Fern. Find out if Stefan's changed his tune.'

'Why would he bother to lie?'

'He'll be in denial. You'd be surprised how common it is. Criminals hate facing up to reality.'

'Perhaps that's why they are criminals?'

'Yeah, Stefan's a violent man, but as far as I know, he never killed anybody before. Once the red mist lifted, he's panicked and done a runner. On his way down to London, he probably decided it was safer to opt for Plan B.'

'Which is?'

'Fern may not find it easy to build a watertight case, especially if his brief advises him to keep his mouth shut. With any luck, Forensics will produce a few aces, but if he admits he was present at the crime scene, and just denies that he harmed a hair on Terri's head, we'll need evidence to persuade a jury. Linking him to the murder weapon may be the key.'

'We didn't see anything lying near the . . . the body.'

Louise's voice wavered as the memory of discovering Terri's remains came back to her. Stumbling across a disfigured corpse was a long way out of an academic lawyer's comfort zone. Not that Hannah would ever become comfortable about murder. Each death hurt as much as the last, each wasted life left her with a nagging ache of frustration and loss. Did this inability to detach herself from the horrors of the job explain why her career had stalled? She hadn't been close to any of the other victims whose murders she'd tried to solve. God alone knew what would have happened if she'd been the one to discover Terri lying battered to death on the sodden ground. She began to clear the table.

'The rain won't have helped, washing away footprints, and making life harder for the forensic people. Fern isn't sure what Stefan used to kill Terri, some sort of blunt instrument is all I know. The odds are, he brought the weapon to the scene. I suppose he might have found a stone lying around and used that, but it seems unlikely. And why would he take it away with him, if it wasn't easy to connect it to him? Assuming he did take it from the scene, and not just chuck it away?'

'It could be lying at the bottom of the beck, or hidden somewhere in the undergrowth. Ravenbank's a small area, but it's densely wooded and thick with ferns and bracken. I suppose your people will make a fingertip search?'

'If the weapon's there to be found, we'll find it. Worst case scenario, it was something small enough for him to throw into Ullswater, and we have to think about bringing in divers. The pathologists should be able to give us a clue about what we are looking for. Mind you, he drove from Ravenbank to Glenridding after the murder, and there are countless potential dumping grounds on that route.'

'So there's a risk you'll never lay your hands on it, unless he's prepared to co-operate?'

'It's not the end of the world. For the sake of argument, suppose the wounds were inflicted by a baseball bat, and we can prove he bought one yesterday, he may struggle to give a credible explanation of why it's vanished. Trouble is, building a case takes time, even when you reckon it's open and shut.'

'Gertrude Smith was battered with a stone, Daniel told me. What about the Australian woman?'

'As far as I know, the weapon was never found. The assumption was that Craig Meek disposed of it. Perhaps he threw it into Ullswater, nobody knows. The forensic people reckoned a piece of wood was used, but what it was, nobody knew for sure. Since there was never going to be a trial, it wasn't worth losing sleep over precisely how the victim died. Besides, there's always pressure from on high to save the cost of in-depth forensic work.' She mimicked outrage. '"Where's my money going?" With a live suspect, this case is very different.'

Louise joined Hannah at the sink as the kitchen door opened. 'Good afternoon. Welcome back to the land of the living. You'll be pleased to know, Hannah's staying with us again tonight.'

Daniel rubbed bleary eyes. 'Great. Any coffee in the pot?'

'Better make some yourself, we've been drinking tea.'

Hannah watched him spoon coffee into a filter. In white

T-shirt and blue jeans, he could have passed at first glance for a teenager. A skinny man with tousled hair, whose manner suggested boundless curiosity. He liked finding things out; if he looked straight at you, it seemed he could read your mind. When they'd first met, he'd been haggard, as if he'd not had a decent night's sleep since the suicide of his partner Aimee. Since then he'd put on a few pounds – but only a few – and started to laugh again. It lifted her heart to see the change in him, to recognise the proof that you could overcome terrible loss, that life truly does go on.

He interrupted her reverie. 'So what are your plans for today, Hannah?'

'Off to Carlisle in a few minutes. Fern is there today, conducting a press conference, and reporting to the top brass. What about you?'

'I thought I'd dig into the murder of Gertrude Smith. See if there's anything in Melody's theory.' He hesitated. 'You're still confident Stefan killed Terri?'

'Why, do you doubt it?'

'How did he know where to find Terri? Not even you knew about Robin Park, or that she was spending Hallowe'en in Ravenbank.'

'Presumably he followed her there.'

'On Hallowe'en? She turned up at Fell View during the afternoon, I heard. So Stefan hung around there, all that time, waiting for his chance to strike?'

'He's a deranged stalker, that's how they operate.'

'So he kept well hidden. All the time we were wandering about in the early hours, trying to spot the ghost of Gertrude Smith, he was nowhere to be seen.'

'It was dark, and you'd all spent the night drinking.'

'Sure, but what about his car? A Ford Fiesta, didn't you say? Where would he have parked it?'

Hannah wasn't familiar with the east side of Ullswater; she'd last called at Howtown on a steamer trip with an early boyfriend fifteen years ago. 'There must be plenty of places you can leave a car unobtrusively. Somewhere between Martindale and Ravenbank?'

'How could he be confident of finding Terri on her own?'

'Your guess is as good as mine. He got lucky because Robin Park was taken ill. Otherwise, Terri would have been with Robin.'

'What if,' Louise said, 'Terri and Stefan arranged to meet in the small hours, after the party was over?'

'No way. One thing I can promise you, Terri had no wish to see Stefan ever again.'

'She was a creature of impulse, wasn't she? Robin's illness might have given her an opportunity. Suppose Stefan rang up and persuaded her, for one last time . . .'

'He can't have called her mobile,' Daniel objected. 'Don't you remember? She'd lost it earlier that day. I suppose he might have contacted her before then, but . . .'

'Lost it?' Hannah raised her eyebrows. 'Terri loved that wretched phone, never went anywhere without it. How did she come to mislay it?'

'No idea.' Daniel drank some coffee. 'She didn't know herself. I can't imagine he called on the landline, at the house of the man who'd taken his place. Whilst we're debating little mysteries, why did Stefan try to imitate the previous killings?'

Hannah shrugged. 'Trying to establish a connection with Shenagh's death, taking himself out of the frame?'

'Mmmmm . . . maybe.'

'Look, are you suggesting that Stefan didn't kill Terri?'

'Historians are just as bad as prosecutors,' he said. 'We don't jump to conclusions, we look for evidence.'

Hannah flinched. 'Ouch.'

'Hey, Daniel,' Louise said. 'This isn't some university debating society, you know.'

He coloured. 'Sorry, Hannah. This whole business is heartbreaking for you. I should have . . .'

'Forget it,' Hannah said. 'It does Terri no favours if the wrong man is accused of killing her. I just can't believe Stefan is innocent. She was genuinely frightened by him, and Terri didn't scare easily.'

'What if,' Daniel said, 'someone in Ravenbank took advantage of that, to pin the blame for the murder on an outsider?'

His question echoed in Hannah's head on the journey up the motorway to Carlisle. She liked his reluctance to settle for easy answers. Long before they'd met, she'd heard enough about him from Ben to be intrigued. She couldn't imagine lecturing to large audiences, or making a name for herself on TV, but Daniel took it all in his stride. In person, his quiet self-assurance was daunting. She could never match it. Ben used to berate her for underestimating herself, told her it was simply a matter of having belief.

Whatever. One thing she did believe was that Terri, her own worst enemy, had allowed the unspeakable Stefan to take revenge for her desertion. He was selfish enough to believe that if he couldn't have the woman he wanted, nobody else could.

When she reached Carlisle, Fern was waiting for her. They found a cubbyhole near a vending machine, and Fern gulped down a black coffee before making inroads on a Mars bar. The rings beneath her eyes testified to a night with little sleep. Like most detectives leading a murder inquiry, she was fuelled by adrenaline and junk food.

'Do you want the good news or the bad news?' she demanded.

'I'm in the mood for good news, to be honest.'

'He's instructed Dizzy Gillespie to act for him.'

At last, a stroke of luck. The dead jazz trumpeter himself would make a more formidable adversary. Gervase W. Gillespie owed his nickname less to flair for music than to a lifelong love of alcohol matched by his lack of ability to cope with it. Rumour had it that he'd never learnt to drive, on the basis that he realised he'd never keep his licence, so he travelled everywhere by taxi. He was a sole practitioner, mainly because nobody had ever wanted to take him into partnership, and ran a tiny office above a fishmonger's in Keswick. He earned a crust in the criminal and divorce courts of Cumbria, taking the cases that didn't offer enough profit to bigger firms. Somehow he'd managed to avoid being struck off the roll of solicitors; the word was that the Law Society thought that keeping a sad old drunk in business demonstrated their commitment to diversity within the profession.

'Wow, a lucky break. Has he advised Deyna to confess yet?'

'That's the bad news I mentioned. The man is sticking to his story like glue. At first, we thought we were quids in, when Dizzy said he was happy for his client to answer our questions, not hide behind a wall of no-comments. But Stefan is fighting tooth and nail.'

'What does he have to say for himself?'

'Maintains he's the victim of a mysterious conspiracy, would you believe?'

'Does he deny stalking Terri?'

'He admits they had issues. He's latched on to the phrase "unfinished business", claims that's why he kept pestering her.'

'And stealing her cat?'

'He's coughed to that, and to sending Terri the decapitation photo. Said he did it to teach her a lesson. Reckons she wasn't into pets, and didn't take good care of Morrissey. He found Morrissey roaming around when he called at Terri's, so he took it home. Never meant to harm the creature, on the contrary. He sent the photo as a kind of rebuke. I gather the cat's well nourished, and he's done his best to look after it.'

'A candidate for sainthood, eh? What about the murder?'

'He claims Terri texted him and said she was willing to meet.'

'Lying toad.'

'Wait a minute.' Fern finished her Mars bar and bought another. 'It's not quite as ridiculous as you may think.'

'Have you seen the text?'

'Nah, he deleted it.'

'Surprise, surprise. What did it say – allegedly?'

'He says she offered to meet him at Ravenbank at two in the morning.'

'And he believed that? Jesus, he must think we're soft.'

Fern crushed the chocolate wrappers in her hand. 'His story is, he was desperate to see her again. He'd bombarded her with calls, and never had a response.'

'A rendezvous in the small hours on a freezing autumn night, in the middle of nowhere?' Hannah shook her head. 'It makes no sense.'

'He didn't see it that way. She was with another bloke, it might be difficult to get away from him to see her ex. He thought she was going to sneak out while Park was snoring.'

'Bollocks. Why should she?'

'His wasn't to reason why. When she changed her mind about seeing him, out of the blue, he didn't ask questions, just grabbed his chance.'

Hannah groaned. 'All right, then what?'

'His story is that she asked to meet him at Ravenbank Corner, where two lanes cross.'

'How far is that from Park's house?'

'Three hundred yards at most. You can't see Fell View from there, because the lane bends. The Corner is overlooked by one house, but it's empty at present.'

'How many houses are there in Ravenbank?'

'Six in total, but two haven't been occupied for some time. Stefan says he showed up in good time, half an hour early, but there was no sign of Terri.'

'I can't believe he expects us to fall for this crap.'

'According to him,' Fern said, eyes fixed on a patch of damp on the wall, 'he became restless, and decided to wander up the lane, to see if he could spot her. He'd never been to Ravenbank in his life, and he thought he might have misunderstood what she'd said about where to meet.'

'And then he conveniently stumbles on her dead body?'

'Pretty much. He followed the course of the beck, and a few minutes later he found her. She was lying in a dip in the ground, with a blanket over her face. He says he recognised her shoes, but he lifted the blanket to make sure. And saw that someone had bashed her face in.'

'What about the murder weapon?'

'Says he didn't see anything that might have inflicted the damage. He dropped the blanket back on her face – and legged it. Close to where his car was parked, he threw up.'

'We're looking to find where the blanket came from?'

'Sure – if we can link it to him, he's toast. His story is, he didn't know if the killer was still lurking at the scene. He says he was in a state of shock. Petrified, and overwhelmed by shock and grief. So he jumped into the Fiesta and drove like the clappers, desperate to get away from Ravenbank.'

'He admits clipping the Mercedes?'

'Oh yes, and doing a runner from his bedsit in Glenridding. He admits he wasn't thinking straight, but he says he thought he'd been set up. Someone had lured him to Ravenbank so that he'd be blamed for the crime. He had to get away. Halfway to Euston, it dawned on him that he'd made matters much worse for himself by running away. He claims it came as a relief when he was picked up yesterday evening. By then, he was trying to get up the nerve to hand himself in.' Fern paused. 'And set about clearing his name.'

Hannah ground her teeth. The farrago this man had

conjured up to try to save his miserable skin made her tremble with anger. Stefan must have realised he couldn't escape justice for long. So he'd spent the time he'd bought in cooking up a tale designed to explain away any forensic evidence linking him with the crime scene. If only they could find the missing weapon.

'You can't seriously believe he has any chance of that?'

'One thing you need to know.' Fern fiddled with her collar. Why was she so uncomfortable? 'Deyna says Terri sent the text from her mobile. Yet Robin Park says that Terri mislaid her phone yesterday, so at the moment we have no way of disproving Stefan's explanation.'

'Does Park know where the phone is?'

'Uh-uh. He assures us he's turned their cottage upside down, but no luck.'

Hannah scowled. 'You're worrying me, Fern. Last night you seemed so confident. Of course it's a long haul to assemble the evidence, but . . .'

Fern digested the last of the Mars bar. 'You're not going to like this.'

Leaning back in her chair, Hannah said, 'I'm waiting.'

'It seems insane, but . . . I'm starting to wonder if he really is our man, after all.'

'You were a bit rough with her,' Louise said. They were standing in Tarn Fold, watching Hannah's car disappear from view. The sun had vanished, and Daniel felt the first drops of rain on his cheeks. 'Don't forget, she's the professional detective. Not you.'

'All right, I got carried away. But the easy answer . . .'

'Is sometimes the right answer,' she interrupted. 'That's what you don't get, Daniel. This isn't an intellectual chess game. Talk to any practising criminal lawyer, and off the record they'll admit ninety-nine per cent of their clients are guilty. The same will be true of Stefan.'

He put his hands up in mock-surrender. 'You win. Let's go back inside. If we stay out any longer, we'll get drenched.'

He turned back towards the cottage, but she caught him up with a few brisk strides. 'You don't fool me. When you give up so easily, and change the subject, I can tell you're not really listening.'

'I was listening. just not agreeing. The mere fact something happens nearly all the time doesn't mean it happens always.'

'What makes you doubt Stefan's guilt?'

He waited to reply until he'd closed the front door behind them, shutting out the incipient downpour. 'Does lightning strike three times in the same place? I don't think so.'

'What's your theory – that Gertrude Smith's faceless ghost walks on Hallowe'en, and every once in a while she inflicts on some poor woman the same fate she suffered herself?'

'If so, she certainly kept out of the way when we went searching for her. No, there's a simpler explanation.'

'Which is?'

He leant against the kitchen door, and looked her in the eye. 'That five years ago, someone took Gertrude's case as a template for a brand new murder. And the night before last, that same someone killed Terri.'

'But why?'

'As you say, I'm not a professional detective. I hardly knew Terri, and I've no idea why anyone would want to murder her. She struck me as a life-enhancing person.'

'Hannah cared a lot for her. She's obviously shattered by what's happened.'

'If Terri upset someone, she wouldn't do it deliberately. So why react so violently?'

Louise folded her arms. 'Are you planning to do anything about it, or just sit back and await developments?'

'Like you said, I'm a historian, not a cop. Better leave it to the police to worry about Shenagh Moss.'

'Meaning that you still want to research what happened to Gertrude Smith? But how? Miriam Park was no help.'

'The only way to understand what happened to Gertrude is to understand the people she was close to. Roland Jones, and the Hodgkinsons. Any history student knows, it's a mistake to rely too much on word of mouth recollection, especially when nobody's left alive who remembers the people concerned. So – time to scout for documents.'

Fern stomped off to resume command of the investigation while Hannah grabbed another coffee, and asked herself how anyone other than Stefan could have hated Terri enough to kill her. Surely she hadn't just been in the wrong place at the wrong time? Not in the small hours in Ravenbank, it was inconceivable. She must have been targeted.

Hannah was shivering, and she couldn't blame Cumbria Constabulary for skimping on the cost of heating. The cubbyhole was stuffy and claustrophobic. Time for a breath of fresh air as she marshalled her thoughts. Five minutes later, with gusts of wind blasting rain into her face and making a complete mess of her hair, she'd begun to doubt the wisdom of braving the elements, but she turned up her coat collar and walked on until she reached the castle.

A coach was disgorging a party of children. Hannah heard an enthusiastic teacher announcing that this vast medieval stone fortress had once imprisoned Mary, Queen of Scots. But what kids who came here really loved was the story of the Licking Stones. After Bonnie Prince Charlie captured Carlisle Castle, the English inflicted brutal reprisals. Thirsty Jacobite prisoners had to resort to licking the stone walls of their dungeons to get enough moisture to stay alive. The survivors' reward was to be taken to Gallows Hill, and executed. To this day, you could still see the marks where the tongues of the doomed prisoners had worn away the stone.

No Police and Criminal Evidence Act in those days, no civil liberties, no worries about whether the forensics would survive scrutiny in court. Hannah spun on her heel, leaving the school party to their tour. Despite the weather, the walk had cleared her head. It was dangerous to acquire a taste for revenge. Fern was right. However much she hated Stefan for his cruelty to Terri, the evidence against him needed to stack up.

Back at the station, she sought out DC Josh Higginbottom, and asked him to join her for a bite of lunch in the canteen. Josh had been an up-and-coming colleague of Fern's, until the day he'd tried to break up a fight between two teenage thugs in a car park a stone's throw from the station. One of the kids, a broken beer glass in his hand, slashed Josh several times across the face and throat. He'd lost one eye and only an emergency operation saved some of the sight in the other.

Even then, it took eighteen months for him to admit defeat in his efforts to resume operational work and accept a job in Communications.

'You can get used to anything in time,' he said, when she asked how he was doing. 'I won't deny that I still have black dog days. When the lad who glassed me was let out of prison, the urge to track him down and give him a taste of his own medicine was almost impossible to fight. But I got pissed and got over it.'

Hannah smiled. 'Not exactly what the doctor ordered, but if it works . . .'

'Yeah.' He rubbed the livid scar on his neck. 'Sorry to hear about your mate.'

As usual when she was with Josh, she felt ashamed of being unnerved by his gaze. One glass eye, one that didn't seem focused, peering out from damaged flesh. He could be moody, Josh, he was well known for it, but nobody had more right. He was a man she admired, and whose company she enjoyed, yet whom she always found strangely intimidating.

'Thanks. I'm still in denial, to be honest. But like you say, getting your head round bad stuff takes time. The unfairness of it all, the sheer . . . finality. I've often wondered how you've coped.'

'Me too. You can't simply rely on the passage of time. You need to force yourself to carry on. However reluctant you are. If that seems tough, trust me, it's better than the alternative.' He studied his fingernails. Badly bitten, she noticed. 'As you can probably guess, I did think long and hard about the alternative, but life's short enough as it is.'

'You were on the team with Fern five years ago when another woman was murdered at Ravenbank. Shenagh Moss, an Australian.'

'You know something? The last major case I worked on before . . .' He gestured at his face. 'I'll never forget it. When I heard someone else had been killed in Ravenbank, I couldn't believe my ears. It's so tiny, you wouldn't expect two bike thefts, let alone two murders.'

'Last time, the assumption was that Shenagh was killed by her ex, but Fern wasn't convinced.'

'Me neither. But Fern didn't agree with my theory.'

Hannah felt her heart pounding. 'Who did you think killed Shenagh?'

'The bloke who kept pestering her. Not Meek, the neighbour.'

'Which neighbour?'

'The smarmy bloke she'd dumped for old whatsisname who lived in the big house. Knight, he was called. Oz Knight.'

The Armitt Museum and Library stood just beyond Ambleside's constantly photographed Bridge House, on the route to Rydal Water and Grasmere. Set back from the road, it was a modern stone building, designed to house an eclectic assortment of books, manuscripts, paintings, geological specimens, and miscellaneous unclassifiable bits and pieces. There were even second-hand books for sale.

A young Dutch volunteer called Trijntje was on duty. She recognised Daniel from his television series, which had been screened across Europe, and five minutes spent chatting about historians as detectives was the perfect prelude to the questions he wanted to ask.

'This man you're interested in, Roland Jones, what would you like to know?'

Good question, not easy to answer. 'I want to know more about him. What sort of man he was.'

'He was an educator, yes?'

He nodded. 'It's a long shot, but I wondered if he features in the papers you keep in the archives?'

Charlotte Mason was already well known in the world of education when she moved to Ambleside in the late nineteenth century. Here she'd established the House of Education, dedicated to training governesses and others who taught the young; to this day, homeschoolers follow the methods she advocated, seeking to educate the whole child, not just the mind. Mason lived to a ripe old age, dying five years after the end of the First World War. Roland Jones had become prominent in liberal education, and Daniel wondered if the tutor had studied Charlotte Mason's pioneering methods. Might he even have had a personal connection with her, and the training institution she'd founded, which once occupied premises next door to the Armitt? But this was tougher than looking for a needle in a haystack; Daniel wasn't sure what to do with the needle, even if by a stroke of luck he found it.

'We have so much material upstairs,' Trjnitje warned him. 'Even to skim through will take many hours.'

'I've got all day. If I don't find what I'm after, I'll come back tomorrow.'

She treated him to a brilliant smile. 'So Roland Jones is a famous man in the history of Cumbria, yes?'

'Not famous, no, but finding out about him might just help me to rewrite a page of that history.'

'Amazing!' She was thrilled. 'Then we must give you all the help we can!'

The PACE detention clock kept ticking. Fern could obtain an extension of the basic twenty-four hours for which Stefan could be held without charge, but ninety-six hours was the absolute maximum, and she'd want to make a decision long before then. Over a coffee, she reported to Hannah that she was losing hope of making the case against him stick.

'Looks like we're back to square one. This time yesterday, I'd never have believed it. When he claimed Terri texted him, asking for a meeting, I thought he'd overreached himself. Then what happens? His story checks out.'

In his haste to catch the train down south, Stefan hadn't noticed that his mobile had slipped out of his pocket. An honest passer-by had found it lying in the road in Oxenholme, near to where he'd parked his car, and handed it in at a nearby shop. A lucky break – but for Stefan, not the detectives aiming to prove his guilt. He'd deleted the text message, but the techies had retrieved it easily enough.

'It might all be some elaborate stunt to throw us off the track.'

Fern made a face. 'No point in wishful thinking.'

'Any joy with the murder weapon?'

'Nothing. It's over to the lab people. The plan is for them to mock up the scenario. They'll try to replicate Terri's injuries, along with all the evidence from the scene, and experiment with all kinds of possible blunt instruments.'

'There must be cast-off marks on the ground, near where she was lying, and maybe on the sacking?'

Drips of blood from the weapon, Hannah meant. Her gorge rose every time a picture of Terri's body swam into her mind. Sometimes in the lab, they used slabs of pig meat to mimic the wounds. She couldn't bear the thought of it.

'Yeah, yeah. Should give us something to go on. Eventually. The snag, of course, is time. Even if I persuade the powers-that-be to pay whatever is needed to prioritise the lab investigation, it's bound to take several days. Worst case scenario if the work takes its place in the queue is – weeks.'

'They have to pay,' Hannah snapped. 'This isn't a case of a teenager nicking a car, it's a murder.'

Fern stifled a yawn. ''Scuse me, it's been a long, long day, and if I take in any more caffeine I'll turn into a junkie. We need a lucky break. Without that, or Deyna changing his tune, we won't know about the murder weapon any time soon. Certainly not before it's time to decide on whether to charge him on the basis of what we've got.'

'You're not going to release him?' Hannah's voice was tight; she was struggling to contain her fury.

'Not yet,' Fern said. 'We worked so hard to find him. I hate the thought of him slipping through our fingers. Fact is, though, it's even worse if he's not the man we're looking for, and the real culprit is getting away with murder because we can't see beyond Deyna. We can't overlook the fact that this isn't the first case of its kind in Ravenbank.'

'We don't have a shred of proof that there's any connection between the deaths of Terri and Shenagh Moss.'

'You're right. For the moment, anyway.'

'But?'

'I don't believe in that level of coincidence. Think about it, the MO is identical. Attractive woman abandons no-good lover for a better bet, only to finish up battered to death in the manner of the village legend. The only difference this time is that the obvious suspect lived to tell the tale. Doesn't seem like a copycat to me.' Fern exhaled noisily. 'I'd say we have a double killer on our hands.'

CHAPTER THIRTEEN

Hannah took a breath. 'Okay. So what are the other possibilities? Do you go along with Josh Higginbottom? He told me he thought Oz Knight might have killed Shenagh Moss.'

Fern nodded. 'Oz and Shenagh had a fling. This was before she moved in with Francis Palladino. The affair was no secret, even though Oz wasn't long married to a pretty woman who worked for him. He revelled in his image as a Casanova, and Melody Knight turned a blind eye. As far as we could tell.'

'Why was that? Was she playing away as well?'

'My take was, she was just happy to have snared the boss.' Fern didn't hide her scorn. She had no time for women whose idea of a career plan was to marry the richest bloke they could find. 'Trouble was, Knight couldn't let go. He kept pestering Shenagh.'

'How do you know?'

'When we checked her phone, we found she'd saved his

texts. Not very edifying. An uneasy mixture of pleading and bullying. Didn't seem to get him very far.'

'Did Francis Palladino know anything about this?'

Fern shook her head. 'He had no illusions about Shenagh's past, but he was convinced she was a reformed character. Possibly he was right. Like Melody, she'd got what she wanted. She didn't tell Palladino about the texts, possibly because she didn't want him to make a fuss. He wasn't in the best of health. If you ask me, she saw their relationship as a five-year investment, give or take a bit. Once he was safely in the grave, she would be free to do as she pleased. And rich.'

'Did Knight have any sort of alibi for the killing?'

'That was the other problem. He and Melody had spent that Hallowe'en night in bed together, or so they both said. We found nothing to link him to the crime scene. Whereas there was no doubt that Meek had been on the spot.'

'Terri worked for Oz,' Hannah said. 'And she'd fallen for another bloke. Are you thinking that Oz wanted her, and when he realised he couldn't have her . . . ?'

'Stranger things have happened.' Fern finished her coffee, and checked her watch. The press conference was due to start in ten minutes. 'But without any evidence, we're just pissing in the wind.'

Hannah had promised to take Daniel and Louise out for a meal, as a thank you for their hospitality. Their chosen destination was the Brack Arms, lavishly revamped after a change of ownership, and recently lauded by *The Good Food Guide*. Ten miles away from the Cricketers, it might have been in a different country. And century.

A slinky Greek waitress called Efthalia took their order. Hannah noticed her giving Daniel the once-over; he seemed unaware of the scrutiny. Like Ben, he had no ego. Over their starters, Hannah supplied a carefully edited account of progress – or lack of it – in the case. Much the same information, she assured herself, as would have been put out at the press conference. That a 38-year-old man who had been helping with enquiries had been released without charge.

'If, by any chance, Stefan didn't do it,' Daniel said, 'there aren't many suspects. Just the people who live in Ravenbank, and the guests at the Hallowe'en party. Including us.'

'Daniel.' Louise's eyes flashed. 'How could anyone imagine . . . ?'

Her outrage amused him. 'Even solicitors aren't automatically above suspicion. We were both on our own after we went up to bed, it would have been easy for one or both of us to go out via that separate staircase without disturbing Quin or Jeffrey. Are your bosses happy about your staying with us, Hannah?'

'Fern's relaxed about it, and it's not a breach of any protocol. The fact your dad was very popular up here still counts for something, and it's not as if we weren't already friends. You two were on the spot, any information you can provide is likely to be trustworthy, and might just make all the difference. So if, for the sake of argument, we rule out the pair of you . . .'

'Your colleagues went through the guest list with the Knights yesterday morning. We were at the Hall, with Jeffrey, Quin and the Parks. Coming to terms with the shock of finding Terri's body. Most of the party guests were ferried away by coach at midnight, but a few went home under their own steam.'

'The Knights didn't have anyone staying at the Hall overnight?'

Louise said, 'No, I talked to some friends of theirs who live at Silloth, and had arranged to spend the night at Ravenbank Hall. During the evening, their son called. His pregnant wife had been rushed into hospital, so they shot off to lend him a hand.'

'And the catering staff had gone by the time you went ghost-hunting?'

'Yes, they were bussed in from Penrith, and left before midnight. Nobody who works at the Hall lives in. Though one of the guests may have parked down the lane, and then hung around waiting for Terri to show.'

'All the people who drove home themselves were couples,' Daniel said. 'Not a solo murderer among them.'

'Someone might have come by water,' Louise said

'Nobody could swim from any distance,' Hannah said. 'That stretch of the lake is a challenge for swimmers even in the height of summer. People have drowned close to the shore on perfect days, and the water's freezing cold.'

'But arriving by boat . . .'

'At that time of night, and year, you'd have to be tired of life to make the attempt.'

Louise said, 'Ravenbank Hall has its own tiny harbour. Melody said they have a boathouse. Oz Knight fancies himself as a sailor. But . . .'

'Fern hasn't quite ruled out someone arriving by boat,

and it's also possible that the killer drove to Ravenbank, as Stefan did, in the hope of finding Terri. But both scenarios seem unlikely, to say the least.'

'If you rule out Stefan, and don't count us,' Daniel said, 'that leaves just the Knights, Jeffrey and Quin. Together with Miriam Park – and son Robin, if you don't accept that he was out of action due to sickness.'

'This stomach bug,' Hannah asked. 'Any reason to think he might have faked it?'

'Quite the opposite,' Daniel said. 'Terri was in no doubt that he was genuinely ill, and she didn't strike me as easily fooled.'

'No,' Hannah said. 'She may have been hopeless at picking men, but she wasn't gullible. And she could see through malingerers.'

'She said she'd have stayed with Robin, but he only wanted to sleep. So she and Mrs Park went to the party.'

'Terri was a party animal, but what about the old lady?'

'She spent years working for old man Palladino as a sort of part-time housekeeper, and jumped at any excuse to go back to Ravenbank Hall. The legend of the Faceless Woman fascinates her. If you ask me, she actually believes it.'

'Robin's illness was crucial to what happened,' Hannah said. 'A stroke of bad luck. It created the chance for someone to murder Terri. If he'd been fit and well, the two of them would have stayed together and slept together.'

'An opportunistic murder, then?'

'Sort of.'

'Most crimes are opportunistic, aren't they?' Louise said, as Efthalia brought their food, giving Daniel a broad smile as she shimmied around the table. 'Suppose the murderer acted on the spur of the moment. He or she somehow seized the chance of a late-night get together with Terri, and it didn't go as planned.'

'Maybe,' Hannah said.

'You don't sound convinced.'

Hannah tasted her moussaka – aubergine, spinach, and lentil, Fern would have hated it – before explaining that, if Stefan was telling the truth, he'd been lured to Ravenbank by a fake text message purporting to come from Terri. It was always a judgement call, where to draw the line, how much information to dole out in order to get something in return. She didn't plan to drop any hint that Oz Knight had come under suspicion in the case of Shenagh Moss.

'You believe the murder was premeditated?' Louise's eyes widened. 'Someone wanted to make Stefan a scapegoat?'

'Just like Craig Meek.' Daniel said. 'And possibly like Letty Hodgkinson, all those years ago.'

'I'm not saying there wasn't an element of opportunism, taking advantage of Robin's illness. Did anything unexpected happen at the party?'

'Nothing,' Daniel said. 'As you'd expect from a couple who specialise in events management, Oz and Melody are very good hosts. They've invited me back to the Hall tomorrow.'

'Really?'

'Melody rang. She and Oz are still reeling from the shock of Terri's murder. I told her I was researching the Gertrude Smith case, and she invited me over for lunch.'

Hannah sipped her wine, thinking about what Josh and

Fern had said. Was it possible that Oz Knight had fancied Terri, and been so jealous of her relationship with Robin that he'd begun to stalk her? Or had Melody been the jealous one?

'I find it so hard to believe someone we met that night could do such a thing,' Louise said. 'Everyone we met was pleasant company. No deranged lunatics, no monsters. What would drive an ordinary person, not only to kill Terri, but also to disfigure her so horribly?'

Hannah forced herself not to think about the damage done to Terri's lovely face. She didn't care whether Stefan was responsible, or one of the supposedly pleasant partygoers. Never would she rest until the killer paid the price. It wasn't simply a matter of doing justice. Her grief was so raw that she wanted revenge. She caught Daniel's eye, and felt herself blushing. It was as if he could read her mind.

'Hey,' he said softly, 'let's not talk any more about murder, shall we?'

'What you mean is,' Louise said, 'you don't want to be distracted while you gorge on your Chateaubriand.'

He grinned at Hannah. 'Can't get away with anything, can I?'

The moment they arrived back at Tarn Cottage, Daniel brought out a bottle of cognac. Not Hannah's favourite tipple, and it was years since she'd last tasted the stuff, but she let him fill her glass to the brim.

'Tell me about your day,' she said, curling up in the vast armchair like a well-fed cat. After feasting at the Brack Arms, she felt as though she'd put on half a stone. Worth it, though.

And the brandy tasted silk-smooth. 'What news of Gertrude Smith?'

'We agreed we wouldn't discuss murder any more.'

'Terri's murder is one thing. Gertrude Smith's is different. None of the people involved is alive. It's much more remote. What Miriam Park overheard seems like a puzzle, a challenge to be solved.'

He nodded. 'I've been piecing scraps of information together about the *dramatis personae*. I found some titbits at the Armitt this morning, and a few more this afternoon in Kendal. The Carnegie Library holds the archives of most of the county's old newspapers.'

'And?'

'Are you sitting comfortably?' he said with a grin. 'Then I'll begin.'

His sister contrived an elaborate yawn. 'I've already heard the edited highlights. To be honest, I'm knackered, must be delayed reaction after the horrors of yesterday. Daniel, you finish off my brandy. I'll . . . leave you two to it. Goodnight.'

Her parting smile was almost as suggestive as Efthalia's. As the door closed behind her, Daniel uttered a low groan.

'Sorry about that. You'll have gathered, Louise fancies herself as a matchmaker. Worst possible timing, and horribly embarrassing. She's not usually this insensitive. Just ignore her.'

The food and the cognac and the company had mellowed Hannah. Just as well, after recent events. Not that she was mellow enough to make a fool of herself with a man twice in quick succession. She waved away his apology.

'Louise has been great. I'm just interested to hear about your researches.'

He cleared his throat. 'It wasn't hard to put together biographies for Roland Jones or Dorothy Hodgkinson. They were both sufficiently well known to merit obituaries in the local press. Roland made quite a name for himself as an educator, and specifically for writing about Robert Southey. I guess he was drawn to the Lakes by his love of one of its major poets.'

'I don't know much more about Southey than his name.'

'Most people don't, but he was a celebrity in his day. Chum of Wordsworth and Coleridge, and a radical supporter of the French Revolution who mutated into a pillar of the establishment. So much so that he became Poet Laureate. His sarcastic line "'twas a famous victory" belongs to one of the first anti-war poems ever written. He recognised Charlotte Brontë's talents, but told her a woman shouldn't pursue a literary career. Shades of the guy who said The Beatles would never amount to much.'

'Any idea why Southey's work appealed to Roland Jones?'

'I'm sure it's because they were both romantics. I've not read Roland's book about Southey, but a Google search suggests it's devoted to the poems, not his biographies or his politics. Unlike Southey, Roland never married.'

'Gay?'

'Not necessarily. What if he never got over the death of Gertrude Smith?'

'You think he was tormented by guilt after killing her?'

'It's possible. Or he may simply have been devastated by the loss of someone he adored. Grief takes people in different ways.'

'Like guilt,' she said softly.

'Immediately after his wife committed suicide, Clifford Hodgkinson sent his daughter to stay with relations in Pickering, in North Yorkshire. Roland was out of a job, but once war broke out, his life changed forever. He joined the Army, but although he was a member of the officer class, he didn't hide away at a safe distance from the enemy lines while his men were blown to smithereens. By the time he was severely wounded in heavy shelling, he'd twice been decorated for bravery. As soon as he was discharged from hospital, he returned to the Somme, where he promptly lost a leg and almost died. Only then was he invalided out for good.'

'Losing Gertrude may have made him reckless whether he lived or died.'

'Again, that could be due to grief or guilt.'

Hannah pictured those young men in France, risking sudden death or catastrophic injury, while fighting over a few inconsequential yards of muddy and featureless land.

'What a transition. From teaching a thirteen-year-old girl in a comfortable rural environment, to the terror of the trenches.'

He nodded. 'After the war, he met Charlotte Mason, and worked at her House of Education in Ambleside, training governesses in Charlotte's philosophy of teaching. Later, he was a senior master at a number of small private schools in Cumberland and Westmorland, and found time to turn his love of Southey's lyrical ballads into a book. Despite his wartime injuries, he lived into his late eighties.'

'And he and Dorothy met just before he died.'

'I'll come on to that. The first major event in her life

after Gertrude's murder was the death of her father. Clifford sank his fortune into the Ravenbank project, and when it collapsed, he had to sell the Hall to stave off his creditors. He died of TB not long afterwards. A life insurance payout meant Dorothy had no need to dirty her hands with a job, or feel compelled to find a rich husband. She became a lady of leisure, passionate about climbing and walking the fells. All the same, she bore a stigma. The daughter of a woman who had murdered her father's mistress won't have been regarded as absolutely respectable.'

Hannah savoured her brandy. The fire was blazing, the cottage was snug, and this seriously charming guy had turned into her own personal storyteller. How long was it since she'd last felt so much at ease with herself, and with a man?

'That's appalling. She was a victim, like Gertrude.'

'Dorothy's solution was to involve herself with good works. Over the years, she became a mover and shaker in the charitable world. Her death notice listed a dozen pet causes, ranging from the Cat Bells Climbing Society to the RSPCA. I've seen her photograph – hair in a bun, gimlet eye, hatchet chin. A formidable character, and it sounds like she put a few noses out of joint along the way.'

'What makes you say that?'

'One or two of the tributes sounded double-edged. Plenty of talk about her strength and her iron will, nothing about her compassion or generosity of spirit. Her climbing days came to an abrupt end when she fell off Helvellyn and broke her back. Her doctors said she'd be crippled for life, but she taught herself to walk again. If she set out to win people's respect, rather than their love, she achieved her aim.'

'But she failed to clear her mother's name.'

'She may have decided it was too late, even before her path crossed again with Roland's.'

'Strange how things come round full circle.' Just as she'd learnt about police work from Ben Kind, and now she was talking murder with his son.

'Yes, the Ravenbank Trust, which ran the home, was wound up when it merged with a bigger charity. The Hall was too remote for it to be easy for people to visit residents, especially in winter. So Francis Palladino bought it and turned it back into a private home. The Trust's main aim had been to look after patients with serious lung diseases, and towards the end of his life, Roland suffered from emphysema. That's why he finished up at Ravenbank.'

'So Dorothy was involved with the Trust?'

'She chaired the board of trustees. The fact that her father had died of TB, and that the Trust owned her old home meant it was a cause dear to her heart.'

'Must have been a shock, seeing Roland Jones there. A face from the past.'

'A real-life ghost, yes.'

'If Roland killed Gertrude – in a fit of jealous passion, say, because of her affair with Hodgkinson, or her pregnancy, or both – he may have been ready to make a deathbed confession.'

'Miriam didn't hear it.'

'But did she say he *didn't* confess? If he did, Dorothy may have decided to do nothing about it. The satisfaction of being sure that her mother wasn't a murderer may have been enough.'

Daniel finished his drink. 'Suppose there's a totally different explanation.'

'Such as?'

'What if Dorothy and Roland shared a secret? That Gertrude was killed by Dorothy's father?'

Lying in bed, Hannah found sleep elusive. What happened at Ravenbank a century ago would tell her nothing about Terri's murder, but wrestling with the puzzle offered a form of escapism. Had Clifford Hodgkinson murdered Gertrude Smith, and then committed the ultimate betrayal, allowing his wife to commit suicide and posthumously take the blame for his crime?

Daniel's suggestion had startled her. 'What's your evidence?'

'Give me a break. It's a century-old mystery. It's asking a bit much to crack it in twenty-four hours.'

She'd had to laugh. 'Sorry. Once a police officer, always a police officer.'

'I'm the first to admit, it's pure guesswork.'

'If you're right, and Roland Jones knew that Clifford Hodgkinson killed the woman he'd loved, why keep his mouth shut all those years?'

'Perhaps he didn't have any evidence, either. Or perhaps he kept quiet for his pupil's sake. Bad enough to lose one parent through suicide – for the other to be hanged would be the stuff of nightmares.'

'You're sure Letty did commit suicide?' It was almost a game. So very different from a savage killing in the here and now. 'Suppose Hodgkinson poisoned her . . .'

'If only I could track down Letty's suicide note. But none of the newspaper accounts of the case shed light on what it said.'

'If Clifford was the killer, and Dorothy guessed as much, it might explain why she didn't campaign to clear Letty's name.'

'Precisely. Not much reputational benefit in having an innocent mum if you wind up with a guilty dad.'

'Was reputation all she cared about?'

'I may be doing her an injustice, but the signs are that she enjoyed having her photograph in the local press, opening a youth club or day centre, or whatever it might be. The glow that gave her was a payback for all the time and effort she put in.'

A woman like Dorothy must have hated being typecast as the daughter of a killer, Hannah thought. The Faceless Woman had become a legend, the Frozen Shroud part of Lakeland folklore. No wonder she'd done her best to build a life in which she commanded respect. If not, perhaps, love.

She shifted under the duvet. The bed was comfortable, and she felt exhausted, but her mind couldn't stop roaming. What motive could Clifford have for killing Gertrude? Suppose she'd got above herself, and started making demands that he couldn't or wouldn't meet. Even if Roland was the father of her unborn child, Clifford might not know the truth. What if she wanted him to dump his mentally disturbed wife, and make his pretty young mistress the second Mrs Hodgkinson? She might have tried her hand at a spot of blackmail. Hard to see the prosperous businessman reacting well to pressure from a servant. In those days, rich men shagged the staff, but rarely married them. You didn't need to be a professional historian to know that.

Or perhaps Gertrude had fallen for Roland Jones, and Clifford had taken it badly. Suppose she'd mocked his lovemaking, or she told him they were running away to start a new life together. He might have erupted with jealous rage.

Murder had so many motives. Her thoughts drifted back towards the one question that she meant to answer, whatever it took. Even as she drifted to sleep at last, her fuddled brain could not let it go.

Terri never harmed anyone. So why would someone want to murder her?

Next morning, Hannah was up at six. Fog was forecast, and the journey through the twisting lanes of Brackdale was bound to take an age. When she opened the bedroom curtains, Tarn Fell was invisible, and she could barely see the spiky branches of the monkey puzzle, poking through the mist.

She and the Kinds had croissants and coffee together before going their separate ways. Louise was scheduled for a teaching day, and Daniel was due back at Ravenbank for his lunch with Oz and Melody.

'Let's speak at the end of the afternoon,' she said, buttoning her coat. 'I'm not asking you to spy on your friends, but . . .'

'Listen,' he said. 'Anything I can do to find out what happened to Terri, I will do. Promise.'

They brushed each other's cheeks with a kiss. He smelt good; his aftershave had the faintest tang of citrus. She picked up her case, and hurried out into the cold without a backward glance.

Greg Wharf found her at the water cooler five minutes after she arrived at Divisional HQ. His eyes travelled up and down her body, more out of habit than lust, she thought. His mood seemed to match the weather.

'What's this I hear about that shit who killed Terri? Word on the street is that Fern's bottled out of charging him.'

'She's never bottled out of anything in her life. It looks like he was set up. Someone nicked Terri's phone and texted him to come to Ravenbank in the small hours after the Hallowe'en party.'

'You can't be serious. Why would anyone other than Deyna want to hurt her?'

'If Fern knew that, she'd have made an arrest by now.'

A theatrical noise of despair. 'I hope she knows what she's doing.'

'You can bet on it.'

He slurped down some water. 'You've come back to work too soon. You look like death warmed up.'

'Thanks, that makes two of us. See you at the team meeting.'

She marched off in the direction of her office, but he kept pace with her. 'Sorry, Hannah, but someone had to say it. Better me than some people.'

She halted in mid-stride. 'Thanks for your concern. Now, I've got things to do and so, I expect, have you?'

He grimaced. 'Back to DCI and DS, eh? Is this about the other night?'

Hannah returned his gaze, trying to choke back her anger. 'Nothing will ever be about the other night.'

He blinked first.

'I give up.'

'Good plan.' She swept away down the corridor, leaving him to stare at her back view. She was sure he was no longer admiring it.

Hannah was tempted to slap a 'Do Not Disturb' sign on the door of her office. Uninterrupted thinking time was in short supply, but she needed some. But the familiar strains of *Doctor Who* broke in before she had a chance to start marshalling her thoughts. The caller's number was unfamiliar.

'Is that Detective Chief Inspector Scarlett?'

A man's voice, eager, and tinged with anxiety.

'Yes, who's calling?'

'My name is Robin Park.'

Hannah squeezed the phone in her palm. Robin, the man whose bout of sickness meant that, instead of being by his side or in his bed, Terri had been wandering around Ravenbank on her own, easy prey for someone with murder on their mind.

Or had his ailment been bogus, a crude ploy to avoid suspicion?

'Hello? Are you there, Chief Inspector?'

'Sorry. I . . . didn't expect to hear from you, Mr Park.'

'It's such a shock, isn't it? What happened to Terri.'

A pause. 'Yes.'

'Devastating, impossible to . . .' His voice faltered. 'You were her oldest friend, she often spoke about you.'

'We went back a long way.'

'I wondered . . . would you mind if we talked? Not over the phone, but face to face.'

'If you have any evidence that's relevant to the inquiry into Terri's death, anything that can cast light on what happened, you should speak to DCI Larter or someone on her team. Straight away.'

'No, it's not that. God, I only wish I knew what happened. I'm in a daze. The sense of loss . . . it's overwhelming. You two were so close, you must feel the same.'

'Yes, it's . . . hard.'

'So – can we meet? Not in your capacity as a police officer. But as Terri's friend.'

Hannah made a quick calculation. What were the risks? The chance of finding some clue to Terri's fate had to be worth taking. She'd square it with Fern. Of course, she was itching to set eyes on Park. Was he any improvement on his hopeless predecessors? Above all, she needed to discover what had led to Terri's death. Nobody was more likely to know than this man.

'All right, Mr Park.' She took care to sound offhand. 'I can spare you an hour after lunch. When shall we meet, and where?'

CHAPTER FOURTEEN

Daniel slammed on the brakes as a car careered through the gloom towards him. He'd almost reached Ravenbank Corner, but the fog was lingering, and the hatchback's lights were on. A man in a hooded jacket was hunched over the wheel, driving as if he were fleeing for his life. The car came to a shuddering halt a few feet short of his front bumper. Daniel recognised it as Quin's VW hatchback. He reversed to a muddy passing place, and the hatchback eased forward before pulling up alongside him.

Quin wound down his window. 'Sorry about that. My fault. Jeffrey keeps saying I'll kill someone one of these days.'

He was striving for jauntiness, but his features were pinched and nervous. Did that shadow on his cheek hint at a bruise disguised by a touch of make-up? When he saw Daniel flinch, he said quickly, 'Sorry, not in the best of taste after what's happened. He means, we see so little traffic, I get careless.'

'No worries.'

'For goodness sake, I'd have thought you'd have seen enough of Ravenbank to last a lifetime. Let alone on a vile day like today.'

Daniel was in no hurry to satisfy his curiosity. 'It's autumn in the Lakes. Fog and rain are par for the course.'

'Yeah, it lingers in Ravenbank, even when Martindale is bathed in sunshine.' He sighed. 'At least five years ago, we had closure. Craig Meek was dead within an hour of killing Shenagh. But the stuff happening now . . .'

'What stuff?'

'Robin tells me the police have carted Terri's computer away. There's a CSI and a family liaison officer at Fell View even as we speak. The police are picking through Terri's stuff. God alone knows what they hope to find. He's moved back in with Miriam to get out of their way. As for the journalists, they doorstepped the poor man until he agreed to give an interview. Disgusting, after he'd asked them to respect his privacy, to give him space to grieve. They didn't take a blind bit of notice, the parasites.'

'They'd say they are only doing their job.'

Quin narrowed his eyes, as if unsure where Daniel's loyalty lay. 'So what brings you back here?'

'Melody invited me to lunch. I promised her I'd help research the Gertrude Smith case.'

'Never mind a crime committed a century ago.' Quin grimaced. 'Have you heard the latest?'

'What's that?'

'It's been on radio and TV. The police have let Terri's stalker go. Can you believe it? They wrapped it up in police-speak, but the bottom line is, the scumbag hasn't been charged. Incredible, you couldn't make it up.'

'The police know what they are doing.'

'You reckon? A polite young woman rang up half an hour ago, wanting to book appointments with Jeffrey and me for further interviews. "Just to clear up one or two points, sir."' He mimicked a Geordie falsetto with cruel accuracy. 'The case is open and shut. What the fuck are they playing at?'

'Your guess is as good as mine.'

'Not really, my friend.' Quin's cheeks reddened, like a teenager with anger management issues. Was the Celtic charmer just one more part he played? 'You're the murder expert, on first name terms with the local plod. I saw you chatting to the fat chief inspector the day before yesterday, while they put the rest of us through the mill.'

'I was questioned too, remember. If they have let Stefan Deyna go, there will be a reason. To do with gathering more evidence, I suppose.'

'How much fucking evidence do they need? He did a runner, didn't he? Everyone knew he made Terri's life a misery. After they tracked him down to London, now they're letting him walk out the door. It's crazy, why catch a dangerous killer, and then let him loose again?'

'They don't confide in me.' Well, it was more or less true. 'So where are you off to in such a tearing hurry?'

'To Keswick. Jeffrey and I intended to go together, but . . . we had a bit of an argument, and he went off in a huff. He'll be at the theatre by now. We're rehearsing this afternoon. The show must go on, and all that crap.' Quin rubbed his cheek. 'I'm worried about Jeffrey, badly worried. For once, I'd have been glad to hear his bloody awful snoring last night, but he didn't sleep a wink. He's still devastated after finding the body.'

So devastated, he'd vented his feelings by slapping his partner? 'Sorry to hear that.'

'The sooner the police lock that man up, the sooner we'll be able to get on with our lives. If they keep on like this . . . nothing will ever be the same again.'

He wound up his window, and they set off in opposite directions. At Ravenbank Corner, the crime scene was still cordoned off with police tape. The fog was thicker here. Crawling towards Beck Cottage, he saw Robin Park, well wrapped up in Barbour and scarf, step out of the side porch, and raise a gloved hand in greeting. He pulled up on the verge by the low garden wall.

'How are you, Robin?'

A grimace. 'I still can't believe what's happened. It's Mum I'm most concerned about. She thought the world of Terri. The shock has hit her very hard.'

'I'm sorry.'

'Oh, she'll get through it. She's a strong lady. A survivor.' He clenched his fist, willing himself to believe. 'Going to the Hall? You must be, there's nothing else the other side of this cottage.'

'Lunch with the Knights.'

'I'm due to meet your friend this afternoon. Hannah Scarlett. What's she like, by the way?'

'A very good detective, that's all I can say.'

'How discreet! Come in, why don't you? It's freezing out here.' As Daniel checked his watch, Robin added, 'I'll only keep you a moment.'

The interior of the cottage was cramped but immaculate. All the curtains were drawn, an old-fashioned mark of respect for the dead. Through an open door, Daniel glimpsed a neat kitchen dominated by a wood-burning stove. The smell of freshly baked bread wafted out, inducing pangs of hunger. Robin called up the stairs to his mother that they had a visitor, and led him into a low-ceilinged living room. Horse brasses and an embroidered child's sampler from the nineteenth century hung on the wall, and a glass corner cabinet was filled with old sporting trophies, silver plate cups, and crossed hockey sticks made from gold resin. A dozen photographs stood on a mahogany sideboard. A single publicity shot showed Robin posing at a piano; the rest were assorted family snaps from his younger days, when his father was still alive. The male Parks bore a strong resemblance to each other, with their regular features and ready smile. Where they lounged, Miriam stood to attention. Her stolid features habitually wore an expression of wariness, as if she expected the camera flash bulb to explode in her face.

'Mum's been resting. She's not as young as she was.'

'I'm sorry. You shouldn't have disturbed her on my account.'

'No, she'd be mortified if I invited you in, and she didn't show her face. Anyhow, she told me you wanted to know about that conversation she overhead between Dorothy Hodgkinson and Roland Jones. By the way, how is Hannah Scarlett coping? I've been dying to meet her, just never expected it to be in these circumstances.'

'Terri will have told you all you need to know. She was much closer to her than I am.'

Robin raised his eyebrows, and Daniel felt his cheeks burn. What had Terri said about Hannah and him?

'Terri's not here,' Robin said quietly, as Miriam Park came into the room. 'Oh, Mum, there you are. How are you feeling?'

Miriam's face was drained of colour and her shoulders had a stoop. She'd looked better dressed up as a witch.

'What can't be cured, must be endured.' She gave a heavy sigh. 'Hello again, Mr Kind.'

'Daniel, please. It's very hard, to endure the murder of two people you knew.'

'I was very fond of Terri, you know.' She sounded defiant, as though she'd suffered a personal injustice. 'She and Robin could have been so happy together here.'

Robin put a hand on her shoulder. 'And she cared for you, Mum.'

'You were friendly with Shenagh Moss, as well?' Daniel asked.

'Oh, she was good company. The two of us were talking, the very day she died, about the Faceless Woman.' Miriam bowed her head. 'Shenagh didn't believe in ghosts, but you have to wonder, don't you?'

'I'm still curious about what happened to Gertrude Smith. That conversation you overheard . . .'

She shook her head. 'It was such a long time ago. Like I said, I can't swear to exactly what was said.'

'But – roughly?'

Her features contorted as she dug into the recesses of memory. 'Mr Jones said something like . . . "Your mother didn't kill Gertrude, we both know that."'

'And she agreed?'

'Yes, I'm sure she did. That was really all there was to it. Miss Hodgkinson left a few minutes later. She was obviously upset, didn't even stop for a chat with any of us. Normally, on her visits, she liked to have a conversation with the staff. If you ask me, she'd always had a suspicion that Mr Jones killed Gertrude, but no more than that. She couldn't take it in.'

'You didn't get the impression that they both thought . . . Clifford Hodgkinson murdered Gertrude?'

'What?' Miriam's eyes widened. 'That never crossed my mind. I just assumed . . . well, I suppose you may be right. But we'll never know now, will we?'

'Sometimes the truth comes out, long after the event, and it's not what everyone expected. The same may happen over the murder of Shenagh Moss.'

'We all know who killed Shenagh,' Miriam insisted. 'That man Craig Meek, may God forgive him. I'm not just talking about Shenagh. He as good as put a bullet through poor Mr Palladino's head, as well. To say nothing of poor Hippo.'

'Hippo?'

'Mr Palladino's dog. Adorable, he was. Poor Hippo was getting on in years, and the shock was too much for him. The vet had to put him down not long after Shenagh's body was found.'

One more victim, then. 'What if there is a connection between Shenagh's death and Terri's?'

Miriam stared. 'Impossible. It's no secret who battered that dear girl to death. That vile Polish . . .'

'We can't fathom why the police have released him,'

Robin said quickly, as if to forestall a potentially racist rant. 'I'm praying it's just a temporary manouevre, that they're playing for time while they make sure the case against him is watertight.'

Miriam passed a hand over her forehead. 'It's a nightmare.'

'Mum,' Robin said, 'you need to get back to bed.'

'And I need to get out from under your feet,' Daniel said. 'I'm sorry to have pestered you about what you heard from Roland Jones.'

Her face was ashen. 'I used to feel sorry for Gertrude Smith, and her ghost, endlessly walking down Ravenbank Lane. She deserved justice, that's what I thought. Now I'm older and wiser. It's not the dead we need to worry about. It's the living.'

'You timed your arrival to perfection.' Melody greeted him with a delicate kiss on the cheek. Her lips were cold. 'The mist is clearing over the lake, though it's only a temporary respite. Freezing fog is forecast for later on. I almost feel sorry for those journalists, shivering outside the gates.'

'I used to live with a journalist,' he said. 'If she was here, she'd tell you not to waste your sympathy, it's like commiserating with a school of sharks.'

'Yesterday was surreal – a helicopter whirling overhead, reporters on a boat, taking photos of our grounds. Did they expect to spot another dead body, dumped in the old boathouse, or draped over the pergola? I thought they'd leave us alone today – we've told them everything we know. I took them a tray of tea and biscuits, to remind them we're human beings, not creatures to gawp at in a zoo. And now, the police have phoned to say they want to talk to Oz and me again. Will it ever end?' She closed her eyes for a split second, as if gathering strength. 'Come on. Quick tour of the garden, before we eat?'

'Thanks, I'd love that,' Daniel said.

'You can see where poor Letty is buried.' She yanked a black Barbour waterproof jacket from a coat rack on the porch wall, and pulled on a pair of muddy wellingtons. 'Some of our visitors think it's creepy, having someone's grave in the grounds of your house. To me, it's sweet. This was where she and her husband and child expected to live happily ever after, before her mind started to give way. At least Clifford made sure that she would never have to leave her home. Whatever else, I respect him for that.'

'Guilty conscience?'

'Yes, he must have felt rotten about his affair with the girl.'

Melanie's brow furrowed as she zipped herself into the jacket. Thinking about her own husband's lapse with Shenagh Moss? Apparently, it hadn't crossed her mind that Clifford might be a murderer as well as an adulterer.

'Oz is due back soon,' she said, as if reading his mind. 'He's spent the morning with our bank manager.'

'Expanding the business?'

'I wish.' She locked the front door, and led him along a path which wound around the Hall. 'This is between you and me, right? I've seen enough of you to know you can keep a secret.'

'Sure.'

'I hate to sound selfish, but this dreadful business about

Terri has come at the worst possible moment. You've seen the newspapers, the TV bulletins?' Daniel nodded. 'Our names are all over them. People say no publicity is bad publicity, but that's simply not true. Not when you're running an events company, that is, and all of a sudden you find yourselves associated with a murder case. And this morning we hear that the Polish guy has been let out. Things are getting grimmer by the hour.'

The fog had cleared to allow them to see the bulk of Hallin Fell, looming up on the other side of the narrow strip of water separating it from the Ravenbank promontory, but patches of mist still obscured its upper reaches. Melody led Daniel under a pergola swathed in winter jasmine and honeysuckle, onto a paved area overlooking a fish pond, rose garden, and a huge spherical water feature made from stainless steel. Stepping stones meandered across a lawn cut in elaborate circular stripes before disappearing through an archway in a neatly clipped holly hedge.

'Wow,' Daniel said. 'Even at this time of year, everything in your garden looks lovely.'

She sighed. 'No expense spared, that's our problem. Until August we had two gardeners working full-time. If things don't look up, this time next year, I'll be the one pruning the roses and feeding the Koi carp.'

Daniel murmured something vague and non-committal. Surely there were worse fates than pruning roses and feeding fish?

'I tell a lie!' she exclaimed. 'We'll be forced to sell the Hall before then, you wait and see. It's what happened to Hodgkinson, all over again.'

'Surely things won't come to that.'

'Oh, the economy is in such a dreadful state, I can't see a way out. Don't believe what you hear about recovery, people are still watching the pennies. Umpteen of the events we manage have been scaled down, others have been cancelled altogether. Oz asked you to speak on the Caribbean cruise, didn't he?'

'Yes, I . . .'

'Well, forget it. We won't be handling that contract after all. We heard this morning, we've been undercut on our tender. The truth is, the cruise line took fright because of what happened to Terri. Two other clients have cancelled their retainers. They come up with endless excuses, but it's all about the murder. It's done us untold damage.'

'Nobody can sensibly blame you for . . .'

'Business isn't sensible,' Melody hissed. 'It's stupid. Everything's falling apart. We have two holiday homes abroad, mortgaged up to the hilt, and we can't even sell them at a knockdown price.'

Her slim body was rigid with tension, and she looked to be about to dissolve into tears. He didn't know what to say, a sure sign it was best to keep his mouth shut.

'I've always hated it, to be honest. It wasn't so bad when I started out as the hired help, with no responsibility except to schmooze the clientele. When you start worrying about whether the bank is going to renew your overdraft, fun goes out of the window.'

'The Literary Lakeland conference was a huge success.'

'Thanks, but we were hired for that job nine months ago. Business has been going down the plughole ever since. Why do you think I was desperate to get out? We found

Terri's salary by closing our office in Penrith, and running everything from here. It was never going to work, I see that now. When Terri announced she was leaving to go and live with Robin, it was a blessing in disguise. Otherwise we'd have had to make her redundant.'

'I'm sorry. I had no idea.'

A bitter laugh. 'Well, you wouldn't, would you? In our line, it's vital to keep up appearances. And we thought we managed that pretty well. Even Terri never guessed we were close to skint. It never rains but it pours. Now we can't even host a small private party without having a guest battered to death at the end of it.'

The branches shivered in the wind, as if fearing for the owners of Ravenbank Hall. Melody started down the low flight of steps to the lawn, and beckoned him to follow.

'Watch your footing. The York stone is slippery when it's damp.' A brittle laugh. 'You breaking your neck really would be the last straw.'

He followed her across the lawn. There were strict limits to his sympathy. He'd never forget discovering Terri Poynton's ruined body, abandoned on a wintry night, for foxes and insects to do their worst. For Hannah Scarlett, Terri's death was a personal tragedy, for the Knights, a flimsy excuse for financial headache caused by spending money as if it were going out of fashion.

Or was this all some huge kind of bluff? Making a fuss about the dire consequences of Terri's murder to conceal the fact that Oz was guilty of it?

'You disapprove of me, don't you?' she asked.

He dug his hands deep in his pockets. Melody might be

naive, but she wasn't stupid, and she didn't lack intuition.

'I'm not sure what you mean.'

Two strides short of the archway, she stopped in her tracks, and looked over her shoulder.

'Be honest. You think I'm a spoilt woman, playing at one thing after another, because I've nothing better to do. At one time it was knitting, now it's journalism. If my husband and I have run out of money, it's our own silly fault for being so bloody greedy, and borrowing up to the hilt to renovate the Hall at the same time as trying to run a small firm in a dog-eat-dog business environment.'

'What I think is this,' Daniel said in a low voice. 'Crimes of violence, most of all murder, harm everyone they touch. Not just the victim, and the victim's family and friends. Witnesses, suspects, people who were simply in the wrong place at the wrong time.'

'Collateral damage, eh?' she sighed. 'The woman in charge of this case, your friend Larter, we met her when Shenagh was killed. She interviewed Oz and me. She didn't like us, specially not Oz. If Craig Meek hadn't been so obviously guilty, she'd have made our lives a misery.'

'She was only doing her job.'

'Oz isn't a murderer!'

'I never said . . .'

'No!' She held up a hand. 'Don't say any more. We've talked enough about Terri – and Shenagh. Let me show you Letty Hodgkinson's last resting place.'

A weathered slate slab bore Letitia Hodgkinson's name and dates, nothing else. It stood beneath a copper beech at the end of a neat gravel path laid between vast, dripping rhododendrons. Through the trees, Daniel glimpsed Ullswater's inky depths. The wind was rippling through Melody's hair and she had to keep brushing it out of her eyes.

'When we bought the Hall, this was a jungle. Nobody would believe it if we hadn't kept before and after photographs.' She waved in the direction of Hallin Fell. 'The old boathouse is over there, can you see it through the trees? When we came here, it was a ruin, in need of complete restoration. Now it's Oz's pride and joy, he loves to go out rowing on his own. As for poor Letty's headstone, it was invisible. Covered by a mass of bindweed and brambles.'

'Looks like Clifford tucked his wife's grave as far out of sight as possible.'

'The poor, poor woman,' Melody said. 'Coming here, and wondering about what drove her to kill Gertrude, set me thinking about whether she'd suffered a terrible injustice.'

'I promised to tell you what I discovered about Dorothy and Roland. Not that it explains what happened to Gertrude.'

She listened with lips slightly parted. It was difficult not to feel flattered when an attractive woman hung on your every word, but Daniel did his best. Her loveliness was just another mask. He still couldn't figure her out. Shallow and self-absorbed, selfless and smart, or subtle and scheming? Or simply a mass of baffling contradictions?

'Fascinating,' she breathed. 'You've discovered so much in twenty-four hours. I suppose that shows the difference between a professional and a dilettante. I didn't know where to start. I just want to find out what happened here a hundred years ago. When we met, it was simple curiosity. Now, after Terri's death, and all the angst about money, it seems like a lifeline. Something to take my mind off . . . all the other crap.'

'The conversation Miriam overheard proves nothing,' he said. 'There's no proof that Letty didn't kill Gertrude. I'd love to know what her suicide note said. If she knew Clifford had murdered Gertrude, and she was determined to cover for him . . .'

'How could she go so far – however much she loved her husband? I know I wouldn't take the rap for Oz.' She flushed, and added hastily, 'Not that I'd ever need to.'

The wind stung Daniel's cheeks. He kept quiet, content to let her talk.

'I mean, even when he picked up penalty points for speeding on the M6 that meant he lost his driving licence for six months, he knew better than to ask me to pretend I was behind the wheel. He has his faults, but he's no bully. Anyway, I simply wouldn't do it. He had to pay his dues.'

'Things were different a century ago.'

'I guess so. Letty had mental health issues. It must all have become too much for her. Perhaps she simply couldn't face living, knowing her husband was an adulterous killer, and that everything was about to fall apart. Whatever the truth, I'm grateful to you, Daniel.'

She switched on a smile, as sudden as it was ravishing. He recalled that before her marriage, she'd not only been a model, but also an actor. 'I needed you to show an interest, to convince myself I wasn't simply romanticising about Letty because she and I had stuff in common.'

So she identified with Letty Hodgkinson. Two women married to men with a wandering eye. Two women whose rivals had been beaten to death with raw and unforgivable savagery.

'You're frowning,' she said. 'Not convinced? It's true, I've been so much luckier than Letty. But . . . I know what it's like to feel suffocated by depression, as if a thick towel is pressing down over your nose and mouth. I know what it's like to go to bed hoping you won't wake up the next morning.'

Above the trees, a buzzard squealed. A squirrel that didn't want to become its next meal scampered down an oak trunk, and vanished into the safety of the undergrowth.

'I had a very rough time in my teens. I can't bear to go into details, but it was horrendous, I promise you.' Her voice had dropped to a whisper, and he had to move closer to hear. 'My uncle was sent to prison for what he did, and I had a lot of problems. Partly physical – I was pretty messed up, and I can't have children. But the doctors were wonderful, and a fantastic social worker helped me regain confidence.'

If she'd kicked him in the stomach, he couldn't have felt worse.

'Melody, I'm so sorry.'

'Oh, shit happens. I was never going to make the big time as a model or an actor, but the work helped me escape from the past. Start a new life.' She drew breath. 'Yet I never quite got over my habit of getting mixed up with untrustworthy men. Trust me, compared with his predecessors, Oz is a saint.'

Daniel heard screaming. The buzzard was being mobbed by a gang of hooded crows intent on defending their territory.

Sometimes it wasn't easy to tell who was the predator, who the prey. He glanced at Melody's profile. Heedless of the birds, she was staring towards the lake. Barely holding herself together. He had to stifle the urge to put his arms around her. The silence between them was uncomfortably intimate.

'There you are, darling!'

Oz Knight was standing in the archway. A man with more to worry about than the weather, to judge by his gaunt appearance. In the past couple of days he'd aged ten years. That once-magnificent mane of hair was flapping in the wind, straggly and grey. Perhaps he'd had too much on his mind to remember to dye it.

His wife groaned. 'Oh God, back to reality. Come on, Daniel. Time for lunch.'

'Hannah – a word?'

Les Bryant's dour features never betrayed emotion, but his voice had a scratchy quality that Hannah hadn't heard before. She nodded, and he followed her into her room, closing the door behind them with exaggerated care.

'Terri was a decent kid,' he said. 'I know how much she meant to you. And you to her, believe me.'

'Thanks.'

She tried to decipher his inscrutable expression. In one of the least likely romantic pairings conceivable, Les had once gone on a blind date with Terri. Once and only once, needless to say.

'She told me you drove her crazy, forever doubting yourself. Her opinion was that you were wasted on Amos.

Reckoned you'd do far better with Ben Kind's lad.'

'There you are, then.' She tried to keep her voice steady. 'Poor old Terri, she had no idea.'

'You're wrong,' he said. 'She was a smart lady. No good for me, obviously. Too young, too good-looking, too bloody dizzy. We'd have killed each other within a week. Tell you what, though.'

'Go on.'

He cleared his throat. 'Before we did kill each other, I'd have enjoyed that week more than any I can remember.'

Daniel swallowed the last of his casserole and said how much he'd enjoyed it. His host and hostess had only picked at their own portions. It was as if Terri's murder had robbed them of their appetites.

'Credit where it's due,' Melody said. 'This is Miriam Park's recipe. Such a wonderful cook. Francis Palladino used to say she was worth her weight in gold. She's in a bad place at the moment. Robin, finally on the brink of settling down with someone, and then . . .'

'You think his relationship with Terri was strong enough to last?' Daniel asked.

'Why not? You only had to spend five minutes in their company to see they were very much in love. He was besotted, and so was she.'

'Miriam jumped the gun about their getting married,' Oz muttered. 'Wishful thinking, if you ask me. Terri was a sweet lady, but she'd already divorced three husbands, and Robin's never come close to tying the knot. They'd only known each other a few weeks.'

'You proposed to me a fortnight after we first met,' Melody said.

'And you turned me down flat.' Oz turned to Daniel. 'Not that anyone could blame her, with the age difference and everything. Took a long time to wear down her resistance.'

'I never planned to marry the boss,' Melody said. 'It just worked out that way in the end. For better, for worse . . .'

'For richer, for poorer.' Oz grimaced. 'Definitely for poorer after this morning, I'm afraid.'

At Melody's confession that she'd told Daniel about their financial problems, he'd flinched, as if she'd poked him in the eye, before rallying with a tirade about greedy bankers and the havoc they'd wreaked on the world's economy. As well as on the Knights' prospects of keeping their business afloat. The overdraft facility had been renewed this morning, but on punitive conditions. He feared the stay of execution was only temporary.

'How will you put things on an even keel?' Daniel asked.

Oz spread his arms. 'Your guess is as good as mine. Neither of us has taken a wage out of the business since April; we're living on our investments, and they are shrivelling fast. The situation's out of my hands, that's what I hate. We need to stop the haemorrhage of clients and revenue. And pray the police get their finger out, so we can start putting our lives back together.'

Daniel concentrated on Melody's rum-and-raisin pudding. Oz was a control freak, and he'd yet to meet a happy control freak. Was that need to be in charge a source of tension in their marriage?

'I can't believe they let that man go.' Oz drained his third glass of Rioja, and raised his voice a little, as he warmed to his theme. 'Terri was scared stiff of him, we were concerned for her safety, like any decent employer. She said he'd beaten up his wife, and hit the woman so hard she was lucky not to lose an eye. Someone like that shouldn't be roaming the streets.'

Daniel said, 'The police will be working night and day on the case. Don't forget, Terri was best mates with one of their senior detectives.'

'And she's a friend of yours,' Oz snapped. 'How does she feel about letting loose the man who almost certainly killed her friend?'

'No one wants justice for Terri more than Hannah.'

'Justice!' It was almost a snarl. 'Then I wonder why she let—'

'Hannah isn't part of the investigating team.' Daniel fought back a rising anger. 'It wasn't her decision to release the man.'

Oz said, 'This uncertainty makes people think there's no smoke without fire. None of us can relax.'

He poured himself and his wife yet another glass of wine. Daniel was glad he'd stuck to orange juice. With a touch of malice, Oz added, 'Even you must feel uncomfortable, Daniel. You were at the party with the rest of us.'

'I feel worse than uncomfortable,' Daniel said quietly. 'I liked Terri, though I didn't know her well. I'd like nothing better than to see whoever did this put behind bars.'

Melody forced a laugh. 'Before long, rumours will start flying that everyone who came to the party was in it together. Like that film, you know, on the train.'

'Robin and Terri didn't quarrel, did they?' Daniel asked.

'Is there any reason for him to worry about the police?'

'None whatsoever,' Oz said wearily. 'She was vivacious and good-looking, but – how can I put this? – more mature than Robin's previous girlfriends. At least those I've met.'

'Did any of them last long?'

'Nope, there was never any question until now of Robin settling down with someone, far less setting up home somewhere new. But if you ask me, he's scared stiff. When one person in a relationship is killed, the other partner inevitably comes under the spotlight.'

'Better take special care of me, then, darling.' Melody's smile was strained, her voice cracking. Daniel frowned; she was too close to the edge for comfort. 'We're deep enough in the shit as it is.'

'Fern's right, if you ask me,' Les Bryant said. 'I don't believe that bastard killed Terri.'

He and Hannah were taking a quick bite of lunch together in the staff restaurant, Les feasting on a bacon, egg and sausage bap while she dipped her wholemeal toast in a pot of hummus.

'What makes you so sure?'

'Think about it. It's clear he was set up. Two women killed in identical circumstances, five years apart? Why would he try to repeat history, what would he have to gain?'

'And your preferred solution is?'

He chewed furiously. 'We both knew Terri. The murder victim's personality is the biggest clue to the motive for the crime.'

'It doesn't say that in the Murder Investigation Manual.'

'No, but it bloody well ought to.'

'I'm not sure I like the idea that Terri brought her own murder upon herself.'

'You're a DCI, and your mate's been beaten to death,' he growled. 'You can't afford to be prissy about this. I'm not saying Terri was killed because of anything she did consciously. Maybe it was because someone had reason to be afraid of her.'

'Where are you going with this?'

He wiped the runny egg from his grizzled chin. 'She was a livewire, right? Into everything, like a little kid.'

'Yes.' That was Terri's gift, her boundless enthusiasm, her love of life. 'She was incorrigible.'

'What if her curiosity led her to find out something she wasn't meant to know?'

'Such as?'

'Suppose she stumbled on a clue to what really happened at Ravenbank five years previous? Something that pointed the finger at one of her new neighbours?'

'She'd have told someone, wouldn't she? Me, for example. She was hiding something from me, yes, but it was the fact that she'd teamed up with this man Robin Park. Daniel and Louise say she was just very happy, looking forward to a new life with him.'

'What if she didn't appreciate the significance of what she'd learnt? Whoever killed Shenagh Moss would have to move quick, to get her out of the way before she tumbled to the truth. Park's stomach bug was a gift, it offered the chance to get Terri on her own late at night, when she'd had too much to drink.'

Hannah smeared margarine on her last piece of toast. 'Maybe it's worth someone taking a look at the paperwork on Shenagh's death.'

He reached into his inside jacket pocket, and pulled out a dog-eared notebook. 'Mission already accomplished. Just as well I got in quick, given that Fern's team have just requisitioned the old file. Well, it's a cold case, any road, so I thought I'd make a few notes on the SIO's Blue Book, and the investigators' rough books. Take 'em, for what they're worth.'

She stretched out a hand. 'You're a star. Though I guess you've broken half a dozen of Lauren's rules about information security.'

'With any luck.' The craggy face relaxed into a rare grin. 'What's the worst that can happen? She's already given me the sack. That's why I leaked the restructure to the press. Just on the off chance it might save the jobs of everyone else.'

Oz saw Daniel to the door after Melody announced she felt a migraine coming on, and was going upstairs for a rest. At the front step, Oz halted.

'I'm worried sick about her, you know.'

Daniel mumbled something bland and sympathetic, but his host interrupted. 'Don't be fooled by that cool elegance, underneath she is fragile. Long before we ever met, she had a spell in a psychiatric unit. It was to take her mind off our money worries that I encouraged her interest in writing, and the legend of the Frozen Shroud. Big mistake. It's backfired horribly.'

'If—'

'No!' Oz raised a hand. 'Let me finish. You and she are never going to prove Letty's innocence, not after all these years. An ancient murder is the last thing Melody needs on her mind right now.'

'Yet she could be right about Letty.'

'What if she is? Who cares?'

Daniel gave a shrug. 'If someone can be cleared of committing a brutal murder, even long after their death, isn't that worth caring about?'

'So you are persisting with this?'

'Why not? This afternoon, I'm going to Keswick Museum. Roland Jones donated some papers to their archives. I'm hoping to pick up more information about him there.'

'Letty was sick. If she hadn't killed herself, she'd never have hanged, not even in Edwardian England. Doesn't what happened to Terri make what happened years ago seem pretty trivial?'

'Any historian believes the past can tell us something about the present. Take the murder of Shenagh Moss.'

Oz stiffened. 'What has Shenagh's death got to do with anything?'

'Three women have been battered to death in Ravenbank.'

'Over a period of a hundred years!'

'Two of them in the past five. You don't have to be a conspiracy theorist to suspect there's a connection.'

Oz strode out into the drive, and Daniel followed to where his car was parked.

'Far-fetched, if you ask me. Copycat killings are commonplace. Craig Meek hated Shenagh because she'd dumped him, and killed her because of it. End of.'

'If the obvious suspect has been released from custody, the police are bound to cast their net wider. When you talk to them, I'm sure they will be asking questions about Shenagh. What was she like, did anyone else hate her?'

'Hate her?' Oz exhaled, and Daniel smelt the alcohol on his breath. 'Listen, I'll tell you something about Shenagh. You'll have heard that she and I were close? It wasn't exactly a clandestine affair. She was funny, clever, a vibrant personality. Fabulous to look at, and even better in bed, I don't mind saying it. It was a miracle old Palladino never had a heart attack. But she had a hell of an appetite, there was no way the old feller could keep her satisfied.'

'But your relationship with her didn't last long?'

'Melody and I – we've had an understanding from day one. She knows what I'm like. When she finally agreed to marry me, we both signed up to the deal. We're a good team, she's a sweet lady, and utterly gorgeous into the bargain. But she's had a hard life . . . look, we're both men of the world. She's a lady to look at rather than touch, if you get my meaning.'

'She said your flings never last for long. And she did seem pretty relaxed about them. But – was Shenagh different?'

Oz bent his head, and Daniel noticed a bald patch on the crown. Until today, he'd always combed his hair with such care that you couldn't see it.

'Shenagh had a low boredom threshold. Once she'd reeled Palladino in, she didn't need me. An ongoing affair with a married man was a complication too far. She wanted fresh fields to conquer.'

'Did she find them?'

'You bet.' Oz chewed his lower lip. 'It was insane, but . . .'

A gust of wind smacked the trees; soon there would be no leaves left on the branches. A crow yelped and flew out from its hiding place in a copper beech. Daniel watched it circle overhead for a few seconds before it headed for the lake.

'Did she become involved with Quin?'

Oz Knight stared at him. 'Jesus Christ. How did you know?'

CHAPTER FIFTEEN

Robin Park's fingers drummed on the varnished pine table top. 'I've heard so much about you, Hannah.'

It always induced paranoia in her when someone said that. She tried to suppress her curiosity by taking a sip of her latte. The game plan was to listen, not talk.

'Sorry, I can't say the same.'

He'd asked her to meet him here in the Jazz Lounge at Pooley Bridge. They were sharing a discreet corner with a piano and stool. Not that there was any need for discretion, with no other customers. When she'd arrived, Robin had been killing time at the piano, playing a few bars over and over. A sixties jazz waltz, a maddeningly familiar lounge lizard's song. She couldn't remember what it was called, but a couple of lines echoed in her mind. *Day after day, there are girls in the office / And men will always be men.*

He gave a fractional bow, as if encouraging her to break into applause. When she offered her hand, his long fingers clasped it for a moment longer than necessary. She must call him Robin, he said, adding that they'd both lost someone so very special. He fancied himself, for sure, but he was also needy; she recognised the type, having lived with one for years. You indulged men like that at your peril.

The ground floor was spacious but draughty; a pair of sliding glass doors weren't properly closed, so the cold from outside seeped in. She kept on her lined jacket, and watched him sashay over to the counter for coffee and millionaire shortbread, a slinky mover in skintight Levi's and thin blue T-shirt. She could just picture Terri ogling the bloke's backside. Her second husband had been a part-time underpants model, and Robin was in very good shape. Yet waiting to be served, he seemed twitchy and ill at ease. Unless it was just the lack of a warm top that made him shiver.

'This place is pretty special to me,' he said. 'Believe it or not, I sat at the back of this very room as a boy, and listened to my dad playing the trumpet in his band. Of course, it was all so different then. Spit and sawdust, no polished floorboards or fancy lighting, but he and I both loved the place. I may not have inherited the family sports gene, but music's always been special to me.' He paused, as if expecting a response, but Hannah wasn't in the mood for nostalgia. 'A brilliant trumpeter, Dad, wonderful ear for a tune. Mum swears he would have made it big, if he'd kept his feet on the ground. But no, he was seduced by the idea of owning a bar. Big mistake – he was a much better musician than he was a businessman.'

He swivelled in his chair to gaze into her eyes, and then, as if disappointed with what he saw, looked away through the glass doors. She followed his gaze. Outside, a paved terrace overlooked the river and wooded lower reaches of

Dunmallard Hill. Years ago, she and Marc had walked up there, and picnicked by the remains of the Iron Age hill fort at the summit. The Jazz Lounge's patio must be idyllic when the sun shone, but all the parasols had been dismantled for winter, and the tables and chairs were cocooned in waterproof sheets. Not even the hardiest local would fancy al fresco snacking on a day so misty, cold and damp.

'You mustn't be cross with Terri for not telling you about us.'

'I'm not cross.' Was that true? Didn't she feel somehow let down, as well as puzzled? 'Just surprised.'

'She was about to break the news to you. The day after the party.'

'I'm not sure what difference the party made?' She shrugged. 'Anyway, doesn't matter.'

'She was worried . . .' He fiddled with his napkin, folding it again and again before squashing it in his palm. 'I think she was worried how you would react. To her starting a serious relationship again, so soon after breaking up with Stefan.'

'All I wanted was for her to be happy and safe.' Shit, why did she sound so defensive, like an overprotective parent mithering about an unreliable offspring? And was he right about Terri? 'Her love life was her own business.'

'Terri was the first to admit she'd made a lot of wrong choices. Especially when it came to men. She assumed you'd think I was just one more good-for-nothing.'

'She used to say I was bossy. Meddling with her life, wanting her to play everything by the book. Getting in the way of her indulging her instinct for having a good time.' Hannah hadn't meant to say what was in her mind, but the words just spilt out. She'd been wrestling with this ever since learning of Robin Park's existence. 'That's why she kept schtum, isn't it?'

'Don't punish yourself, it's not your fault.' Reassurance so swift and so slick that she was sure he'd used that line before. True or not, it was the sort of thing people liked to hear. 'She looked up to you, put you on a pedestal. It was always Hannah this, Hannah that. To be honest, I was in awe of meeting you. The paragon.'

She waved away the bullshit. 'I simply didn't want her to be hurt again. So many of her Prince Charmings turned into frogs.'

Robin's grin made him look like a cheesy TV presenter. Very white teeth, tanned skin. Easy not to notice his anxiety. But those pianist's fingers kept tapping the table top.

'The worst kind of frogs, from what she told me. Idle, penniless wastes-of-space. And then the last one turned violent. When she told me her life story, I finally realised how she could tolerate being with a two-bit jazz pianist.'

Easy to understand what Terri had seen in him, Hannah had to admit. It wasn't just the dazzling blue eyes and the trim bum. Terri would have found his self-deprecating manner and hint of vulnerability equally hard to resist. Just as she'd fancied Marc, another handsome man whose affability concealed a streak of weakness.

'How did you meet?'

'At a jazz concert the Knights organised. In Ambleside, at a place that had just opened up.'

'Not Balotelli's? She took me there for a drink, last time we went out together.' God, it seemed like half a lifetime ago. 'The night before Hallowe'en.'

'Yeah, she told me. Our original plan was to spend that night together, even though she hadn't moved in with me on a permanent basis. You know Terri, she cherished her independence. With all the hassle from Stefan, I hated the thought of her being on her own. God knows, how right I was.'

Hannah waited.

'Unfortunately, it was the anniversary of my dad's death. Mum's always a bit low when that day comes around, and she wanted me to spend the evening with her at Beck Cottage. I couldn't let her down. When Terri phoned me, and I explained, she decided to stay with you instead.'

'That's one mystery solved. She didn't tell me who she'd called.'

'Oh, she loved being mysterious, didn't she? Said she was matchmaking, but you wouldn't play ball. In her opinion, you and Daniel Kind were perfect for each other. Small world, eh? Who would have thought I'd meet him for myself at the Knights' party?'

Hannah swallowed some more coffee. She had no intention of discussing Daniel, especially not with a man she'd only just met. This mustn't become a cosy chat between two people sharing their grief. Robin had been present in Ravenbank the night Terri was killed. His sickness had given someone the chance to commit the crime. And there was an alternative that she couldn't yet rule out. Sickness could be feigned. It was too early to presume he had nothing to do with her death.

In her head, she heard Terri speaking. 'Hey, kid, relax. Can't you forget, for once in your life, that you're a police officer?'

Oh sweetheart, easier said than done.

'Tell me what Terri did on Hallowe'en.'

'She and Oz called in at the Theatre by the Lake to discuss Quin and Jeffrey's premiere. Later, she spent an hour setting up a Hallowe'en party in Keswick. By half two, she was back at my cottage – by which time I'd well and truly succumbed to the bug.'

'Did any of your neighbours know you'd been taken ill?'

'Probably all of them. Terri popped round to the Hall to pass on my apologies to the Knights, and she called at Watendlath to give an update on the discussion about the show. Between you and me, Oz didn't keep her fully occupied. There wasn't much business coming in, and they were helping with the show mainly as a favour to Jeffrey and Quin. She'd heard Oz the day before, ranting at his accountant, something about an overdue tax payment.'

'Was the company in trouble?'

'Sounded like it. But I've never taken much interest in business or money.' And he hadn't needed to, Hannah thought, once his mother used the legacy from Palladino to buy him a home. 'Anyway, I was out for the count, but I didn't want that to spoil Hallowe'en for Terri.'

'Or your mother?'

'Exactly. Mum was looking forward to the party. Until Francis Palladino died, she worked at the Hall, and she still helps Melody out every now and then. It's not about money, she just loves the Hall, and she's never minded getting her hands dirty. Any excuse to relive the old days. I insisted the two of them go without me.'

Ah, the selfless invalid. The more they talked, the more he

reminded her of Marc. 'While you stayed at home in bed?'

'Well, I was staggering back and forth to the loo every two minutes. Or that's how it felt. Ghastly, trust me. You really don't want to hear the details.' The cheesy grin reappeared. 'All I could do was obey Mum's words of wisdom. Drink gallons of water and get as much rest as possible.'

'Ravenbank is a dangerous place at Hallowe'en. Weren't you worried about Terri? Bearing in mind the murder of Shenagh Moss, and the legend of the Faceless Woman.'

He made a performance of choking on a mouthful of shortbread. 'Are you seriously suggesting that Terri's death is connected with that Frozen Shroud rubbish?'

'I'm not suggesting anything. In a murder case, it's essential to explore every avenue.'

'Including a barmy story about the ghost of a woman without a face?'

'Almost the last time anyone saw Terri was during the ghost hunt.'

'They just did that for a laugh, everyone was pissed, by the sound of things. Nobody in their right mind would take the story seriously.'

'Is your mother equally sceptical?'

He sighed. 'Mum belongs to a different generation. You have to realise, she's spent most of her life in this small corner of Cumbria. She can barely use a computer, and probably thinks One Direction is a road sign. They may be a dying breed, but there are still people like that, you know. As for the legend, Esme Palladino swore she'd once seen Gertrude Smith's ghost walking down Ravenbank Lane, and that was good enough for Mum.'

'But not you?'

'Esme was an old soak. She'd probably been on a bender the night she claims she saw the Faceless Woman.' He closed his eyes. 'Don't get me wrong, the legend is fun. But – it's a ghost story. Not real. It has nothing to do with what happened to Terri.'

She wiped shortbread crumbs from her mouth. 'How can you be sure about that, Robin?'

Daniel squeezed his car keys in his palm. Quin's affair with Shenagh had tormented Jeffrey Burgoyne. Five years after her death, he wasn't over it. At The Solitary Reaper on Saturday, a mere expression of sympathy – 'poor Shenagh' – had been enough to get under Jeffrey's skin. Daniel remembered their exchange of looks, charged with meaning, yet inexplicable to anyone who didn't know. As soon as they were alone, recriminations must have begun, and the upshot was that Jeffrey slapped his partner on the face.

'Whenever Shenagh is mentioned, it's obvious Jeffrey despised her, but Quin was a fan. I wondered if that made Jeffrey jealous.'

'Jealous as hell.' Oz Knight's gaunt expression twisted, as if he had toothache, and Daniel saw that he too had been devoured by jealousy. 'He didn't understand that Shenagh was playing a game. Seducing a gay man was a challenge, like I said. To her, it meant nothing more.'

He wasn't trying to hide his bitterness, any more than he'd bothered dying his hair or combing over that bald patch. It was as if he'd abandoned the persona he'd adopted for so long, leaving in its place just one more miserable middle-age man. Like Clifford Hodgkinson and Francis Palladino before him, the murder of a woman had ripped up his life. In the space of a few days, he'd segued from lord of the manor to sad old loser.

'Are you sure?'

'She as good as admitted it. When I told her it was wrong to treat people as playthings, she told me to fuck off. Said she'd spent half her life being treated as a plaything. Now it was her turn.'

'You don't think she'd have left Francis Palladino for Quin?'

'No way!' Oz scoffed. 'She'd tied everything up so cleverly with Francis. Shenagh was sorted, believe me.'

Was that true, or what he wanted to believe? 'Did the relationship with Quin fizzle out?'

Oz frowned as leaves gusted across the lawn. 'She'd stopped confiding in me by then.'

'Was she still seeing Quin at the time of her murder?'

'This is a game to you, isn't it?' Oz didn't sound angry, just defeated and disillusioned. 'Next stop, Keswick Museum, to see what stones you can lift up. For some of us, it's not an intellectual puzzle. It feels like a blade, ripping through my guts.'

He turned on his heel, and strode out across the lawn, boots squelching in the wet grass. His gait was uncertain, and Daniel didn't think it was just down to the Rioja.

Five years after her death, Shenagh's ghost still haunted Ravenbank. She'd played for high stakes, but in the end she'd lost. Perhaps she'd pushed one of her playmates too far.

* * *

'Terri's murder is horrific,' Robin said. 'It's destroyed everything we dreamt of together. I'm not sure I'll ever get over it. But her death has nothing to do with what happened five years ago. Surely there's an overwhelming case against Deyna?'

He ventured a tentative smile. Hannah wasn't giving him any encouragement. She sampled the millionaire shortbread: pretty good.

'I mean, the man can't deny he was at Ravenbank that night. Or that he made a run for it. What more proof of guilt do your colleagues want? Why would anyone act like that, if he had nothing to hide? It's bizarre that they've let him go. A scandal. I don't suppose you're able to explain what the hell your people are up to?'

'You suppose right. Besides, it's not my case.'

'Oh, Hannah, please.' He was finding it a struggle to remain Mr Nice Guy. Those fingers started drumming again, louder than before. *Tap, tap, tap*. 'I'm not a total simpleton.'

'I never thought you were.' True enough, but she couldn't yet decide whether he was bewildered and distraught, or had some ulterior motive she was yet to fathom.

'Well, then. You're matey with this Larter woman, aren't you? And she's in charge of the investigation. I met her five years ago, and she struck me as pretty smart. So why would she free the prime suspect?'

'You're right, DCI Larter is a first-rate detective. They don't come any better. If she's made a decision, she'll have her reasons.'

'So where do we go from here?'

'You tell me.' She stifled a yawn. Although the bed at Tarn Cottage couldn't be more comfortable, she hadn't slept properly since the night of Marc's car crash. 'Terri's mobile went missing on Hallowe'en, I hear.'

'That's right.' *Tap, tap, tap.*

'I couldn't get my head round that. Terri was constantly messing with her phone. Calling friends, texting, playing games. She hardly ever let it out of her sight.'

He gave a helpless shrug.

'Any idea what happened to it?'

'I don't have a clue!' Two pink spots showed on the tanned cheeks, as if she'd accused him of petty larceny. 'Before she got ready for the party, she mentioned she'd mislaid her phone. She was upset, as you'd expect, but by that time, I was out for the count. Feeling awful, and very sorry for myself.'

'So you've no idea when she lost it, let alone how?'

He shook his head. 'Might have been when she was with Oz, in Keswick. Or she may have dropped it in her own car. Though the forensic people have gone over that with a fine toothcomb, as well as all the possessions she kept in my cottage. Her handbag, her computer, you name it.'

'She didn't mention calling Stefan that night, to arrange a clear-the-air meeting with him?'

'Do you seriously believe I'd have let her run the risk?'

Hannah folded her arms. 'Let's assume for a moment that Stefan didn't kill Terri.'

'For God's sake! Why should we assume that?'

'Because his guilt hasn't yet been established. And we do want to get at the truth, don't we?'

'Of course.' He reminded her of a sullen little boy. Or

Marc, on occasions when things didn't go his way.

'In which case, the murder of Shenagh Moss is bound to come under scrutiny.'

'What makes you say that?'

'Because,' Hannah said, 'it's impossible to believe that two more or less identical killings, committed in the same place five years apart, are not connected.'

'Everyone knows Shenagh was killed by Craig Meek! He was as bad as Stefan. A mad stalker, with a grudge against a pretty woman who'd made a few bad judgements in her life.' His voice wavered. 'But who didn't deserve to die.'

'Did she make a bad judgement with you?' Hannah asked quietly.

'For God's sake! Are you suggesting that I slept with Shenagh?'

'It's a question that is bound to be asked.'

'Okay, the answer is simple. Watch my lips.' He tried to mimic Bill Clinton. 'I did not have sexual relations with that woman.'

She studied his white, distraught face, and decided he was telling the truth.

'Sorry. I felt I had to ask.'

'I wanted to meet you,' he said in a muffled tone, 'because we had Terri in common. Terri meant the world to me. Okay, we'd only known each other a short time, but that didn't matter. And before you ask, we never had a cross word. No rows, no tantrums, nothing but love and laughter.'

He stared out through the sliding doors. Had she done him an injustice? It was selfish to assume her suffering was more intense – selfish and almost certainly wrong. He'd been

Terri's lover, the man she'd chosen to spend her life with. The latest in a long line, admittedly, but that didn't mean they hadn't fallen head over heels. The depth of Terri's passion might explain her reluctance to mention him. Perhaps she'd wanted to see Hannah fixed up with Daniel before boasting about her own new relationship.

'I'm sure she did, Robin. Is there anything you can tell me about Shenagh? Did anyone in Ravenbank have reason to want her dead?'

'Dead?' He shook his head. 'I'm not saying she was everyone's cup of tea, but – for someone to want to murder her, and in such a brutal way? It's incredible. I refuse to believe it.'

'She'd shacked up with a lord of the manor twice her age. A sexy woman, with lots of money, and time on her hands. It's a recipe for trouble.'

'You're barking up the wrong tree.' He was beginning to sound more confident. 'The femme fatale with the boring old bloke who takes a younger lover? Shades of *Double Indemnity* and *The Postman Always Rings Twice*. Surely that would make Francis Palladino the prime candidate for a murderous attack on a dark night? The poor old boy found her body, after all.'

'Suppose Shenagh was happy with Francis, and that made someone else jealous?'

He gazed at her in silence. Making, she thought, some kind of calculation.

'Is this Oz Knight we are talking about? Or Alex Quinlan?'

Jeffrey Burgoyne couldn't control his temper. Sitting behind the wheel, waiting for a chance to get past a tractor lumbering along the narrow road, Daniel flinched at the memory of the stinging blow he'd witnessed. An aberration, perhaps – but its casual brutality suggested otherwise. This morning, the imperfectly concealed mark on Quin's cheek suggested another bust-up. Plenty of apparently respectable men still assaulted their wives because they'd deluded themselves into imagining they had the right. Jeffrey was no different, except that he was gay.

He held the purse strings, and that might be all that kept the couple together. If he had a violent streak, Shenagh's seduction of his partner might have provoked him into losing control. Quin was stylish and sexy, and twenty years his junior. If he felt insecure . . . suppose he'd killed Shenagh, and then – somehow – Terri had discovered what had happened five years earlier. He'd have a motive to silence her before she betrayed him.

At last, the tractor turned off down a muddy farm track. Daniel put his foot down. Optimism surged inside him. At last he was making progress. The truth about the Ravenbank murders wouldn't stay hidden much longer.

Hannah savoured the last of her shortbread. The caramel and chocolate gave her a buzz. It wasn't only outdoors that the fog was lifting. Links between Terri's death and Shenagh's were starting to connect in her brain.

'Let's take Knight first. I hear his wife is very attractive. Yet still he strayed?'

'Leopards don't change their spots, do they? There are no kids – Melody told Mum that she can't have them, and presumably they never considered adoption. Oz is a super guy, don't get me wrong, but he needs to be the centre of attention. An ego that size needs constant feeding.'

'And Quinlan? I thought he was gay?'

'With a civil partnership certificate to prove it. But Quin swings both ways. And he's not faithful. Not long after he arrived in Ravenbank, he tried flirting with me.'

'But he didn't get anywhere?'

He gave her a chilly smile. 'It's women who turn me on. Attractive women, like Terri. But I'm sure Quin leads Jeffrey Burgoyne a merry dance.'

'Are you positive that Shenagh had a . . . dalliance with Quin?'

'Hey, I wasn't lurking in the undergrowth with a long-lens camera like some paparazzo hoping to catch a celebrity with her top off. Ravenbank is such a tiny place, it's hard to keep secrets, however much you try.'

He sighed, as if he had cause to regret it.

'How did that particular secret leak out?'

'Melody Knight overheard a quarrel between Jeffrey and Quin one afternoon when she popped round to their cottage for something.'

'And Melody told you? You're good friends, I take it?'

He'd just said how much he liked attractive women. Was it possible that he'd had something going on with Melody? Surely all the residents of Ravenbank couldn't be shagging each other? The Lakes' long dark winter nights had a lot to answer for, but there were limits.

'Hey, don't get the wrong idea. We get on fine, we even indulge in some mild flirting every now and then, but there's nothing in it. In fact, it was Mum she told. And Mum mentioned it to me.'

Hannah pictured an elderly crone, outwardly good-natured, inwardly gleeful at any chance to spread a scandal, even if only as far as her own son. Robin seemed to read her mind.

'You mustn't get the wrong idea about Mum. She's no blabbermouth. In her book, people should keep themselves to themselves.'

Hmmmm. Maybe.

'That's why she agonised over what Melody told her. Much as she liked Shenagh, she was outraged, on Francis's behalf. I think she even contemplated grassing Shenagh up, but in the end, she decided there was no point. Shenagh would deny everything, and Francis would take her side. It might even have wrecked her relationship with Francis, and she wouldn't have wanted that. So she just hoped the affair would blow over.'

'Perhaps Quinlan took it more seriously?'

'Not as seriously as his boyfriend, if you ask me.' Robin grinned nervously. 'At least it entertained Terri when I told her about all these shenanigans.'

Leopards don't change their spots. Hannah remembered wondering if Terri had become romantically entangled with her new boss. 'I don't mean to be tactless – but there's no chance that Terri and Oz Knight might . . .'

'What are you implying?' His colour rose. 'That Oz was shagging her behind my back?'

'He's a leopard, isn't he? You said so yourself.'

'You don't get it, Hannah, do you? Terri and I had something very special. Over the years, we'd both gone down enough blind alleys to recognise the real thing when we saw it. There's no way she'd have messed about with Oz. Anyway, she worked for him, it would have been unprofessional.'

Unprofessional working relationships, oh dear. Hannah didn't want to go there.

'Were you planning to get married?'

For once, he seemed unsure how to answer. 'Mum was keen for that to happen. I hear she said something at the party about us getting hitched. But we had no need to jump the gun. She was only just settling herself into the Ravenbank community. Everything in good time.'

Now for it. Hannah leant forward. 'In the course of settling into Ravenbank, did Terri stumble onto something which identified Shenagh's killer?'

He opened his eyes very wide, and she saw the thought had never crossed his mind until now. He blinked hard, as if calculating odds in his head.

'You think that's what happened? That she came across some sort of clue, and she was murdered by someone desperate to keep their guilt secret?'

'It's possible.'

'I suppose . . . but Terri never said anything to me.'

'Perhaps she only found out on the day of the party, perhaps after you were taken ill.' Hannah took a breath. 'How about you, is there any gossip in Ravenbank about your secrets? Or don't you have any?'

'Me?' He sat bolt upright. 'What do you mean?'

'You were a young man, roughly the same age as Shenagh Moss. Not bad looking, and unattached. A musician, presumably with a relaxed lifestyle. Didn't the two of you . . . ?'

He mustered a grin. 'Thanks for the kind words. At least – I *think* I'm flattered. And if that's a dig about my lifestyle, I can promise I'm no dope fiend. Weed gives me a headache. Though . . .'

'Yes?'

'Terri smoked the occasional joint. That surprises you? It was one of her darkest secrets, given your job. She said you were a puritan when it came to drugs.'

Hannah gritted her teeth. 'You haven't answered my question.'

'I liked Shenagh, and she liked me. That's as far as it went, you'll have to take my word for it. I'm different from Oz. I was lucky enough to grow up with two parents who were happily married. Mum and Dad were polar opposites in personality, but they were a couple who believed in till death do us part. I don't believe in breaking up other people's relationships, and I wasn't interested in muscling in on Francis Palladino's territory.'

Quite a speech. Hannah couldn't keep the sarcasm out of her voice.

'Very commendable.'

He didn't seem offended, even allowing himself a sliver of a grin. 'Besides, she wasn't my type.'

'Okay, what is your type? An extrovert like Terri?'

'She was nothing like my previous girlfriends. Apart from anything else, she'd been married three times before. Until now, I've steered clear of women who want long-term commitment. Most of her predecessors have been in their early twenties. I guess I was just looking for the right person to settle down with.'

She wanted to keep pressing him, see if he faltered. 'And Terri was that person?'

He hesitated, as if searching for the right form of words. 'I hoped so. She was easy-going, someone who believed in live and let live. I can't bear neurotic, frigid women, or predatory types. I don't wish to be unkind, but women like Melody and Shenagh scare the pants off me. But not literally.'

In the last few minutes, despite her intrusive questions, he'd seemed calmer, and more candid. No more table-tapping; for whatever reason, he'd relaxed. As if he'd accomplished his purpose in arranging this get together. Had he simply been curious to meet her? He leant back in his chair, curiously pleased with himself. Hannah decided to risk wiping the smile off his face.

'Your mother received a legacy when Francis Palladino died. Such a generous bequest that she could afford to buy you a cottage.'

Robin's face darkened. 'Hannah, please. I'm really disappointed. You are seriously implying that the money gave either my mother or me a motive to get Shenagh out of the way?'

'Only flagging up a question that you're bound to be asked.' She gave him a shamelessly disingenuous smile. 'Giving you advance warning, if you like.'

'Excuse me for not prostrating myself with gratitude. Better do your research more carefully before you start flinging accusations around. It's verging on slander. I don't care about myself, but I won't have you slagging off my mum. You haven't the faintest idea about the terms of Francis Palladino's will, have you?'

His anger was genuine, no question. A bilious feeling in her guts told her she'd blundered. Risked making an enemy of the man Terri had loved.

'Care to enlighten me?'

'Francis drew up a new will when he fell for Shenagh. Previously, four-fifths of his estate went to charity, and the rest to Mum. In recognition of all she'd done for him, and for Esme. A hell of a lot of money, but he didn't have any close family. With Shenagh on the scene, he arranged that she'd take half the estate. Mum's share was unchanged, the legacies to charity were scaled down pro rata. After Shenagh's death, the original provisions kicked in again. The murder didn't make a ha'p'orth of difference to Mum financially.'

'I see.'

'No, I tell a lie,' he said fiercely. 'It made my mother sick with distress, she was so distraught about what had happened. Shenagh was her friend, and Francis she idolised. The poor old boy never recovered from losing the woman he loved. He lost the will to live. Even the poor old family dog died. It was a disaster all round. Satisfied?'

Ouch. No question about who had seized the moral high ground. Time to beat a hasty retreat. 'Sorry, but I had to ask.'

He put his head in his hands. Theatrical, yes, but effective. 'It's a mucky job, yours. Terri never understood how you could stomach working for the police.'

Terri had never said that to her. She knew how much the job meant. And yet his jibe had the ring of truth. It hurt like a poke in the eye, that Terri had confided in a man she'd only known five minutes things that were taboo between two best friends. Hannah dug her nails into her palm. Urging herself not to fall into the biggest trap of all, and succumb to jealousy of Terri's relationship with this man.

'I don't like it myself, sometimes.'

'You don't seem capable of trusting anyone.'

Twisting the knife, but probably she deserved that. She bit her tongue.

'I trusted Terri. Now she's gone, I want to find out why she died, and who killed her. If that means asking embarrassing questions, too bad. All I care about is the truth.'

He looked up, and she saw a teary glistening in his eyes. 'The truth is that Stefan Deyna killed her. Why can't we leave it at that?'

'We can't settle for a solution just because it suits us. Rough on the innocent, but there's no alternative.'

'There's no persuading you, is there?' He shook his head, as if making a decision. 'That's it, then. I'd better not waste any more of your afternoon.'

This time, their handshake lasted a nanosecond. Hannah said, 'I'm still not clear why you wanted to meet.'

'I only met Terri in August,' he said. 'You grew up with her. How I envy you, knowing her since you were both kids. There's so much I don't know about her. I hoped we could talk, you could help me fill in the gaps. I was expecting reminiscences, not the Spanish bloody inquisition. Stupid of me, I should have realised a police inspector has different priorities.'

Hannah glanced outside. The fog was coming down again. Already it was hard to make out the trees on the opposite side of the river. Perched on the beer garden wall of the pub next door, two crows were quarrelling, like an old couple who'd been together too long.

'How well do any of us know anyone else? Another time, when all this is sorted, we can talk about Terri.'

Almost to himself, he said, 'I doubt there'll ever be another time.'

He moved back onto the piano stool. This time he chose 'Cry Me a River', humming softly as he played. Hannah listened to the first verse, before slipping away into the unforgiving cold.

Daniel's phone shrilled. He had hands-free, but a lay-by was a hundred yards ahead and he decided to pull up.

'Hello?'

'Daniel! Thank God you answered!'

'Melody, you sound frantic. What's the matter?'

'It's Oz.' Her voice faltered. 'I'm so scared.'

'What of?'

'I'm frightened of what he's going to do.'

CHAPTER SIXTEEN

Hannah rang Fern from her car, and they agreed to meet at Undercrag that evening for a catch up. Hannah offered to cook, but Fern refused to let her go to any trouble.

'You've got enough on your plate without worrying what to put on mine. Besides, you'd only make me eat something healthy, and I can't be bothered to count the sodding calories. Ring for a pizza from that Italian on Rydal Road. Mine's a Stromboli De Luxe with double pepperoni and garlic bread on the side. Long, long day, got to cater for the inner woman. Must dash, see you later.'

From her vantage point outside the Sun Inn, Hannah saw Robin Park come out of the Jazz Lounge. The weight of the world seemed to be pushing down on his narrow shoulders as he squeezed into his natty little sports car. Ravenbank was only five or six miles away, and Hannah felt a sudden urge to follow him and see it for herself. She must, she absolutely must, make a pilgrimage to the place where Terri's body had been found. Not this afternoon, however. The fog would soon return, and she had plenty of work to do before she talked to Fern.

On the way to Kendal, she replayed the conversation with Robin Park in her mind. If Stefan was innocent, then Robin had to be a prime suspect. If the relationship with Terri had imploded, or if she'd found out something linking him to Shenagh's death, he might have had a motive for murder. Yet her death seemed to have stunned him, and though he was too self-absorbed for Hannah's taste, she hadn't detected a lurking predisposition to the rage and violence necessary for two such brutal killings.

But, she reminded herself, she'd been surprised once or twice before about what a seemingly decent human being is capable of when pushed beyond endurance.

She was supposed to progress the Cold Case Review Team's reorganisation this afternoon, but as soon as she reached the sanctuary of her office, she buried herself in the material Les Bryant had supplied. She wouldn't have the sanctuary much longer, might as well use it as a bolt-hole whilst she could. She managed twenty minutes' reading before a bang on the door broke into her concentration.

Greg Wharf didn't wait to be invited in, or to take a seat once he'd shut the door.

'Sorry to burst in, but you'll be receiving an email from HR any minute now, and I wanted to speak to you first.'

He seemed purposeful yet defiant, as if bracing himself for an onslaught.

'This had better be quick.'

'Fine.' His jaw was set. 'In a sentence, I've asked to be redeployed.'

She stared at him. 'What for?'

'I thought you wanted me to be quick. I've said what I came here to say.'

She groaned. 'Please, Greg, I'm not in the mood to be messed about.'

'And I don't want to mess you about, which is why I'm moving on. Lauren was right – hey, I never thought I'd say that. If I go, you'll be able to keep someone else. Les Bryant is lower cost, there's no pension to factor in. If I go, there will be no complications.'

'Complications?'

He gave an exaggerated sigh. 'You-and-me complications. People are whispering about us already. You're a detective, you must have picked up on it. My fault, my reputation goes before me. You've had enough to contend with, I don't want you damaged on my account.'

'So this is a noble act of self-sacrifice?'

'Don't get stroppy, Hannah, I'd rather part on good terms.'

She counted to ten. 'You're a good detective too, Greg. I'd want you in my team any day. What happened the other night doesn't change anything.'

'It does, actually,' he said. 'For me, anyway.'

'What are you talking about? We agreed, we can be mature adults.'

'Yeah, but I thought it over and I realised I'm no good at being a mature adult.' A glimmer of a smile. 'That's the difference between us. Zanny used to complain that I can't control myself, and for once, she was right. I can't – but you can, and that's too much to bear. Okay?'

Heart sinking, she shook her head. It was very much not okay. But what could she say that wouldn't send the wrong signal?

'Anyway, HR have put the wheels in motion, so it's a done deal. Public Protection can't be that bad, can it?' He jumped to his feet, pausing as he opened the door. 'Thanks, Hannah. I mean – thank you, ma'am.'

Daniel raced along the road to Ravenbank, taking the zigzag bends of the Hause so fast that twice he nearly came off the road as he came over the top and began his descent towards the little church and the valley. No farm vehicles in the way this time, thank God, but the respite from the weather had proved short-lived. Fog was rolling down the slopes of the fells above Martindale, wrapping itself around the scattered farm buildings, fences and huddles of sheep.

Melody had sounded fuzzy and incoherent on the phone. She'd probably washed down her Rioja with pills to cope with the migraine. All he could make out was that Oz had gone missing, and she feared the worst. Whether she was afraid for her husband or herself, he couldn't tell.

The traumas of her youth had left a mark deeper and longer lasting than any of Quin's bruises. Until now, Daniel had assumed that she and Oz slept together, handily providing each of them with an alibi for murders committed in the middle of the night. But if she wasn't interested in sex, perhaps they occupied separate bedrooms. In which case . . .

The same might be true of Jeffrey and Quin. The Irishman had moaned about Jeffrey's habitual snoring, and said that his partner hadn't slept a wink. But if someone suffered from insomnia, what more natural than to get out of bed and go downstairs? Once you looked beyond Stefan, all kinds of possibilities opened up. Because Terri had never returned to Fell View Cottage, Robin Park had no alibi, but neither, he suspected, did anyone else.

Bumping over the little bridge, he found himself looking towards Ravenbank. The tops of the trees were wreathed in mist, the beauty spot had become lonely and forlorn. On a day as dark as this, the Faceless Woman might be tempted to resume her melancholy promenade.

He drove past Beck Cottage, with its drawn curtains. The journalists had finally departed; they must have decided that if they didn't get away before the fog returned, they might wind up stranded for the night on Ravenbank Lane. A solitary figure stood guard outside the gates of the Hall. In the gathering gloom, he felt like Walter Hartright, catching a glimpse of the Woman in White. As he drew closer, she pulled down her hood, and he saw that in fact it was Melody, enveloped in a vast white puffer jacket.

He jumped out of the car, and she ran up, and flung her arms around him. She was sobbing wildly, and he felt her body convulsing against his chest. He could smell alcohol on her breath. After a moment, he took a step back, taking hold of her shoulders and gazing into her reddened and tear-filled eyes.

'What happened to Oz?'

'He . . . he's disappeared!'

'Has he gone somewhere in the car?'

'No, all our cars are locked in the garage. I checked.'

Jeffrey had mentioned that, for some reason, the Knights

had three cars, a couple of SUVs and a natty little open top sports car. No wonder money was tight.

'When did you last see him?'

'As you were leaving. Not long after, my mobile rang. I was half asleep, and didn't answer. Some time later, it rang again and this time I took the call before it went to voicemail. It was Oz.'

'What did he say?'

Melody gulped in air. '"I'm sorry."'

'Sorry for what?'

'That's all. He sounded distraught, and rang off. I called him back, but couldn't get through. I ran downstairs, and the front door was still open. Did you see where he went?'

'As I drove off, he was walking across your lawn.' Daniel pointed. 'As if he were heading to the gardens. He's probably gone for a stroll around the shoreline, a breath of fresh air to clear his head.'

'We're not . . . we're not a pair of drunken sots, you know.'

'Hey.' He hushed her. 'I never said you were.'

'You thought it, though, didn't you?'

It hadn't crossed his mind till now, but he'd seldom seen either of them without a drink in their hand. Even at Amos Books, he recalled. During lunch, they'd worked their way through a couple of bottles, and Oz had knocked back the greater share.

'You think he's gone for a walk and had an accident?'

'Oz isn't much into walking. I tease him about how he drives to the pillar box on the other side of Ravenbank Corner, when he wants to post a letter. Whilst I was waiting for you, I realised what's happened. He's gone out in the boat.'

He put his hands on his hips, unable to hide disbelief. 'In this weather?'

'Yes. I found his mobile, he'd tossed it away on the path near to Letty's grave. I went down to the boathouse. *King Ulf* is missing.'

His head was spinning. 'King Ulf?'

'Oz named the boat after the Nordic chief who gave his name to the lake,' she said impatiently. 'He fancied himself as Ulf's modern day successor.'

She was speaking in the past tense. He hoped it was just that she was thinking back to when Oz bought the boat.

'Please, come on,' she said. 'We need to find him.'

'If Oz didn't moor the boat securely, it may have broken loose in one of the storms we've had lately.'

'Oz wouldn't make a stupid mistake like that.'

Daniel blinked. Oz had surely done nothing but make stupid mistakes for far too long.

'Have you called the police?'

She shook her head. 'Not yet. I'd rather not get them involved if there's no need. That's why I called you. I need your help, your advice. I don't know who else to trust.'

'Ring them now. They have people at Robin's cottage, they can be here in two minutes.' He looked into her eyes, but didn't see any hint of a meeting of minds. 'It's the logical thing to do.'

She shut her eyes. 'Haven't you figured it out yet, Daniel? I'm really not a logical person.'

You can say that again. Fighting to contain his frustration, he dug his mobile out of his inside pocket. 'Let me phone them, if you won't.'

'Okay, I'll call them. But come with me to the boathouse first. Let's see if we can figure out what he's done. Maybe we can catch sight of him.'

She set off without him, breaking into a trot as she headed across the grass for the path they'd taken together on the tour of the Hall grounds, waving for him to follow her lead.

A crazy thought flitted into his mind. Nobody else knew he was here. The fog was descending over Ravenbank, and soon darkness would fall too. Suppose he was walking into a weird kind of trap?

Fantastic. Yet not impossible? What if Melody was afraid he was about to give them away, what if she or her husband had let something slip that would link them to Terri's murder, or Shenagh's, or both? He'd already worked out they might sleep in separate rooms. What if . . . ?

No, no, *no*.

He couldn't bring himself to believe it. Now wasn't the time to get carried away by his obsessive interest in the drama of murder. Melody was many things, but she wasn't a deranged psychopath. In a momentary flash of bravado, he told himself he'd stake his life on that. Whatever her failings, this was a woman who did not betray; she had suffered betrayal. A victim, not a culprit.

Melody reached the path and turned to face him.

'Come on!'

He sucked cold Cumbrian air into his lungs, and set off after her.

* * *

Hannah's brain was hurting by the time she packed her notes into her briefcase and locked her office. She didn't have the time or inclination to agonise about Greg's resignation. He was a grown man, and had to take responsibility for his own decisions. The notes Les had given her raised endless questions, and she'd decided to beat the deteriorating weather and try to work out some answers at home. His experience meant that he'd distilled a handful of telling details from the morass of information facing him as he waded through the Blue Book and the background papers.

Half a dozen people were on the spot in Ravenbank at the time of both murders. Whatever else he'd done, Stefan probably wasn't guilty of bludgeoning Terri to death. He'd been someone else's cat's paw. And if that was true of him, it was likely true of Craig Meek. The key to the mystery lay in the killing of Shenagh. Find the motive for that crime, and you'd find the culprit.

The fog was closing in, and the journey back to Undercrag took twice as long as usual. She decided to invite Fern to stay for the night. The last thing she wanted was for Fern to risk driving home later in lousy conditions after a long and exhausting day. She didn't fancy any more visits to the bedside of RTC victims. Besides, she could do with Fern's company. After a couple of nights at Tarn Cottage, the prospect of tossing and turning in her lonely bed at home had zero appeal.

Once at home, she made herself a coffee and resumed her study of Les's notes. Fern called to say she should arrive in another half an hour, the cue for Hannah to order the pizzas and garlic bread. When the doorbell rang, she thought the pizza delivery man had made it in record time.

Marc stood on the doorstep, his face muffled by a scarf his mother had knitted, a padded envelope in his hand.

'Here are the keys. I thought I ought to let you have them, so you won't be worrying that I might make any more unwanted calls now I'm out of hospital.'

She'd seen him look prettier, but he was in one piece, and so far as she could tell, the cuts on his face were beginning to heal. She held out her hand.

'Thanks.' No way was she going to invite him in. 'You needn't have bothered to deliver them in person, especially on a night like this.'

'I felt I had to do it, as soon as I was discharged. Sort of symbolic, if you know what I mean. End of an era, and all that.'

'Uh-huh.'

'I'll speak to the estate agent tomorrow. I'm assuming you don't want to make me an offer to buy out my share?'

She shook her head. 'This isn't a house for one person. I rattle around too much. I need a change. A small cottage, maybe.'

'Greg isn't moving in?'

She gritted her teeth. Even when he tried to be on his best behaviour, he couldn't resist a dig.

'As a matter of fact, he's moving on. He's applied to be redeployed as part of the team restructure.'

'Are you serious?'

'I told you, the other night was a dreadful mistake. I know it, and so does Greg.' Though that wasn't quite the point he'd made earlier this afternoon. 'Anyway . . .'

'I'd better get back to Grange, before this fog worsens.' He paused. 'It's rotten about Terri, I know you thought the world of her.'

'Yes, I did. Thanks very much for bringing back the keys. Give my love to your mum.'

He gave her a look, as if to say: *Who are you kidding?*

'Goodbye, Hannah.'

'Take care.'

She closed the door, and tossed the envelope onto a small table in the hall. Well, well, her life was getting less complicated by the minute. First Greg, now Marc. And it might be foggy outside, but her head was clearing.

There was a reason why she felt nervy and excited – though she'd refused to admit it, even to herself – each time she heard Daniel's voice. It wasn't because he was his father's son. He was interested in her, but he was determined not to show it, because he felt she wasn't ready. Considerate of him, but clever as he was, he'd miscalculated. The truth was simple. He meant more to her than Marc and Greg put together.

'See what I mean?' Melody demanded.

She and Daniel stood side by side on the shore, peering into the empty boathouse. It jutted out over a tiny inlet, close to the tip of the promontory. The Knights had replaced the rotting timber, and given it a fresh coat of white paint, as well as tiling the roof with new green slates. Daniel dared not guess the cost. A rich man's whim, but now the rich man had gone AWOL.

'What do you think is in his mind?' Daniel asked.

'I daren't imagine,' she said. 'I'm so afraid.'

'Does he often row over to Patterdale, or Glenridding?'

'Hardly at all these days, the novelty has worn off. And never in weather as foul as this.'

The chill air nipped at Daniel's skin as if it had teeth, but she wasn't talking about the temperature. Fog was rolling down from the fells that circled Ullswater, anonymising familiar scenes, blotting out fields and houses with a relentless tide of grey. Visibility was shrinking by the minute. Soon the lake would disappear beneath a cold and eerie blanket.

Yes, nobody in his right mind would row out on such an afternoon, but Daniel was no longer sure Oz Knight was in his right mind. It still wasn't impossible that he'd simply wandered off on his own to blow away the cobwebs. Melody couldn't be one hundred per cent certain he had taken the boat out, but he'd thrown away his mobile close by, and *King Ulf* was nowhere to be seen.

'Is something preying on his conscience?'

'What?' She almost choked with anger. 'He's facing bankruptcy, and the last time I let him try to make love to me, he couldn't even get it up. So much for the smart businessman and the smooth Lothario. Is that enough to satisfy your curiosity, Daniel, is that what you want to hear?'

Her venom made him flinch. 'About Terri's death. If there's anything . . .'

'No!' She cried out as if in pain. 'What are you suggesting? Oz isn't a violent man. He liked Terri. He'd never have harmed a hair on her head.'

'What about Shenagh – might he have harmed her?'

'Don't be stupid!' she shrieked. 'My husband would

never kill anyone. Let alone a woman who drove him almost insane with lust. He's beaten, don't you see? Everything he's worked for is in ruins, and Terri's murder is the final straw.'

He clenched his fists, fighting for calm. 'Sorry, Melody, but we won't help Oz by arguing. Will you ring the police or shall I?'

She pulled out her mobile. 'I'll do it. And I'll go and fetch the people from Fell View. It will be quicker if I run along the shore, than going back down Ravenbank Lane.'

'Okay, I'll stay here till reinforcements arrive.'

She hurried away down the shore path. He saw her speak into the phone, and when the call was over, break into a graceful, loping run. He watched until the path climbed upwards and away from the water, and she vanished into the trees.

He gazed out across the lake. The fog was freezing, and denser than it had been even five minutes earlier. What was Oz Knight playing at? Was he intent on suicide? His throat dry, Daniel wondered if he might yet come face to face with a corpse for the second time in a week. For all the warm lining of his jacket, he found it impossible to stop shivering.

He strained his eyes, peering into the murk. An image sprang into his mind from the macabre story he'd read at Watendlath. A flesh-creeping picture of a misshapen oarsman, a great grey nodding sponge, rowing to his doom.

The fog, like the nameless evil in 'The Voice in the Night', was slow and silent and remorseless, consuming everything it encountered. Soon it would devour Ravenbank. All the landmarks he could identify were disappearing, one by one. The clawing intensity of the cold gnawing at his skin possessed a vindictiveness he'd seldom experienced before; it had become an enemy, intent upon destruction.

He realised now that to think of the fog as a blanket was too cosy, too comfortable. There was nothing homely about this scene. He might be anywhere, or nowhere. Sinister and irresistible, the fog was spreading and stretching. Soon it would devour Ravenbank, as if in punishment for a history of one hundred years of violent death.

Already the lake had disappeared. Buried beneath – how eerily appropriate – a frozen shroud.

CHAPTER SEVENTEEN

'They must find him soon,' Melody whispered. 'He wasn't wearing any waterproof gear and he's been on the lake for over an hour now. How long can he last . . . in this?'

They were standing on the shore, peering out into fog and darkness, because they didn't know what else to do. Quin and Jeffrey Burgoyne had joined them; so had Robin and Miriam Park. Like mourners at a graveside.

The police officers at Fell View Cottage had triggered a Lake Rescue Plan. There was an established routine when someone got into trouble on Ullswater, starting with a ring-round of declared resources. The volunteers from Patterdale Mountain Rescue Team were at the heart of things, coordinating operations along with the coastguard team, and the fire brigade.

The team leader, himself a former cop, had quizzed Melody, looking for flesh to clothe the bare bones of a whereabouts feasibility study. Was there a particular destination that Oz would make for? What might be in his mind? Flailing around like a rag doll, Melody offered no clues. Oz had never done anything like this before. She felt she was living a nightmare from which she'd never wake up.

'There's no shortage of boats out looking for him,' Jeffrey said. 'The Outward Bound Trust, the steamship company, the Mountain Rescue team, they're all on the case. Searching the shoreline, traversing the lake. The police have organised divers, the Mountain Rescue Team's dogs are searching the shore to see if he's run aground. They will find him, you can depend on it.'

'They'll find his dead body, you mean.'

Melody buried her head in her hands. The cool, elegant woman from the conference – was it really less than one week ago? – had become flaky and frightened. She began to wail, a hideous, keening sound, like an animal caught in a trap.

Miriam Park wrapped a strong arm around her, squeezing tight, trying to hush her. The family liaison officer had offered to stay with them, but Miriam had said there was no need; she'd spent a lifetime looking after people.

'You have to grit your teeth, dear,' she said. 'It's the only way to survive when things go wrong.'

'You don't understand. It's . . . over.'

'Hush, you don't know what you're saying.' Miriam hesitated, and Daniel imagined her mental cogs whirring. 'In any case, what on earth do you mean?'

'We're both ruined. Our business is dead in the water.' A bitter laugh. 'And so will Oz be, if this goes on any longer.'

'You don't think that he had anything to do with . . . what happened?'

Melody shrieked, as if a knitting needle had been stuck into her stomach. 'I don't know *what* to think any more!'

One of the police officers had told Daniel that, within minutes of receiving the call, the Mountain Rescue team was in the thick of the action. They'd launched their rigid inflatable craft from the pier at Glenridding. Twenty feet long, with massive lights rigged up on a gantry, he said. But in a white-out as dense as this, light scattered when it hit an object – you couldn't see further than the hand in front of your face. Melody needed to cling to the volunteers' years of experience, and their track record of saving countless lives, often out when all else failed.

'The rescuers will find him soon.' Jeffrey was in tower-of-strength mode, as if playing a part in a British stiff-upper-lip movie made just after the war. 'Depend upon it. He may have found a sheltered spot. Near the bay at Howtown, perhaps.'

'The prevailing wind rushes down from the top of the Kirkstone Pass,' Robin muttered. 'It would blow a boat further on, towards the north end of the lake.'

His mother said, 'If he has any sense, he'll be lying down in that boat, trying to keep warm.'

'In weather like this,' Jeffrey pronounced, 'your core temperature can drop like a stone.'

'It's getting darker,' Robin said. 'Chances are, they'll call off the search until first light tomorrow.'

'Oh God!' Melody said. 'They can't do that, surely? He won't survive a night out in . . . that.'

'They won't give up easily, take it from me,' Jeffrey said. 'All we can do is wait for news.'

'The lake is so deep,' Melody said. 'I can't bear to think of it . . .'

'Ullswater is deceptive,' Quin said. 'Only sixty metres deep, but under the surface, it's like . . . well, the Mariana Trench. Tiered, like a huge jelly mould, the sides don't taper away gradually. Anyone who goes overboard will likely finish up on one of the shelves.'

'That's enough!' Jeffrey snapped. 'Can't you see what Melody is going through?'

'Sorry. I didn't mean . . .'

Quin's voice trailed away. Difficult to make out his expression, in conditions as vile as these, but he didn't sound apologetic. Daniel thought he was more like a small boy, thrilled by the drama, moving restlessly up and down the shoreline, barely able to contain his excitement.

Was he hoping Oz wouldn't make it?

'Major new development.' Fern tried in vain to suppress a note of jubilation. 'Sorry I'm running late, but I had to stop on the road and take the call.'

'No worries,' Hannah said into her phone. 'What's up?'

'Oz Knight is lost on Ullswater. Apparently he set off in a rowing boat with the fog coming down. Melody and Daniel raised the alarm. An intensive search is under way.'

'Jesus. Suicide attempt?'

'Looks that way. I hope to God they find him soon. Out there on a night like this, he won't last too long. Drowning himself in lieu of a confession would be deeply unsatisfactory. Though look on the bright side, it would save a lot of paperwork.'

‘Yeah,’ Hannah said coolly. ‘Like Craig Meek’s car crash.’

‘Ouch.’ Fern hesitated. ‘Of course, you’re right. Don’t want to jump to conclusions, do we?’

‘Perish the thought.’

‘Okay, my wrists are duly slapped. I’ll get to Undercrag as soon as I can.’

After much patient coaxing, Jeffrey convinced Melody that the six of them were doing no good, standing outside in the freezing cold, staring into nothingness. Better to get into the warm, and await developments. At first, she insisted on remaining there on her own, keeping a vigil on the shore, but her resolve crumbled, and in the end she trudged back with them through the fog towards the safe haven of the Hall.

Once they were inside, Miriam took charge, making strong tea, and fussing around as if Melody was a patient from the days when the Hall was a care home. She’d nursed Esme Palladino here, and the thought struck Daniel that Francis Palladino might have ended up happier if he’d made a new life with his unprepossessing but capable housekeeper, rather than glamorous Shenagh Moss. But experience had taught him that life and love have little to do with logic.

He shared the colossal L-shaped sofa with Jeffrey sprawling on one side of him, Quin and Robin Park on the other. Robin said *sotto voce*, ‘If you ask me, this could be a blessing in disguise.’

‘Too right,’ Quin murmured. ‘Frankly, he had this coming.’

Daniel glanced at Jeffrey, and saw that he’d heard the exchange. He was keeping his counsel. Brow furrowed, lips clamped shut. A faint sheen glistened on his forehead. He must be out of condition if the mild exertion of walking up from the shore made him sweat.

Both Robin Park and Quin were constructing narratives that cast Oz as Terri's murderer. Daniel wasn't sure whether they genuinely believed this or simply found it convenient to have a fresh scapegoat in place of Stefan. As for Melody, how much did she know, and what did she believe? Sitting in a vast recliner, with her eyes closed, she looked unexpectedly at peace. Impossible to guess what thoughts were spinning through her mind.

The phone rang, shattering the quiet. With a muffled cry, Melody opened her eyes. She put her hand to her mouth.

'I'll get it.' Miriam picked up the receiver. 'Hello? Do you want to speak to Mrs Knight?'

Melody shook her head frantically. Miriam listened to someone speaking at the other end of the line. Her eyes flickered with anxiety.

'Yes? . . . yes, I see. Well, thank you . . . I'll tell her, of course.'

She put the receiver down and heaved a sigh.

'They've found Oz . . .'

'Thank God!' Jeffrey interrupted, wiping his forehead with a theatrical flourish.

Miriam's frown of reproach reminded Daniel of a teacher rebuking an ill-mannered pupil. 'The wind had driven his boat to Sharrow Bay.'

'How is he, Mum?'

Robin sounded nervous, and Quin was chewing his fingernails.

'He's still breathing, but barely conscious. They reckon he's suffering from hypothermia. An ambulance is taking him to hospital right now. He's in a bad way.'

Fern was still tucking into her Stromboli De Luxe when Hannah took a call from Daniel. Leaning against the kitchen table, she listened to the latest news, along with an outline of the Knights' troubles, and Jeffrey Burgoyne's habit of inflicting domestic violence on Alex Quinlan.

'Interesting,' Hannah said. 'Fern is spending the night here, so I'll brief her. I'd be glad of full chapter and verse about your conversations with people who were at the Knights' party. Can we get together tomorrow? Will you be at Brackdale, or are you on your travels?'

'I was planning to go back in time. I've decided the history of murder suits me much better than homicide in the here and now. When Melody begged me to come back to Ravenbank, I was on my way to Keswick Museum. I meant to go there tomorrow morning, but if . . .'

'No, no, don't change your plans. Let's meet in Keswick.'

'Fine, lunch at the theatre? With any luck, we'll bump into Jeffrey and Quin, so you can kill two birds with one stone. Their show launches next week, and they will be rehearsing.'

'Perfect.'

Fern refilled their glasses with Chablis as Hannah updated her. Marc had laid down some cases of fine wine a few weeks before moving out, and she'd come across them at the weekend during a clear-out of the cellar. It would be rude, as Fern agreed, to let them go to waste. And absolutely stupid to hand them back to him.

'Well, well.' She washed down the last of her pizza with a large gulp of wine and burped happily. 'So Ben's lad is doing some detective work of his own?'

'He's in the thick of this case, after helping to find Terri's body. Possibly he'll get more out of one or two witnesses than we can. People find him easy to talk to, he's a brilliant listener. Plus, I suppose, they enjoy rubbing shoulders with someone who used to be on telly.'

'Yeah, yeah, I'm not complaining. We keep running these campaigns to ask members of the public to help us, after all. Daniel's one of the good guys.' She chortled. 'Wouldn't kick him out of bed, either.'

'Behave.'

'Just saying.' Fern guffawed, but a piece of pizza stuck in her throat, and she half-choked herself. 'Oh God, serves me right, I know. All right, where are we up to? Let's kick off by leaving Deyna out of the equation. Odious creep, but I'm sure he was set up.'

'Like Craig Meek.'

'Yeah, yeah, déjà vu all over again. Daniel guessed right, by the way. The Knights sleep in separate rooms. They were totally upfront about it when they were interviewed. According to their statements, they went straight to bed after the ghost hunt. With an estimated time of death in the early hours of that morning, neither of them has an alibi.'

Hannah fished a couple of Mars bar ice creams out of the freezer. Fern's ideal dessert recipe involved having her Mars bars deep fried, but this was the best she could do. 'Five years ago, they were sleeping together. At least, that's what they said at the time when they made statements and gave each other alibis. Question is whether they were telling porkies.'

'Why would they lie last time, but tell the truth now?'

'Relationships change over time,' Hannah said. 'Cold case work has brought that home to me. Love fades, loyalties shift.'

'Ha! Tell me about it.' Fern had had her share of romantic disasters.

'Say Oz was afraid of being suspected of Shenagh's murder, and spun Melody a yarn, asking her to lie for him. I bet she was under his thumb. He was rich, powerful, controlling. With Shenagh out of the way, she'd have him to herself again. It's different now. If his business is stuffed, she'll need to make a new life. He's lost his hold on her, she doesn't need him any more.'

Fern sank her teeth into the chocolate. 'Mmmm, just what the doctor ordered. The stress counsellor, anyway. Seems to me, we need to have a word with Mr Knight, as soon as he's in a fit state.'

'Assuming he recovers.'

'He'll recover,' Fern said briskly. 'Mild hypothermia won't kill him, he won't so much as lose a little toe. His body has a decent layer of fat. All those expense account meals have come in handy, even if he couldn't afford the expense account.'

'I'm assuming you see this as attempted suicide?'

'Well, he wasn't admiring the scenery on a day like today, was he?'

'So it's a sign of guilt?'

'I'd prefer a signed confession approved by his lawyers,

but beggars can't be choosers. This little mishap will take some explaining. Oh, if he doesn't cough when he wakes up, I expect he'll say he couldn't face the prospect of financial ruin, and decided to row off into oblivion. But I'll get the truth out of him, one way or another.'

'You're confident he did it?'

'He has to be a strong favourite. Obsessed with Shenagh, unable to let go.'

'I see from the old file that Francis Palladino said she'd persuaded him to go out to Australia with her.'

'Yeah, that tickled me. She was giving up Oz – so she could go to Oz.' Fern's massive boobs wobbled as she guffawed. 'Francis said the Hall held unhappy memories because of his wife's long illness, and a warmer climate would benefit his arthritis.'

'According to the notes Les made, Oz had already put in an offer to buy the Hall.'

Fern rubbed her chins. 'Actually, you're right. I remember now. Though with Shenagh dead, Francis stayed put until he died.'

'Which means Oz had conflicting emotions about Shenagh's impending emigration. He'd lose an ex-lover, and gain a big posh house.'

'Swings and roundabouts, huh? I see where you're going with this. If Oz meant to buy the Hall, he'd reconciled himself to losing Shenagh.'

'Exactly.'

'Unless the offer to buy was a sham, to cover his tracks.' Fern ingested the last piece of chocolate, and leant back in her chair, well-fed and content. 'If he simply couldn't face losing Shenagh . . .'

'What about Melody's motive? Shenagh had shagged her husband, and even thought the affair was supposed to be over, Oz was still slavering after the woman. You'd have to be a saint not to be pissed off.'

'If Oz had offered to buy the Hall, she must have known Shenagh would soon be out of temptation's way, on the other side of the world. The same goes for Jeffrey Burgoyne. You say Daniel has some evidence that Jeffrey has a violent streak, and he was jealous because Quin had something going with Shenagh. But Shenagh wasn't going to stick around much longer.'

Hannah switched on the coffee maker while Fern replenished her glass. 'Perhaps he simply lost the plot. It happens.'

'Yeah, murder is a desperate act, but don't forget, there are different kinds of desperation. Whoever killed Shenagh did a fair amount of planning. Especially as regards luring Craig Meek to the scene.'

'From the notes I've seen, I'm not clear whether he received a call or text to his mobile, in the same way as Stefan.'

'Pass.' Fern shook her head. 'I'll check, but I'm not sure we ever worked that out.'

'You take the point?' Hannah took a couple of mugs out of the cupboard. 'It's hard to see why Jeffrey Burgoyne would kill her in that particular way.'

'Isn't he a ghost story fan? He fancied imitating the legend of the Frozen Shroud.'

Hannah thought about it. 'Yes, that makes psychological sense. But it's equally true of Quin. Suppose Shenagh's decision to waltz off to Australia tipped him over the edge.

He couldn't face losing her, so he killed her. Murder's often paradoxical.'

'Can't get my head round that.' Fern grunted. 'How about Robin Park? I mean, I know he was Terri's squeeze, but that doesn't mean he didn't have a guilty past. Suppose he was a secret admirer of Shenagh's, who couldn't handle rejection? If he let something slip to Terri . . .'

'Hard to see it.' Hannah poured the coffee, while Fern emptied what was left in the Chablis bottle into her glass, downing it in one. As they moved into the living room, she continued, 'Robin's a mummy's boy. Beneath the charm lurks a spoilt kid's ego, I'm sure. If Shenagh snubbed him, he'd have taken it hard. But there's no evidence he took a serious interest in her – is there?'

'He denied they ever got beyond low-key flirting.' Fern's amiable expression hardened. 'Then again, he would, wouldn't he? For Shenagh, Miriam Park was a sort of mother-substitute. What if that made Robin jealous?'

'I doubt he's that unbalanced, frankly. But I can't see from Les's notes whether he had any sort of alibi for Shenagh's murder?'

'Only what you'd expect. He and his mother were living together in Beck Cottage. She said she was a light sleeper, and she'd have heard if Robin had been up and about that night. It's a tiny place, and all the floorboards creak. But he's her son, her only child. She's bound to want to protect him. The so-called alibi wasn't remotely watertight.'

'Whereas Jeffrey and Quin presumably swore they spent the night in bed together.'

'You presume right.' Fern yawned. 'God, I'm shattered.

Early night for me, kid. As for Quinlan and Burgoyne, if one of them did kill Shenagh, the other knows the truth, and helped in a cover-up.'

The wine and the warmth from the fire were making Hannah drowsy too. The fog was as thick inside her brain as outside Undercrag.

'But?'

'But as of this moment, the smart money has to be on Oz Knight. He murdered Shenagh in a fit of passion, and then Terri came across something – maybe through working for the man – that incriminated him.' Fern scowled at the flames. 'So he didn't dare let her live, and tried to frame Deyna just as he'd done with Craig Meek. When we released Deyna, he saw the writing on the wall.'

She drank a mouthful of coffee before adding in a savage undertone, 'Pity they rescued him.'

CHAPTER EIGHTEEN

Keswick Museum called itself 'a cabinet of curiosities', and with good reason. A late Victorian building in the arts-and-crafts style, it housed a bizarre and extraordinarily diverse collection, ranging from Musical Stones and a man-trap to a giant cobra skin and a skeleton of a cat that was nearly seven hundred years old. The Robert Southey archive was its most extensive special collection of manuscripts, letters, maps and other documents, but there was also a wealth of material concerning De Quincey, Wordsworth, Coleridge, Walpole, Rawnsley, and Ruskin. Daniel had first visited the museum while researching De Quincey for *The Hell Within*, and promptly fell under its spell. Every time he turned his head, something different caught his eye.

'Cutting it fine, aren't you?' Lita Bosman, the Principal Archivist, pushed a hand through her frizzy dark hair. 'Talk about leaving it to the fifty-ninth minute of the eleventh hour.'

He grinned. After Oz Knight's brush with death on

Ullswater, returning to the calmer waters of historic research was a joy. This morning, the mist clinging to the valley of Brackdale had little in common with the opaque grey morass of last night. He'd crawled home from Ravenbank along the endless winding roads at little more than walking pace, and by the time he reached Tarn Cottage, he was fit for nothing except bed.

'You close on Monday?'

'Yep, and we've barely started packing. The weekend's gonna be a write-off. Nightmare!'

The Heritage Lottery Fund had coughed up a couple of million to fund a refurbishment that would bring the museum into the twenty-first century, and Lita and her colleagues were determined that modernisation would not affect its character and charm. A likeable South African from Kimberley in Cape Province, Lita had fallen in love with the Lakes while studying at Lancaster Uni, and her passion for the museum was fierce and unyielding.

'Thanks for sparing your time when you're up to your eyes.'

'No problem, Daniel, though I can't imagine why you've jilted old Thomas in favour of Southey?'

'Long story,' he grinned.

'Me, I prefer Coleridge. So you want to inspect what Roland Jones donated to the museum? Trust me, there was a shedload of material. You'll need to be selective if you're not planning on an overnight stay.' She handed him a couple of sheets of paper. 'I printed off this schedule of documents. You said you were keen to read any diaries he may have left. This lot will keep you out of mischief.'

'You're a star.'

On the phone, she'd said she was sure there were personal diaries among all Roland Jones's working papers covering everything and anything to do with Southey. Holding his breath, he scanned the long list of items. 'Is this right? "Private Journals, 1910 to 1974"?'

She hooted with laughter. 'Yeah. Donors are often – shall I say overgenerous? They don't just leave essential manuscripts, but reams of peripheral stuff as well. When we receive gifts by way of a legacy, the executors are usually desperate to wrap up the estate, and they throw in the kitchen sink.'

'You're not tempted to refuse?'

'I'm just a girl who can't say no,' she sang. 'As you well know, there's always the outside chance of finding a nugget in amongst the dross. Not that we can possibly sift through everything ourselves. I'm a custodian, not a researcher. If I'm lucky, I'll have time to delve into the detail to prepare a catalogue or exhibition. Otherwise, we just make sure everything is carefully preserved in case one day it comes in useful. We can't afford to get too engrossed. Not that I'm complaining, I'm a hoarder by nature.'

'Me too.'

'You look thrilled with my schedule. That's wonderful, people usually groan and roll their eyes.' She waved to a desk piled high with leather-bound journals and commanding a view of Fitz Park, still green despite the time of year. 'I've reserved you a place, and the first ten volumes are waiting there for you. Now, if you don't mind, I'll leave you to it, and carry on writing out labels for packing cases.'

Too right, he was thrilled. He'd suspected that a studious Edwardian like Jones might have kept a diary, but had hardly dared hope that it had been preserved, and found its way into the archive bequeathed to the museum. Feeling like a prospector panning for gold, he sat down to read.

The eureka moment came twenty minutes later. His cry of delight had heads turning in bewilderment.

He didn't care – where better for a historian to make an exhibition of himself than in a museum? At last he'd found the truth about the Faceless Woman.

'So the answer was lying in the archives of Keswick Museum all the time?'

Hannah bit off some pitta bread. They'd found a quiet corner in the theatre's café. Daniel looked and sounded exhilarated, more so than she'd ever seen before. Despite the aching void created by Terri's death, her own spirits were lifting. His gift for communicating his passion for historical research must have inspired countless students, let alone telly viewers. Now she had him all to herself, and she was determined to make the most of it.

'Archives are treasure trove, you never know what you may turn up.'

'Thousand to one chance, though?'

'No, the odds weren't as long as you'd think. Lita at the museum checked the terms of Roland's bequest. Apparently, he added a codicil to his will a week before his death, saying that the diaries should be included in the papers given to the museum.'

'Why not tell what he knew much sooner? Come to that, what exactly did he know?'

'He had precious little evidence. The question is, what did he believe, what did he work out for himself over a period of time? Remember, I've only read segments of the diaries so far, but enough to piece his story together.'

She leant towards him. 'Okay, you've built the tension to fever pitch, I can't bear it any longer.'

He teased her by taking a mouthful of spiced falafel, followed by a swig from a glass of sparkling water, before uttering another word.

'When Roland Jones arrived at Ravenbank to take up his teaching duties, he was twenty-four years old. After public school, he'd studied English at Cambridge, and was a devotee of Robert Southey. A comfortable and sheltered life, with minimal experience of the opposite sex. My impression is of a reserved, academic type, a decent young man who seemed aloof unless you got to know him.'

'And you think you've got to know him?'

He took another sip from his glass, milking the suspense, but Hannah suppressed her impatience. It was no hardship to let his warm, husky voice wash over her.

'When you read someone's private thoughts, you develop a personal connection to them. He was writing for himself, not posterity. Describing his daily life, as he experienced it, without the benefit of hindsight or the wisdom of experience. That's why I find archives so fascinating. Southey fans who want to see how Roland pieced together his thoughts on their hero will love wading through the notes he made for his book. But reading his own private diaries is like peeking over his shoulder.'

He held her gaze for a moment before looking away, as if suddenly embarrassed by his excitement. There was something she found intensely attractive about a man with a thirst for knowledge. Marc's obsessive love of books had been – she realised now – a huge part of his appeal, even though she would still rather read a pristine trade paperback than a grubby first edition.

'Please, go on.'

'Coming to a remote spot to teach a rich man's daughter, he expected to have plenty of time to indulge his interest in literary research. He didn't bargain for falling head over heels for a pretty young servant, but that's what happened.'

'And did she fall for him?'

'Tricky question. I've spent the morning immersed in Roland's inner life, and it's tempting to see her through his eyes. He needed to be discreet, which complicated his pursuit of Gertrude, even though he was crazy about her. It wasn't the done thing for a young girl's private tutor to fall for a housemaid. Mind you, I bet he was more transparent than he realised, and that everyone at the Hall knew how the land lay. But although she was flattered by his attentions, she was aiming higher.'

'She made a play for Hodgkinson?'

'She figured out she could do better for herself than a gauche young academic. Day after day, poor Roland frets about her increasingly distant manner. She became reluctant to pass the time of day with him, let alone allow him to take any liberties. He was hopeless at reading between the lines.'

'How did he get on with the Hodgkinsons?'

'He gave Letty a wide berth. Her mood swings made

him wary, though he mentions her devotion to Dorothy more than once. No hint that she was equally devoted to her husband. The marriage had soured long before Roland came on the scene. Letty had said some unpleasant things which caused his predecessor to walk out. A successful entrepreneur like Hodgkinson must have hated the situation. He was a winner, and a mentally screwed-up wife dented his image. Dorothy was a conscientious student, but Roland never warmed to her. She frustrated him because, he said, she lacked a sufficiently enquiring mind.'

'A plodder, in other words.'

Daniel was enjoying telling the story. Leaning back in his chair, using his slim hands to emphasise points, relishing the role of raconteur.

'She committed the cardinal sin of disliking Southey's poetry, and to make matters worse, she idolised her father, whereas Roland found him overbearing and self-important. To him, Hodgkinson didn't deserve Dorothy's adulation – he showered her with expensive presents, in lieu of spending quality time with her. What Roland didn't realise was how, exactly, Hodgkinson was spending his time.'

'By seducing Gertrude?'

'The affair seems to have been taking place under Roland's nose for weeks, yet he never got wind of it.'

'How did he find out?'

'Dorothy told him.'

Hannah put down her knife and fork. 'You mean, she egged him on to kill Gertrude?'

'Hey, don't jump to conclusions.' He grinned. 'And don't steal my thunder. This is a once-in-a-lifetime opportunity, to reveal a murderer's identity in a conversation with a DCI.'

'Your dad would have been proud,' she laughed.

'The day Gertrude died, Dorothy didn't show up for her first lesson. She was invariably punctual, so Roland went to search for her. He found her near the boathouse, crying her eyes out. When he'd calmed her, she said she'd overheard a row between her parents. Clifford had told Letty that he was leaving her – and Dorothy. He and Gertrude were lovers, they used Beck Cottage – which was newly built and unoccupied – for their trysts. Now she was expecting his baby, and he was going to sell his business and the Ravenbank estate, and make a new life with her.'

'Quite a bombshell. How did Roland take it?'

'He wrote up his journal that same night. He said he found it almost impossible not to burst into tears himself. All he could do was to have it out with Gertrude. Which he promptly did.'

Hannah groaned. 'With disastrous results?'

'You said it. She gave him a severe kicking. According to her, Hodgkinson was putty in her hands. She'd always wanted a baby, and now she would not only achieve her ambition, but live in luxury to the end of her days. She was determined that Hodgkinson must drive a hard bargain with Letty. She and Dorothy would have enough to live on, but not a great deal more.'

'How did Roland take that?'

'Her onslaught sent him into a tailspin. He was losing the woman he loved, and a comfortable, well-paid job into the bargain. Not only had he never had any luck getting into Gertrude's knickers, she'd been two-timing him with the master of the house. There was no hope of winning her back. Soon she would be out of reach in every possible respect. Her dream was to return to Edinburgh as a lady of leisure, and Hodgkinson had promised to make it come true.'

Hannah pursed her lips. 'Did Roland decide to stop them?'

'Nothing so decisive. He crumpled into a heap. He actually wrote in his diary that evening that it was the last entry he would ever make. Not true, as things turned out – he said it in the heat of the moment – but six weeks passed before he picked up his pen again. By then, he'd left Ravenbank, and was trying to make sense of what had happened. So his account of Gertrude's death and its aftermath weren't contemporaneous.'

'Gertrude was the love of his life, he can be forgiven for crumpling.'

Terri's face came into Hannah's mind; she'd come close to falling apart herself after her friend's death. Roland Jones was unaccustomed to the cruelty of crime, and Gertrude's betrayal of him, and subsequent murder, must have felt too much to bear.

'Presumably that's why he never married in later years. It's abundantly clear from everything I've read that he could never have harmed her.'

'You're sure of that?'

'He was a gentle, introspective man. Violence horrified him. Dorothy was obviously desperate for him to intervene somehow, that's why she confided in him, but from her point of view, he proved a broken reed. Later that day, she sought him out, and he had to admit she was right. Gertrude had

Hodgkinson in her clutches, and wasn't letting go. Dorothy became hysterical, and beat him with her own little fists. Of course he sympathised, he was on her side, but he had to be firm. There was nothing either of them could do.'

'Except that somebody did . . . do something.'

'Yes. This was Hallowe'en, but the occupants of Ravenbank Hall weren't in the mood to party. The weather was bitterly cold, and Roland went to bed early, but he was so stressed, he hardly got a wink of sleep. Next morning, he was greeted with the news that Gertrude's body had just been found, covered with the Frozen Shroud. He wrote afterwards that the whole day was a blur. The police were called, the Hall was in uproar. And then Hodgkinson went to Letty's room, and discovered that she'd committed suicide.'

'There's no doubt it was suicide?'

'None. According to Roland, she did leave a note, written in her own shaky hand. Just five little words.' He paused. '"I had to do it."'

Hannah considered. 'Ambiguous.'

'Precisely. Those five words offered a narrative to suit the survivors. Letty had killed Gertrude out of jealousy, and for fear of what would happen if Clifford threw her and Dorothy onto the scrapheap.'

'But?'

'Roland was confined to bed with a fever for a week after the two deaths. Nerve-related, I guess. As soon as he was fit enough, he had to pack his bags and leave. Over time, he began to put pieces together. On Hallowe'en, because he couldn't sleep, he'd got up just before midnight, and gone downstairs to make himself a drink. From the window, he glimpsed a slight figure wrapped in a heavy coat and scarf, sneaking out of the house. The figure stayed under the trees, skirting the open drive, but heading for Ravenbank Lane.'

'Gertrude, off to meet Hodgkinson?'

As she spoke, instinct told her she was on the wrong track. So did the look on Daniel's face.

'Dorothy, on her way to kill Gertrude.'

For a moment, Hannah was lost for words. He grinned. 'Okay, let me get the coffees.'

When he returned from the counter with two steaming cups, Hannah said, 'Call myself a detective? I should have seen that coming.'

He didn't patronise her by arguing. 'Roland didn't recognise Dorothy at first, but the more he mulled it over, the more convinced he became that he'd seen his pupil, setting out to murder her father's mistress. And she was carrying something. Roland's theory was that it was a large stone, wrapped in a blanket.'

'Right.' Hannah exhaled. 'The murder weapon and the Frozen Shroud.'

'Once his suspicion focused on the girl, everything made sense. In particular, Letty's note. Of course, in her mentally and emotionally fragile state, she felt she had to do it. She had to kill herself and take the blame for Gertrude's murder, because otherwise her daughter's guilt would be discovered.'

'Why did Letty suspect her own daughter of murdering a servant?'

'Letty knew Dorothy better than anyone, much more than doting Daddy. She had an idea what the kid was capable of. She was also an insomniac. The doctor had prescribed heavy duty sleeping pills, but she kept refusing to take them. Roland suspected that she'd looked outside and spotted Dorothy, just as he'd done. He also wondered if Dorothy had said something to her mother that gave the game away.'

'I hate to be a damp squib, but aren't there holes in this theory? How did Dorothy lure Gertrude out onto Ravenbank Lane?'

'She didn't. Gertrude was due to head for Beck Cottage that night, as usual, for her rendezvous with Hodgkinson. But Hodgkinson was out for the count. When news came that Gertrude's body had been found, he had to be roused from a deep sleep, though he was usually an early riser. Roland reckoned Dorothy slipped some of her mother's sleeping pills into her father's cocoa. Having knocked him out, the coast was clear for her to kill the housemaid.'

'Dorothy was only a little girl.'

'Five years younger than Gertrude, but fit and strong. Her obituary mentioned she was a keen mountaineer. Polio had withered Gertrude's right arm, and if she was attacked out of the blue, she couldn't have defended herself.'

'But the brutality of the murder . . .'

'Children are as capable of hate as any adult. Dorothy battered Gertrude's face with the stone, and then she draped the blanket over the bloody mess. My guess is that the enormity of her crime struck her as soon as she took a look at what she had done, and she couldn't bear the sight of it. Hence the shroud.'

'Why in God's name did Roland keep his mouth shut?'

'He recorded his agonies in the diary. Harrowing to read, but also frustrating. Poor Roland made Hamlet look decisive. To be fair, he had no corroborative evidence. It was all guesswork, and he baulked at accusing a child of a brutal murder when everyone blamed it on her mother. Besides, he felt personal responsibility. When he told Dorothy what Gertrude had said to him, he robbed her of the last hope that her family could remain intact. She blamed Gertrude, not her father. I suppose she couldn't face the thought that he was prepared to abandon her for someone she regarded as a trollop. Roland took his duties seriously. He was *in loco parentis*, and he'd failed to understand the extent of Dorothy's desperation. If he spoke out, he ran the risk of making a catastrophic situation even worse.'

Hannah said slowly, 'And when the war broke out, he joined up, reckless as to whether he lived or died.'

'Correct. Afterwards he forged a new life as an educator. Trying to atone? I dunno, I need to read the rest of the diaries. It wasn't until he was dying that he met Dorothy again.'

'When they had the exchange that Miriam Park overheard.'

'Hence the codicil to his will. He couldn't expose Dorothy at that late stage, and probably he didn't want to. She acknowledged her guilt to him, if only tacitly. Nor did he want the truth to be buried forever. He was dying, and it mattered little to him whether the story came out in five years or fifty. He settled for leaving it to be dug up by a researcher who shared his academic interests, and had the time and inclination to wade through his journals.'

'Enter Daniel Kind.'

'It had to be someone. It just so happened it was me.'

She tasted her coffee. 'It's taken a very long time.'

'Unravelling secrets of history often does.'

'Meanwhile Dorothy salved her conscience by involving herself with good works?'

'It's not such a bad way to pay your dues. The murder was horrendous, but she was only a child. I'm sure she killed Gertrude because she couldn't imagine how else to prevent the destruction of everything she held dear.'

'So Melody Knight got it spot on,' Hannah said. 'Gertrude was denied justice, because her murderer was never identified. No wonder her ghost has continued to walk. Will you tell Melody what you've discovered?'

'I doubt she still cares.' He shrugged. 'Right now, Melody has more to worry about than a mystery that's taken a century to solve.'

CHAPTER NINETEEN

'How is Terri's father coping?' Daniel asked, as they made their way to the Studio Theatre. 'She said he'd been unwell lately.'

'No idea, to be honest. I've never had his contact details, but he left a message at Divisional HQ for me yesterday, saying he wasn't fit enough to fly back to England for the funeral. It was the first time I've heard from him since Terri and I were kids, before he ran off with another woman. Terri's mum died some years ago, and so did her brother, who was older. Neither of our families was close-knit, it was one of the things we had in common.'

Daniel halted outside the entrance to the Studio. 'Fly back to England? Is he on holiday abroad?'

'No, he lives in the States. After his second marriage broke down, he met a Spanish-American woman, and followed her back to Florida, where he found a job in a bar. As Terri said, his twin passions were beer and sex, so he had the time of his life until his lady died of cirrhosis of the liver. Last I heard, he'd been diagnosed with cancer. Terri was upset, naturally. She reckoned she'd not been a good enough daughter, but that was rubbish. He wasn't a good enough father.'

'Did you know Terri and Robin Park were planning to move to be nearer to him?'

'What?' Hannah almost choked in disbelief. 'They meant to emigrate to Florida?'

'If that's where he still lives, yes. All she said was that because of his illness, she wanted to be closer to him.'

Hannah felt as if someone had slid a needle into her flesh. Was it childish to feel betrayed? Over the years, they'd shared so many secrets, yet all of a sudden, she realised she hadn't a clue about Terri's life.

He put a hand on her arm, a simple gesture that gave her a frisson. 'Are you okay?'

'Yes, yes. It's just . . . a surprise, that's all.'

Why hadn't Terri said anything sooner, when she was happy to tell strangers at a fancy dress party? One of the world's great blabbermouths hadn't dropped the tiniest hint to her closest friend of her intention to move to America. Then again, late at night after they'd both had plenty to drink, she'd come close to saying something, until Hannah's reaction discouraged her. The clues were there. She knew Terri's dad was ill, she should have realised that blood was thicker than water. Perhaps Terri feared Hannah would be jealous of her new life. After all, her relationship with Marc was shot to pieces, her cold case team was about to be ripped apart.

Hannah felt anger surge inside her as she realised Terri must have pitied her.

Quietly, Daniel led the way through a gap in the long black curtains that ran around the Studio. With a hundred seats, and set up in traverse, the Studio was less than a quarter of the size of the main house, but ideal for smaller-scale local productions. At the back, a technician hovered, making tiny adjustments to the lighting to keep it subdued.

Script in hand, Quin stood at the rear of the stage. Jeffrey was sitting three rows back on the right. Quin cleared his throat before speaking in a hushed tone.

'I sat up, my heart hammering, and then to my horror discerned, slinking against the farther wall, the evillest-looking yellow mongrel of a dog that you can imagine!'

'Just turn your head a touch towards me, love,' Jeffrey said. 'Let me see more of that gorgeous profile!'

Quin twisted his neck a fraction, and repeated his line. As Jeffrey called out, 'Perfect!' Quin caught sight of Daniel and lifted his hand in greeting.

'Don't be shy, we're pretty much finished, aren't we, Jeffrey?'

'Absolutely. And this must be Hannah! Or should I be formal and say DCI Scarlett? We've heard so much about you, do come and say hello!'

Daniel whispered, 'All sweetness and light again, by the sound of it.'

He and Hannah walked down to join the two men in seats on the front row. After introductions, Jeffrey launched into an explanation of the way he and Quin had been checking to make sure both of them could be seen and heard.

'You need to include the whole audience in a space like this, not just favour one side. Thankfully, everyone is close up, and the acoustics are nice. You're on the swivel, on the balls of your feet, all the time you're on stage.' Jeffrey beamed, segueing into lecturer mode. Daniel wondered if, beneath the bonhomie, anxiety was making him talkative. 'Playing here demands loads of energy, but it's worth it. There's no other place quite like this. When we tour the production, we'll adapt it for conventional venues, but the Studio is unique, you'd be amazed how we turn it into a claustrophobic black box. A ghost story is perfect for somewhere quite small, where you can take the volume down low, and draw the audience in. Do come and see the show. We've kept a few tickets back . . .'

'I'm sure Hannah has other things on her mind,' Quin interrupted. 'Can you tell us the latest on Oz? Has he been arrested?'

She gave a brisk, impersonal smile. 'The doctors say that he should make a good recovery, but so far, he hasn't been questioned further.'

'Is it safe to assume he's your prime suspect? Or is Terri's stalker still in the running?'

'It's not safe to assume anything in a murder investigation,' Hannah said. 'I did want to ask you something, though.'

Jeffrey exchanged glances with Quin, and said in a tone of forced jollity, 'By all means! We don't need our lawyer present, do we?'

'It's about Terri and her plans. She and Robin were going to move away from Ravenbank, weren't they? To America.'

'I never heard that,' Jeffrey said. 'Frankly, I'd be astonished.'

Daniel said, 'Melody told me that Terri had resigned to

go and live with Robin. She wouldn't need to pack in her job if she was staying in the area.'

'But they'd only known each other five minutes, and Robin has always been tied to his mother's apron strings.'

'How would Miriam Park have reacted?' Hannah asked.

'She would have put her foot down, make no mistake. Whatever Terri may have had in mind, I'm sure Miriam saw the two of them making a life together in Ravenbank, and in due course presenting her with grandchildren to idolise.'

'That's why they kept quiet about putting Fell View on the market,' Quin said.

Jeffrey gaped. 'You can't be serious!'

'Never more so. I saw the pair of them coming out of an estate agents in Station Street on Monday.'

'You never told me!'

'Didn't I? Must have slipped my mind.' Quin's grin showed his pleasure in reminding Jeffrey that he could keep a secret. 'I asked what they were up to, and they said they wanted to sell up and move to Florida. Terri's dad lives there, and he's been poorly. But they asked me to keep it to myself for a few days. Miriam still needed to be won round.'

'She'd have gone into the stratosphere!'

'Yeah, I wished them luck as far as that was concerned, and Robin said he'd certainly need it. He was dreading the conversation. It was the anniversary of his father's death, and his mother was bound to be upset.'

'Yes,' Hannah said slowly. 'Terri spent Monday night at my house. He decided it was better to break it to Miriam one-to-one, rather than have Terri by his side.'

'Very wise,' Jeffrey said. 'It could have become quite . . . difficult for all concerned.'

'Which estate agent was it?' Hannah asked.

Quin told her. 'I suppose Robin will be staying in Ravenbank for good now.'

'Not necessarily,' she said.

'What do you mean?'

She stood up. 'Daniel's done some brilliant detective work, discovering the truth about Gertrude Smith. Fascinating story. Why don't you listen to him explain while I get back to the job? He's proved once and for all that history does repeat itself.'

'Don't go in there on your own,' Fern said on the phone.

'It's only an idea. We don't have enough evidence to make an arrest.'

'Ashok and Jodie are on their way. Two of my young stars. And Ashok's built like a bull.'

'I'm not expecting any trouble.'

'Better safe than sorry.' Fern paused to let the advice sink in. 'Okay?'

'See you later.'

Hannah killed the call, and switched on the ignition. She'd parked at Ravenbank Corner, and, through the crime scene tape, she'd contemplated the muddy ground by the beck for fully five minutes before ringing Fern. So this was where Terri's life came to its sad and futile end. It was tempting to walk over to the spot, but she'd stayed in the car. Later, there would be time to pay her respects. Now there was work to do.

Soon the whole sorry business would be over. A thrill of anticipation rippled through her. She was convinced she knew the truth.

'So there is a connection between the murders of Shenagh and Terri?' Quin asked.

He and Daniel were in the foyer, while Jeffrey talked business with one of the theatre trustees. Both the actors were in high good humour. The first night was a sell-out, and there was only a handful of seats left for the other performances.

Daniel nodded. 'You were close to Shenagh, weren't you?'

'We used to meet late at night in the woods. Her excuse was taking the dog for a walk, mine was that I couldn't sleep. Jeffrey thought I was downstairs, learning my lines, when I was with Shenagh. She wasn't going to leave Francis, any more than I planned to dump Jeffrey. It was harmless fun for both of us, just a break from the routine. Exciting – made a change, you know?'

'Uh-huh?'

'Unfortunately, one night Jeffrey came down, and discovered I wasn't there, so there was hell to pay. This was only a couple of nights before the murder. Otherwise – we'd have met up on Hallowe'en.'

'Did you think Jeffrey killed her?'

'I hadn't a clue what to think.' In an unconscious gesture, Quin rubbed his cheek. 'He has quite a temper, you know. But everyone seemed to think Craig Meek was responsible, and that was good enough for me.'

'But Terri's death changed things.'

'Of course. Old wounds opened up again.'

'Just as you suspected Jeffrey, he suspected you.'

Quin nodded. 'Crazy, isn't it?'

Hannah drove a hundred yards along Ravenbank Lane, coming to a halt opposite Beck Cottage. A variegated ivy smothered the front wall, and even at this time of year, the window-box flowers were a mass of blue and yellow. She imagined Terri falling in love with the place. At every window, the curtains were drawn.

One of the ground floor curtains twitched. The sound of her car engine must have attracted attention. She'd thought it might. Her gaze bored into the front door, straining to penetrate the secrets hidden behind it.

As the door opened, she wound down her window. Robin Park's slim figure appeared. He was wearing a scruffy T-shirt and jeans, and hadn't shaved. In the space of twenty-four hours, he'd aged years. She was pretty sure he hadn't slept, and also that he hadn't kept awake fretting over Oz Knight. His eyes widened, in something more than astonishment. Her spine tingled with excitement. Robin was frightened of her.

'What brings you here?'

'One or two more questions I'd like to ask, if you don't mind.'

He blinked. 'You'd better come in.'

She could wait, of course. Ought to wait, actually. Ashok and Zoe wouldn't be long. Usually, she could be patient, and sometimes she even managed to be sensible. But not today, not when justice for Terri was within touching distance.

She opened her car door. There'd be time later, lots of it,

to worry about Fern's outrage at her cavalier disregard for procedure. But this was about Terri, nothing else.

Robin stood aside, and waved her past him, into the hallway. With a bang, he slammed the door behind her.

'Who is it, Robin?' A woman's voice, coming from the kitchen. So Miriam Park was here. Hannah had hoped she would be.

'Terri's friend, Mum.' He took a breath. 'Detective Chief Inspector Scarlett.'

Miriam plodded out into the hall, wiping her hands on her apron. A grey-haired woman, not wearing a trace of make-up. Hannah knew she was sixty-five, and she looked every day of that, but her build was sturdy, her jaw square and uncompromising. Hadn't Robin said something about his failure to inherit sporting skills? His father had been a musician who owned a bar; his mother must be the sporty one. Deep lines were etched into her face; bags hung below her eyes. The woman was exhausted, and only sheer will power was keeping her on her feet.

Hannah offered her hand. Miriam's grip was firm, her fingers thick and powerful.

'I gather you were a sportswoman in your younger days.'

The older woman straightened with pride. 'I played hockey for the county when I was only seventeen. People said I could go on to play for England, but my parents weren't well, and I was working long hours to keep things going, so that all went by the board. After Mum and Dad died, I joined the Army. Before long they sent me to Belfast, at the height of the Troubles. One or two things I saw there, no young woman should have to see.'

'I can imagine,' Hannah said softly.

'I was homesick, and had a bit of a . . . well, a breakdown, I suppose you'd call it. But I got over it, and got out of the Army. Then I came back to the Lakes for good.'

'Your husband was a musician, Robin told me.'

'I met and married him within six weeks of leaving the Army. Before he could change his mind.' Miriam wasn't smiling, and there wasn't a hint of sentimentality in the faded grey eyes. 'I've never believed in messing about, it gets you nowhere. Believe me, Bobby had his faults, but it was the best thing I ever did.'

Her gaze settled on her son, who shifted uncomfortably. 'Would you like to come into the living room, Hannah?'

'Kitchen's warmer,' his mother said. 'Thanks to the stove.'

Without waiting for a reply, she turned on her heel and marched through the kitchen door. Robin's shoulders drooped in despair. Hannah followed Miriam, and after a moment's hesitation, he joined them.

The kitchen looked as though it had been extended by knocking through into an old scullery. The units were pine, some built-in, some free-standing, and Hannah recalled seeing something similar in a brochure when she and Marc had been planning the renovation of Undercrag. The price had been out of their reach, but Francis Palladino's will had left Miriam a wealthy woman. She might not have invested in her own appearance, but she'd spent lavishly on her domestic kingdom. As promised, the wood-burning stove gave off plenty of heat. Hannah's arrival had interrupted the preparation of a steak casserole. Two succulent fillets lay on a chopping board on one of the work surfaces. The smell of garlic, and of an onion chopped into half a dozen wedges, hung in the air.

A large rectangular table occupied the middle of a stone-tiled floor. Miriam walked round to the far side, and took a seat close to the stove, with her back to the window. Hannah and Robin sat facing her. Over Miriam's shoulder, Hannah looked through a gap in the blinds into a neat garden, with a rockery full of purple and white late-flowering heathers.

'So what can we do for you, Detective Chief Inspector?' Miriam asked.

'I wanted to meet you, Mrs Park.'

They gazed at each other, and Hannah realised they were each trying to read the other's mind. But it was as much in vain as if they were time travellers from different centuries.

'Oh yes?' Miriam was sitting bolt upright, arms folded, a study in defiance. Hannah was conscious of Robin beside her, shuffling around on his chair.

'You might like to know that Daniel Kind has discovered the meaning of the conversation you overheard between Roland Jones and Dorothy Hodgkinson. She killed her father's mistress, and her mother took the blame for it.'

Miriam nodded. 'I did wonder if was something like that.'

'Dorothy couldn't bear the prospect of her world falling apart.'

'You can understand it,' Miriam snapped. 'Being separated from someone she loved. Even if her father was a good-for-nothing. Blood's thicker than water.'

'But the price she paid for refusing to let go . . .' Hannah clicked her tongue. 'She lost her mother, and her father didn't live long. While she had to live with the consequences of that crime to the end of her days.'

'What did you come here for?' Robin's voice was cracking. 'To boast about solving the mystery of the Faceless Woman? Shouldn't you be fully occupied, interrogating Oz Knight?'

'There's nothing I want to ask him. Knight didn't kill Terri, any more than Stefan Deyna did.'

'Ludicrous. The police have two perfectly good suspects, and they aren't making any effort to . . .'

'There's no panic,' Hannah interrupted. 'I'm confident an arrest will be made before the end of today.'

He opened his mouth to speak, but his mother beat him to it. 'Why did you want to tell me about Dorothy Hodgkinson?'

'You kept her secret, didn't you?'

'I felt sorry for her. The others who worked at the Hall didn't like her. Too severe, they said, too stuck-up. Not somebody you could have a laugh with. But each to his own. We can't all be comedians.'

'Did you feel equally sorry for Gertrude? Murdered for falling in love, and then cheated of justice?'

Miriam pursed her lips. 'Some might say she brought it on herself.'

'Was that true of Shenagh Moss?'

'Craig Meek killed her. He was one of those men who always had to get his own way. She gave him the run-around and he made her pay for it, everyone knows that.'

'Just as everyone knows Letty Hodgkinson murdered Gertrude Smith?' Hannah sighed. 'Ravenbank is an unlucky place. No wonder they called it Satan's Head in the olden days. In the last five years, the old story turned into a template for murder. The same pattern recurred. A young woman came here, and disturbed the peace. Someone with no loyalty to Ravenbank, and a yearning to move away. Regardless of whether she was tearing people apart.'

Miriam's expression was as bleak as the fells above Wasdale. 'You don't understand.'

'Actually, Mrs Park,' Hannah muttered, 'I think I do.'

'No, you have no idea! Shenagh was good company. Terri was . . . a very nice woman.'

'So you say. But it didn't count for much when you faced the prospect of losing someone you loved. Nothing could compare with your devotion to Francis Palladino, could it?' Hannah banged her fist on the table. She was losing the battle to contain her fury. 'Except for your worship of Robin?'

Robin laid a restraining hand on her shoulder. 'What do—?'

Hannah shook off his hand. 'I suppose you put something in his breakfast, or in his dinner the night before, to make him ill? Nothing harmful, just something to get him out of the way for half a day, so that you were able to do what you wanted?'

Miriam's features froze. 'I'm saying nothing.'

'You stole Terri's phone, so that you could text Stefan Deyna, and invite him to Ravenbank. I guess you played a similar trick on Craig Meek, and then had an extra stroke of luck when he died in a car crash.'

'Good riddance, if you ask me,' Miriam said. 'He was a bully, a good-for-nothing.'

'Mum—' Robin began.

She put up a gnarled hand to hush him. 'I was sorry about Shenagh, but really, she was her own worst enemy. The way she played around with Oz Knight was bad enough, but to betray Francis with that *queer* – it really was disgusting. And yet, you know, I could have forgiven her.'

'Really?'

'Yes, really. If she hadn't insisted on taking Francis away. He was an old man, not in the best of health. He wouldn't have lasted five minutes in Australia.'

'Shenagh's death killed him,' Hannah said. 'What's more, it killed the dog too.'

'That wasn't meant to happen.' Miriam's voice rose in anguish. 'I loved Hippo! But of course, he'd seen everything, and he couldn't understand. For ever afterwards, he looked at me with such sad eyes, I couldn't bear it. He was getting old, and I said to Francis it was kinder to have him put down.'

'You wanted Francis all for yourself.'

'All my life,' Miriam said, 'the people I've loved have been taken from me. My mam and dad. My husband, Bobby. Francis. As for Robin, who meant most of all, I couldn't bear the thought of . . .'

Robin said hoarsely, 'We would still have been in touch. There are aeroplanes. Phones. Skype. In this day and age . . .'

'It's not the same,' Miriam said. 'You know that, darling. Deep down.'

'But why—?'

The doorbell cut off his question. Hannah said, 'My colleagues have arrived. Can you let them in, please?'

Out of the corner of her eye, she saw Miriam rise from

her chair. In the same instant, Robin's face twisted in horror.

'No!' he shouted.

Half-hidden behind a bread bin at the back of the work surface beside the stove was a wooden knife block. Miriam reached over, and plucked out a steak knife. Her eyelids didn't flicker as she held it up, serrated edge glinting under her nose.

Hannah tensed. Thank God the large table stood between them.

'Put the knife down, Mrs Park.'

'Mummy!' Robin cried. 'Mummy, please, no!'

Holding the knife in her iron grip, Miriam plunged it into her throat. As the blade penetrated the vein, she let out a gurgling howl that filled the cottage kitchen. An outpouring of agony, and defeat.

The doorbell shrilled again, and Robin started to scream.

CHAPTER TWENTY

After an overnight frost, Saturday morning dawned bright and crisp. Sunshine played on the surface of Ullswater, as Hannah caught sight of Daniel standing on the wooden pier at Glenridding. She felt light and free, as if a dead weight had been unstrapped from her back, and she found herself skipping like a child as she made her way to join him. A phone conversation with Fern had delayed her, but he cut short her apologies.

'Occupational hazard. I'm the son of a policeman, remember?'

'How could I forget?'

She enjoyed watching his cheeks redden. A bright guy, Daniel, and a minor celebrity, yet unexpectedly easy to embarrass. Not like his dad.

Or had Ben, beneath that grizzled exterior, been much shyer than she'd realised? Was that why . . . ?

Daniel was talking; she must stop daydreaming about what was dead and gone. Including Ben.

'. . . and the steamer doesn't sail for a few minutes. I've

already bought our tickets. Let's walk along the shore while you tell me everything.'

'In a few minutes? A few hours, more like.'

'Fine, we've got all day.' He clapped her on the shoulder as they passed the ferry terminal. 'So – how are you?'

'Still alive, thanks. Unlike Miriam Park.'

Miriam had died in the ambulance from that single stab wound. In Northern Ireland, she'd learnt about ruthlessness, and working in a care home had supplied enough anatomical know-how to ensure the knife found her jugular vein. Her death was for the best, everyone agreed – even Robin, it seemed. But there were still procedures to follow. Regulations classified her suicide as a 'death following contact with the police', so Professional Standards were tasked to carry out an internal investigation under the watchful eye of the IPCC.

'You solved the case, why put you through the pain of an inquiry?'

'Strictly speaking, I shouldn't have gone into the cottage on my own. Not that I'm worried, events overtook me. If I bent the rules, I didn't break them. There's no question of a suspension. On the contrary, Lauren Self has been sweetness and light, urging me to get counselling "after all I've been through". Very kind, but I'm not into touchy-feely stuff. I'll make do with a few glasses of wine, preferably in pleasant company. Like I said on the phone, I'm catching up on a bit of leave.' She laughed. 'Speaking of Lauren, she's handed in her resignation. Headhunted by an American firm of management consultants, who want to market her insights into leadership and management. They'll learn.'

'Where does that leave the team restructure?'

'It's feeling more like a slight tremor than an earthquake, thank God. I'm only losing Greg Wharf.' She hesitated. 'He . . . decided it was time to move on. But Les Bryant may stay put. Seems the brass has remembered the value of cold case reviews, now we've solved two murders for the price of one. Not counting your work on Dorothy Hodgkinson, which started everything off.'

'At least that compensates for my messing up over Terri. I should have told you sooner that she planned to move closer to her father. It never crossed my mind he didn't live locally.'

'For goodness sake, don't beat yourself up. How could you know about Florida? Quite possibly Fern's team already filed away that titbit, but unless you know the context, it seems unimportant.'

'The context being that Miriam couldn't let go?'

'Robin told Fern that when she was serving in Belfast, her best friend had her head blown off by an IRA gunman. She threw herself into caring for other people. Robin's dad she adored, but he died young, and left her bereft. Admirable – until it becomes an obsession. Hence her son becoming a spoilt brat. Eventually, she devoted herself to Francis Palladino. Fern reckons she hoped he would marry her, after his wife died. When he fell for a sexy gold-digger instead, Miriam swallowed her pride, and took Shenagh under her wing. She thought she mattered to both of them. What she couldn't bear was the prospect of Palladino abandoning her forever, and moving to Australia with his floozie.'

'So the motive wasn't money?

'No, it was love.'

Their steamship was nearing the pier, and as they retraced

their steps, Hannah told him what Robin had said about Francis Palladino's will. 'Of course, killing Shenagh was utterly self-defeating. The murder broke Palladino, the last thing she wanted. Pity she didn't learn her lesson. If she had, poor Terri would still be alive.'

'Her MO was influenced by Dorothy's killing of Gertrude Smith,' Daniel said. 'Craig Meek was as much a scapegoat as Letty Hodgkinson, and battering Shenagh's face to turn her into a latter day Faceless Woman was Miriam's idea of covering up what the murder was really about. She repeated the pattern with Stefan and Terri.'

'Fern's found out how Miriam smashed Shenagh's face. She destroyed that weapon, but used another one, exactly the same, to kill Terri.' Hannah swallowed hard. 'A hockey stick.'

Daniel stopped in his tracks. 'You're kidding.'

'Robin says she kept a couple of sticks for years, had a sentimental attachment to them. There's no trace of either of them in Beck Cottage now. Robin is in bits, as you might expect, but fighting to save his own skin by cooperating. If he's to be believed, he didn't have a clue about what his mum was up to. Heard no evil, saw no evil.'

'And is he to be believed?'

'Debatable. Sounds like he's rewriting history.'

'Happens all the time.'

'You're the historian, you should know. Anyway, he's admitted starting to become suspicious in the last day or two. He remembers her burning wood on her stove after both deaths. Not unusual in November, but he thinks she burnt the hockey stick she used to kill Shenagh, and did the same after murdering Terri.'

'Jesus.'

'Despite her age, she was strong, and she knew how to use a hockey stick. Her victims were half her age, but she had the advantage of surprise.'

'Like Dorothy with Gertrude.'

'Yes, there are so many parallels. No wonder Miriam felt Ravenbank was haunted.'

'That wasn't her idea, either. She nicked it from Esme Palladino.' They had reached the pier, and he followed her up the wooden steps to join the queue of passengers. 'I suppose that was Miriam's problem, the flaw that wrecked her life.'

'What?'

'She lacked imagination.'

The Lady of the Lake chugged past the wooded tip of Ravenbank on her way to the bay at Howtown, pursued by a flock of noisy gulls. Hannah and Daniel were out on deck, leaning on the rail, a stiff breeze flicking their hair into their eyes as they spotted the boathouse from which Oz Knight had paddled off into the fog less than forty-eight hours earlier.

'I suppose the Knights will sell the Hall,' he said. 'There'll be a positive glut of houses in Ravenbank coming on to the market any day now.'

'I guess Louise won't be making an offer?'

'Not likely. She's given up on her move to Glenridding. The surveyor found the cottage was riddled with damp. Hard to believe, it looks like something from a picture postcard.'

'Rather like Ravenbank, huh?' She sighed. 'Beautiful, but rotten at its heart.'

'At least Jeffrey and Quin are back on an even keel.'

'Until the next time jealousy provokes Burgoyne into giving Quinlan a good slapping.'

He turned to look at her. Hannah's eyes were fixed on Hallin Fell, her expression unreadable.

'How about you? You've had a rough time, what with Terri's death, and . . . everything.'

'I'm not an invalid,' she snapped. 'Oh, shit. Sorry, Daniel, didn't mean to bite your head off. Truth is, I'm dead on my feet.'

'It'll take time to come to terms with losing Terri.'

'At least now I understand why she kept quiet about her plans. She was excited about this new life with Robin, but she realised making it happen would be complicated. The last thing she wanted was me, trying to be the voice of reason, advocating restraint when she was desperate to get away from Stefan, and panicking about how Miriam would react to losing her precious boy.'

'Do you think Robin really meant to make the break and move to Florida?'

'Absolutely – if he's telling the truth. With a man like that, you can never be sure. He told Fern that he yearned to escape from Ravenbank. Mother love was suffocating him. So much for the devoted offspring.'

'Robin didn't deserve her. Neither did Stefan.'

'Sure, but it takes two to tango. When it came to men, she kept making bad choices.'

Not that I can talk, given my recent track record. Time to make a good choice, for a change.

The gulls had flown away, heading for Bonscale Pike.

The leaves left on the trees were countless shades of green and gold. The only sounds were the steady chop of the ship through the water, and the impatient hustle of the wind.

Daniel took his hands out of his pockets. 'So how much do you think Robin knew?'

'Fern reckons he persuaded himself first that Stefan had killed Terri, and then that Oz was to blame. Anything rather than face up to the possibility that Mummy had committed murder, just to make sure she could keep him.'

He nodded. 'Like Quin and Jeffrey, each silently frightened that the other was a killer.'

'He had a double motive for wanting to meet me. Not simply to pick up clues to the progress of the investigation, but to distract my attention from Miriam as a possible suspect.'

Ravenbank was slipping out of sight behind them now, and as they rounded Hallin Fell, the little jetty at Howtown came into view, along with the gentle slopes of Steel Knotts, rising up behind the village. The plan was to have a leisurely lunch in the hotel, and stroll up to the cairn at the fell summit before catching the steamer on its way back.

'Don't rush back to work before you're ready.' He put one of his hands on hers. She liked the way he gently squeezed. 'You deserve a break.'

'Yeah, Undercrag needs an autumn clean, to make it fit for viewing by prospective buyers.' She gazed out across the lake, willing him to make a move. No way was she going to chase him, it would never work. 'Plus, I ought to start looking for somewhere else to live.'

'Plenty of time for that. Why not get away for a few

days? Change of scene. This isn't the only gorgeous place in Britain.'

'Not sure I can be bothered. Too much hassle.'

'An old college friend of mine has a place in mid-Wales, high above the Mawddach estuary. A two-bedroom cottage. Very remote, very quiet. Not a crime scene in sight. He's offered it to me for a few days. I was wondering . . . would you fancy coming along too?'

She blinked. 'You are joking. Aren't you?'

'Trust me, I'm serious.' He grinned. 'Too serious, if Louise is to be believed. By the way, she's staying up here. Tied up lecturing to wannabe hotshot lawyers next week. There's only one snag.'

'This cottage is so remote we might get cut off from civilisation?'

'No, no.' His grin widened. 'That wouldn't be such a disaster. I'm sure we'd find ways of passing the time.'

Hannah laughed. Inside a few breath-snatching seconds, she'd travelled back half a lifetime, and become a carefree, excited teenager again. Two bedrooms? Oh well, she'd see how she felt.

'All right. Break it to me gently.'

'The owner swears blind the cottage has its very own ghost.'

ACKNOWLEDGEMENTS

Ravenbank – fortunately, given its homicide per capita rate – does not exist, but I much enjoyed my visits to Ullswater while researching this book. As usual, I've made some changes to the topography of the Lakes in order to avoid confusion between fact and my fictional world. In particular, the characters who appear are imaginary and not intended to have any resemblance to any living persons. Most of the organisations mentioned are also invented, with a few obvious exceptions. My description of Cumbria Constabulary, and the people who work for it, is intended as a portrayal of an imagined version of the real thing: Hannah and her colleagues do not represent real-life equivalents, and whilst I touch on one or two issues that impact on all police forces today – notably the need to contain costs – I have not based events in the story on anything of which I'm aware in the real, as opposed to make-believe, Cumbria Constabulary. Happily, the Theatre by the Lake, Keswick Museum, and the Armitt Library and Museum all exist in the real world, and a good thing too – I strongly recommend all of them to anyone visiting the area.

Once again, I've been lucky enough to receive plentiful and generous help in writing this book. Roger Forsdyke and Ian Pepper, as so often before, kindly provided me with much information about the work of police officers and forensic scientists, which I adapted for the purposes of fiction. Rachel Laurence, of Hunt and Laurence (www.huntlaurence.co.uk), and a sometime crime fiction reviewer, supplied fascinating insights into the life of an actor in a two-person company.

In the Lake District, David Ward, of Theatre by the Lake, again gave valuable encouragement. Nigel Harling of Patterdale Mountain Rescue Team not only provided me with an insight into how the rescue of Oz Knight would be organised, but was also good enough to read and comment on the draft scenes; here, as ever, the needs of fiction must prevail, but such input does help me in my quest to achieve that indefinable touch of authenticity. Charlotte Stead, the curator of Keswick Museum, gave me a personal tour behind the scenes, and patiently answered many questions. Not long after, the museum closed for its refurbishment, and I look forward to a return visit to this marvellous place when it reopens. Judy Burg's short but excellent article on the work of an archivist in the Autumn 2012 issue of *The Author* informed my account of Daniel's researches, and Kerrie Smith and Bernadette Bean from Australia gave me some clues to Shenagh's early life. I'd also like to thank my agent, Mandy Little, and my publishers for their continuing support – as well, of course, as my readers, whose messages of goodwill and enthusiasm for this series of novels mean so much to me.

THE LAKE DISTRICT MYSTERIES

'Full of twists and turns and some sinister
(and very dangerous) secrets'
Mensa Magazine